Dear Jessi,

May you know
the love of Christ
which passes
knowledge,

Love and God bless,

Joan Deneve

OTHER BOOKS
BY JOAN DENEVE

Saving Eric

Freeing Ellie

LOVING BROCK

Book Three in the Redeemed Side of Broken Series

JOAN DENEVE

Write Integrity Press
Loving Brock
© 2018 Joan Deneve

ISBN: 978-1-944120-48-1

All quoted Scripture passages are taken from the KING JAMES VERSION (KJV): KING JAMES VERSION, public domain.

Published by Write Integrity Press;
PO Box 702852;
Dallas, TX 75370
Find out more about the author,
Joan Deneve, at her website www.joandeneve.com
Or at her author page at www.WriteIntegrity.com

Printed in the United States of America

DEDICATION

For all my dear readers
May you "know the love of Christ,
Which passeth knowledge,
That ye might be filled with all the fullness of God."
Ephesians 3:19

CHAPTER 1

They were in the last week of their trek with only two more villages still to visit. Dr. Brock Whitfield drove away from Mbombi Village with a cloud of red dust swirling behind and mingling with smoke from the inhabitants' morning fires. The strains of their African harmony were stuck in his head, and he rhythmically slapped his open palm against the steering wheel. Beside Brock, Moses, the African national who was his first Christian convert, joined in, using his long fingers to tap out the beat on the dashboard.

Moses's wife, Miriam, rode in the back with the newest member of their team, Joy Stockman, a retired nurse and recent widow, who'd come to Angola for much the same reason Brock had almost thirty years before: to minister to sick and hurting people and to offer hope through Jesus Christ.

Brock had no worries about Moses and Miriam even though they had a good five years on him, putting them somewhere in their early seventies. Ellie, his daughter, referred to them as "hardcore." Their energy and stamina seemed inexhaustible, and they were accustomed to the rigors of village life.

Joy Stockman, on the other hand, was more delicate. A petite woman in her early sixties, Joy had signed up for a one-year stint as a surgical nurse taking the place Ellie had vacated. As hard as it had been to have his daughter relocate, he had to admit that Joy had been a welcomed addition.

Brock had done his best to discourage Joy from accompanying them on this trip. In the end, he relented, mainly because she seemed so excited about experiencing every aspect of mission life, and he hated to tell her no.

Twice a year, Brock and a team of dedicated volunteers loaded the Land Rover full of medical supplies and headed for obscure tribal villages within a fifty-mile radius of their mission compound.

Even though it was the second week of June and the rainy season was technically over, the damage it had done to the back roads made their travel rough, bumpy, and dangerous. Brock swerved to avoid a deep rut, then blurted out, "Sorry. Didn't see that one until we were right up on it."

He shifted in his seat and caught a glimpse of Joy in his rearview mirror. She gripped the grab bar above her door as the Land Rover bounced over another rut. "Holding up okay back there?"

Joy met his gaze in the mirror and shouted above the noise of the engine. "Holding up and holding on for dear life."

He grinned. "We'll be there soon."

Up ahead, a village they'd never visited came into view. Several women plodded along the side of the road with loads of firewood or water pots on their heads. The sun blistered the afternoon sky as they pulled into a clearing with huts surrounding a central area.

Women with babies strapped to their backs tended fires on raised bricks or pounded corn or millet in a large mortar. Their sing-song chanting stilled, and they stopped their work to stare as Brock and the others emerged from the Land Rover.

Brock and Moses approached the largest mud-hut enclosure, assuming correctly it belonged to the chieftain, who strutted from his hut with a clear air of authority. His torso bore traditional cuts and scars, the markings that distinguished their tribe from others. Out of respect, Moses asked permission for their team to enter his village.

Brock listened as Moses spoke in dialect, working out a deal that they would set up a temporary clinic for basic first aid and medical care. In return, the chieftain would provide the evening meal in their honor.

Moses made a deferential bow to the chieftain and said in the village's dialect, "It is well."

There was nothing easy about these trips. It required loading and unloading at each stop and quickly ascertaining the "political" lay of the land, so as not to cause offense or dishonor.

Brock parked the Rover where the chieftain indicated and went around to the back of the vehicle to unload two folding tables and set them up side by side. "Okay, Joy, you're all set."

"Thanks." Suddenly all business, she brushed her palms down her khaki shorts before lifting one of the heavy crates from the Rover.

Half-naked—and sometimes completely naked—children stood close by, their large eyes wide and curious as they watched Joy deftly arrange the donated supplies on the tables.

He couldn't blame them. He'd stopped a time or two to watch her himself. She seemed to be faring well, far better than he'd anticipated.

They worked steadily through the afternoon. Under a canopy tent, Brock performed outpatient surgery. With Joy assisting, they were able to lance boils, remove a goiter from an elderly man's neck, and even extract several teeth. Moses and Miriam performed basic first aid, treating scrapes, cuts, and burns with antibiotic ointment and gauze.

As the sun inched toward the horizon, Brock and Moses unloaded their tents and set them up while the two women packed up supplies and stacked crates in the back of the Rover.

The villagers waved them over to the chieftain's courtyard under the largest tree in the village. Women, dressed in bright, flowing material wrapped snuggly around their slender bodies, layered rice on large banana leaves. They demonstrated how to roll the sticky rice into a ball and dip it in a community bowl of hot peanut oil. His first try, Brock dropped his rice in the oil, and it dissolved into tiny kernels. The native women ducked their heads and giggled, but after a couple of tries, he mastered the process.

Brock sat beside Joy and nudged her with a whisper, "Keep your left hand in your lap."

She quickly did so, mouthing a silent thank-you.

He smiled so as not to arouse suspicion. "I learned that little etiquette tip the hard way. It seems the left hand is used only for wiping the nose and other unmentionable areas. On my first trip to an outlying village, I was labeled a *kaquito,* a common person with no manners. Actually, the exact words were something like 'What? Were you raised by baboons?'"

Joy chuckled under her breath. "Thanks for watching out for me. My mother would turn over in her grave if I was accused of being raised by baboons."

After the meal, Brock nodded to Moses who asked the chieftain for permission to tell a story. The chieftain gave his consent as Brock knew he would. Along with singing and dancing, storytelling was the main entertainment at night.

Brock rose and moved to the large tree and leaned against it, facing the entire village of perhaps sixty-five people of all ages from suckling babies to the elderly who had to be helped to the courtyard.

The people listened as first Brock spoke, then Moses translated into their dialect. Brock told them of the great Creator who made the world and everything in it.

"*Mmbaa.*" The oldest man in the group sang out what must have been the equivalent of Amen.

Moses turned to Brock and explained. "It means to go on and tell us more. We are with you."

Brock was happy to comply. He went through a simple version of the "Fall of Man" and man's need for a savior. After each phrase, the men would add another resounding "Mmbaa." Then the women chanted, "Mmmmm. Mmmmm."

Brock had Moses lead them in a prayer, knowing some would respond, but others would have to think on this a while. Still, the seed had been planted. God would have to cause it to grow.

The chieftain reclined on bamboo slats shaped like a chaise lounge. He wore a coarse robe, with a sword tucked into a leather strap at his waist. With a flick of the finger, he motioned for Moses to approach. As Moses did so, a warning went off in Brock's spiritual radar. Something wasn't right.

Moses returned, his face giving nothing away.

"Is something wrong?"

Moses's face remained passive, but he leaned closer and whispered in Brock's ear. "Perhaps it would be wise to leave at first light."

The hairs on Brock's neck stood at attention. "What did he say?"

Moses nodded toward Joy, then pulled Brock to the side, out of her earshot. "The chieftain expressed interest in the silver-haired woman with the beautiful smile. He asked if she was your wife."

Adrenaline surged through Brock's veins. "What did you tell him?"

"I say, 'No, she is a *kamba,* a friend only.'"

"And?"

"He requested that the silver-haired one share his tent and his favors this night."

Brock curled his hands into fists. If Abraham could lie about his wife being his sister, why couldn't he lie and say Joy was his wife? "Maybe we should leave now."

"My brother, all will be well. I explained that Joy is a princess and the daughter of a great king who would not welcome advances on his child. The chieftain reluctantly withdrew his request."

In spite of his anger, Brock broke into a smile. "Brilliant." He shifted and cut his gaze over to the chieftain who continued to ogle Joy. "But I agree with your earlier assessment. We must leave at first light."

"I will let the ladies know."

Brock grabbed Moses's arm and tugged him back. "You can tell Miriam to be on the alert tonight, but I'd rather Joy not know."

"As you wish."

Brock encouraged the women to go to bed early. He and Moses did the same, but Brock couldn't shake the uneasy feeling in his spirit. He tossed on his cot until he finally sat up with a huff. "Moses, wake up."

"I am already awake. You are troubled?"

"Yes. We need to move our tent."

Without asking for an explanation, Moses rose, unzipped the tent flap and bent, backing out. Brock folded his cot and helped collapse the tent.

They moved it directly in front of Joy and Miriam's tent, effectively blocking the entrance. Both men had set up the tent so many times, they had no problem working in the dark of the moonless night.

When they finished, Brock followed Moses back into their tent and stretched out on his cot, still stewing over the audacity of the chieftain. At least, now if the man wanted to get at Joy, he'd have to go through Brock to do it.

As much as he needed sleep, Brock stared at the seams in the top of the tent as the hours wiled by.

If tomorrow ever came, they would leave this place and go to their last village on this trip, and he would be able to breathe again. The good chieftain of that village loved and appreciated their team and never tried to make advances on the women.

Brock lay on his back, his ears alert to any sound outside his tent. Tomorrow could not come fast enough.

CHAPTER 2

Tonight of all nights, Joy Stockman had to be ready for anything—like maybe a flash flood. Earlier this morning, Brock seemed to be in a great hurry to leave the previous village. Perhaps he knew more than he was saying. Torrential rains began not long after they arrived at this last village on their trip, and intermittent downpours occurred throughout the day.

The rain now pelted the top of her tent and quickly intensified into a Niagara-sized roar. Refusing even to take off her heavy-duty hiking boots, Joy stretched fully-clothed on her cot, then shined her mini-flashlight on the floor by the zippered flap. No wet spots. Yet. She prayed the plastic vinyl separating her from the monsoon force gale would hold up through the night.

Miriam lay on a cot next to Joy's. She stirred but continued her slow and steady breathing, seemingly oblivious to the storm.

Oh, to be able to sleep like that. Joy closed her eyes and tried to slow her own breathing. Maybe the racing thoughts that kept her awake most nights would take a break and let her tired body get some much-needed rest.

She groped for the bag containing the few clothes and

toiletries she'd packed back at the mission hospital and plopped it on her chest. At sixty-two, she wasn't a woman easily frightened. Of anything—especially a hearty storm. Back home in D.C., the forecast of a good Nor'easter sent a frenzy of excitement through her. A quick trip to the market for essentials like coffee or hot cocoa, and, of course, batteries, and she was all set to enjoy the show.

But that was in her cozy recliner well within the confines of her solid brick home with her rock-solid husband somewhere in the house as well.

Frank. Her eyes flew open. First time she'd thought of him in days. He had never been a fan of short-term mission trips. *No way. You might pick up some kind of disease. Just write them a check.* Frank's answer to everything. A practical self-made man, quite vocal with his cynical opinions, who would roll over in his grave if he could see her now somewhere in the wilds of Africa.

Joy turned to her side and hugged the bag she still held close to her chest. Two years and she still missed him. Missed the safe predictable life she'd shared with him. With all of his faults, he'd been good to her, and except for mission trips, denied her nothing. Though he'd never have admitted it, Frank Stockman had needed her, especially near the end, when cancer snatched the career he'd built his life around. He'd wanted her near him at all times. Said he felt better when she was in the room. Even asked her to read the Bible out loud to him, and affirmed that the faith he always said he had, was, in fact, genuine.

For one brief year, as hard as it was, she finally had the husband she'd always dreamed of having.

Then he died.

A tear escaped and slid across the bridge of her nose.

God carried her through that time, just like He had when their daughter died the summer after high school graduation. Just like He carried her now. God, her faithful friend, the One who would never leave her or forsake her, even in her darkest times.

And if she was going to get any sleep, she had to close the door of grief she'd inadvertently opened. With purpose, she slowed her breathing and silently quoted a familiar passage guaranteed to still her thoughts and quiet her spirit. *The Lord is my shepherd; I shall not want. He maketh me to lie down in green pastures. He leadeth me beside still waters.*

Still waters? She smiled into the darkness. Not very still tonight ... *He restoreth my soul ...*

A slight touch to her arm jolted her out of the best sleep she'd had since beginning the two-week trek to outlying Angolan villages.

"Sorry to startle you." Miriam's lithe body dominated the tent's limited space. "Dr. Brock feels we should leave ahead of schedule."

"Thank you." Joy swung her legs over the side of the cot, careful not to kick Miriam. "I'll be right out."

Miriam smiled and gave her arm a gentle squeeze. "I'll let him know, but take your time. He and Moses are loading the Rover."

"Has the rain stopped yet?" Joy spoke to the stooped figure backing out through the unzipped flap of the tent.

"Yes, but more is on the way."

Left alone, Joy shined a mini-flashlight on her watch. A few minutes before five. Way ahead of schedule. She zipped up the flap again to use her personal bedpan. Primitive but at least more private than the open ditch behind the village. Hopefully, a deep one that wouldn't flood during storms like the one last night. She shook the tube of antibacterial gel, her most precious possession at the moment, and willed it to last one more day.

With a quick finger comb, she twisted her silver hair in the back and secured it with a clip, grateful it was long enough to wear up off her neck. She rifled through her bag of toiletries for her toothbrush and toothpaste. Most of the people she'd met on this two-week itinerant mission had beautiful smiles with strong white teeth. She made a mental note to add toothbrushes to the items to bring on the next visit and used the last of what was left in her water bottle to rinse. She swished the tepid water in her mouth, then spit into her multi-purpose "chamber pot." Not something she relished but better than unzipping the tent and spitting into the mud puddles outside.

She had committed to serve a year at Brock Whitfield's mission hospital in Angola, located south of Luanda. He'd warned her that a visit to outlying villages was primitive and sometimes dangerous, which, in hindsight, might have been an understatement. They weren't "home free" yet, but all things considered, she'd held up pretty well so far.

She was thankful. The past two weeks had given her a deeper glimpse into the heartbeat of this African mission and of the caliber of man who'd started it. With two months left of her original commitment, she was praying about signing up for one more year.

Joy stood, her short frame barely needing to stoop in the tent, and smoothed the wrinkles in her khaki shorts as best she could.

A slight drizzle sprayed her face as she exited the tent. She gingerly stepped around puddles to empty the contents of the bedpan a discreet distance away.

Moses met her on the way back and gave her a deferential nod. "Good morning, Ma'am. May I enter to get your cot?"

"Yes. Of course."

Dogs, goats, and curious children joined the crowd of about thirty men and women clustered on the rain-drenched area in the midst of their thatched huts. A more somber group than the day before when they had greeted the team's arrival with a happy chorus of clapping, songs, and wide smiles. Good humble people who appreciated the smallest gestures of kindness shown to them. Joy hated to leave early, but no doubt, Brock would find a way to make it up to them.

She scanned the area for the leader of this expedition

and found him at the back of the Rover loading supplies. As usual, Brock wore a brightly colored short-sleeved shirt untucked over regulation khaki shorts much like the ones she wore as well. He was taller than she, but not by much, and he had silver hair, like hers, which, according to Miriam, caused more than one villager on this journey to assume they were a couple.

Her boots made a thick suction sound as she trudged through the mud to the vehicle.

Brock turned and smiled as he took her bag. "Good morning. You look nice and rested."

Her spirits rose as they usually did whenever she was with Brock Whitfield. "Thank you. Once I finally went to sleep, I don't think I moved the rest of the night."

He placed her bag on some boxes in the back of the Rover, then turned and gave her his full attention, something Frank Stockman with his Type A impatience had rarely done. She immediately felt guilty for comparing the two.

"I'm sorry we had to wake you, but if we don't leave before the next rash of rains hit, we may not make it across some of the streams we'll encounter on the way back."

"Really?" The flash flood scenario popped into her mind again.

"But don't worry—" he broke off as Moses approached with the folded tent. "Thank you, brother." Together the men positioned the tent in the back and strapped it down with bungee cords.

Brock shifted back to her. "As I was saying, I'm not that concerned. We're doing God's work with a magnificent Land Rover, which happens to be equipped with a powerful wench." He leaned closer as if telling her a secret. "That I really hope we won't have to use."

A sentiment she shared. Her gaze drifted to the front even though the wench attached to the front bumper was out of her view.

Moses joined them again. "I think we have everything."

Brock flashed the charming smile that his daughter Ellie had inherited. "Wonderful." He gave Moses a friendly clap on the back. "Let's say our goodbyes. This time I'll let you translate for me, if you don't mind."

Brock led the way with Moses following a respectful distance behind. They stood on a slushy mound of dirt that seemed more like a tiny island surrounded by an ocean of brown water.

Joy moved to the side where Miriam stood on another clump of mud. Brock's expression softened as he scanned the crowd. A hush fell over the group, and as if on cue, they moved closer, wide-eyed and apparently unconcerned that they stood ankle-deep in murky water.

Brock extended his hands, open-palmed, "My beloved friends."

Moses mimicked Brock's gestures and repeated his words in the tonal dialect.

"I am sorry we must leave earlier than planned. Before

we go, I want to remind you that we visit in the name of Jesus Christ, our Lord and Savior."

Brock paused until Moses finished the phrase.

"We come because we love you."

None of the words spoken by Moses bore any resemblance to Brock's English words.

"We come because God loves you and sent us to tell you so. God sent us with this message:" Brock pointed to the darkened clouds in the sky. "There is only one true God, and He sent His son Jesus to be sacrificed for your sins."

Brock paused to let Moses catch up. Even then, Brock remained silent, his jaw working and his expression radiating love and compassion. No one, not even the animals moved.

He reached into his shirt pocket and held up a pocket New Testament. "God wrote His words in a book for us so we could find Him. Listen, my friends." He read from the page and spoke louder, emphasizing each word. "And this is life eternal, that they might know thee, the only true God, and Jesus Christ Whom Thou hast sent."

As Moses translated, Brock moved into the water to be closer to the crowd, and that was when the tears spilled over and coursed down Joy's cheeks.

Brock pointed. "You, Uduak, have believed in Jesus." The young man nodded before Moses finished translating. "And you, Etiene, have believed in Jesus." Brock stepped back and extended his arms to the group, his voice choked with emotion. "And many others. But God desires for all of you to come to Him for forgiveness so that you can live forever with Him." Brock paused and pointed to the sky again. "In heaven, where He lives."

Brock backed away even farther. "We must leave you now. But we will pray to God for you. And we will return. With food and medicine and more stories about the one true God who loved us enough to die for our sins." He looked pointedly at Uduak and Etiene and the others he'd called out. "My brothers and sisters, teach your people. Share with them how you believed."

Brock bowed his head and lifted his hands to heaven. "Gracious Father, help them to understand Your truth. Continue to speak to their hearts long after we are gone."

At that moment, the mud-drenched area where they stood transformed into holy ground, and Joy's fears for their journey home dissipated. She bowed her head and offered a silent prayer of her own. *Help these dear people, Father. Thank you for letting me be a small part of this great work.*

After many hugs and tears, Brock pushed his way through the throng of people who seemed reluctant to let him go. Joy and Miriam had taken their places in the backseat of the Rover, and Moses sat up front next to Brock.

"All set?" Brock joined them and clicked his seat belt into place. He eased the Rover through the crowd taking care on account of the children and dogs running alongside. With a final wave, Brock picked up speed.

Joy turned for one last look. The people would begin their day, content to go about their mundane tasks of living and surviving. She settled back into her seat, thoughtful and profoundly moved. She would find a time to thank Brock and tell him what this trip had meant to her. How it had changed her with a whole new perspective on what being Christ's servant entailed. But not now, when she'd have to shout over the roar of the engine.

A steep hill loomed ahead. Brock slowed and downshifted. The vehicle jerked and slid a few times. Joy and Miriam collectively leaned forward in a vain attempt to aid the struggling vehicle, then together released their breath as they crested the hill.

"I'm going to take a different route back. A road carved out by a logging company some years back. May take longer but—" Brock broke off mid-sentence as the Rover fishtailed around a curve.

Miriam reached over and clasped Joy's hand, whether to comfort herself or to offer comfort, Joy wasn't sure.

The four of them maintained a tense silence as Brock tackled another hill, smaller but with deeper ruts. Descending the hill proved even more difficult with the vehicle skidding sideways to the bottom.

The next couple of kilometers were relatively uneventful until Brock came to a halt before a rickety log bridge spanning a deep ravine. Rapid moving water from a stream swollen with torrential rains made the crossing a formidable endeavor. The bridge, scarcely wider than their vehicle, afforded no room for mistakes.

Both men left their seats, not bothering to close the doors and stood in front of the vehicle for a long time. Finally, Brock pointed to the bridge, his face grave, then shook his head and said something to Moses.

Joy chanced a look at Miriam, whose serene countenance offered no clue what the men might be thinking.

Brock returned and leaned in far enough to address them both. "Ladies, I'm afraid you'll have to walk across."

Joy swallowed the lump in her throat. Probably not the best time to let him know she was terrified of heights.

CHAPTER 3

The ramshackle set of crossbeams and logs sent a sick thud to the pit of Brock's stomach. The bridge, the only way across this deep ravine, left few options, but driving across with the women on board was not one of them.

Brock forced a pleasant expression, a skill he'd perfected as a doctor, and opened the back door. "As soon as we get you girls over safely, Moses and I will come back for the Rover."

At her first good look at the chasm underneath the bridge, Joy gasped and placed a hand over her heart. "Oh, my. It's ... very high."

Brock nodded, unsure how to respond. The center of the bridge was indeed high, at least twenty feet above the water. He slung the strap of her bag across his shoulder and gave what he hoped was a reassuring smile. "Take my hand and try to step where I step."

The men paved the way, gingerly testing and then taking the next step on the roughhewn logs. On a good day in excellent conditions, crossing this particular bridge would be a gamble. Unthinkable on a day when the mist and mud made each step a precarious exercise in solid nerves and balance.

Joy inched behind him, a death grip on his hand. Moses and Miriam could easily have made it across but stayed close, pausing at regular intervals to give them a chance to catch up.

"We're halfway there." Brock spoke in a soothing tone. "You're doing great." The words had barely left his mouth when Joy slipped. Her left foot shot up propelling her backward. She gasped and tried to compensate, flinging her body forward. Brock grabbed her shoulders before she plunged over the edge. Fear and adrenaline surged through him as he yanked her back with enough force to knock him off his feet. Still gripping Joy, he fell back hard, with her crashing on top.

Joy struggled to rise, her arms and legs flailing like a turtle stuck on its back. "I'm so sorry."

"Please don't apologize." Brock huffed out the words, still trying to recapture the breath that had been knocked out of him. He remained in a semi-sitting position, his neck muscles straining to keep his head out of the muck. "This one is on me."

Literally on him. Slimy mud oozed under his shirt and down his back. At least, he'd taken the brunt of the fall, a fact his joints and muscles would no doubt remind him of for days to come.

Moses stationed himself at their feet. "Would you like some help?"

"Yes, please."

Moses's face crinkled in amusement as he pulled Joy

to her feet, then offered his hand to Brock. "Are you hurt?"

"Mostly my pride." Brock swiped thick mud from his backside and turned to face Joy. "What about you? Are you all right?"

Joy brushed off a clump of mud still stuck to her cheek. "A little shaken but very thankful Moses didn't have to fish us both out—" She stopped mid-sentence, her expression changing from grateful to somewhat shocked.

Brock followed her gaze, hoping there wasn't some blood-sucking leech or worse attached to his leg. With relief, he found only mud. Actually, a massive mudslide, working its way south down his calves and into his boots.

"I really am sorry." Joy placed her hand over her mouth, he suspected to hide an amused grin. "But I might have some wipes in my bag."

Her bag. The one that used to be on his shoulder. "I'm afraid it's my turn to apologize."

She gave him a puzzled look.

"Your bag. I might have accidentally tossed it when you slipped. I'm sorry."

To his surprise, Joy laughed. "No worries. Given the choice, I'd rather you save my life than my bag." She took his hand, "And I'm counting on you to get me off this bridge in one piece."

"I'll do my best."

They started forward, but Moses brought his arm down like a railroad crossing bar, blocking their next step. "Not there." Moses pointed to a log and pried up a loose board

26

with the tip of his foot. "Come to this side. I will lead Miriam, and you can follow her."

Brock nodded, more than happy to comply. Pivoting back to Joy, he switched the hand that held hers and placed his other hand on the small of her back to offer extra support as they made the lateral move. "We're going to make it. Just a few more feet now."

Joy's mouth tightened to a thin line, her focus on the next step.

Moses with his lanky legs cleared the bridge, propelling Miriam with him.

Not the kind of move Brock wanted to risk. Moses reached out and gripped Brock's forearm, giving him enough support to catapult himself and Joy over that last big step.

Relief ruled the moment. Not waiting to think it through, Brock broke his self-imposed code of ethics and pulled Joy closer, hugging her tight. "Home free," he whispered, more for his sake than hers.

She nodded, her damp hair cool against his cheek. "Thank God." She stepped back but took both his hands in hers. "And thank you." Before he could respond, she released his hands and walked toward Miriam.

Not quite home free yet. Brock joined Moses, who squatted at the side of the bridge studying the under pilings.

"Well, my friend. What do you think?"

Moses straightened, his lower lip jutting out. "It will be tight, but we can do it."

They had to do it. What other option did they have? The rain picked up and pelted his face. It would be a wet, miserable ride home. That's if he managed to get the Rover across the bridge.

Brock scanned the area for the women. They stood well away from the bridge beneath gnarled branches of a massive baobab tree. A pitiful pair, huddled under a shared poncho stretched over them like a makeshift tent. Joy peeked under the rim through rivulets of water running down the sides.

Her smile cheered him, made him stand a little taller until he remembered how ridiculous he must look with mud coating most of his back. For one brief second, he considered immersing himself fully clothed in the water below, but with his current luck, he'd need the wench from the Rover to pull him back up the slippery slope.

So with a nod and a two-fingered salute, he swallowed his pride and turned, giving the ladies full view of his mud-caked backside.

The trek back across the bridge proved uneventful and faster than the first time. Moses remained as guide in the middle of the bridge.

Brock climbed into the seat and took time to pray aloud what he'd already prayed in his heart. "Father, guide my hands as you do every time I perform surgery. Keep me steady. Get me and this vehicle safely across."

He revved the engine and backed the Rover up a few feet to make sure he was completely centered, then switched to low four-wheel drive.

The truck and his own life were in Moses's hands. Big hands, now held straight up and down and motioning him forward. Brock held his breath as he inched onto the bridge with little leeway for error.

Moses nodded, urging him to continue. Brock complied until the front wheels came to a log jutting above the rest. To get over, he'd need a quick surge of power.

He backed up about three feet and stepped on the accelerator. The back wheels spun and slid sideways. He jerked his foot off the gas, turning the wheel in the opposite direction. The truck straightened, and he eased forward again, holding his breath until he cleared the offensive log. Thankfully, the back wheels cooperated and scaled the hurdle with no problem.

Sweat streamed down Brock's temples and into his close-cropped beard. He took a moment to catch his breath. He'd learned long ago that God didn't always make things easy and effortless, and he'd quit expecting Him to.

Instead, he strove to be grateful for favor and blessings and to be gracious when things went wrong.

But right now, his well of grace had run as dry as his mouth. He grabbed his water bottle from the console and drained the rest of the lukewarm liquid.

"Father, You know how weary I am. How anxious I am to get the team, especially the women, home safely."

He paused and rubbed some of the fog from the windshield. Moses stood in the center of the bridge with no hint of impatience, waiting for Brock to make his next move. It was a lesson in self-effacing respect and humility Brock could stand to learn.

"Father, forgive me. I know You are always right and always on time. I trust You to send exactly what we need, even if it means more setbacks and challenges."

With renewed purpose, Brock eased the Rover forward, not sure what might lie ahead.

CHAPTER 4

Joy woke before dawn, totally disoriented. A couple blinks later, her vision adjusted to the dimness, and her brain fog cleared. What had seemed a tall ominous stranger and a fat dwarf lurking in the corner became the pole lamp nestled between the overstuffed tan recliner and the three-drawer dresser.

Her own bedroom back at the mission. She turned on her back and blew out her breath in a long grateful sigh, extending her arms behind her head until her fingertips grazed the headboard. Every stiff joint protested her attempt at a full-body stretch and reminded her of the one part of the trip she'd rather forget, the inglorious mishap on the bridge with Brock going down and her landing on top of him.

Joy flipped back the cover and rolled out of bed, the concrete dormitory floor cool under her bare feet. She clicked on the light and rummaged in the top drawer for lavender scrubs, the nice ones she hadn't taken on the excursion into the wild. She flossed and brushed her teeth and then moved closer to the mirror, her teeth bared for inspection. Maybe not flawlessly white like Miriam's, but certainly passable.

Fix up first thing in the morning, her mother had drilled her, *then walk out the door and forget yourself.*

A seeming contradiction to a twelve-year-old especially when her mother, with finger raised, added, *But always remember: the most important asset a woman possesses is her smile.*

The memory itself made Joy smile until she caught her first real glimpse of morning bed hair. What had possessed her to crawl into bed without drying her wet hair first? Her fingers tried to coax life into the limp sheet of hair plastered flat against the right side of her head.

She would need more than a smile to be able to face people today.

So, she showered again, too good to pass up after a two-week stint of sponge baths.

At least five years earlier, she'd quit fighting the inevitable gray. Turned out to be one of the best decisions of her life. The agonizing process of going natural revealed a stunning platinum silver, not the dingy yellowish gray she'd feared. Had she known, she would've made the switch a lot sooner and saved hundreds of dollars from needless salon visits.

Wet hair slicked back, she applied tinted moisturizer, a hint of mascara, and a dab of lip gloss. Putting on her face, as Frank used to call it. Far less "face" than she wore in America, but enough to make her feel presentable.

Her mother would approve.

She left the steamy bathroom and blow-dried her hair

in front of the full-length mirror on the back of her bedroom door. Thank God for easy hair.

A quick double-knot to her Nikes and she was out the door, intent on her mission to join Brock on the terrace for his morning sunrise ritual.

Something she rarely did even though she'd been given an open invitation. Shyness and perhaps a fear that he was offering out of politeness made her hesitant to overuse the privilege.

Today, she had some news that would affect them both, and she was eager to share it. With a hefty shove, she opened the terrace doors.

Brock whipped around and rose a little too swiftly, knocking a reluctant cat from his lap.

As usual, his smile warmed her entire being.

"Good morning." With a quick swipe, Brock brushed the seat of a chair and gestured for her to sit. "This is a nice surprise, but I meant to tell you to sleep in today."

She returned his smile and pretended not to notice she'd startled him. "As much as I'd like to, I've never been able to sleep past five."

Brock backed to his usual chair and paused until she was seated. "A plight we both share, I'm afraid."

A faint hint of citrus drifted her way. His full silver hair was still damp and combed. His close-cropped beard neatly trimmed. A rather attractive man. Not the first time she'd tried unsuccessfully not to notice.

She let her head rest against the back of the chair, the

eastern horizon getting brighter with no hint of clouds. "Hardly looks like the same sky as yesterday's."

Brock followed her gaze and sighed. "The calm before the storm."

She jerked upright. "Another storm?"

His soft chuckle was sweet and oddly reassuring. "Not a rainstorm, but just as daunting. The clinic seems to be slammed whenever we return from a trip." He leaned forward and propped his arms on his thighs. "Every so often the monsoons dig in with one last show of force. It rarely rains in June, but, in hindsight, I should've planned the trip for later." His words sounded more like an apology than observation.

"The trip was perfect, Brock."

He grinned, giving her a sideways glance. "Even the bridge fiasco?"

She laughed, "Even that. In fact, I made a decision that I wanted to discuss—" A sliver of sun inched into view, and she clamped her mouth shut.

No way would she interfere with what his own daughter called a *near obsession to never miss a sunrise*.

Within minutes, the sun cleared the cragged hillside with a brilliance that was indeed breathtaking.

They enjoyed it in silence for a minute before Brock shifted back. "You were saying?"

It pleased her more than a little that he seemed not just politely interested but actually eager to hear what she had to say.

She opened her mouth and was again interrupted, this time by a panting golden retriever that raced across the terrace and skidded into Brock's legs.

"Lady! Hello, girl!" Brock's enthusiastic welcome made the dog even more hyper. She probably would've jumped onto his lap had he not leaned down to tousle her fur. "I know. I missed you, too."

Toby came soon after. "I tell you what. That girl's been moping around ever since you left."

Brock stood and gripped Toby's extended hand, pulling him closer into a hearty embrace. "Good to see you, Toby."

"Good to see you, too, Doc." Toby stepped around Brock to get to her. "Miss Joy."

"Hello!" She stood, her full height barely reaching Toby's shoulders, and slid her arm around his waist. "How's Nicci feeling?"

"Better. Her morning sickness is 'bout gone." Toby looked back to Brock. "Hope you're hungry. She's in the kitchen now fixing your breakfast, and you know what that means."

Brock laughed. "I do indeed." He patted his flat stomach. "But after two weeks, I think I can do it justice."

Toby's wide smile lit his dark face. "That's good, cause trust me, you don't want to mess with a pregnant woman. Hey, I'll be flying out later this morning for the supplies Iyegha ordered. Let me know if you want to add anything."

"Thank you. I'll check his list and let you know. Tell Nicci we'll be there in a few minutes. Can't wait to get some of her coffee and cinnamon rolls." Brock waited until Toby cleared the double doors. He gave her an apologetic grin. "Now, where were we?"

"I've decided to stay another year." She blurted before anything else could stop her. "That's if you want me to."

"Oh, I want you to. I've been wondering how I was going to manage around here without you."

"You're kind. I think you'd manage just fine." She dropped her gaze to her hands. "But I'm not sure I'd manage so well if I left." She shifted to face him, fighting the tremor in her voice. "The trip to the outlying villages confirmed my decision to stay. God flooded my heart with love for these sweet, humble people. I almost feel as if I was born for this time in my life."

A slight breeze cooled her hot cheeks. Brock listened, his eyes soft, expressive and so full of understanding, she wanted to tell him more. Tell him things she'd barely acknowledged even to herself. That like everyone else in this entire medical compound, she had fallen under his spell. That she admired him above any other man she'd ever known and that he was a big reason she had started to feel alive again.

Would his razor-sharp perception see the things she'd left unsaid? She prayed not. The last thing she wanted was to sabotage the easy friendship that had developed between them.

She could be content just to be here and work with him in this great ministry. After much prayer, the peace had come the last day of their trip when Brock said his final goodbye to the rain-soaked village.

She rose, having said all she dared to say.

He stood, too, and took her hand, placing his other hand on top, a gesture she'd seen him use many times with patients, as well as staff. Simply an act of kindness and affirmation, but it warmed her heart, as did his smile. "I'm very thankful God sent you here, Joy."

"Me, too." To keep from melting into a puddle at his feet, she said the first thing that came to mind. "I'll need to stop by your office for my personnel folder to look up my son's phone number."

His forehead wrinkled as he shook his head. "You've lost me."

"I hate to confess it, but I never memorized my son's number. I always just hit speed dial."

Brock nodded, then his eyes widened. "Your phone." He covered his mouth, his face stricken as if he'd committed murder. "It was in the bag I tossed into the river. I'm so sorry."

Her big mouth. If she'd been in her right mind, she would've asked Miriam to get the folder, and Brock would never have known. "Please don't apologize. Absolutely no harm done. I'll return to the States in a couple of months to take care of some business. I was planning to upgrade anyway." Not exactly true but considering the circumstances, definitely plausible.

"I'll fly back with you. Ellie's been begging me to visit. I'll replace the phone and anything else that was lost."

She opened her mouth to protest, but he held up his hand. "Please. I insist."

"Brock, you really don't have to."

"I want to."

They faced off, then she relented, if only to make him feel better.

"Good." He took a deep breath and blew it out. "Now, we'd better get in there before Nicci comes looking for us."

Breakfast proved to be a short, but sweet reunion. Joy ducked out ahead of the others to brush her teeth and use the restroom. Within minutes, she rejoined the team as they filed out the side doors to the compound.

Mac, the compound mechanic and general handyman, held the door. "Step right out, little lady. You don't want to miss the show."

"The show?"

"Just watch." He grinned and gestured with the Styrofoam coffee cup in his hand. "Doc gets an enthusiastic welcome when he's been gone a while. Some of the nationals won't let anyone but Doc treat them. Some even camped out the whole two weeks waiting for him."

Show indeed. Joy stood on tiptoe, then sidestepped the team for a better view. Barefooted children with heads bobbing raced across packed-down red gravel and barreled into Brock, grabbing his legs and almost knocking him over.

Brock laughed and patted their heads. A host of adults caught up and blocked her view.

Mac nudged her arm. "See what I mean?"

Joy nodded. "It's like he's a rock star."

Like one giant organism, the crowd inched toward the clinic. Moses moved ahead and motioned for the medical staff to follow.

"And there goes the bouncer to run interference. Better catch up, Miss Joy, so you won't get trampled." With a wave, Mac veered to the left, followed by Al.

Moses stood on the second step facing the crowd while she and Miriam squeezed into the clinic behind him. Brock made it inside and then Moses, who pushed back wiggling fingers before easing the door closed.

"Whew." Brock wiped his forehead with a hanky and smiled at her. "Sweet people. They get a little excited when the team returns from a trip."

The team? Not likely. She grinned but didn't bother to correct his assessment. "Mac gave me a heads up. Was that the storm you told me was coming?"

"I'm afraid it's just getting started."

With that, Brock made the switch from celebrity to the single-minded doctor she worked with every day. He stepped over to a window and peeked through the blinds. "Iyegha?"

Iyegha, his most trusted African assistant, joined Brock at the window.

"See the woman with the child strapped to her back?"

Iyegha shook his head. "There are three such women. Which one do you mean?"

Brock edged closer and pointed. "That one. Move her to the front of the line, please."

Iyegha nodded and hurried out, but soon returned. A woman, her face etched with weariness, followed close behind. The limp body of a small girl was strapped to her back.

Brock took the woman's hand and gave her an encouraging smile, then lifted the makeshift bandage from the child's leg.

The odor that had already permeated the room became so powerful, it took all Joy's resources not to gag.

Saving this child would take a miracle, and from Brock's pained expression, he knew it.

CHAPTER 5

Brock lifted the unconscious child from the mother's stooped back and placed her on the examination table. Such a frail little being, probably no more than four. Below the left knee, shreds of rotting flesh held the stench of putrid decay.

The child remained unresponsive, a few short breaths from death. Normally, this would be the time he would nod to Miriam. With her superior skills with dialects, she would take the relative to a private room to explain there was nothing more they could do.

The woman fell to her knees, her hands folded as if in prayer. "*Giumbo.*"

Machete. She was pleading for him to cut off the diseased leg. The child would most likely die, but that was God's call to make, not his.

Brock swallowed back his own tears and bent to enclose her rough leathery hands in his own. His knowledge of Angolan slang was sketchy at best. He requested her name in his best Portuguese. "*Como se Chama?*"

She dropped her gaze and mumbled. "Kasemba."

He eased her chin up to maintain eye contact and spoke

in a soothing tone. "Kasemba, I will try."

She lunged forward and clutched his leg, resting her damp cheek against his thigh. "*Obrigado.*"

In response to her gratitude, he placed his hand on her head, her hair coarse and matted from sweat and layers of red dust. She must have come a great distance. She slumped against him as if she could no longer hold herself upright.

Miriam bent and took great pains to gently pry loose the woman's grip on his leg. He nodded and gave a reassuring smile as Miriam led her from the room. Iyegha had already begun intravenous fluids and antibiotics.

Joy went with him to scrub, her quiet presence a comfort. No need to speak or state the obvious. One of the things he appreciated the most about working with her.

He scoured his hands and forearms, mechanically scrubbing every inch, while his mind mapped out the procedure. They returned to the surgery table within minutes in sterile surgical gowns and masks, although outside germs posed the least threat. The toxicity of the decaying leg had most likely poisoned the child's entire body.

Iyegha removed disposable gloves and stepped away to prepare himself for surgery. Joy slid into place and applied lidocaine to the entire area of concern.

Brock had performed many amputations in his years at the mission, always as a last resort, and always with regret. He took the scalpel from Joy and made the incision, feeling the cut in the pit of his stomach.

"She's not breathing." Joy spoke with quiet urgency. She fingered the wrist in search of a pulse, then shook her head.

The scalpel clanked on the tray as he switched to CPR counting thrusts to the tiny chest. He stayed with it, probably longer than he should have, praying life back into the inert form on the table. "Come back. Sweet child." He blinked away sweat stinging his eyes and leaned in, repeating in Portuguese. "*Volte, crianca doce.*"

The bluish hue of the child's slack lips confirmed what he had feared all along.

Joy fingered the pencil-thin wrist and shook her head.

For one brief moment, they both stopped and looked at each other, the heavy hush of regret forming an unspoken bond.

Joy smoothed back a wisp of curly black hair from the tiny forehead. "I'll stay."

Brock lowered his mask and turned toward the double doors. He stuffed his blood-spattered surgical gown into the receptacle before he entered the waiting area.

Both women raised large hopeful eyes as he entered the room. He closed the distance to their bench and addressed Miriam. "Let her know her daughter has gone to God."

Miriam nodded and turned to the wide-eyed young woman.

The woman looked up at him, her expression full of

agony.

He knelt in front of her and covered the cold, limp hands folded on her lap. *"Sou Wawè."*

His apology brought out an anguished cry that seemed to come from the deepest part of her core. She collapsed against Miriam who wrapped both arms around the woman and spoke in soothing tones.

Brock slowly released a deep breath. Life and death were in God's sovereign hands. He'd made peace with that long ago, but informing loved ones never seemed to get any easier. Kasemba, crumbling beside him in exhaustion and grief, would need their support and help.

"Does she have family?"

Miriam spoke over Kasemba's drooping shoulders. "Only an uncle. He forced her to take the child from the village. Told her there was bad blood. She does not want to return."

"She won't have to." His jaw tightened. "Tell her we want her to stay here."

Miriam paused and scanned his face.

This wasn't an invitation he extended often and never without a clear prompting from God. Brock squared his shoulders. "Tell her we will be her family now."

Miriam nodded and repeated the message.

Kasemba stilled. Her sorrow-filled eyes now held a faint glimmer of hope.

He stood and gestured. "Come with me."

She took his extended hand and shuffled behind him

like a meek child, but then stiffened as they neared the double doors. Miriam embraced Kasemba from behind and nudged her forward.

Joy had cleaned the child and bandaged the leg that mercifully he had not yet severed from the little body.

The child lay as if she were sleeping with tiny hands folded on her chest, her once-furrowed brow, now relaxed.

Kasemba gathered the child in her arms and rocked her back and forth.

Brock moved closer and encircled both mother and child in an embrace that became tighter as Kasemba sagged against him. Slowly, her sing-song keening stilled, and the room became as quiet as the chapel sanctuary.

He glanced up, searching for Joy's eyes. She met his gaze, her eyes now dry, but reddened and puffy. Her smile warmed him, bolstered him as much as he now bolstered the weary woman in his arms.

Behind Joy, the wall clock read 9:03. Only fifty-three minutes since they'd entered the side door through the crush of people. A tiny soul had already entered eternity.

The storm he had described to Joy had hit early and hard with many more patients and challenges to come before they could call it a day.

CHAPTER 6

Joy lumbered across the compound, kicking herself for baling out.

She grabbed some water from the dining hall cooler and downed four ibuprofen, the maximum number allowed, then rolled the cool bottle across her forehead, praying the jackhammer in her head would take a break. At least, she'd made it through most of the day.

She entered her dormitory room, closed the door, and leaned against it, willing the pills to stay down. Maybe a little rest before dinner. She eased onto the bed, as if her head were a case of nitroglycerin, and blew out her breath in a grateful sigh. There. Just a little rest—

"Joy?"

She opened her eyes and blinked a couple of times. Miriam sat beside her on the bed, her dark form blending into the blackness of the room. "Are you unwell?"

"I have a headache." Pain pulsated behind her eyes. Joy rubbed them and attempted to sit up. "Sorry. I must have dozed."

Miriam's cool fingers pressed against Joy's cheek. "You have a fever."

"Hmm. Your hand feels good."

"I'll let Dr. Brock know you are unwell."

Joy grabbed Miriam's arm. "Please don't. I'll be fine by morning."

Miriam sat again and smoothed the hair back from Joy's forehead. "It was he who sent me. If I do not return, he will come himself."

Joy closed her pain-filled eyes and nodded. Of course, he would have to know, but she'd rather crawl into a cave and die alone than bother this man who'd already been stretched to the limit today.

Miriam left quietly and within seconds, there was a soft knock on the door, then Brock entered, followed by Miriam. "Hello." He sat beside her on the edge of the bed. "What's going on?"

He used his doctor voice, the soft one full of tenderness and compassion, which seriously threatened her resolve to remain calm and stoic.

"Just a headache. Not worth making a fuss about."

He and Miriam exchanged amused glances. "I promise I won't make a fuss. How long have you been feeling bad?"

"Since mid-morning." She tried unsuccessfully to keep the quiver from her voice. "The pain started behind my eyes. Might be a migraine."

Brock nodded, all traces of amusement now replaced with concern as he took a mini flashlight from his pocket. He leaned closer and shined it briefly in each eye. "Do you get many migraines?"

"No."

Miriam handed him a thermometer. He placed it under Joy's tongue, then reached for her hand, fingering her wrist and applying gentle pressure to her pulse. He removed the thermometer and held it up sideways to catch the light from the hallway. His face remained unreadable as he handed the thermometer back to Miriam. "How's the pain now?"

"Not much better."

He studied her for a long moment, then gave her the Jesus smile, the one he gave all his patients. "I think we'd better move you to the clinic."

Miriam returned his almost imperceptible nod and left the room.

The searing pain had steadily become more intense. Joy closed her eyes and wondered if it were possible for them to explode out of her head.

"I want to draw some blood. Do some tests."

It hurt too much to nod. Joy offered a weak smile instead and mumbled, barely moving her lips. "If I die in Africa, my son will kill me."

Brock chuckled. "It's me he will kill."

He took her hand and squeezed, speaking so softly she barely heard the words.

"And I'm not going to let you die."

Bloodwork confirmed what Brock had most feared. Chart in hand, he walked down the darkened hallway, a cycle of "if only's" marching in formation around his guilt-ridden conscience.

If only he hadn't taken her to the outlying villages.

If only he had waited longer, well past the rainy season.

If only it was he and not Joy ...

He knocked softly and entered the cubicle-sized room.

Joy stirred and opened glazed eyes that quickly fastened on him. "If I have the flu, I don't want you to get it."

"Not the flu. Dengue fever."

"Dengue." Joy stared at him, her wan face expressionless. "I remember the name, not much else."

"An illness with no known vaccine." He raked a hand through his hair. "In spite of every precaution, one infected mosquito somehow got through. The virus has been percolating in your blood anywhere from four to seven days."

She looked at the ceiling as if calculating when she'd been bitten, then turned back to him. "Maybe I shouldn't have prayed to experience all Africa had to offer."

Her self-deprecating chuckle tightened the knot already crushing his gut. "I'm so sorry. I regret—"

"No. Don't apologize." She placed her hand on his arm then pulled it back. "It's not contagious, is it?"

"Only if the same mosquito bites someone else." He reached for the hand she'd snatched away and held it firmly in his. "Don't worry. Moses, Miriam, and I have all had our bouts with dengue, so we're immune."

"How long will it last?"

"About two weeks." He had to level with her. He owed her that much. "The first week will be the roughest. High fever. Nausea. Body aches. It'll feel like the flu times ten. We'll keep you here as a patient and try to make you as comfortable as possible."

"The clinic is already so busy." Her voice became more tremulous. "I hate to be a bother."

The arm she flung over her eyes did not hide the lone tear trailing down her temple and into her hairline. He smiled in spite of himself at the fragile pathetic picture she made and without thinking it through, Brock raised the hand he still held and brushed it against his lips. "Joy. You are no bother."

She had either drifted off again or was too weak to respond.

His throat tightened. Dengue fever was rarely fatal, but it could be. He shifted and placed her hand back on the sheet. "I'm going to check your vitals, then let you rest."

She remained unmoving and quiet as he clicked a plastic sleeve onto a thermometer and leaned in, whispering close to her ear. "I need to take your temperature." He already knew it would be bad, judging from the heat radiating through the sheet. He guided the instrument under her tongue and waited.

One hundred four point nine. Brock's jaw tightened. Any higher and they would have to pack her in ice.

Miriam pushed open the door enough to peek in. "How

is she?"

"Resting. I'm glad you're here. I need to take care of a few things. Can you stay with her for a little while?"

"Of course." Miriam grabbed the padded chair from the corner and set it beside the bed.

He placed his hand on Miriam's shoulder and whispered, "Thank you." With one more glance at Joy, he left the room.

The clinic hallway extended like a long dark tunnel with one faint nightlight halfway, signaling a turn leading to the staff dormitory hall. Usually a very welcomed sight to a worker much in need of rest.

Tonight, he bypassed the familiar path and continued noiselessly down the tunnel to the last room on the right. He maneuvered through the room and around the oversized desk without turning on a light.

His office. One of the many places on the compound he could go for sanctuary. He sank into his leather desk chair and blew out a long, grateful sigh. The first quiet moment he'd had since early morning to pause, think his own thoughts, and connect with God. Moments as essential as food and water for him to function in this ministry—and something he would give up sleep to preserve.

He rested his head against the back of the chair, his brain too tired to form a prayer. The faint sound of footsteps in the hall indicated that his brief moments of solitude were about to end. A familiar gait and stride that could only belong to Moses.

Brock spoke as the dark, shadowy form filled the doorway. "Hello, my friend."

The usually unflappable Moses let out a gasp.

"Sorry. I didn't mean to startle you." Brock clicked on the desk lamp and blinked as his eyes adjusted. "You're up late tonight."

"As are you." Moses took the chair in front of the desk, his long fingers still splayed against his chest. "Miriam told me the unfortunate news. Joy will have some rough days to come."

"Yes."

Moses leaned forward resting his forearms on his thighs. "God sends dengue to those who belong to Africa."

Brock smiled. "As I recall, those words brought little comfort when you nursed me through my bout of fever. Perhaps it would be wise to hold that information from Joy until she feels better."

"Indeed." Moses's easy laughter split the muffled stillness of the night air. He stared into space, a wide smile creasing his face as if he were cherishing the shared memory.

"But I must confess, I regret my decision to take Joy to the outlying villages."

Moses looked at him, his expression now sober. "This woman. She is special to you. More than a worker?"

Brock dropped his gaze to his clasped hands. With one simple statement, Moses had zeroed in on what he'd been dancing around for weeks. Moses knew him too well.

Would be pointless to deny it.

"Yes. I find I enjoy her company very much."

"Joy finds your company a pleasure also."

Brock leaned forward, feeling like an adolescent, waiting for him to say more.

Which Moses seemed happy to do. "Her face brightens when you enter a room."

Brock assessed, then shook his head. "Joy has a gift for making people feel valued. She brightens when anyone enters a room."

"Like the moon." Moses gave him a knowing smile. "For you, she becomes the sun."

Brock could not argue, and truth be told, he didn't want to. In that split second, he entered a new awareness. Uncharted territory that seized him with new feelings and brought back old ones he'd thought long dead. Possibilities he would have to sort through when he was more rested and less vulnerable. And when they had gotten Joy through this crisis.

"You do not have to reach the shore tonight."

Brock shook from his reverie and gave his friend a questioning glance.

Moses rose, "You are tired, my brother. Don't try to reach the shore tonight. Pull in the oars and let God steer the boat."

Simple but profound advice. Brock stood, too, and walked around his desk. "God must have sent you tonight." He placed his hand on Moses's shoulder and walked with him to the door. "Words I needed to hear. Thank you. You are a good and wise friend."

Moses bowed his head in humility. "I pray it is so. God sent the very best man to teach me." Moses turned and gripped Brock's upper arm. "I will leave you now. Do you plan to stay up all night?"

"No. I have a few things to take care of first, but I will make it to bed soon."

"Then I bid you good night."

"Good night."

Alone again, Brock returned to his desk and the task that had brought him to his office in the first place. He pulled Joy's personnel folder from the bottom right drawer and scanned the pages for emergency contact numbers. Not a call he looked forward to making especially after the kind of day this had turned out to be.

Pacific Northwest. Midnight here would make it three, maybe four in the afternoon where David Stockman lived. With a long sigh, he replaced his glasses and tapped out the numbers.

Not surprisingly, after three rings an automated voice clipped out, "Please leave a message after the tone."

"Hello. This is Dr. Brock Whitfield. I need to speak with you concerning your mother." After a short pause, he added, "No emergency, but please call me back at your earliest convenience."

Brock ended the call, and stared blankly, the adrenaline he'd been running on, now bone dry.

Brock re-entered Joy's room without bothering to knock. Miriam remained erect in the chair with only her bowed head bobbing.

He leaned in to whisper. "I'll take over now."

She jerked upright, her eyes wide and slightly bloodshot.

Without meaning to, he'd managed first to startle Moses, and now Miriam, within the span of a half hour.

Miriam shook her head. "No need. I can stay. You need your rest."

"We both need rest." Brock took Joy's chart and scanned the numbers. "I'd better grab some ice packs from the storeroom fridge. As soon as I get her fever under control, I'll let the night nurse take over. It's Sonja tonight, isn't it?

"I'll go." Miriam was out the door before he could protest.

Joy lay perfectly still in the same position as when he'd left over an hour ago. At least she was resting.

Miriam returned with four ice packs submerged in a basin of ice water. "I brought some extra cloths."

"Wonderful." He took the basin and set it on the table beside the bed. "Did you speak to Sonja?"

"I will do that now. Is there anything else I can get for you?"

"No. Thank you. Get some rest."

With a feather touch to Joy's arm, Miriam left the room.

Brock picked up the chair and moved it out of the way. Then he wrung out one of the cloths and placed it on Joy's furrowed brow.

Her lips curled into a slight smile. "Feels good."

"You're awake?"

"Hmm. Trying not to move. Hurts too much."

Brock's jaw clenched, all too aware of the skull-splitting pain she was experiencing. It was a memory still vivid even after twenty-plus years. He dropped the now-warm cloth back into the basin and left the room. Within minutes, he returned with a syringe loaded with codeine.

He took her limp arm and dabbed the inside of her elbow with an alcohol swab. "A little stick." He whispered as he eased the needle under her skin. "I called David."

For the first time since he'd entered the room, she opened her eyes and looked at him.

He nodded, answering the unspoken question he saw in the glassy depths. "I'll give him daily updates. When you feel up to it, you can talk to him yourself."

Joy started to nod, then closed her eyes again.

Brock reached for the petite hand now clutching the edge of her sheet. "The pain will ease soon."

She responded, barely moving her lips. "Thank you."

For calling her son? For some drug-induced relief? Or could it be for taking her hand? He smiled and tightened his grip around her limp fingers. "You're welcome."

His own fatigued muscles started to cramp from the awkward stance he'd taken. Only after her brow eased and she had settled into long measured breaths did he let go of his hold to place her hand under the sheet.

Sonja peeked in. He grabbed the chart and motioned for her to join him in the hall, thankful she hadn't walked in a moment earlier. After a quick briefing, he left Joy in Sonja's care.

Within minutes, he fell across his bed, too drained to bother undressing. If he fell asleep right away, he could squeeze in three hours.

His frazzled mind drifted back to Joy. Could he dare to hope that after all these years, God was giving him another chance to love and be loved in return?

Moses was right. There would be no reaching the shore this night.

CHAPTER 7

Brock tied off the last suture and stepped away from the gurney. He drew off his surgical gloves and rubbed the back of his neck. Three days had passed in a blur with hardly time to breathe. He crossed the hall to Joy's room hoping for news of a breakthrough.

He eased the door open. Miriam stood at the head of the bed bathing Joy's face with a wet compress.

Kasemba stood on the opposite side. She looked up as he entered, her face beaming. "Doktor Borock."

He gave Miriam a sideways glance. "English?"

Miriam broke into her trademark smile without looking up. "She has something else to tell you."

Brock shifted his attention back to Kasemba and gave an encouraging nod.

Kasemba placed her hand over her heart and looked at Miriam before stammering out, "Je'sus."

"Yes!" Brock laughed and repeated, "Jesus!"

She waited, smiling broadly, and it took a couple of seconds for the news to register. He turned to Miriam. "You're saying Kasemba trusted Christ today?"

Miriam nodded, her smile matching Kasemba's.

"Wonderful!"

Miriam dropped the cloth back into the basin of water and inched closer to him. "We talked a long time today. Kasemba prayed for Jesus to wash her clean and make her His child. She asked me to teach her enough English to tell you herself."

His throat constricted. "Very good, Kasemba!"

Less than a week had passed since they'd lost the precious little one Kasemba had brought in strapped to her back. *Sweet Jesus! How like You to give beauty for ashes.*

He placed his own hand over his heart and spoke to Kasemba. "Boa! Kuyava!" His praise in both Portuguese and Angolan dialect did not touch the depth of his emotion.

Kasemba looked from Miriam back to Brock and spoke again in a halting voice. "Tank yu."

Brock raised steepled fingers to his lips, his heart too full for words.

Miriam and Kasemba stared at him, their large eyes wide and bright with unshed tears mirroring his own.

He stepped around the bed and placed his arm around Kasemba in a sideways embrace. His touch brought on an avalanche of epic proportions. Her thin shoulders convulsed as pent-up tears gushed without restraint. With a choking sob that seemed to come from her very core, she turned and buried her wet face in the crook of his neck.

Compassion flooded his heart. This poor love-starved girl had known more than her share of abuse and heartache. He held onto her, gripping tighter as she sagged against him. "Sim." Yes. Cry it out, sweet one. Maybe now true healing could begin. "*Boa. Ta Fiche.*" He repeated soft words of affirmation until the torrent ended. He held Kasemba a moment longer, then released her and took a step back.

Kasemba dropped her gaze, her short, jerking breaths becoming steadier as she wiped her wet cheeks. "*Obrigado Je'sus veio para dentro e levou a minha tristeza.*"

If he heard right, Kasemba already had a good grasp of what true Christianity was all about.

Miriam joined them and took Kasemba's hand. "Yes. She thanked Jesus for coming inside and driving out her sadness."

"My heart is overwhelmed. I came in here hoping for good news. This was even better than I expected."

"The fever has been high." Miriam handed him Joy's chart and jolted him back to the pressing business at hand. "She talks out of her head."

"Any vomiting or nosebleeds?"

Miriam shook her head and handed the bowl of melted ice packs to Kasemba.

He took Joy's arm and turned it over. A rash but no abnormal bruising. He prayed it stayed that way. High fever, even delirium was to be expected. Nosebleeds and bruising could mean something much more serious. He pulled reading glasses from his shirt pocket, then scanned the numbers on the chart. "I'll take over the rest of the evening."

Miriam guided Kasemba to the door, then paused and

touched his arm. "Our Joy is a fighter. She will come back to us."

He knew in his heart she was right. In twenty-five years on the field, he'd lost only one to dengue.

But he also knew God didn't always work according to the odds. He placed the chart on the bedside table and managed a smile. "I pray you are right."

"I'll have Nicci send you a tray."

He thanked her even though the thought of food turned his stomach. Left alone, he fished the cloth out of the basin and wrung it out.

Waiting. Probably the hardest part of his job. Give him any operable tumor, and he could deliver. Abscesses, broken bones? Not a problem. All things he could fix.

But fever wasn't so cut and dried. As untamable and unpredictable as the black mamba rearing its deadly head.

A shudder rippled through his spine. Thank God it was dengue and not venom infiltrating her bloodstream.

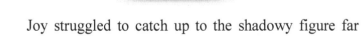

Joy struggled to catch up to the shadowy figure far ahead. Each time she got close, he disappeared over the next dune. *"Frank."*

He did not turn or slow down. She cast off her shoulder bag and walked faster, careful to plant her feet in the hollowed-out footprints he left behind. The scorching sun felt like a laser splitting her head in two. The sand seared her bare feet.

"Frank, please."

He turned, and his scowling face disintegrated before her eyes.

She stood, unable to move or respond. The sand between them disappeared as if it were sifting through a funnel. She tumbled with it, sliding into the vortex. Flailing about, she grasped for anything to slow her descent, then hurtled forward, freefalling into a black chasm.

Strong hands caught her, gripped her arms, and set her upright. A stranger. A man, whose face was blurred and out of focus. He steadied her and brushed loose sand from the folds of the African tunic she wore.

Her legs gave way beneath her. When she came to, she lay on her side beside a crystal-clear lake. The stranger now sat in the crook of her body, his back pressed against her thigh. He bathed her face and dropped water from a sponge into her mouth. She swallowed, eager for more.

The stranger's presence comforted her, made her feel safe. His shadow fell across her and blocked the searing sun. He placed the palm of his hand on her cheek.

She wanted to cover his hand with hers so he couldn't remove it from her cheek. More than anything, she wanted to thank him, for rescuing her, but her lips were unable to respond.

"I won't leave you."

She stilled.

Had he read her mind and answered her silent plea?

His presence filled her with a sense of overpowering

love that wrapped around her like a warm cocoon. She craved more, even more than the water he dropped on her lips.

She curled around him and let herself drift off, finally at peace.

Brock waited, unmoving, for over an hour, until he was sure Joy's fever was fully broken, then moved gingerly from her side.

He eased beside her bed and knelt, not caring his angry knee would give him fits when he tried to rise again. He rested his forehead against clasped hands. *Look inside my heart, dear Father. Read the overwhelming gratitude and love I feel for You at this moment.*

He raised and caught a glimpse of his watch. Four in the morning. Soon, Sonja would be making her last rounds of the night shift. That would leave just enough time.

Brock winced as he pushed back from the bed. A nice hot shower for these stiff muscles.

And then the sunrise, which could not be anything but glorious.

CHAPTER 8

Joy's pulse sped up as the familiar footsteps she had anticipated for the past hour came closer. Not to seem too eager, she waited a few seconds after the soft knock before answering, "Come in."

Brock entered and with him the invisible aura that seemed to surround him and fill the room with a sense of peace. He smiled and crossed the room to stand beside her chair. "Hello." He took the hand she held out to him and gave it a gentle squeeze. "How was your day?"

"Surprisingly good."

He released her hand and pulled a chair from the corner a little closer.

"Kasemba can now say five complete sentences."

"Impressive." Brock's crooked smile held a hint of amusement. "Toby made a mail run today." He handed her a bright yellow envelope with her name printed in neat, precise letters. "Eric's handwriting."

She chuckled and slid her fingernail under the back flap. "Stick around. You may have to interpret anything Ellie wrote inside."

Two photos tumbled out as she opened the card. "The twins!" She leaned closer and centered the picture between them. "How cute. Look at that hair."

"There's a caption on the back." Brock took his reading glasses from his shirt pocket and handed them to Joy.

"Thanks." The glasses slid down her nose. She tilted her head, then handed them back. "Sorry. I can't make out what Ellie wrote."

Brock held one side, his head almost touching hers. "Not sure." He took the photo and squinted. "I think it says Bek is chewing Nicky's chin. Good thing she doesn't …?" He gave it back to her. "Can't make out the last two words."

She examined it again. "Teeth! Doesn't have teeth." She flipped it over and leaned in for another shared look. "Too cute. I can't wait to get my hands on those babies."

Brock took the other photo from her lap and held it out for her to see. "Family photo from their living room."

"Beautiful family." Brock's family that she loved like her own. A wave of homesickness washed over her. "They look happy."

Brock's phone rang. He fished it out of his pocket and checked the caller ID. "It's David." He handed her the phone and stood. "Would you like to sit on the terrace after dinner?"

She nodded and smiled to the retreating figure, then pressed the green button on the phone as the door closed. "Hello."

"Hey, Mom. How are you feeling?"

"Almost back to normal."

"That's good to hear."

"I'm back in my dorm room now. One of the national girls kept me company today. I'm teaching her some English."

She heard his soft chuckle and the ding of his car door. Of course. It was morning in Seattle and he would be on his way to work. "So, now that I have my wits about me again, catch me up. What's been going on with you?"

He didn't answer right away which could have been due to all sorts of things. Maybe he was maneuvering through traffic. Or maybe the sheer distance between them caused a delay.

"I'd rather talk about you, Mom. The doctor called with daily updates. You had me pretty worried. One more day and I would've booked a flight."

The uncharacteristic concern in his voice made her throat prickle with unshed tears. "That's sweet, but I'm glad you didn't. There wasn't anything you could've done, and I'd much rather you visit when I'm well enough to enjoy it. How's Abby doing?"

Another long pause. This time, her mother radar went off like a five-alarm fire. "David?"

"Abby's gone, Mom."

"What?"

His long sigh held resignation, and something much worse. Defeat. "She left me."

"Oh, David. No. When? What happened?"

"About a month ago."

He left the other question unanswered. She sat there stunned, not knowing what to say. "I'm so sorry."

"Me, too."

"But … there's hope, right? That you can work things out?"

"I don't think so. One of those things, I guess."

He sounded like her son again. Humble. Approachable. Not the distant, driven business mogul like his father. "What can I do?"

He paused, then said, "You seem to be one of God's favorites. Say a good word for me."

"I will." A spark of hope flickered. She resisted the urge to press for more details or offer advice. "Listen, I'll be back in the States in about four weeks. Would you be able to break away for a visit?"

She waited, praying he wouldn't say no.

"I'll try. Listen, I'm pulling into the parking deck. I'll call you again tomorrow. I'm glad you're feeling better. I love you, Mom."

Her throat constricted. It had been a long time since he'd said those words. She answered back, trying not to gush. "I love you, too, son."

Joy set Brock's phone face down on the bedside table and stared numbly at the floor.

Her relationship with Abby had always been cordial but not close, no matter how many times Joy had tried to tighten the gap. She'd even thought of relocating to Seattle shortly after Frank's death. Thank God, she hadn't.

Still, her heart was heavy, for David and for Abby. Couples seemed to give up way too easily these days.

What went wrong? Her first thought went to an extramarital affair, either his or hers.

Difficult to overcome, but not impossible, as she had learned so many years before. She had never regretted her decision to stay and work things out.

Was the sin of the father now being visited on the son? The thought made her sick. To her knowledge, David knew nothing of his father's infidelity. Maybe she should tell him and also tell him that forgiveness and restoration are possible with God's help.

She had prayed a long time for David to return to the faith that had once been such a strong part of his life.

When dengue struck, she'd had the crazy thought God might even use her own death to touch his heart and bring him back. But the breakup of his marriage?

"Dear God, my boy."

Tears, that seemed to hover near the surface since her illness, now poured down her cheeks. She bowed her head and wrapped her arms around her body, rocking back and forth. "Please, God. Bring him back. Fix this. Fix him, before it's too late."

CHAPTER 9

Brock took a sip of water and nodded to something Moses had said, his mind much more focused on the quiet woman to his right. Maybe he should've insisted she have a tray sent to her room. Rushing recovery, especially from dengue, could bring a serious relapse.

Brock wanted more than anything to find a way to bring back the spark he'd seen earlier this afternoon. He stood and held Joy's chair as she pushed back from the table. "Would you like a raincheck for the terrace?"

"A raincheck?" She blinked up at him. "No—I mean—but if you'd rather not."

"I don't want you to overdo it."

She gripped the edge of the table and pulled herself up. "I think cabin fever has replaced dengue."

He laughed and fell into step beside her. "Then I definitely prescribe some terrace therapy."

She took the arm he offered with a grateful smile. "Thank you. I'm still a little unsteady."

He liked the feel of her hand resting on the inside of his elbow. "You're making a remarkable recovery."

"Really? I'm starting to think I'll never get my old pep back."

Aha. She was just tired, understandably so. "I know what you mean, but you'll get it back, I promise."

"You have a wonderful bedside manner." Joy smiled up at him, her eyes soft. "It felt good to be back in my own room again." Joy slowed her steps and faced him. "You arranged for Kasemba to stay with me today, didn't you?"

"I did." He adjusted his pace to hers. "Was it too much? Would you rather be alone?"

"Oh gracious, no! I loved having her with me. She's precious. There must be so many others like her out there." Joy made a sweeping gesture with her hand. "Girls who are starved for love and for the truth about the Savior. It's crazy, Brock, but it made me want to visit those villages again."

She spoke with a passion that touched him, especially since she'd been so quiet at dinner. He smiled and covered the hand still wrapped around his arm with his own. "You don't know how many times I've regretted taking you into those villages."

She stopped and turned to him. "You can't be serious."

He met her gaze. "When you were out of your head with fever, I vowed to never again take you to the outlying villages."

She released her hold on his arm and stared at him, her eyes wide. "Why not? You said I can't get dengue again."

"Joy, I love your spunk and courage and your heart for these people."

"But?"

His mouth went dry. How could he tell her about the *soba,* the sleazy village chieftain who'd tried to bargain for a night with the *mwatu wawa kwuiba,* the silver-haired beautiful woman? Or the million other dangers she might be subjected to. "I couldn't live with myself if something happened to you on one of those trips."

Her expression softened, and she slid her hand back into the crook of his arm. "That's kind of you, Brock. But I'm willing to take that risk."

He wasn't. But it was God's and Joy's call to make, not his. He managed a smile as they resumed walking. "I think Moses was right."

"Moses?"

"The night I told him about your fever. He said dengue attacks the ones who are meant to be in Africa."

Her eyes widened with the sparkle that had been absent for quite some time. "I had hoped God would send an easier confirmation that I was supposed to return for another year."

Brock laughed, "I'm glad to hear you haven't changed your mind."

They reached the end of the hall. Brock pushed open one of the double doors and was hit with a gust of easterly wind. "July evenings can be chilly. Would you like a wrap?"

"No, it feels wonderful." Joy spoke as she breezed past him.

A chorus of crickets and tree frogs greeted him as he

followed her out to the terrace. Most of the field, with its clumps of natural vegetation and scrub brush now covered in shade, gave off a pungent, musky smell he particularly loved. The sun, setting behind the mission, highlighted the treetops on the other side of the field with a golden glow.

Joy took a deep breath and let out an appreciative sigh. "I've missed this."

"So have I."

He stopped short of adding not just the terrace but time with her, in the quiet of the evening after a busy day. The two of them, alone, away from the rest of the team.

He angled a patio chair for her, then pulled another one closer and sat beside her. They both remained quiet as the tranquility of the evening settled over them.

After a long while, she shifted in her seat and smiled. "How was your day? Any interesting cases?"

"The usual infections. Abscesses. Oh, and a knee that was severely out of joint. A man, probably in his late forties. Tough guy. Barely let out a grunt when I finally yanked it into place. Had I known it would take five tries, I would've sedated him."

"Any surgeries?"

He shook his head. "I've postponed most surgeries until I get my assistant back. I'm afraid you've spoiled me."

"Aww. I bet you say that to all your assistants."

He grinned and raised three fingers. "Just you, scout's honor." Then as quickly changed the subject. "Hey, I had good news today."

"Tell me. I could use some good news."

"A group of volunteers scheduled a visit."

"Reinforcements! Will they arrive before I leave?"

Feline tail held high, Lucy rounded the corner followed by the younger version of herself.

Brock held up a hand. "Excuse me. These two will give no peace until they get what they came for." He scraped back his chair and walked to the storage shed, raising his voice as he spoke over his shoulder. "Anyway, there's a man and wife in this group who came a number of years ago."

The two cats weaved between his legs as he opened a plastic container and scooped cat food into two metal bowls. He eyed both bowls, then transferred a few nuggets from one to the other. "Here you go, girls."

He brushed off his hands and returned to his seat. "Great guy. Gifted surgeon, recently retired from the air force. I mentioned leaving him in charge while I visit the States."

"That's wonderful." She nodded, then fell silent, staring out into the field.

Brock regarded her. Recovering from a fever often left one blue and out of sorts. Not that she was anything but gracious. Just uncharacteristically quiet.

He settled back in his chair and wracked his brain for a subtle way to fish out what was bothering her, then blurted the first thing that came to mind. "I guess David was glad to finally to talk to you in person."

"Hmm?" She roused from her trance. "Yes, I think he was." She dropped her gaze and picked at one of her cuticles.

His skills at reading women were at best rusty, but whatever was eating at her had something to do with her son. He'd put money on it.

"He mentioned you called with daily updates." Joy shifted and gave him a serious look. "That was kind of you. Thank you."

"I was happy to. He seemed very concerned."

"He has a lot on his mind right now. I'd like to ask you to pray for him."

"Of course."

She sighed and added in a flat voice. "His wife left him."

He closed his eyes. A long-suppressed memory surfaced … a time when his own wife had stormed from the house with his two little girls shuffling behind. "I'm so sorry, Joy. Are there children?"

She shook her head and wiped a tear before it reached her chin. "As much as I've prayed for grandchildren, I'm thankful there are none that have to go through this." She leaned forward and gave him an anguished look. "Dave's a lot like his father. Driven. Too self-sufficient to need God."

"Is he a believer?"

Joy shrugged. "I honestly don't know. I took our

children to church. Both made a profession of faith and were baptized. Our daughter died suddenly when she was seventeen."

The news made him gasp. "Whoa, wait a minute. You had a daughter that died?"

She nodded. "Savannah."

He scooted closer and reached for Joy's hand, hungry for clues into her life that by some unspoken agreement neither had yet shared. "What happened?"

"A boating accident. She and a group of friends dove into the water to cool off. Another boat came out of nowhere at top speed and plowed into them. She was the only one—"

The pain in her voice was killing him. He swallowed hard, his thumb absently massaging the side of her hand. "I'm so sorry."

"Thank you. It was a dark time. I clung to God to get me through, but my husband and David seemed to run the other way, immersing themselves in work. It's been over twenty years, and I don't think David's been back to church since." She seemed to regain her composure. "But he did ask for prayer, in a roundabout way, I think. Maybe this separation has jolted him enough to be receptive." She continued, her voice choked with emotion. "Please, help me pray that God will do whatever it takes to break Dave's stubborn will."

God knew how to break a stubborn will, and no one knew that better than he. Brock squeezed her hand. "Would you like to pray now?"

"Yes. Very much."

They leaned in until their shoulders touched, both bowing their heads. He prayed, his heart full of love and gratitude for the grace God had shown in his own life. Beside him, Joy occasionally sniffed and whispered "Yes."

He ended the prayer, and she withdrew her hand from his to wipe her wet cheeks. "Thank you. My son is my heart. He's the only family I have left."

"Would you mind if I ask the team to pray for him during staff devotions?"

"Please do. The more people praying, the better." Joy crossed her arms and shivered.

"You're cold. Let's get you inside."

Joy took his hand and stood, but just as quickly buckled.

Brock lunged and diverted her back into the chair. "I could kick myself for keeping you out here too long."

"I'm fine. I stood up too fast, that's all."

He knelt beside her chair and studied her, unconvinced. He brushed the back of his hand across her forehead, then let his hand linger on her cheek. "You're warm."

She placed her hand on his and gave a pitiful smile that sent an unexpected jolt to his heart. He let himself stay a moment longer, ignoring the twinge in his stiff knee, then pushed himself up. "Come on. I'll help you back to your room. I don't want to have to call David with any more bad news."

She smiled, took his hand, and rose without incident.

Neither spoke in the hall. When they reached her door, he didn't attempt to go in. "Will you be all right?"

She turned. "Yes. Thank you."

He wanted very much to take her in his arms and kiss her good night. Instead, he reached to smooth a strand of hair away from her face. "Get some rest," he whispered. "I'll check on you in the morning."

She nodded and closed the door.

Brock walked down the dark hallway to his own bedroom and fumbled for the knob on his lamp. He grabbed a water bottle from the case he kept by his bed and settled into the brown leather recliner. He took a drink, draining half the bottle in one long swig, then took his prayer journal from the stack on the table beside his chair. After a quick check mark beside the request to heal Joy's fever, he started a new page.

David Stockman.

The pen remained poised above the name as Brock digested the latest piece of information.

Two children. A daughter who had died as a teenager.

A son, most likely the older of the two, who according to Joy had thrown himself into a career.

What kind of mother had Joy been? When had she come to Christ?

More details would be nice. Brock filled in the gaps with what he already knew about her. Definitely, a woman who loved people and was capable of showing great compassion. A skilled nurse who could hold her own no matter the challenge.

And transparent—a quality he valued above most.

He wanted to know more, but in exchange, he would have to tell her more about himself. Could he risk telling her the truth about the man he used to be?

Could he bear the disappointment on her face once he did?

CHAPTER 10

Joy awoke completely relaxed. Headache gone. Forehead cool. She lay in the center of the bed, smiling at the ceiling and in a way, smiling at God.

What a change in her. Almost like she'd been reborn.

Not at all like the impressionable girl who had married the dynamic Frank Stockman and molded herself to his driving personality until she had become almost invisible. No regrets, though. Could she relive her life, there was little she would change.

But this year in Africa had released something of her former self. The pre-Frank version of herself who laughed easily and felt free to be spontaneous.

She flipped back the sheet and coverlet and swung her legs over the side of the bed careful to give the blood a chance to catch up to her upper extremities. No Brock around to catch her if she buckled. The memory released a host of butterflies and not even David's marriage problems could dampen her spirits. If God could bring her through Frank's illness and death with all its ensuing depression, He could navigate David through this dark time, too.

Joy headed to the shower and undressed. She slid dusty bathroom scales from the corner while the water warmed up. Habit forced her to ease onto the scales wearing next to nothing, even though she'd already lost nine pounds since coming to Africa. Her eyes gawked at the result. She stepped off the scales. The needle returned to dead-level zero. Another try produced the same number. Eight more pounds. If she lost any more, her son would frown and swear she had AIDS.

The small bathroom felt like a sauna by the time she finished her shower. She wrapped the towel around her wet hair, then leaned against the pedestal sink, swiping away steam on the mirror to examine her face. Dark circles and pasty complexion. A little foundation should handle those dengue remnants.

She dressed in scrubs and cinched in the waist as far as she could to keep them from slipping down as she walked.

By the time she left her room, the breakfast crowd had vacated the dining hall that still bore the wisps of coffee and bacon. Her sneakers made a faint squeaking sound on the concrete floor as she pushed through the double doors leading to the kitchen. Nicci stood at a counter, her back to the door. From behind, no one would suspect she was almost six months pregnant.

"Hello, Nicci." Joy said above the drone of the industrial-sized dishwasher. "Would you mind if I make myself some tea?"

Nicci whirled around, chef knife in hand, her perfectly round stomach like a medium-sized pumpkin.

"Miss Joy!" Nicci dropped the knife on the counter and rushed to grab a stool and shove it closer to Joy. With a gentle push, she maneuvered Joy down on the seat. "You sit, Ma'am. I will make your tea."

Joy resisted the urge to protest and simply smiled her thanks. Nicci heated the kettle, and minutes later, poured boiling water over loose tea leaves. She turned and leaned against the counter, her hands folded on top of her protruding belly. "We can talk while the leaves steep."

"Let me pull over the other stool so you can sit too."

Nicci waved her hand in dismissal. "It feels better to stand."

"I hear from Toby that your morning sickness is better."

"Yes." Her smile broadened the ridged scars on her cheeks. "Now, I eat all the time." She brought both hands to her mouth and chomped the air.

They both laughed. Then Nicci gave her a serious look. "But you? You are feeling well?"

"Yes. I am well."

Nicci turned and poured steaming amber liquid through a strainer into a clean cup. She added honey and stirred as she closed the distance back to Joy. "That is good. Dr. Brock will now smile again."

"Smile again?" Joy took a quick sip to cover the shameless pumping for information.

"He could not rest. He would not eat. He stay by your side. Night and day." Nicci returned to the counter and continued chopping onions with the skill of an accomplished chef.

Joy cradled the cup in her hands and kept it close to her face. Nicci was known to exaggerate a bit, but even so, the words sent a little jolt to Joy's pulse. So many days of her illness were lost in a haze of jumbled fragments. Had he really stayed by her side? It seemed each time she awoke, it was Miriam or Kasemba beside the bed. He must have slipped from the room like a phantom each time she started to regain consciousness.

The honeyed tea soothed her stomach, still a bit queasy from the aftereffects of the fever. Joy finished it off and put the empty cup in the stainless steel sink. "Your tea is as good as your coffee."

"I'm glad it pleases you." Nicci turned and wiped her hands on a dish towel. "And now, I must ask a favor from you."

"Of course. What can I do for you?"

Nicci filled a Styrofoam cup with fresh coffee and handed it to Joy. "Would you please take this to Dr. Brock? It's almost time for him to come for a break. I must decorate this cake before he sees it."

Joy glanced at the counter. "His birthday cake?"

"Yes. Two days from now. But he does not take the time to acknowledge. Toby is planning a big surprise for him." Nicci's eyes widened as she put her hand over her mouth. She spun back to the counter and began scrubbing down her work area with quick deliberate strokes that jostled her whole backside.

Joy smiled and started to tell her not to worry, that Toby had no doubt already told most of the compound. Instead, she eased closer and slid her arm around Nicci's expanding girth. "Don't worry." She leaned in and whispered. "I'm good at keeping secrets."

Nicci's stiff shoulders relaxed for the briefest of seconds.

"And thank you for the wonderful tea." Her well-timed compliment earned a smile from Nicci. With a wave, Joy backed through the double doors out of the kitchen.

Brock's birthday. Two days to come up with the perfect gift, special and meaningful, but not too personal. Impossible.

She slowed her steps to keep from sloshing the scalding coffee onto her hand and pushed open the side door. The air was cool. A slight breeze tousled the side bangs of her upswept hairdo. Across the compound, Brock squatted beside a man who propped against a muldane tree. Brock once again wore his Jesus smile, as if that one patient was the most important person in the world.

She was almost upon them before he noticed her presence.

He patted the man's shoulder, then stood. "Hello. How are you feeling?"

"Much better." She returned his smile and handed him the coffee.

"Thank you. You must have read my mind."

"Can't take credit. Nicci asked me to bring this to you."

He took a sip, his eyes crinkled in amusement. "She spoils me."

Of course, she does. For lack of anything better to say, she blurted out, "You've already been in surgery."

Brock nodded and looked down at his somewhat soiled scrubs. "Yes. I could've used your skills this morning. Iyegha doesn't quite anticipate my next move like you do."

"I'm dressed and ready for business."

He stopped and gave an apologetic look. "I didn't mean to rush you. We can handle things until you are stronger."

"You're not rushing me. That's why I dressed in scrubs. Please. I'd like to get back to work."

His eyes softened as he released a heavy sigh. "You sound like Ellie. She begged to return to work not two days after her miscarriage."

"Did you let her?"

"Of course. I find it impossible to say no to her."

Joy smiled, thinking how blessed Ellie was to have such a father.

"But I made her promise to stop and rest when she got tired. Can I get the same promise from you?"

She raised her hand. "I promise."

"I'm going to hold you to that. A relapse is not fun. Don't ask me how I know." Brock opened the door of the clinic and gestured for her to go in first.

Every chair around the perimeter of the room was filled, some with children sprawled across the laps of their mothers. Men and older children sat cross-legged, dominating the concrete floor. All sick, hurting people waiting patiently for their number to be called.

Open windows and two ceiling fans going full blast did little to fumigate the rank smells of open wounds and body odor. Joy tried breathing through her mouth, then stifled an involuntary gag.

"Having second thoughts?" Brock gripped her forearm and maneuvered her through the crush of prospective patients.

"No, but when did you say those reinforcements would arrive?"

Brock chuckled, choking on the sip of coffee he'd just taken. "Not soon enough."

Joy followed his path to the large room with curtained cubicles.

Iyegha approached, with a tired but welcoming smile. "It is good to see you, Miss Joy." He backed away and gestured to the patient he'd left, an unconscious man with blood covering the left side of his face.

Joy inched closer as Iyegha spoke to Brock. Apparently, the man had constructed his own gun and had loaded too much powder. It exploded and drove metal shrapnel into his skull.

Brock listened, his expression calm but grave as he

donned green plastic gloves. She did the same and moved to the opposite side of the gurney to await Brock's assessment.

One of her favorite moments, to watch the master at work. Brock's fingers gingerly parted the hair, matted with oozing blood, to examine the point of entry.

She saw what she had missed before. Dark metal protruded from an area about an inch above the man's left earlobe.

Brock shook his head and stepped away from the gurney, peeling off his soiled gloves. "Feel up to surgery?"

"Absolutely."

His grateful smile was like a dose of B-12.

Iyegha signaled two aides to transfer the patient to surgery room one. By the time Brock and she had scrubbed, a surgery team had prepped the man, cleansing away the blood and had laid out surgical instruments which to her surprise included a pair of Craftsman pliers. The area around the protruding metal had been shaved and doused with lidocaine.

Brock looked up and met her eyes as Iyegha helped secure the safety goggles over his face. A brief glance but long enough to make her feel good, like he was really glad she was back.

Brock went to work and within minutes extracted the metal from the man's skull. She leaned in and dabbed the gaping wound. Only fresh red blood flowed. No cerebrospinal fluid or even worse, brain tissue.

"I'm going to leave this open for a while." He spoke as if to himself. "The blood will drain and carry away any contamination from the metal. Iyegha, use pressure dressings to control the blood flow. I'll stitch him up later tonight."

He backed out of the way as aides pushed the gurney to post-op, then removed his gloves and pushed the goggles to his forehead. "Ready to take a break yet?"

Joy removed her gloves, folding one inside the other, and decided to honor her promise. "I think I will. Great work, by the way."

"We have an outstanding team here."

Of course, he would downplay his part. "Yes. Yes, we do." A team she loved being a part of. "Life is never boring here, is it?"

"No. Never that." He walked her to the hallway. "Get some rest. See you tonight at dinner." He gave her elbow a little tweak and turned back to the clinic.

She returned to her dormitory room, an idea for a birthday present kicking around in her brain. But she would need Toby's help and his phone to make it work.

CHAPTER 11

Brock pulled on his standard khaki shorts and chose the tan button-up shirt covered in bold crimson geometric shapes. Not as bright as his usual attire but his favorite nonetheless. His one nod to his birthday.

A day he'd like to ignore if only his staff would let him. They had something cooked up for sure this time. Too many times over the past week he'd entered a room to have all talking suddenly stop, replaced by furtive glances and barely hidden smiles.

He sighed as he double knotted his shoelace. The dear folk seemed to revel in it, so he'd play along. At least they limited it to one day. He could stand anything for one day.

Brock slid the French door back and stepped onto the terrace. He felt his way to his chair and angled it toward the east, then sat, eager for the show. The shed door creaked open and within seconds, Lucy jumped on his lap. He winced and pried loose the razor-sharp claws that kneaded his thighs. "Take it easy, girl. My thin skin can't take the pain anymore."

He nudged her off his lap, then stood, easing to the edge of the terrace. A blanket of fog hovered over the field giving it a mystical look.

Sixty-seven. Funny. He didn't feel that old.

He'd been thirty-three when he left that party too drunk to drive. It should've been *him* that died that night.

His stomach still twisted in knots at the horror of what he'd done. Tight pricking in the back of his throat signaled the inevitable tears the memory evoked yet was always accompanied by overwhelming gratitude.

A sliver of sun inched above the hillside and split the dimness with a ribbon of light kissing the treetops. A sight that never ceased to take his breath away. Within seconds the light fell full on his face, much as it had done in his prison cell so many years before. "Thank you, Jesus. Every day of life since that time has been nothing but grace."

God's amazing grace.

Brock lingered, his full heart not ready to leave his quiet reflection. So many good things had sprung from that tragedy. If he could go back and change the past, would he?

From nowhere, his thoughts drifted to Rozalynde the way a tongue seeks out a sore tooth.

Rozalynde. The socialite wife who'd stormed from his life before he ever went to trial.

Not that he blamed her. Nor did he miss her. Quite possibly the most physically beautiful person he had ever seen, but a shell of a person, whose flawless exterior hid the bitter, acid-tongued woman underneath. A woman who did not try to hide her disdain of him or anything to do with him … except his money.

And yet he prayed for her. A somewhat faithless

prayer but one he'd committed to years ago. For her to come to know Christ. For God to change her, just like God had changed him.

The same prayer he prayed for his two daughters, the only good thing that came from their marriage.

So why had Rozalynde invaded his thoughts now?

The answer came as quickly as the question, and punched him in the stomach.

Joy.

He had fallen deeply in love. He'd fought it. Tiptoed around it. Denied it and had even tried to ignore it. "Who am I kidding?" He looked at the sky. "Certainly, not You. What are you trying to tell me? Why don't I have peace?"

The still, small voice He'd come to count on was silent.

"You know my heart, Father." Brock slowly released the breath he was holding and held out his hands, palms up. "And I know You won't withhold anything from me unless it is for good. Make it plain. I'll wait for Your green light."

Brock lingered, savoring the last moments of solitude he would get until well into the night. Then he turned, entered the hallway and moved past Joy's closed door.

Was God closing a door that hadn't even been opened yet?

Brock tied off the last suture and left the next few cases in Joy's and Iyegha's very capable hands.

He scanned his text messages. One from Ellie arranging a Skype session after dinner. One from the short-term mission team finalizing plans for their upcoming visit.

His paperwork was stacking up and weighing on him. Details he should probably delegate. He glanced out the hall window on his way to the office. Miriam mingled with the visiting patients and their families. Kasemba stood nearby, crouching low to speak to a little girl, not much older than the daughter she had recently lost. He paused and quietly observed, well aware the smile and look of compassion masked the pain Kasemba still felt and would continue to feel, for the rest of her life.

Three hours later, Brock closed the last patient file and removed his glasses, taking the time to massage his tired eyes. A good stopping place with most of the pressing paperwork done. He might even make it to dinner early. His stomach responded with a rumble.

Beans and rice. If he could have only one meal for the rest of his life, it would be Nicci's black bean soup and rice, seasoned with her blend of saffron, turmeric, and cayenne. His favorite, and Nicci knew it. He could count on it for dinner tonight.

Something else was cooking, too, he felt sure.

Brock entered the dining hall at his usual brisk pace and pulled up short. Everyone was already seated. All eyes went to him, then looked away.

"Hello, everyone. I hope you weren't waiting for me." Brock scanned his watch as he pulled out his chair between

Moses and Joy. Five minutes early.

At the back of the room, Mac pushed through connecting doors from the kitchen carrying a large platter, a job normally delegated to Toby. Nicci followed with a smaller tray and shot Brock a tentative glance that almost looked guilty. Poor girl. He could at least act like nothing was out of the normal.

"Bean soup and rice! I was hoping I'd get my favorite." Brock reached for Moses's and Joy's hands. "Shall we pray?"

He blessed the food and tried to keep the tremor from his voice as he thanked God for the hands that prepared it. No one could've made this dinner with more love.

Moses picked up the first serving bowl and handed it to Brock. Brock thanked him and handed it off to Joy, choosing to serve himself last. By the time the food made it back to him, Toby's heavy tread sounded in the hallway and from the sound, he was not alone.

From behind, Toby cleared the doorway with a booming, "Surprise!"

Brock shifted in his seat and almost choked on a mouthful of beans as Eric came into view followed by Rocco.

Eric closed the distance and grabbed him in a fierce hug. "Happy birthday, Dad."

Brock, with his face wedged against the rock wall of his son-in-law's chest, gave a muffled, "Thank you. So wonderful to have you here!"

"Dude, give somebody else a chance."

Eric loosened his hold and stepped aside.

Brock gripped Rocco by the arms, pulling him into a hearty embrace. "Rocco, one of our favorite volunteers! Welcome back!"

"Yes, sir. Couldn't miss out on the party."

From then on, the room erupted into a cacophony of sliding chairs, laughter, and back-slapping welcomes.

Brock swiped his wet cheeks and glanced at Toby, who at the moment was adding two chairs to the already crowded table. As their eyes met, Brock placed his hand over his heart and mouthed "Thank you."

Toby edged around the crowd and gave him another hug. "So you were really surprised?"

"Oh, my, yes. Thank you. Thank you so much."

Everyone began to settle in at the table again. Eric sat next to Joy.

Rocco, who sat on the other side next to Miriam, eyed Toby. "I just want to know one thing. How'd you pull this off without spilling the secret?"

Toby's eyes widened. "What you talking 'bout? I can keep my mouth shut when I have to."

Eric laughed and turned to Joy. "The smug guy over there is Rocco, who helped keep me alive two summers ago. Rocco, Joy Stockman, the new angel of the compound."

Rocco spooned some beans over the rice on his plate and nodded. "Good to meet you and put a face to the name.

Looks like the Africa bug bit you, too."

Brock chimed in. "Yes. Literally. She's still recuperating from dengue."

Rocco winced. "I see I haven't lost my knack for saying the wrong thing at the wrong time." He winked at Eric. "It's a gift."

Eric chuckled. "One that keeps on giving." He wiped his mouth with a napkin and shifted in his seat. "By the way, Ellie sends her love and some cookies."

Brock nodded and washed down a spicy bite with a sip of water. "I'll thank her tonight. We're supposed to Skype after dinner."

"She mentioned that. Her strategy to keep you from guessing the surprise. I'd like to join you, if you don't mind. She'll want to know that she won the bet."

"The bet?"

"She bet Nicci would serve bean soup and rice. I put my money on Muamba De Galinha."

"Chicken stew! Definitely on my top ten list, but Nicci knows my absolute favorite is bean soup. Never get enough of it, do I?"

At his reassuring smile, Nicci nodded and pushed back from the table. "And after you speak to Ellie, come back for dessert."

The easy conversation continued, making dinner go by fast.

Eric passed a pile of empty dishes down to Nicci. "Did you make coffee?"

"Ya. Ya." Nicci nodded. "All you can drink."

"Perfect. Let me guess. For dessert, you made Bolo de Ginguba?"

Nicci grinned, widening the ridges on her face.

Toby took the stack of dishes and spoke over his shoulder as he followed Nicci to the kitchen. "You should've put your money on that one. Everybody knows that's Doc's favorite."

"Dude, it's everybody's favorite. Sorry, Doc, but Nicci's peanut sponge cake is the real reason I came back for a visit."

"I understand completely, Rocco." Brock's jaw ached from smiling as he pushed back from the table. "It's been a perfect day. Thank you all so much."

He stepped behind Joy, as usual, to help pull back her chair from the table. She thanked him, but instead of following him out, she went toward the kitchen.

"You will join us for the Skype, won't you?"

Joy turned with an apologetic smile. "Not this time. Please give Ellie my love and tell her I'll touch base with her soon."

He nodded and tried not to read too much into her refusal. Something he found impossible to do.

CHAPTER 12

The double door leading to the kitchen swung open with a force that almost knocked Joy off balance.

Nicci barreled out, then pulled up short, grabbing Joy's hand. "Wawe. Sorry, Miss Joy. How clumsy of me."

"No, no. I'm the clumsy one." Joy leaned in and hugged Nicci. "I'm looking for your husband."

"Ya, ya. He has something for you." Nicci held the door open and pointed to Toby who towered over the industrial-sized sink rinsing dinner dishes.

Joy gave Nicci's hand a squeeze. "Thank you."

He looked up, shutting off the spray of water as she approached. "Hey, Miss Joy. I was wondering how I was gonna get this picture to you." Toby dried his hands and grabbed a package from the counter. "Here you go." He handed her a large envelope. "I opened it. Hope you don't mind. Didn't want to get all the way back here with the wrong one."

"No. Of course not." She slid the photo from the open slit on the side and gasped at her first glimpse of the glorious sunrise she'd snapped. "Oh, my. It looks better than I'd hoped. Thank you so much for lending me your phone and going to the trouble to pick up the photo for me."

"Glad to. Doc's gonna love this." Toby leaned in for a closer look. "I wouldn't mind having a copy for myself. Doc's all caught up in the moment. Look at his face. Practically glowing as much as the sun. Did he know you were taking it?"

She shook her head and slipped the photo back into the envelope. "I felt like a spy on a covert mission. I didn't want Brock to know so I eased your phone from my pocket, aimed and shot. Maybe's that's the secret. I didn't have time to overthink it."

"You did good." Toby returned to the sink and started scouring rectangular cooking pans. "I never know what to give him."

She grabbed a stack of rinsed dishes and placed them in the dishwasher. "Oh, I think you found the perfect gift. It must have taken weeks for you to work out the details to get Eric and Rocco here."

"Yeah. Took some doing. Shot the idea to Eric, then Mr. Do-Everything-Perfect took over. Told me when to show up."

"I know it meant so much to Brock. He and Eric seem to care a great deal for each other."

"Crazy, ain't it? You'd think Eric would hate the man who'd killed his parents."

Joy almost lost her grip on the plate in her hand. She looked at Toby who seemed unaware he'd just dropped a bombshell. She couldn't have heard him right. "I don't understand. I was with Eric the night his father died."

"Oh, that was his uncle. His real dad died when Eric was two."

Her shocked expression must have jolted Toby back to reality. "Wait a minute. You didn't know, did you?"

She shook her head too stunned to speak.

"Me and my big mouth done did it again. I'm sorry, Miss Joy. I figured you already knew, you being so close to Eric and all."

"I—um—no." She reached for his hand. "Please don't apologize. This explains some questions I had." But left even more unanswered ones.

His mouth twisted as he shook his head. "Yeah, but the news shouldn't have come from me."

He was right, and she realized there was very little she knew about Brock. Apparently, Brock wanted to keep it that way or he would've told her himself.

She placed her hands on her cheeks, feeling very foolish.

Toby handed her a bottle of water. "Here. You look like you're gonna faint. I sure wish I could eat my words. Don't be thinking bad of Doc. He'd be the first to tell you he ain't the same man he was when he went into that prison."

She jolted upright. "Prison?"

He grimaced. "I done stepped in it again. Might as well keeping walking."

She gave him an encouraging nod and took a fortifying sip of water.

"Yeah. Doc did jail time. He'd been drinking when he plowed into that car. Folks in Texas frown on drunk driving especially if it kills a pastor and his wife. He got ten years, but they let him out early for good behavior."

Joy's intake of breath sent water down her windpipe. She coughed and sputtered.

Toby slapped her on the back, looking worried. "Hey, I know how hard it is to wrap your head around all this. Same for me. When I flew Eric here a little over two years ago, I had no clue Doc had been praying for Eric for years. Doc fought like crazy to keep Eric alive."

Toby wedged the last pot into the overstuffed dishwasher. "I guess that's all she'll hold. And I guess I done said too much. Don't let what I told you change your opinion of Doc. He's a good man. Loves God more'n anybody I know."

Joy placed her arm around Toby's waist. "I'm glad you told me, and it won't change my opinion at all." She was surprised to realize that, if it were possible, it made her admire Brock even more, but that was not something she wanted to share with Toby.

"I think I'll go to my room now. Thank you, Toby. For everything."

"Yes, Ma'am."

Nicci re-entered the kitchen, this time backing in, a stack of dirty dishes in her hands.

Joy stepped aside and resisted the urge to take the stack from her and place them on the counter. Nicci would only wave her away. "Good night, Nicci. Dinner was delicious."

Nicci pulled up short. "You must stay for dessert."

"Thank you, but my headache is back."

She handed the stack to Toby. "I will get an icepack for you."

"Please don't bother. I just need to lie down."

"Then I must tell Dr. Brock to look in on you."

"No." She spoke too quickly, then tried to cover it with a smile. "Thank you, but I want him to enjoy his party. I'll be fine."

With a quick hug to Nicci and a wave to Toby, Joy pushed through the double doors and scanned the dining hall. Brock and Eric were still gone. Mac and Al stood near the coffee counter, Styrofoam cups in hand. Joy smiled and nodded as she went by. Several clinic assistants clumped together near Moses, Miriam, and Kasemba. Their animated conversation kept them from noticing her at all.

In the hallway, she slowed her steps and breathed deeply. Thank God for dengue. She massaged her throbbing temples. At least her excuse was legit. All she wanted was to be alone.

She eased into her bedroom, closed the door, and locked it. Without pulling down the covers, Joy stretched fully clothed on the bed. Toby's news had left her shaken, but that wasn't what was really bothering her.

So Brock had a sordid past. Granted, the news took her off guard. But deep down, it didn't matter a hill of beans to her what he had done.

The fact that she'd learned about it from Toby and not from Brock himself stung a little.

Stung a lot. And there could be only one reason. Brock wanted to keep their relationship professional and not personal.

How had she misread the cues? Brock had only ever been kind and above reproach, just as he was with everyone else who worked here. He'd done nothing to encourage her growing feelings for him.

Except be the best human being she'd ever known.

She placed her hands on her hot cheeks. He was probably very aware of her infatuation with him. It was all over her like the rash dengue had spread.

Maybe if she acted completely normal around him. Looked him square in the eye. Worked like the professional she was. Business as usual.

But what about his present? Should she still give it to him?

She sat up and took the envelope containing the photograph from the bedside table. She held it in one hand and then switched to the other, weighing the pros and cons.

With a resolute breath, she placed the picture in a frame, wrapped it in brown paper, and wrote a note, taping it to the back. She left her room and moved down the hallway once again in stealth mode. Brock's bedroom door was open, the lights out.

Checking the hall to make sure she was alone, she stole into his room, double-checking to make sure no light shone under his bathroom door. What would he say if he saw her sprinting from his bedroom? A rush of adrenaline ripped through her as she left the package beside his bed, then hightailed it out of there, not stopping to see if the coast was clear.

Thank God it was. She made it back to her bedroom and closed her door, the pounding in her head keeping pace with the racing of her heart.

It was the right thing to do. She owed him that.

Nothing had changed, really. She would return to Africa. God had already confirmed that much. But she would return a much wiser, and more cautious woman than she'd been over a year ago.

CHAPTER 13

Brock left the office flanked by Rocco and Eric, the Skype session cut short by two very hungry twins.

Rocco swung his arm around Brock's shoulders. "You mind if I duck in to say hello to the night crew?"

"Of course not."

Rocco laughed and cocked his head. "I hear Toby. Sounds like the party's revving up. Save me a plate."

Eric cut off Brock's reply. "Can't make any promises there, pal. Every man for himself."

"Hey, don't make me pull the 'you owe me' card."

Eric threw his hands up in surrender. "You've got me there. Just don't be all night."

"Deal."

With a wave, Rocco disappeared down the dark hallway leading to the inpatient wing of the clinic.

Brock and Eric paused as if by mutual consent, savoring their first moments alone.

"The twins get bigger every time we Skype."

"What day is this?" Eric pulled out his phone. "I thought so. Nine months today. They're still small, but developmentally, you'd never even know they were preemies. That's mostly thanks to Ellie."

Brock grinned. "I knew she'd make a great mother."

"Wait'll you see her in action. Ellie was born to be a mother." Eric leaned against the wall and crossed his arms. "You remember Rocco's wife?"

Brock nodded.

"Jess and their little girl are staying with Ellie while we guys are here having fun. Erica just turned one, but next to the twins, she looks half grown. I have a feeling the girls will be ready for a break when we get home."

"How long do you plan to stay?"

"A week. Hope you don't mind that Ellie arranged for the Gulfstream to fly us over."

"Of course not. In fact, it works out better this way. I had planned to fly back with Joy in a couple of weeks. This way, Joy can go back when you do."

Eric's face fell. "You're not coming?"

"Yes, but later. I've got a couple coming out in two weeks. I need to be here to help set things up for them. Then, if you and Ellie are willing, I might spend a month with you."

"Are you kidding me? Ellie will be on cloud nine. But you might change your mind. Some days it's like a circus at our house."

Brock laughed. "I've always loved a good circus."

Toby's laughter filtered down the hall. Eric grinned and gestured with his head. "Good ol' Tobe. Some things never change. I guess we'd better join the party."

Brock fell into step beside Eric. "I have a job for you

before you leave."

"Sure. What's up?"

"I'd like for you to go into Luanda and buy a hunting rifle and some ammunition. Something simple and functional."

"Thinking of taking up hunting?"

Brock shook his head. "It's for one of my patients. He should be released before you leave. I'd like for you to teach him how to use it."

"What happened? Did he accidentally shoot himself?"

"Worse."

Eric stopped walking. "Oh, I didn't mean—"

"Don't apologize. This guy's lucky to be alive. He made his own makeshift gun. It exploded when he shot it. Maybe a good reliable gun and some training from an expert like yourself might keep it from happening again."

"I'd be glad to. As a matter of fact, I was hoping to go hunting myself."

"The villagers will be happy to hear that. They keep asking when the mighty hunter with one leg will return."

"Mighty hunter." Eric chuckled. "I like that, but they could've left the one-leg part off."

A group of clinic assistants swooped around him as soon as Brock cleared the door. Eric caught his eye and mimicked holding a coffee cup. "Heading for the coffee. Want me to grab a cup for you?"

Brock spoke over the crowd. "No thanks. I'll get a bottle of water in a few minutes."

Nicci elbowed her way through the mass of people surrounding him and handed him a plate with a giant piece of cake.

"Thank you." Brock wrapped his free arm around her thin shoulders. "You've worked harder than anyone to make this day special for me."

Nicci leaned into his embrace and like a child craving affirmation, looked up, her eyes wide and searching. "You were pleased?"

He smiled and kissed her forehead. "Yes, I was very pleased. With the food. With the cake. It was a wonderful day. But I need a favor."

"Ya. Ya. I will do anything for you, Dr. Brock."

"Not for me. Rocco said to be sure to save him some cake."

"I will do that now." She left him, her tiny frame parting the crowd like a missile.

The group still lingered around him and had now formed a line for a chance to talk to him one on one. He set the plate Nicci had given him on a side table and greeted each one with a hearty handshake or sometimes an embrace. Hard-working men and women, many of whom he'd trained himself. Dear, humble people who worked long and hard because they loved God and loved this ministry.

As soon as he'd spoken to the last person in line, Eric came over and handed him a bottle of water.

"Good timing." Brock opened the bottle and took a

long drink. "Hmm. I was thirstier than I realized."

Eric turned and gave a two-fingered hand motion to Toby who nodded and shuffled over, keeping his head down. The chiseled set of Eric's jaw spoke volumes as did the sheepish glance Toby gave to Eric as he approached.

Brock looked from Eric to Toby. "Is everything all right?"

Toby licked his lips. "Eric says I'd better tell you what I did."

Eric's stern expression gave away nothing. Brock nodded to Toby. "Of course."

"Doc, I'm sorry. I thought she knew."

Brock shook his head. "I don't understand."

Toby cracked his knuckles and blurted out, "I told Miss Joy about you."

"I see." Brock swallowed hard and tried to keep his face from revealing his disappointment. "Exactly how much did you tell her?"

Toby dropped his gaze and rubbed his forehead. "I don't know. We was talking about how close you and Eric are. And then I said something about that was kind of a miracle, you killing Eric's parents and all."

Brock gave an inner groan. "Oh." He glanced at Eric whose grim expression mirrored how he felt himself. "What did she say?"

"Nothing. She just looked kinda shocked." Toby looked up, his eyes wide and pleading. "I swear I thought she knew already. I told her how you got saved in prison then I handed her a bottle of water 'cause she looked like she was gonna faint. She left not long after that. Said she wasn't feeling too good."

Brock took another sip of water, not feeling so well himself.

Toby splayed his hand across his chest. "I'm sorry, Doc. I really am."

He'd had every intention to tell Joy himself, but somehow never found the time. Or the right words. Thanks to Toby, the right time had moved to priority status.

Toby's stricken face stabbed at Brock's heart. He'd have to let Toby off the hook and make at least one less casualty from this unfortunate situation. "Don't give it another thought, Toby. My past is no secret. In fact, it's a testament to God's grace. Thank God, I'm not the man I used to be."

"That's just what I told her." Toby perked up. "And I told her not to think bad of you, and she said she didn't."

That at least was something.

"Sure wish I could go back and undo it all."

Brock smiled and placed his hand on Toby's shoulder. "You will never know how often I've thought the same thing."

Eric remained quiet but edged closer as if to offer support. Brock felt, more than saw, the look of compassion coming from Eric. But Brock couldn't risk making eye contact. The moment was too charged with emotion.

An overwhelming sense of gratitude washed over him.

God loved him. Eric knew the truth and had forgiven him. It was time for Joy to know the truth, too.

"Now." Brock rubbed his hands together. "I'd better put a dent in that slice of cake."

Toby took a deep breath, inflating his cheeks like a balloon, then slowly blowing it out. "Yes, sir."

Brock somehow found the grace to stick around and mingle, even though every part of him wanted to find Joy and explain. Maybe she'd return to the party. His eyes kept straying to the dining hall door.

She didn't return, and he could only guess what that might mean.

He stayed around until only Rocco, Eric, and Toby remained at the table. Brock eased over to stand behind them and placed his hands on Toby's shoulders. "You and Nicci made this the best birthday I've ever had."

Toby reached up and patted Brock's hand. "You deserve the best."

"Thank you, Toby. And now, gentlemen, I'm going to call it a night."

All three stood and gave him another hug. He left and moved slowly to his room at the end of the hall. He clicked on the lamp and sat on the edge of the bed, too physically and emotionally drained to undress.

A package wrapped in brown paper and tied with yellow yarn was on the bedside table with a folded note taped to the outside. From Joy. Somehow he knew even before picking it up.

He took it and ripped the paper, revealing a framed picture, a profile shot of himself gazing at a glorious sunrise. Most photos could never capture the true beauty of the original, but this one came close. He removed his glasses and held it closer, studying every detail. Quite possibly the best gift he'd ever received, made all the more meaningful because of the one who was sharing the moment with him. How had she managed to take the picture without his noticing?

He picked up the note and held it for a long time. Had she written it before or after that fateful revelation about his past?

With a deep breath to steady himself, he gingerly unfolded it, finding neat, precise words as dainty and beautifully scripted as the person who had written them.

Forgive me for leaving the party before you made it back, and forgive me for my intrusion into your bedroom.

He paused and pressed his palm to his chest. She'd written it after.

I wanted to give you this small token of appreciation. This year has been life-changing for me, and I've loved every minute, especially those shared sunrises.

Thank you, Brock. The love of Christ shines through all that you do.

God bless,

Joy

"Let them that love God be as the sun when he goeth forth in his might." Judges 5:31

He read it through again, and then again, his anguished heart hungry for the affirmation, especially now. Each time the words became more blurred. He taped the note to the back of the frame, wanting to keep it and maybe read it again sometime.

His shoulders started to convulse with the release of long restrained tears. He slid from the bed and knelt, burying his broken sobs in the bedspread, his heart too full for words.

CHAPTER 14

Joy gave a lazy stretch and rolled out of bed, in no hurry to face Brock again.

A piece of paper under the door caught her eye. Had she dropped it last night in her haste to get back to her room unnoticed?

She picked it up. Brock's unmistakable scrawl, almost as illegible as Ellie's.

Don't wear scrubs today. I'm taking the day off, and I'm taking you with me. That's if you feel up to it. I have something fun planned. Call it an extension to my birthday. See you at breakfast. PS LOVED THE PHOTO!

Oh, my. She placed her fingers over the silly grin widening her face. Could this be considered a date?

She took extra pains putting on her makeup, fixing her hair. The goal was to look her very best without making it too obvious.

Now. What to wear? Most of her slacks hung loose. She stood at the closet and studied each item before sliding it aside. She paused when she came to the African sarong Miriam had made. Did she dare wear it? The lightweight, silky material slipped easily over her head. She looped the sash over one shoulder, cinched it at the waist and checked herself out in the full-length mirror. The effect was decidedly Grace Kelly, with the deep aqua bringing out the blue of her eyes.

She looked good. Almost too good. Maybe she should change. She returned to the closet to grab baggy slacks and sensible pull-over top with three-quarter sleeves. Instead, she stooped and rummaged for the silver sandals she had thrown into her luggage at the last minute before leaving for Africa.

She slipped them on and squared her shoulders. At least she could wear the sarong to breakfast. If Brock's fun day meant hiking to some remote part of the compound, she could always come back and change.

All eyes went to her as she entered the dining area. Eric stood the moment she entered, which spurred the other men to do the same.

Joy gave a nervous smile and shook her head, motioning for the men to remain seated. They looked to Eric, who not only remained standing but was now pulling out her chair.

"Thank you." Joy gave his arm a pat and slid into place as quickly as she could.

Brock entered within minutes wearing long Khaki pants and a button-up shirt. He apparently had taken as many pains with his appearance as she had, a fact not lost on the group.

Rocco whistled. "Looking spiffy, Doc. I take it you aren't planning to operate today."

Brock sat next to her and placed the napkin on his lap. "No, Rocco, I decided to take Joy to the coast before she returns to the States. A little sea air therapy to speed up her recovery."

Brock leaned closer and looked at her for the first time since entering the room. "That is, if it's okay with you."

She nodded, maybe a little too enthusiastically. "More than okay. I would love it."

His smile was as warm as the platter of eggs he handed her. When the platter made it full circle, everyone joined hands. Brock blessed the food and gave her hand an extra squeeze as he ended the prayer.

A whole day with Brock Whitfield. She should be nervous, but she wasn't. The man had a way of putting people at ease.

The past two years had been a rough time of transition for her. Maybe God was giving her this opportunity to relax and just have a great day with a great person.

Why not take it and enjoy it as the gift God meant for it to be?

Brock checked two post-op patients, gave Iyegha and Rocco last minute instructions, and left through the side doors of the clinic before some crisis could pop up that might keep him from leaving.

Toby exited from the dormitory hall and sprinted over, wearing headphones wrapped around the back of his neck.

"Ready to roll?"

"Ready."

Apparently, Joy was, too. She stood by the helicopter laughing at something Eric said. She really had a radiant smile. Warmed him to see it, and made him smile, too. She turned as they approached, looking so pretty with her hair blowing in the morning breeze. Sort of took his breath away. And his ability to swallow.

At least the problem of whether or not to share details of his past was now solved, thanks to Toby. It was the green light he'd been waiting for and one of many reasons he wanted to get away for the day—from interruptions and well-intentioned curiosity.

He had things to say. Maybe Joy did, too. He couldn't help but think today might be a turning point for both of them.

"I hope we didn't keep you waiting too long."

She smiled up at him. "Not at all. Eric's been amusing me with stories about the twins. I can't wait to get my hands on them."

"I'm jealous."

"I don't blame you. By the way, Nicci loaded us up with snacks. From the feel of it, we won't need to buy any food." Joy slipped the bag from her shoulder, and their heads almost collided as they peeked inside. "No wonder it's so heavy. Nicci threw in some water bottles."

"I've got it." Brock took the bag, then turned and gave Eric a friendly pat on the back. "I guess Iyegha gave you the supply list."

Eric chuckled. "More like a file folder. I hope Toby knows his way around Luanda."

"What's this about me?" Toby rounded the corner of the chopper wiping his hands on a shop rag.

"I was just saying I hope you can maneuver Luanda traffic without getting us both killed."

Toby punched Eric's shoulder. "Aw, now. You gonna get Miss Joy scared to fly with me." He took the bag from Brock and stored it behind the seats. "All set?"

Brock helped Joy into the back and then took the seat next to her. Eric sat up front. Toby pushed some buttons and the blades rotated slowly, revving up to full speed.

Toby set his headphones into place, then shifted to look back at them. "Okay, you two, behave back there."

Brock stifled a groan. Joy, however, took it in stride. "No worries." She spoke louder above the roar of the engine. "I'll be busy checking out my bird's-eye view of this beautiful country."

She wasn't exaggerating. From the moment of liftoff, Joy leaned toward her window like a child on her first airplane ride.

Brock found watching her animated face far more satisfying than looking out his own window.

Toby became a self-appointed tour guide, pointing out various landmarks along the way.

During a lull, Joy touched Brock's arm and leaned closer, asking in a soft voice meant only for him, "What do you have planned?"

He opened his mouth but stopped when Toby blurted out another spiel about the herd of antelope scattered on a field to their right.

Eric turned and gave Brock an amused look. "If you like, I'll tackle this list by myself and let Toby hang with you today."

"No thanks. I think you need him more than we do."

Toby droned on, his headphones making him oblivious to the secondary conversation going on around him.

Forty minutes later, Toby landed at an airstrip west of Luanda—not the larger, commercial airport, but one that elite tourists used for their private jets.

Eric opened the taxi door for Brock and Joy feeling more like a worried parent than a son-in-law. They turned and waved, looking like excited teenagers on their first date, but to a seasoned pickpocket or con man, they would look like easy targets.

Deference and respect for Brock's experience kept Eric from voicing his concerns, but since he wouldn't be there to act as watchdog, he could at least pray God would raise a shield of protection around them.

Toby walked up, keys in hand. "They gave us one of those European sports cars. Not sure I can scrunch my legs up in that thing." Toby looked around. "I guess they got off okay."

Eric nodded and followed Toby to the rental cars parked on the side of the terminal.

"It's that red one." Toby clicked unlock. "I think Doc's gonna pop the question today."

Eric stopped mid-step. "You're crazy."

Toby paused before getting in and propped his elbows on the top of the car. "When's the last time you saw him in long Khaki pants and a button up shirt?"

Eric shook his head and got in the car. "That doesn't mean he's going to propose."

"Not just that. He's taking her to that swanky place on the beach." Toby settled in his seat and poked Eric's chest. "Where you and Ellie spent your honeymoon, I might add."

"I'm aware." Eric swatted Toby's hand away. "Buckle up, and quit yakking." Eric reached for his own shoulder strap. "Look, he said he wanted to show her the coast before she goes back to the States. I believe him."

"Nah." Toby jutted his lower lip out and shook his head. "That's just a smoke screen. Ten bucks—they come back engaged."

"No thanks."

"Uh-huh. Cause you know I'll win."

"Because it wouldn't be fair to you."

"Admit it, bro. You couldn't handle losing."

"Toby, you're full of you-know-what."

"I'm telling you. I know Doc. I've been around them two a lot more than you have. I think they're crazy about each other."

"So do I."

Toby gave Eric a double-take and almost ran off the road. "But you still don't think he's gonna propose?"

"Not today. And concentrate on your driving, you knucklehead."

"Tell me why not."

Eric turned and stared out the window. There was no way Brock would ask Joy to marry him without talking it over with Ellie first. But that wasn't something the world's biggest mouth needed to know.

"Let's just say I'm good at reading people."

"Then put your money where your mouth is."

Eric looked at him and sighed. "You're really not going to let this go, are you?"

"Nope."

"Fine. But I don't bet money."

"The heck you say. You always betting money with Ellie."

"That's different."

"Name your price then."

Eric tugged at his lower lip. "Okay. If I'm right, you have to bring Nicci and the baby to visit your folks at Christmas."

"Deal. And if I'm right, you and Ellie and the twins have to come here."

Eric reached over the console to shake Toby's hand. "Your sweet mama will be so happy."

"You beat everything, you know that?"

"So you've said. But I give you fair warning. I only bet on sure things."

"Is that so? How come you always having to pay up to Ellie?"

"'Cause it makes her happy to win, and I happen to be addicted to seeing her dimple."

CHAPTER 15

The taxi appeared clean, but the air freshener dangling from the rearview mirror did little to mask cigarette smoke, stale beer, and the lingering smell of previous passengers who'd failed to use deodorant or even soap.

Brock wrinkled his nose and glanced at Joy, which was a mistake. She got tickled, which set him off, too. They giggled and ducked down like guilty children to keep the driver from seeing them in the rearview mirror.

Joy covered her mouth, but her shoulders still shook with suppressed laughter.

He couldn't remember the last time he'd laughed with such abandon, especially over something as silly as a smelly cab.

"Oh, my." Joy fanned herself and turned to him. "Sorry, I got a little carried away."

"So did I. Felt good, didn't it?"

"Yes. Yes, it did." Her eyes sparkled with amusement. "Your therapeutic plan is working. What else do you have up your sleeve?"

He chuckled. "I don't actually have a plan. I thought we'd do whatever we feel like doing."

"A plan without a plan. I love it!" Joy clapped her

hands. "It's going to be the best day ever!"

Brock found her enthusiasm utterly enchanting. "Hmm. Best day ever? Now the pressure's on. So the place is called Ilha de Luanda which basically means island of Luanda. The day's wide open. We can shop, or rent an umbrella and a couple of beach chairs and gaze at the ocean. Your call."

"Okay, but first tell me what you would rather do."

"Spend the day with you." He blurted the words, then wished he could stuff them back into his mouth. Brock cleared his throat. "Going into the remote areas of Africa was hardly a vacation. Thought I'd make it up to you by giving you something fun."

"That's very sweet, Brock. Especially since it was *your* birthday. Thank you."

"You're welcome, but the best thanks you could give me is to relax and have fun." He took her hand and gave it a gentle squeeze. "So what will it be?"

"The beach, please."

He smiled, secretly relieved. "Done." He released her hand and leaned forward speaking to the driver in Portuguese. The rest of the drive passed in companionable silence.

Joy stared out the window, a hint of a smile giving her face a soft glow as if she had some secret joy bubbling up inside.

It captivated him to watch her. He pretended to be interested in the scenery outside her window to steal glances without being too obvious.

The taxi pulled into a circular drive of a large hotel. Brock handed a couple of bills to the driver, then ushered Joy into the lobby. "There's a great restaurant here. We can do lunch now or head to the beach."

"Beach."

"I was hoping you'd say that." He steered her past the pool to the rental cabana.

Sandals in hand, Joy walked barefoot beside him on the golden sand.

Brock checked the tag number. "This one." The sun-bleached wooden chairs looked like chaise lounges with green cushions on top. The adjustable back reclined at a perfect forty-five-degree angle. Brock plopped the bag of snacks on the sand and opened the umbrella situated between them.

Joy leaned back in her chair and propped her feet on the cushion. "Ah." She took a deep breath and slowly exhaled with a soft hum. "This is the way it should always be."

"Yes." The way it should always be, with Joy beside him enjoying life's simple pleasures. He stretched out on his chair and propped his hands behind his head. Not a cloud in the sky. The water a blend of deep blue and aquamarine. A balmy breeze full of the fragrant scents of the beach: salty sea air with occasional whiffs of fried fish from local street vendors.

A perfect day. Except for the African-sized elephant

Toby had unleashed that neither Joy nor he wanted to acknowledge.

Joy was too classy to bring it up. But something had changed. She seemed more reserved around him, like the way she'd been in her first weeks at the mission. A cordial stranger.

Maybe it was his imagination, but he wouldn't know for sure until he discussed the details with her himself. Something he hated to do. He had a feeling what he had to tell her was going to spoil her "best day ever."

His mouth went dry. He rummaged through the bag Nicci had packed and pulled out a bottle of water.

Joy glanced over and smiled as he took a sip.

He wiped his mouth. "It's lukewarm but wet. Want one?"

She shook her head. "No, thank you." She rested her head against the back of her chair and closed her eyes. "You were right, you know."

"That's always good to hear." He screwed the top back on the bottle. "About what?"

She opened one eye and peeked at him. "About the beach being therapeutic. I'm glad you prescribed this little beach trip."

"Me, too." Words welled up, pushing to come out. He had to do it. Or explode. "Joy—"

"Hmm?"

She remained with her eyes closed, a relaxed smile softening her features. Maybe he should wait. At least until after lunch.

She turned her head and looked at him. "Yes?"

"Never mind. It can wait."

Joy swung her legs around and sat, smoothing the folds of her dress as she faced him. "Brock, I know all I care to know about you."

He stared, completely unarmed by her response. Not only had she noticed the elephant between them, she walked right up and confronted it.

"I've worked with you for over a year. I know the caliber of man you are."

He dropped his gaze to his folded hands and blew out a long breath. "All that I am, all that God has allowed me to do, has been a trophy of His grace." He raised his head. "I'd like to tell you my story, but only if you want me too."

Joy grabbed a bottle of water from the bag. After two unsuccessful attempts to open it, he took it from her and twisted off the cap.

"Thank you." She took a long sip and grimaced. "Definitely lukewarm."

Was she stalling for time or now avoiding the elephant altogether?

Finally, she spoke. "Could we go for a walk?"

CHAPTER 16

Joy sensed an almost palpable, electric tension that something was coming. Something that might change the whole dynamic of their friendship.

She pushed up from the chair.

Brock fell into step beside her, carrying her shoes. "These might not be here when we return."

"Oh." She glanced back at the bag Nicci had packed.

Brock added, "I don't mind if somebody wants the food, but I won't let them get your sandals."

"Thank you. I can carry them."

He moved the sandals out of her reach and took her hand instead. "Let's go for that walk."

With Brock still holding her hand, they started down the beach. They dodged a group of children playing tag with the waves. She waited until they reached a relatively secluded area to blurt out, "Brock, I'm afraid."

"I know."

"No, you don't." She stopped and turned to him. "I'm not afraid of thinking any differently about you. I'm afraid you will avoid me because you will think I feel different about you."

"It seems we're both afraid of the same thing." He paused as if unsure of himself, then added, "But I have noticed you've been a little reserved since Toby told you."

Joy inched forward, ready to walk again. "I'm embarrassed to tell you why."

Brock chuckled. "You of all people have no reason to be embarrassed. About anything."

"Oh, I have good reason to be embarrassed." She shrugged and stared out at the ocean to avoid looking at him. "I thought our friendship might be growing into something ... deeper. That night, I realized how wrong I was, or you would have told me yourself. I felt like such a fool for reading more into our friendship than was really there. And please don't think you did anything to make me assume what wasn't there. You've been nothing but gracious." She forced herself to stop babbling so he could respond.

The silence hung between them. Eventually, she swallowed her pride and turned back to him.

He looked into her eyes for a long time as if he was waging some inner battle. Finally, he spoke, his voice so soft she could barely hear above the noise of the surf. "You'll never know how many times I wanted to tell you. Even started to tell you, but then something would happen to interrupt or postpone. I began to think God was stopping me for some reason."

Brock kicked a piece of driftwood sending a spray of sand into the air. "I'm almost relieved that Toby got the ball rolling."

Brock's words started to sound far off and a familiar blackness swirled around her vision. *Not now. Please, God, not now.* She slowed her steps and glanced back. Their chairs were like specks on the horizon. "Brock, I need to eat or drink something, or I'm going to go down."

Brock turned and gripped both her arms, now in full doctor mode. "Your blood sugar?"

She nodded. "I'm so sorry."

"Don't be." He set her down on the sand and gently pressed her head forward. "Lean your head over."

Almost immediately, the lightheadedness passed.

"I don't see anything close by." Brock knelt beside her. "Rest a moment longer, then we'll try to get you back."

She rested her head on the cradle of her raised knees, silently cursing her weakness. Usually, she could feel a sinking spell coming on, but this time, she'd been too caught up in the moment until it was too late.

After a few minutes, she raised her head and gave Brock a shaky smile. "I feel better. We can start back now."

Brock studied her, concern etched on his face. "All right." He took her hand and pulled her up, then looped her hand through his arm. "Hang on to me. If you need to sit again, let me know."

She nodded and leaned her head against him, just for a moment, to let him know how grateful she was. "I see what you mean about those interruptions."

He patted her hand that gripped the crook of his arm.

"I shouldn't have left that bag of snacks."

They didn't talk again until they reached their chairs. The bag lay upside down on the sand. Joy picked it up and shook it. "Looks like you were right again."

She sat and brushed away loose sand before strapping her sandals back on. "Good thing you grabbed these. I'm sure the hotel has a shoes-required policy." She was babbling again.

Brock probably knew it, too. He sat across from her, his eyes crinkled in amusement. He stood and offered his hand. "Ready to find some food?"

"Yes."

Cool air had never felt so good. They walked past the check-in desk and concierge to a corridor leading to a restaurant. Brock steered her to some benches and left to give their name to the hostess. She ducked into the ladies' room to freshen up, then returned to her bench.

Brock was nowhere in sight. She peeked through a clump of ficus trees to see if the server had already seated him, then spied him coming down the corridor carrying two bottles of water.

He sat beside her, twisted the cap off one of the bottles, and handed her a couple of aspirin.

"You blessed man."

"I'm still kicking myself. My goal was to speed up your recovery, not set you back."

"This wasn't your fault." She swallowed the pills and drank a good third of the water.

A woman wearing a turban and flowered sarong approached and motioned for them to follow. She led them to a corner table with an excellent view of the ocean, then gave a little bow with her head. "Your server will be with you shortly."

Brock pulled out the chair for Joy, then sat across from her. "I've eaten here a couple of times. The menu is in Portuguese, so if you tell me what you feel like eating, I'll order for you."

"What do you recommend?"

"This one." He leaned over and pointed. "Grilled grouper and rice. They also serve fried grasshoppers and caterpillars sautéed in garlic butter, but I don't recommend them."

She grimaced and closed the menu. "I'll go with the grouper."

He took her menu and placed it on top of his. "Good choice."

Even before the food arrived, their overzealous server made any meaningful conversation impossible. So they sat in silence, sipping water and staring out the window. Occasionally they exchanged glances that held affection as well as a hint of amusement.

The food provided a wealth of trivial things to comment on. Wasn't the grouper grilled to perfection? The rice delicious, but not as good as Nicci's. The fruit platter big enough to feed the entire staff back at the mission, and maybe they could get the server to box up the leftovers.

The server brought their after-dinner coffee and returned Brock's credit card with a deferential bow.

Brock gestured for the man to lean closer. *"Meus comentarios e gostaria de passer algum tempo sozintho, sem interrupcoes."*

The words flowed from Brock as if he'd been born Portuguese, something Joy found incredibly attractive. She sipped coffee and stared nonchalantly out the window while straining to hear every word.

The server responded with another bow. *"Voce foi muito generoso. Voce e sua senhora amigo fao bem-vindas para tomar todo o tempo que voce preciso. Por Favor entre em contato conosco se precisar de assistencia."*

Lady friend and please. The only words Joy could pick out. From the corner of her eye, she could sense the man looking at her.

Brock nodded and said, *"Muito Obrigado."*

Thank you. That much she knew.

The server clasped his hands. *"Voce faz uma adoravel casal."*

Brock looked at her and nodded. *"Si."*

The man bowed to her and gave Brock a hearty pat on the back before turning to go. Brock chuckled and stared after the man.

"You *are* going to tell me what you said, aren't you?"

Brock smiled. "I told him my guest and I would like to spend some time alone, without interruptions."

"Oh. That would explain the frequent looks my way."

Brock chuckled. "So you noticed that, too."

She grinned back. "Oh, yes. It'd be hard not to. And I guess he agreed to leave us alone?"

Brock leaned back in his chair and nodded, an amused grin filling his face.

Her eyes narrowed. "What?"

He raised his eyebrows and gave an innocent look.

"Brock, what are you grinning about? What else did he say?"

"He said we are a lovely couple. I'm pretty sure he thinks I'm going to ask you to marry me."

She gave him a wide-eyed stare. "Did he really say that?"

Brock held up his right hand. "He said we make a lovely couple. I assumed the rest."

He leaned forward and took her hand. "Joy, I—"

She snatched her hand away and placed it over her heart, which felt like it was going to thump out of her chest.

Brock's grin changed to full-blown laughter. "I wish you could see your face. You look like you're about to bolt. Relax, I'm not going to propose."

"Sorry." She smiled, feeling more than a little embarrassed. "I guess I jumped to conclusions."

"Not really. What I started to say was that you weren't wrong."

She cocked her head. "Wrong?"

"Out there on the beach. You said you thought our friendship was growing into something deeper." He reached for her hand and held it tighter as if he expected her to snatch it away again. "Our friendship *has* grown into something deeper. I've known it for a long time."

She forced herself to meet his gaze.

His expression seemed almost anguished. "I have much more to say about that, but for now, I wanted to assure you that you weren't wrong or jumping to conclusions."

She nodded and was finally able to take a full, deep breath. "Thank you."

He gave her hand a squeeze and then released it. "Now, let's talk."

She placed her hands on her warm cheeks. "Brock, I don't want you to feel like you have to tell me about your past."

"Do you want to know?"

"Of course I do, but—"

A peace settled over Brock, a sure affirmation he was doing the right thing. "I'm not sure where to begin. I don't want to bore you with too many details."

Joy cradled her coffee in her hand and leaned back in the chair as if settling in for a good story. "Start at the beginning. I promise I won't be bored."

He shot her a grateful look. "Okay. Here goes. I'm from Texas. My grandfather owned a large spread somewhere between Dallas-Fort Worth and Houston. I guess like Jed Clampett he discovered some of that Texas Tea and began his own oil company."

"Oh my goodness." Joy covered her gaping mouth. "*You*— are Whitfield oil?"

"Not me personally, but it is the company my grandfather started."

She held up a finger. "Wait a minute while I process that."

Revealing his massive wealth came almost as hard as revealing the sordid details of his past. He propped his elbows on the table and tapped his lips with steepled fingers.

She gripped the table and gave him a direct look. "So the private company you said underwrites and funds the mission is actually your company?"

He nodded, and though he hadn't actually lied, he might need to explain more fully. "I'm sorry. I didn't mean to mislead you. The company is run by a board of some very good men who handle all the business dealings."

She shook her head and gave him a bemused look. "And you thought I might be bored."

"That's just the introduction. There's a lot more."

"I'm licking my lips."

He grinned. "You might be disappointed. Okay. Where was I?"

"The introduction."

"Oh, yes. I was an only child. My parents were good people who indulged me more than they should have. My mother's father was a Dallas physician—a prominent plastic surgeon. I followed his career path much to the disappointment of my own father.

"I met Rozalynde when I was a resident in Houston. A Scandinavian beauty who seemed to be at every party I attended. I found out much later she had set her sights on me, or rather on my money, and had made sure she was invited to all the right events."

Joy's blue eyes sparkled with amusement. "So you had a stalker?"

Brock chuckled and reached for his glass of water. Dredging up memories of Roz always put a bitter taste in his mouth. At least, Joy seemed to be taking it all in stride.

"I didn't mind. In fact, I was flattered. She was the most beautiful woman I'd ever seen."

"She still is."

"That's right. You've met her."

Joy's eyes lost some of their sparkle. "Briefly. She is an … interesting person."

"That's putting it kindly. We had a whirlwind relationship. She got pregnant."

"Ellie?"

"No. Our first. Gwyneth. And we were married within three months of our first date. My parents begged me to reconsider, but Roz was like a fever in my bones. I wouldn't even agree to her signing a pre-nup." He shook his head and muttered under his breath. "Such a fool.

"Roz did a one-eighty before the ink was dry on the

marriage certificate. More likely, she reverted back to her true self. She was a self-absorbed narcissist who made Scarlet O'Hara look like Mother Teresa. It didn't take long before I thought her the ugliest woman on the planet. But I was too proud to admit to anyone what a mistake I'd made. For a while, we kept up the charade. Attended parties together. Then she found excuses not to go. Oh, she still moved in the best social circles, but always without me.

"So I spent long hours working." Brock traced a pattern on the red tablecloth, unable to meet Joy's sympathetic gaze. "Working with my patients was the only good thing in my life. Until Gwyneth came along. What a little beauty. Blue eyes that later turned more turquoise. Fiery red hair with a temper to match."

"So when Ellie came along, you at least had two little girls who adored you."

His mouth went dry again.

Ellie. Their miracle baby. A miracle she was ever conceived. The result of a one night stand when they'd both had one too many cocktails. Roz was furious, but at least she had the decency not to abort. She never let him touch her again.

Not that he wanted to. By that time, the very sight of her sickened him. He retaliated by rarely coming home. So his daughters were strangers to him. And to their mother as well. Two selfish hedonistic people in a sham of a marriage who left the rearing of their daughters to the best nannies money could buy.

A soft hand on his jolted him back from the dark place he'd gone. "Brock, you don't have to say any more."

He flipped his hand over and curled his fingers around hers. "Sorry. I got a little lost."

"I know. Please don't say any more. It's too painful."

"I'm sorry. I didn't want to cause you pain."

Her mouth quivered. "Not for me. For you."

"The pain's a good thing. A good reminder of how much God delivered me from. Are you bored yet?"

"Are you kidding me?"

"Okay. I'll try to stay on track and get the rest out. About a year after Ellie was born, I received word in the middle of one of my surgeries that there was a family emergency. A serious one. An associate stepped in to finish the surgery. My first thought was that something had happened to Roz. I'm ashamed to admit, I was almost hopeful."

He swallowed hard and with his free hand, played with water droplets on the outside of his glass.

"It was my father. Crushed in a freak on-site accident. My mother lost it. She was never the same after that. And, I guess, I lost it, too. I worked even harder. Drove myself into the ground during the week, then partied on weekends.

"A few months later, I left a New Year Eve's party. There was a freezing rain. I remember that much. I was too drunk to drive and too stubborn to admit it. I was told when I awoke in the hospital that I had run a red light. Plowed into the car of a young pastor who was returning from a

New Year's Eve service at his church. The pastor and his pregnant wife were killed instantly. The toddler asleep in the back seat survived.

He paused and added in a flat voice, "My mother died during my trial."

Joy gasped and tightened her grip on his hand.

"My lawyers assured me that she died in her sleep, but I knew better. She'd been taking anti-depressants and other opioids. That mixed with alcohol is what got her. I somehow knew in my gut I'd killed her as surely as I had killed that pastor, his wife, and their unborn baby. And I believe to this day it was suicide." He hesitated and added, "I died that day, too."

Joy folded in her lips and dabbed her eyes.

"A week later, I listened unmoved when the judge sentenced me to ten years for vehicular homicide. Nothing could touch me anymore. I was already dead."

Joy's shoulders shook with quiet sobs. She pulled from his grasp and covered her face with both hands.

Tears streamed down his cheeks, too. He reached for extra napkins and handed Joy a couple as well. "I'm sorry. That's the worst part. I promise. It gets better from here."

"Good." She took the napkin. "I take back what I said. This is killing me."

"Try to smile. The server looks worried. He's been watching us through that cluster of ficus trees over there."

Joy glanced over her shoulder.

"No, don't look. He might come over here to rescue

you. Or beat me up."

Joy burst out laughing. She blew her nose and gave him a breathtaking smile. Her eyelashes were wet and clumped together, but the compassion in her eyes shook him to his core. Joy Stockman was everything Rozalynde was not. And in that moment, Joy had never looked more beautiful.

He continued talking to keep from staring. "Now, where was I?"

"The part where it gets better."

"Oh, yes." He wouldn't tell her the prison horror stories. Not something she needed to know. Ever.

"I guess it goes without saying that I hit rock bottom in prison. Would've had to look up at the belly of a snake. Roz filed for divorce. I signed and agreed for her to receive half the income from the company for life as long as she remained unmarried, my one selfish act of defiance.

"I had lost my parents, my daughters, my medical license, my social standing, and, most of all, my self-respect. But I did not lose my fortune, thanks to the excellent lawyers and board of trustees who valued my father enough to fight for me.

"Prison broke me enough to drive me to my knees. I had a lot of time to think. I had a small radio that kept me company at night when I couldn't sleep. The only station without static had a preacher that talked a lot about forgiveness. Every night, I pulled the radio up close, hugging it to my ear.

"And I know in my soul," he tapped his chest, "that God Himself was speaking right to me from that preacher.

"One of the only kind guards got me a Bible. I looked up every verse I could find about forgiveness. I started to put the pieces together about Jesus. It seemed too good to be true that Jesus would take the punishment I deserved. That's what kept me from coming to Christ. I couldn't let myself accept His free offer of forgiveness. I didn't deserve it."

Joy shook her head, her expression pained. "Oh, Brock."

"Finally, a chaplain visited me. I know God sent him. I told him how I felt and somehow he said exactly what I needed to hear."

"What was that?"

"He said, nothing I could do would ever make up for killing that pastor and his wife."

Joy's eyes widened. "What?"

"He was right. Then he said, 'but that pastor wouldn't want you to go to hell as penance for killing him. Or even his family. And if you refuse to accept God's forgiveness, that pastor and his wife would've died for nothing.' That somehow clicked with me. I read through the entire book of John that night. I cried most of the night, too. And then as the sun began to rise and shine through my cell window, I knelt by my cot and asked God to forgive me, to take all my guilt and the mess I'd made of my life."

Brock held up his finger and placed it next to his lips

to stop their trembling. After a few seconds, he regained his composure. "Sorry. This part gets me every time."

She nodded, smiling through the fresh onslaught of tears running down her cheeks.

"The morning sun shone down upon my head, and … this feeling of love so powerful …" He had to pause once more. After a few seconds, he cleared his throat and tried again. "Love so powerful, it almost took my breath away. And the rest of my time in prison was almost precious to me. I spent hours reading the Bible and praying. Some of the guards gave me a hard time. Said I was faking religion to get paroled." Brock shook his head. "Didn't matter." He pointed to his chest. "Inside, I was already free."

Joy smiled. "It's why you love sunrises."

"Exactly."

"That's the most beautiful thing I've ever heard, especially since I've gotten to know the man you are now." She placed her elbows on the table and leaned forward. "Eric was the toddler in the back seat, wasn't he?"

Brock gave her a quiet smile and nodded.

"And the man that died of cancer a couple of years ago?"

"His uncle. The pastor's brother, who was bitter at God and did his best to keep Eric from learning about Him."

She cocked her head, her forehead furrowed. "Did Toby know all of this when Eric was injured in that attack? Is that why Toby flew him to the mission compound?"

"No. That's a long story and a miracle in itself. One that maybe you should hear from Eric himself. Maybe, before you go back to the States, we'll ask Eric and Toby to tell you all about it. More than ever, it shows how God is able to do exceedingly, abundantly above all that we ask or think."

Brock reached for Joy's hand again, his expression serious. "That's what I think He is doing for me now. With you. All these years, I've been happy and so grateful for the second chance God has given me. The man who walked out of that prison was a new man. God has been more than enough, and I've never considered myself lonely. Then you came and created a new hunger in me. I found myself thinking of you more and more. It happened almost before I realized it. And then I began to consider the possibility that maybe God was in it. That He might be sending me the gift of love in my later years. A gift I had neither sought nor thought I needed.

"But I have to confess, this is all new territory for me. So every day, I prayed for you because I am fully aware you had a long and happy life with your husband."

Her gaze dropped, giving no hint of what she might be feeling.

He glanced out the window, second-guessing his plan to level with her. Maybe he'd said enough. Or too much. How could he explain something he didn't quite understand himself?

"The thing I still struggle with is that God has not yet

given me peace to—"

She looked up, her eyes wide and troubled. "Brock, you don't have to explain."

"Yes, I do. I want to be completely transparent with you." At least, as transparent as God allowed him to be. He caressed the delicate hand he held, staring at it and weighing his next words. "I believe God brought you to Africa, and into my life for a reason. I don't quite know what that reason is, but I can tell you this: I have perfect peace as things are now, and I'm thrilled beyond words that God led you to return to Africa. I don't know what the next step is. I hope you're okay with that, but I completely understand if you aren't."

His heart hammered in his chest. He waited, scarcely breathing, afraid he'd blown any chance he might have had with her.

Finally, she spoke. "The last thing I was looking for when I volunteered was to find love again. But I, too, felt drawn to you. It's been a healing year for me, and God used you so much to bring that healing about. I've soaked up your wisdom. I've watched you love on this people. Save their lives. Lead them to Jesus."

She shrugged and looked down. "I kept telling myself it was the Jesus in you that I was falling in love with." She lifted her head and gave him a serious look. "And I'm telling you the truth, if I can only ever be your friend and work here in this ministry alongside you, I will be more than content. And grateful. So thank you." Tears had filled

Joy's eyes and made them a brilliant blue. "Thank you for telling me your story. It only makes me admire and respect you even more and praise the God who did such miracles in your life." She gave his hand a gentle squeeze. "I think our friendship is God's gift to both of us. I don't know what the next step is either, or even if there is a next step. But right now, I can honestly say, that's okay. It's enough for me."

Brock's throat tightened and he fought hard to keep the emotion from overtaking him. Somehow God kept his mouth clamped shut, for he was ready to swoop her up in his arms, confess his undying love, and marry her on the spot.

CHAPTER 17

A long list of worst-case scenarios had been dogging Joy all morning. They were only her usual pre-flight jitters and not some kind of crazy premonition. At least, that's what she kept telling herself.

Should she pack all her scrubs or leave them here? After all, she would return in a couple months, wouldn't she?

She chewed the tip of her finger. The short-term volunteers might need to use this room so the closet really ought to be empty.

Her indecision had always driven Frank crazy. She could almost hear him huffing, *For crying out loud, Joy, hurry up and make up your mind.* His impatience never seemed to help. Nine times out of ten she wished she'd made a different choice.

She'd gotten better since she'd been on her own. No more second-guessing if what she did was going to make Frank mad.

Joy tapped her lips and stared into the closet. Why not take the scrubs? There'd be plenty of room on the plane for extra baggage. She slid the hangars together then bent to rummage for the garment bag hanging in the back corner of the closet. A soft tap made her go still and crane her ears toward the door. "Yes?"

Miriam opened the door and poked her head inside. "May I enter?"

"Of course, my friend." Joy met her halfway, struck as always by Miriam's perfect teeth and radiant smile.

The two embraced, with Miriam holding tighter and longer than usual. "I am already missing you."

"I will miss your bosom hugs." Joy's words sounded muffled with her face still crushed to Miriam's chest. "I'm trying not to think about it, or I'll cry."

"Ya. Ya. I've been wiping my cheeks all morning." Miriam released her hold and handed Joy a package.

"What's this?"

"A little something I want you to have." Miriam folded her hands at her waist, a wide grin filling her face.

"Aww. How kind of you." Joy peeled back one of the corners, trying not to waste it even though it was standard brown wrapping paper. After the first jagged tear, she gave up and ripped it open.

A bright red sarong with specks of gold woven throughout was tucked neatly inside. Joy gasped and freed the satin folds letting the paper fall to the floor. "This is beautiful." She shifted to look in the mirror holding it up in front of her, then whirled back to Miriam. "You dear, dear woman. You've outdone yourself this time. How can I thank you?"

"You are pleased?"

"Pleased? I love it!" Joy juggled the material in an attempt to try it on.

Miriam swatted Joy's hands away. "I will show you."

Within minutes, Joy was once again transformed into an African princess. She faced the mirror again, pirouetting to view the back. "I must wear this home tomorrow." Tears blurring her vision, Joy grabbed Miriam's hands and squeezed the rough, calloused fingers. "I wish I had something to give you."

"You have given yourself." Miriam pulled her hands free and gripped Joy's shoulders. "You have brought joy— to this place and to our hearts."

Whether the play on words using her name was intentional, it was still quite possibly the most beautiful thing anyone had ever said to her. They embraced, with more smiles than tears, two women from two different worlds, bound together by Christ's love. "Thank you, Miriam. For everything. For nursing me back to health and most of all, for being my friend."

"Come back soon. Bring our Joy back to us."

"I will." She promised despite the nagging fear that something might go wrong.

It made no sense, this feeling of gloom. After all, she wasn't leaving forever. Two months, give or take, she'd be back, ready for another year even better than this one had been.

Wouldn't she?

CHAPTER 18

Eric raced Lady to the terrace. The golden retriever barreled past and almost skidded into Bits, who arched her back and hissed. Eric bent over and gripped his thighs while heaving in gulps of air. Sweat dripped from his forehead, forming blotches of dark circles that quickly dried on the hot concrete.

Ten miles over uneven terrain. A good run, and a good way to end the week.

As much as he loved the place, he was ready to go back home to Ellie and the twins. Ellie was all over this place, pricking him with waves of homesickness every time he turned around.

The week had flown by, and there was only one thing left unfinished. He tousled Lady's fur and gave Bits a tweak to the ear. "You two behave."

In his room, Eric rummaged through the top dresser drawer making a mental note to return the clock to the wall before leaving. He grabbed a towel and sat to detach his prosthesis. He had become somewhat of a master of balance even though, technically, he could shower with his leg attached. He still chose not to.

After the soaking warm water, he dressed and left his

room, an almost nervous excitement racing through his veins as if he were going on a date. The packed red gravel crunched under his Nikes as he crossed the road to the chapel.

The musty smell of wood transported him back to the first time he ever entered this hallowed place. Like a pilgrim visiting a shrine, Eric eased down the center aisle, his eyes never leaving the stained glass. He placed the hilt of his palm against his chest, the place where the risen Christ now lived.

The atmosphere held a holy silence. He sat on the third bench from the front with no agenda but to revisit the place where he had first met his Savior.

His mind drifted back to the morning when he finally surrendered to the truth and asked Jesus to be his savior. How different his life would be if he hadn't been set up for that ambush. He'd still be a CIA operative, with a gaping black hole inside that only God could fill.

He stayed over an hour, in quiet reflection and worship, then rose and nodded, and tapped his heart in a quiet salute.

The door creaked open. The man who patiently loved him and taught him basically everything he knew about God took a step in before glancing up and stopping mid-step. "Eric. Hello." Brock smiled and with a wave, started to back out. "I'll come back later."

"Wait. Don't leave." Eric closed the distance to join Brock at the door. "Please. I'd like to talk something over with you."

Brock turned. "Of course."

Eric returned to his usual spot, and Brock settled in after him.

"This week has flown by." Eric flexed his leg in front of him.

"Still get those leg cramps?"

"Yes, but not as severe. Mostly when I need to hydrate. Should've grabbed some water."

Brock started to rise. "I'll go get you a bottle."

"I'm good." Eric reached for Brock's arm to tug him back down. "I'd rather talk."

"So would I." Brock eased back into his spot. "It's been like old times this week. I wanted to thank you for teaching my patient the proper use of a firearm."

"Glad to. That was quite some head wound. I think he learned his lesson."

"Let's hope so."

The men fell silent, and then both began to talk at once. After a shared chuckle, Brock gestured for Eric to continue.

"I was just going to say that I remember the first time I came into this chapel alone. I had promised Ellie I'd try to get to know God, and I figured this was the place to find him. And you told me to read the book of John, you remember that?"

Brock nodded, his fingers barely covering his smile. "I do indeed."

"And I read it through." Eric shot him a sheepish look.

"I'm usually a fast learner. I figured I'd knock the God thing out in one afternoon. I have to tell you, after I read it through, I was more confused than ever. I closed the Bible and prayed for the first time. You told me praying to God was just like talking to a person in another room you couldn't see." Eric cut his glance back to Brock. "You were right, by the way. So I said something lame, but it was the only thing I could think of. I told God I had never prayed before, but if He was real, could He help me out."

Brock smiled. "I think He answered that prayer."

"Me, too. I was so green back then." Eric switched his gaze to the stained glass image of Christ. "You said that you knew God was real because He talked to you."

Brock nodded.

"That blew my mind. I wanted that so bad, for Jesus to talk to me and let me know He was there. The night before my leg surgery, before you and Ellie and everybody else came in and prayed with me, I spoke out loud to that glass image, begging Him to talk to me, begging Him to say anything that would help my faith, which was basically zero."

"He did speak to you that night."

Eric cocked his head. "What do you mean?"

"If I remember correctly, that is when we all burst in on your solitude. Eric, God could show up at any time as we've talked about before. But He chooses to speak through people. We are His voice, His hands, His feet."

"I see what you mean." Why hadn't he thought of that

before? "I still have so much to learn. But the cool thing is that I can hear God talking to me now." He poked his chest. "I'm learning to listen for that voice like I used to listen to Simon."

"Simon?"

"Simon Do-Right. The name I gave to my gut feeling."

"Oh, yes. I'd forgotten all about good ol' Simon."

"Simon's not very happy with the new arrangement. I've learned to let God's voice trump Simon's."

Brock laughed and threw his arm across Eric's shoulder. "That's priceless. And what has God been telling you lately?"

Eric dropped his gaze. He hadn't told anyone, not even Ellie. "I'm not sure, but I think God might want me to be one of the agency chaplains."

"That doesn't surprise me."

Brock Whitfield was nothing like the man who'd raised him. Bob Templeton, even after becoming a Christian, would've shot down him and his aspirations as soon as the words left his mouth. His tense muscles began to relax. "It's crazy. I'd been toying with the idea, but not very seriously. Then Director McDowall pulled me aside and asked if I'd ever considered applying for the position."

"What'd you tell him?"

"I thanked him. Told him I'd pray about it and let him know. I've been tied up in knots ever since." He turned to Brock. "I'm like the world's least likely candidate for chaplain."

"I disagree. You have a unique ability to read people. It's what made you such an outstanding agent." Brock gave him a gentle nudge with his elbow. "With God's help, I dare say you have the potential to be the best chaplain the agency has ever had."

"So you think I should take the job?"

"Definitely! If God is leading you to do this, go for it."

The big if. Eric sighed and stared at the stained glass. This was one of those times he wished the image of Christ would magically start talking. He turned back to Brock. "How do you know if something is from God?"

"Good question."

Eric waited without interrupting, aware Brock took his time to answer well.

"If you think something only once, on a whim, then maybe that is good ol'Simon talking. But if the thought continues to come to you at random moments, then there is a good possibility it is God nudging you in the right direction."

Eric nodded. "But how do you know for sure?"

"You obey what you think God is asking you to do and trust He will stop you from making a mistake."

"So I should pursue this until God stops me?"

"Possibly. But there is another way you can know for sure."

Eric shifted and looked him full in the face. "I'm all ears."

"Peace. It's the litmus by which I judge every decision

I make. I've learned not to make a move without it. Tell me, what does Ellie think about it?"

"I haven't told her. I know she worries. About you. The mission. Our future. I've been sitting on it until I could talk it over with you."

"Hmm. Well, I can tell you something God has been telling me."

"Okay."

"I somehow knew in my heart when you left Africa the last time, you'd never be back on a permanent basis."

"Really?" Something he'd felt, too, but didn't want to acknowledge, even to himself. "But what about the clinic? I know how much you count on Ellie to help out."

Brock shook his head. "God always provides the help we need. Like Joy. By the way, she's signed up for another year. She's going to take care of a few things in the States, then return after my visit next month."

"She told me. I think that's great." Eric leaned forward, his fingers wrapped around the edge of the bench. "While we're on the subject, I know it's not my business, but—"

"Everything that pertains to me is your business. You were going to ask about Joy and me, weren't you?"

Eric screwed up his face. "Busted. Toby was positive you were going to ask her to marry you at the beach."

"You don't say? So that's why you punched him in the ribs as soon as we arrived back at the terminal." Brock laughed outright. "You know, the server at the restaurant

154

thought so, too, probably because I tipped him four times what he normally would make if he'd give us privacy." Brock sobered, a grim twist to his mouth. "I told her my story."

Brock's story, and in many ways, Eric's story as well. A powerful and painful story to hear. Couldn't have been easy, for either one. "How'd she take it?"

"Better than I could have hoped." Brock hesitated, then added. "You've probably guessed how much I've come to care for Joy."

Eric met his gaze and nodded.

"I shared my feelings with her as well. Figured since I was already telling her my dark secrets, I might as well get everything out in the open."

"Does she feel the same?"

"Amazingly, yes."

To Eric, there was nothing amazing about it. Two of the most selfless people on the planet, cut from the same cloth of total commitment to the Lord and His work. "It would make Ellie happy. She predicted it even at Joy's first visit to Africa."

"Even then?" Brock fell silent.

Eric waited. Brock had more to say—he'd bet on it.

"Remember that peace I was telling you about?"

Eric nodded.

"For some reason that I don't understand, God hasn't given me the green light to take our relationship to the next step. It seems God has brought the perfect person into my life but hasn't given me peace to ask her to marry me. And God isn't telling me why." He dropped his chin and gave Eric a sideways glance. "Believe me. I've asked."

Eric reared back and faced Brock, surprised to learn his spiritual mentor didn't always have the answers either. "So, what's the next step?"

"I wait … and trust His timing." Brock's expression softened. "We're okay, son. Joy and I discussed what God might be asking of us. As I suspected, she assured me she was completely content to accept whatever God had in store." He leaned closer, his shoulder touching Eric's. "Which I have to confess made me fall even deeper in love with her."

Eric managed to smile even though his heart was aching for both of them.

Brock placed his arm around Eric and pulled him close in a sideways embrace. "Thank you for listening. I'll be praying for you and your decision. And you can pray for us when you think about it. My biggest concern is for Joy not to get hurt. She's known so much pain in her life."

This from the man who'd had more than a fair share of pain in his own.

"We will." Eric grinned. "But I have a feeling I know how Ellie will be praying."

CHAPTER 19

Change did strange things to Joy. Even good change. Joy stuffed the last of her toiletries into the bag and plopped it next to the other bags beside the door. She dressed in clothes she'd worn the night before, saving the gorgeous sarong for after breakfast. She paused at the door and turned, giving the now bare room a once over. A familiar heaviness she'd been trying to deny squeezed her chest.

The bright red numbers on the bedside clock clicked over to four thirty. A full hour before sunrise. She slipped out the door anyway and moved noiselessly down the dark hall to the terrace.

Brock was already there, which secretly delighted her. He stood and even in the darkness, she could make out his welcoming smile.

"Good morning. You're up early." Brock eased behind to pull out her chair.

"Thank you." She sat and the clean scent of soap and aftershave drifted over to her, a smell uniquely his. "Do you know, I've never beaten you out here no matter how early I arrive. Tell the truth. You sleep out here, don't you?"

He laughed and slid his chair closer. "No. Just one

minute sooner, you'd have beaten me this time. So you couldn't sleep either?"

She smiled and shook her head. "Too keyed up … and a little sad."

"Me, too." Brock looked out toward the field. "Listen. The birds are showing off for you today."

She closed her eyes, immersing herself in the beauty of the moment. "I'm going to miss these early morning concerts."

Brock didn't respond. She turned and found him smiling at her, his eyes full of warmth. "I don't think they'll sound quite so cheerful after you leave."

Joy forced back tears that could only dampen their last moments together. "I hope it's not too crazy around here until reinforcements arrive."

He held up his hand, his fingers crossed. "I'm hoping for nothing major, especially surgery. A group is coming in a couple of weeks. Good people. I think I might have mentioned the couple who are praying about coming on full-time."

"Yes, you did. Will they still be here when I return?"

He nodded. "They plan to stay six months. If they can survive the rainy season, I think we're home free."

"Oh dear. You remember what Moses said? If they're meant to be in Africa, these poor people might get bitten by the dreaded dengue mosquito."

Brock laughed. "We won't tell them."

They both fell silent, but even the lull was nice. A quiet

connection between them that needed no words.

The sun, at last, made its appearance, a golden promise of a beautiful day. Joy leaned back and let out an appreciative sigh. "You've changed the way I look at sunrises, Brock."

He shifted his gaze and studied her. "You've changed the way I view a lot of things."

Things they normally wouldn't say on an average day. But since this was their last shared sunrise for a while, they'd both let the barrier down, just a little. And it was enough.

They stayed until the sun was fully up, then Brock's voice turned tender. "Ready to go in?"

She nodded, and they both stood. He opened his arms, and she moved into them without hesitation, resting her head against him, loving the thud of his strong heartbeat and the feel of his chest gently rising and falling.

Brock gave a heavy sigh and whispered close to her ear. "We'd better go."

Their private goodbye. A sweet moment that she would relive many times in the weeks to come.

CHAPTER 20

Joy clicked her seatbelt into place and waved to the crowd as Toby lifted off. She kept them in her sight as long as she could, then settled back for the forty-five-minute flight to Luanda airport.

"Never easy to leave this place." Eric's smile told her he knew exactly what she was feeling.

She shook her head, warmed by his empathy, and placed her hand on his. "You remind me of Brock."

"I take that as a compliment. He's an amazing man."

"Yes." She would find time to talk more with Eric. About Brock, and the role Brock played in Eric's transformation. But not now, while she was still too raw to speak without getting emotional. And especially not around Toby and Rocco, who were up front, carrying on a lively discussion of their own.

Eric met her gaze and rolled his eyes at the men's banter, then leaned back and stared out his own window.

The time went more quickly than she expected. Almost too soon, they landed at the same small airport as before. Toby helped transport the luggage to the Gulfstream and gave them all crushing bear hugs.

Eric slapped Toby on the back. "I'll see you in

December."

Joy perked up. "You're taking Nicci to the States?"

Toby looked first to Eric, then back to her. "Yes, Ma'am. Me and Eric had this—"

"Discussion." Eric finished for him.

"Yeah. Discussion about how I needed to take Nicci and the baby to visit my folks."

Joy opted to ignore whatever was going on. No telling with those two. "That's wonderful. I hope I get to see you." She started up the steps, then paused and turned. "What was I thinking? I'll be back at the mission in December."

"Yes, Ma'am. The sooner the better. And I know one person that'll be counting the days 'til you get back."

"That's right." Eric interrupted. "Nicci mentioned last night how much she hated for Miss Joy to leave. Said she hoped you'd make it back before the baby's born."

Toby gave Eric a confused double take, then nodded, not very convincingly. Joy cocked her head and almost laughed out loud. She might be slow, but she wasn't stupid. She eased back down the steps and gave Toby another hug, more fervent than the one she'd given earlier. "Toby, I love you! Please give a hug to 'that person' for me."

"Yes, Ma'am" He gave Eric a smug look. "I'll be sure to do that."

"Yeah, Tobe, give 'that person' a hug for me, too." Eric grinned and slung his arm around Toby's broad shoulders. "Bye, man. Take care of things around here."

"Will do, bro."

Joy started up the steps with a lighter heart than before. She sank into a padded leather seat and reached for her seatbelt.

Eric followed and raised his duffle bag over his head as he eased past. He returned and sat across the aisle in the seat beside Rocco. "Guess I'd better let our wives know we're on the way." He took out his phone and tapped out his text, then scrolled to the group photo Rocco had taken earlier. "Turned out great." He slanted it so she could see.

She took it from him for a closer look. A spontaneous picture that couldn't have been more perfect had it been choreographed. She and Brock, dead center flanked by the entire compound team who'd taken a moment to send them off. Another wave of sadness swept over her. She handed the phone back to Eric. "I don't have a phone yet, so would you email a copy of that to me?"

"Yes, Ma'am." His finger went to work.

"You don't have to do it now."

"Already done." He pocketed his phone with a smile. "By the way, Brock gave me specific instructions about taking you to replace your phone."

"Oh, dear. I hoped he'd forget all about that. Did he tell you what happened?"

Eric nodded, his eyes lit with amusement. "I'm sure he left out details. He did mention something about being caked with mud."

She chuckled. "Yes. I'm glad there was no one around to video it. He's kind, but there's no way I'll let him replace my phone."

"Brock said you'd say that. Told me I may have to use my skills as a former spy to convince you to let him do it."

Joy gripped her neck in mock fear. "Torture?"

Eric laughed. "I think he meant my powers of persuasion." He reached across the aisle and took her hand. "Look, I love you both, so the last thing I want to do is take sides, but I think it would mean a lot to Brock for you to let him do this."

She dropped her gaze and bit her bottom lip.

Eric continued with a nonchalant tone, "And he may or may not have mentioned that if you'd consent, he'd be the first to call and thank you personally."

She covered her mouth to hide her amused grin. "Powers of persuasion, indeed. Oh, all right."

"Mission accomplished." He squeezed her hand, then reclined his seat. "Wake me when we pit-stop for fuel."

"Okay." Which she fully intended to do, but lack of sleep and the drone of the plane hypnotized her. The next thing she knew, a hand on her shoulder roused her from a deep, dreamless sleep.

"Joy?"

She stared dumbly up at Eric.

"We're in Paris. Want to stretch your legs and get something to eat?"

She returned her seat to the upright position and said through a stifled yawn, "I hope the rest of the trip goes by this fast."

"Not likely."

She grabbed her purse, and Eric followed her down the steps. Rocco and the pilots were ahead walking toward a terminal more user-friendly than the larger international airport would be.

So this was Paris. A little anti-climactic with its overcast sky and stifling humidity. At least, she could now claim she'd been to Paris.

The co-pilot waited at the door for them to catch up. "The bathrooms are down that hall. Then we'll grab lunch in the cafeteria."

Eric thanked him and followed her to the restroom. "Will you be all right?"

She nodded, touched by his consideration. No doubt he was prepared to follow her into the bathroom and stand guard at her stall if necessary. She washed her hands and splashed cool water on her face, trying to clear the sleep-induced fog in her brain. That was some good sleep. Best she'd had since her bout with dengue.

Lunch at the airport was a nice but short break. They grabbed an extra chair and crowded five around a table meant for four. She didn't think she was hungry until she took her first bite of a hot ham and cheese croissant. Apparently, even Parisian food at an airport was something to write home about.

Home. She was already making the transition in her head.

Eric touched her arm. "I'm going to grab a coffee for

the road. Want one?"

"Yes, please." She hit the restroom one more time, putting off using the one on board until she absolutely had to.

Back on board, Rocco grabbed his earbuds. "Nap time. I have a feeling the girls will meet us at the door, babies in hand."

Eric laughed and agreed. He looked at Joy. "Mind if I sit next to you?"

"Of course not." She moved to the window seat.

Eric sat and balanced his Styrofoam cup on his thigh. "I wanted to apologize to you."

She turned and raised her eyebrows.

"For not telling you sooner that Robert Templeton wasn't my biological father."

"Oh, Eric." She placed her hand on his arm. "No apology needed."

"You're like family to me. I would've told you the day we mentioned the journal my father wrote, but that would open up things about Brock, too. Things I didn't feel right about revealing."

"You love Brock a great deal, don't you?"

Eric's mouth tightened. "He's literally the dad I never had. Crazy, isn't it?"

"More like amazing. Were you angry when Brock told you the truth about your parents?"

"Yes, but not for long. By the time Brock broke the news to me, I already loved the man and was in love with his daughter." He stared at his cup. "Looking back, I know God was breaking me down, pulling out every prop I had. I hit rock bottom. My identity, my reputation, my future—all stripped from me. It took that to make me turn to God."

Was that what God was doing with her son? *Please, God. David needs a miracle, too.*

They talked for a good part of the trip. Details about Eric's work in the CIA. About growing up with a harsh, demanding father. About the day his mother left the house, never bothering to say goodbye to her adopted son. About how Toby's mother took Eric in and offered him his first taste of genuine love.

All deeply personal things that he probably had not shared with many people. She didn't waste the opportunity. While Rocco snored from his seat across the aisle, she probed, hungry to know whatever he cared to tell her, even though much of his story pierced her very soul.

"I asked Brock the night before my surgery if he thought I would lose my leg. Without batting an eye, he said yes. It was like he kicked me in the gut. Then he said, God could fix my leg if He wanted to. Of course, then I had to ask, 'What if He didn't want to?'"

As a hospice worker, she had been confronted with that very question.

"The answer he gave wasn't what I wanted to hear. He said if God allowed my leg to be amputated, it would be for my good. That God would sacrifice my leg to accomplish something greater." Eric crushed the empty

166

cup in his hand. "I fought it, but deep inside, I knew. In my gut, I knew that God was going to take my leg," his voice broke—"sorry."

Joy waited, too choked up herself to respond.

"And then, when I got to Washington, it all started to make sense. The something greater God wanted to accomplish was Bob Templeton coming to Christ." He chuckled, even with tears streaming down his face. "And I don't know which is the greater miracle: That Bob Templeton became a believer or that I could finally thank God that I lost my leg—and mean it."

"Oh, Eric … I wish I'd known this when I came to your house. I should've been more encouraging to you."

"Are you kidding me? You were wonderful. You seemed to know when to show up, especially toward the end. I'd never have made it without you." He rubbed his hands together, a classic move she'd seen Brock do many times. "Now, enough about me. Tell me more about you."

She turned and stared out the window. The plane had pierced oppressive clouds revealing nothing but blue skies and a foamy white carpet beneath. "My story is not quite as exciting or miraculous as yours."

"I don't know. You told me once about your daughter Savannah. I couldn't imagine losing a child. How'd you get through it?"

"I turned to God. Not because I was so spiritual. I had to. The pain was too great to handle on my own. And I threw myself into my work, too. Fortunately, I was a nurse.

There's something therapeutic about helping people heal when you're hurting, too."

She stopped and gave Eric a serious look. "When you told me how God broke you down, I couldn't help but think about my David. His wife has left him."

Eric frowned and shook his head. "I'm sorry."

"Thank you. He's devastated. More broken than I've ever seen him."

"What happened?"

"I don't know. He's not one to open up." She managed a smile, the first one since reboarding the plane. "He plans to visit while I'm in the States, so I'll be making lasagna. I'd love for you and Ellie and the babies to come to dinner."

"Name the day and time. We'll be there."

"Good. Maybe you can use your skills to draw him out."

"Absolutely. Truth serum or do you want me to rough him up a bit?"

Joy laughed out loud, then clamped her mouth and stole a look across the aisle. Rocco, earbuds in place, remained with mouth slightly open and eyes closed. She leaned against Eric's rock solid arm with a grateful nudge. "Thank you! I needed that laugh."

His eyes crinkled in amusement, then sobered. "Seriously, I'll be glad to do what I can. Did you tell Brock about David?"

Joy nodded.

"Good. Miracles happen when that man prays."

Joy sipped her lukewarm coffee and smiled.

Eric set his empty cup in the armrest cup holder. "We should make it home by ten tonight. I talked to Ellie before we left. She'll open up your house, get your AC going."

"That would be nice."

"And in the morning, if you're not too jetlagged, we'd like for you to come over for brunch. It's a little send-off before we have to take Rocco and Jess to the airport."

"Let me bring something."

"Just yourself. Rocco and I have it all planned out."

"I'll be there. I can't wait to get my hands on those babies."

Smiling, Eric reclined his seat and crossed his arms over his chest. "I'm going to squeeze in a little nap before we land."

"Sure … I should, too." But she stared out the window. The sun they had been chasing now sat low on the horizon and would soon disappear. This morning, as she waved goodbye, she'd braced for the inevitable sadness of going back to an empty house full of memories.

Maybe she'd feel a twinge when she entered the dark house later tonight. But she wouldn't go borrowing trouble. Right now, the sadness was gone, and in its place, a happy feeling, like something good was about to happen.

Nothing had changed back in Washington. But she had, and it was her own little miracle. Someone must be praying for her.

She had a feeling she knew who that someone was.

CHAPTER 21

Brock stood at the operating table with a scalpel poised over a boy's exposed chest. A Buruli ulcer had created a baseball-sized hole so deep, Brock could see the boy's ribs at the base of the wound. The patient was possibly fifteen and had suffered for months. Relatives had tried numerous herbal remedies, all dismal failures.

Brock glanced up, still getting used to seeing Iyegha and not Joy across from him. "More light, please."

Iyegha nodded, his dark, round face almost completely covered by surgical mask and cap. He positioned the lamp to shine more fully on the boy's chest.

Brock's jaw tightened. "Sonya, have Moses bring another pint of blood."

Two hours later, Brock covered the raw surface of the patient's chest with a sterile dressing. He stepped away from the gurney and pulled down his mask as Moses wheeled the patient to post-op. "Have one of the night crew stay with him. Keep him comfortable. Wake me if his fever gets too high."

He patted Iyegha's back and went into the clinic before calling it a night. Busy day. Not that he minded. It kept his mind focused on the reason he'd come to Africa in the first place—and off of the charming person who'd invaded his heart.

Brock picked up a stack of file folders and flipped through each one, sometimes pausing to jot down instructions. Then he took off his glasses and pressed his fingers against tired eyes.

He'd already missed dinner. He left the clinic through the side exit and cut across the road to the terrace. A sliver of new moon shone just above the horizon. It would be a dark night. A hot shower and a glass of milk, then bed, so he could get up and do it all again tomorrow.

His phone pinged. He pulled it from his pocket and checked caller ID. Not a number he recognized. Might be one of the short term group coming next week.

He tapped OK.

Thank you for replacing my phone. As soon as Eric teaches me how to use it, I will love it.

Brock rounded the corner of the staff dormitory and greeted Lady with an overzealous hug, mostly because he felt like hugging at least some living being. He sat in his usual chair on the terrace and tried more than once to save the number to his contacts with Lady nudging his hand for more attention.

"Just a minute, girl."

He gave up and pocketed his phone. "All right. I know. You miss Eric as much as I miss Joy, don't you, girl?"

He nuzzled the fur under Lady's neck and scratched her ears. "There. That's enough for now. Go lie down."

Lady backed up a step and gave him a soulful stare.

"That's all." His voice was quiet but firm. "Go." He pointed to the corner. "Lie down."

She complied but lay close to his feet. That would have to do, for now. He expelled his breath in a long sigh. The first quiet moment alone all day, yet all he wanted to do was talk to Joy.

He retrieved the phone, saved her number to his contacts, then typed out a short text. *Glad you have a phone now. May I call you sometime?* His finger hovered over the send icon. After a few seconds, he tapped and sent it on its way.

He waited, staring at the dark screen, feeling more like an adolescent than a man who'd just celebrated his sixty-seventh birthday. Finally, a responding ping.

YES!!

He punched her name and hit call. Then the lyrical *hello* he'd been waiting for.

"Let me guess," she said. "You're on the terrace with Lady at your feet."

He laughed. "Right on both counts. How'd you know?"

"Lucky guess. It's after dinner, and it's where I'd want to be if I were there. Well, not at your feet, but on the terrace. It was one of my favorite times of the day. I can just imagine the cool breeze and being serenaded by a chorus of crickets. Sorry, I'm babbling. I'm missing Africa."

He would be happy to listen to her babble the rest of the night. He stared into the darkness, a big smile plastered across his face. "Africa is missing you. How are you, Joy? Are you over your jet lag yet?"

"Finally. Eric and Ellie invited me over for brunch the day after we got back. I went, and I know it was rude, but I couldn't quit yawning."

Brock stifled a yawn of his own. "So you got to hold my grandbabies?"

"Oh, my goodness, Brock. Those babies. In fact, I talked Ellie into letting me babysit. She and Eric went on a little date last night."

"That was nice of you." Maybe something they could do together when he visited next month. He almost told her so but stopped himself. "How'd it go?"

"Great. Nicky is teething, so he tries to chew everything in sight, especially his sister. Bek's a little angel. Has a dimple like her mama and a head full of dark curls. Absolutely precious. I'm pretty sure she has her daddy wrapped around her little finger."

Brock chuckled but said nothing, hoping for more.

"So, catch me up. What interesting cases have you tackled lately?"

"Well, I could've used your skills today. Operated on a young lad with a Buruli ulcer."

"Hmm. I probably should know, but refresh my memory. What exactly is a Buruli ulcer?"

"No reason you would know. It's named Buruli after

the town where it was first discovered. It's caused by a bacteria that's like a cousin to tuberculosis, only it affects the skin and not the lungs. The infection had spread farther than I expected. I had to remove skin and fat from his entire chest. Recovery will be brutal, and he'll need some skin grafts. Sorry, now I'm babbling. I'm probably boring you with tedious details."

"Are you kidding me? I love details. Makes me feel like I'm still part of the action."

If she only knew how much he wished she were.

The conversation lagged. "So, what did Nicci serve for dinner?"

He hesitated, then confessed. "The surgery went long. I missed dinner."

"You must be tired. And hungry."

"Definitely tired." He scrambled to think of something else. Anything to keep her talking. "Have you told David about your plans to return to Africa?"

Joy let out a long sigh before answering. "Not yet. He's going through such a hard time, I hate to dump something else on him."

"Do you think he'll object?"

"I do. He's a practical man, just like his father was. But he plans to visit me soon. I'll break the news to him then. Maybe you could meet him when you come to Washington and help sway the odds in my favor."

"I'm not sure how much swaying I'll do, but I look forward to meeting him." Mostly true, even though he pictured himself in a straight-backed chair being interrogated by Joy's stern-faced son.

"David loves me. He'll come around. By the way, while we're on the subject of kids, I took your daughter to lunch yesterday. She has big plans for your visit."

"I have no doubt."

"Brock!" Joy gave a little gasp. "I always forget the time difference. It's almost midnight for you, and I've been chatting away. I'll hush now so you can go to bed."

She was right, even though he'd gladly give up sleep to keep talking. "Okay. But I did my fair share of "chatting away" too. I'll call you again tomorrow if you're up for it."

"Of course! Give my love to everyone."

"I will. Good night, Joy."

"'Night, Brock. Sweet dreams."

The screen went dark. Brock palmed the phone and let it rest on his thigh. Two and a half weeks …

CHAPTER 22

Visiting doctors were nothing new. But Neal Johnson was not just any visiting doctor. He could very well be the man to inherit the entire ministry one day in the future.

Brock waited beside Moses as the helicopter blades slowed. Toby hopped out and opened the rear passenger door. Neal piled out and waved, his shaved head gleaming in the direct sunlight. His wife followed and still had the same easy smile which now dominated her plump round face.

Brock closed the distance and extended his hand. "Welcome, Neal, Dottie." He put an arm around each of them. Two other men rounded the corner of the chopper. Neal turned, "You remember Ben? And this newcomer is John Sanders."

"Of course. Hello, Ben. John, nice to meet you." They shook hands all around. "This is Moses, the man who makes this compound work."

"No. No." Moses, all smiles, also shook hands. "You are all very welcome."

Mac and Al showed up to help Toby carry bags and get everyone settled.

"This way." Brock gestured for the group to follow.

Neal caught up and fell into step beside Brock. "Looks like you've added a couple of buildings."

Brock scanned the compound like a proud father. "Yes. We actually just extended the north wing out farther. We have a fully functional X-Ray room now."

"That's a game changer, I bet. Is that your house on the side?"

Brock followed his gaze. "No. I'm still in my little room off the terrace. Originally, the house was for my daughter and son-in-law. Right now, Toby and his wife live there."

"Toby's married?"

"Yes, to Nicci."

"You don't mean that little waif who—"

"Yes, the same. She stayed and is now our cook. That is, until October. She's expecting their first child."

Neal rubbed a hand over his smooth head. "I've been gone way too long."

"Agreed." Brock placed his hand on Neal's shoulder. "And as soon as you get settled, I'll give you a tour."

"Let's go now."

A few feet ahead, Dottie paused with one foot on the step leading to the dormitory. "Yes, Brock. Take him. He's been antsy for the past three hours."

"Sounds good. Dottie, go through those doors. Miriam should be in the kitchen. She'll show you to your room." Brock led the three doctors to the side door of the clinic. Twenty sets of wide eyes followed the group as they maneuvered through the outer waiting area. An old man, one of their regular patients, latched onto Brock's leg and cried, "*Medico! Pode me ajudar?*"

Brock painstakingly pried the man's fingers loose, leaving five greasy smudges on the side of Brock's shorts. "Sim." He took the man's hand and helped him stand, then motioned for Iyegha. "Take him back next. Make sure he gets some food."

Brock turned to Neal. "You remember Iyegha?"

"Of course." Neal shook Iyegha's hand. "Looking forward to working with you again."

Iyegha, who understood English better than he could speak it, merely smiled and nodded, then led the feeble man to a curtained cubicle.

Brock pushed through double doors leading to the hall. "Those rooms on the left are still used for surgery. More in-patient rooms are down this hallway. My office, which will actually be your office while I'm away, is the last room on the right."

Neal nodded. "Feels good to be back."

Brock took them the back way to the staff rooms. "Would you like to unpack and get settled? Dinner will be at six."

"I'd like to change and dig in at the clinic." Neal shot Brock a questioning glance. "If that's all right?"

"Us, too." John spoke for himself and Ben.

Brock nodded. "Great. I'll meet you there."

Two weeks later, the day before he was scheduled to leave for the States, Brock and Neal lingered after breakfast to go over last-minute details.

The double doors at the far corner of the room opened, and Nicci came into view, a stack of Styrofoam cups in one hand, the other hand splayed under her round belly. She looked up with a start, then retraced her steps. "Sorry to interrupt. I will come back later."

Brock pushed back from the table. "Wait. Don't go." He turned to Neal. "Excuse me for a moment."

Nicci remained rooted to the spot. He caught up to her and nudged her closer to the double doors. "I've wanted to talk with you before I leave tomorrow."

Her shoulders slumped, and she cocked her head to one side.

Body language he knew very well. "No, you haven't displeased me. If anything, you're doing too much. I want you to take care of yourself, Nicci. Sit more, and tell Kasemba or Miss Dottie what you want them to do."

Wasted words, Brock knew, and advice he couldn't take himself. Placing the care of the clinic in someone else's hands, no matter how capable, was not something he found easy.

"Can you do that for me, so I won't worry while I'm gone?"

She nodded but kept her gaze lowered as if

embarrassed to look at him. "Ellie leave. Miss Joy leave. Now you."

Brock's heart melted. "Nicci." He placed his arm around her shoulders and pulled her close. "I will make it back before you have this baby, I promise." He raised her drooping chin with his finger. "Now. Can I get a smile before I go?"

She covered wet cheeks with her hands but managed to give him a tremulous smile.

"That's my girl." He kissed the side of her forehead and nodded to Neal. "Ready?"

Neal pushed back from the table and placed his empty tray on the sidebar for the clean-up crew. Together, the two men left the dining hall to make after-breakfast rounds.

"I still can't get over the change in that girl."

"Yes," Brock agreed. "God has done a great work in her life. Her greatest joy is to serve others."

"Sounds like you." Neal held up his hand, cutting off Brock's reply. "Working with you these past two weeks, I realized that most of the people working here are your converts. That's quite a legacy. You know, Dottie and I were never blessed with children. I guess that's why we're here. We want to be a part of a ministry where lives are not just saved physically, they're changed for eternity."

"I'm glad you feel that way." Brock slowed his steps and faced Neal. "I can't think of anyone I'd rather have in charge while I'm away."

"Thank you. That means a lot to me."

Brock made it back to his bedroom before midnight, exhausted but satisfied he'd left nothing undone. A good feeling, at least on the inside. He sank into the recliner trying to muster enough energy to take a shower and crawl into bed.

He found himself looking forward to this trip with an eagerness he hadn't felt before. Barring emergencies and Bob Templeton's funeral, he could count on one hand the number of times he'd been back to the States since he first came to Africa. Never for purely personal reasons and certainly never for a whole month.

Grandchildren had a way of changing everything. He'd finally get to hold the twins. Something he'd waited ten months to do. Thank God, Ellie had been in the States and not in Africa when she went into labor. Yet another example of how perfect God's timing had always been.

He drew his phone from his back pocket. Call Joy or spend some quiet time with God? His worn-out body couldn't handle both.

With a resolute sigh, he set the phone face down on the table by the chair and picked up his Bible. He opened to Romans 8, one of his all-time favorite chapters.

Nothing can separate us from God's love. Words God had used time and again to answer Satan's attack. Brock made it through chapter 12 before the words started to blur.

He closed the Bible and said a short prayer out loud so he wouldn't fall asleep or let his mind wander. "Lord, I love you. My heart is full, but my body is tired. Take care of this ministry. Take care of all whom I love. Thank you for being so good to me. I trust you, Father, to send just what I need. Bless this trip."

His muscles balked as he pushed up from the recliner. The hot shower helped. He downed a couple of aspirin and eased into bed, expelling his breath in a grateful sigh. *Ah ... the way it should always be ...* He smiled and drifted to sleep thinking of a lovely lady in a turquoise sarong ...

The insistent ringing in his dream finally registered. He groped for his phone, his mind in a deep fog. The screen read Ellie. The time: three-twenty-three. Early even for him, and Ellie would know that.

"Hello." He tried to sound more alert than he felt.

"Dad?" Ellie's voice came through shaky and high-pitched.

Brock bolted upright. "What's wrong, honey?"

"It's Mom. She's had a stroke."

CHAPTER 23

Crises were not unusual. Through the years at the mission, Brock had come to expect them, even welcome them as an opportunity to see God at His best. He sat on the side of the bed and calmly found the number for the hospital and dialed it. As expected, information and access to the attending doctor were denied. Brock sighed and ran his hand through sleep-tousled hair. Setbacks were nothing new either.

Father, tell me what to do.

With a quiet nudging, he reluctantly dialed his daughter Gwyneth. "Hello, honey."

"Oh. Hello." Gwyneth's voice held the same begrudging tightness it always had whenever he called her. "I guess Ellie called you."

"Yes. Do you have any more details?"

"One of the staff found Mom unconscious on the floor of the bathroom. They called 911, then me. They ruled out heart attack."

"Ellie said it was a stroke. Is your mom conscious?"

"Yes. She's in ICU. Looks like she's paralyzed on her right side."

Worse than he thought. "How are you doing?"

"How do you think? I'm the only one left to deal with this mess." Her voice became shriller. "Ellie's got her own perfect little life, and you were never here."

Brock's gut twisted. At least, she didn't hang up.

Gwyneth's heavy sigh cut his reply. "Listen. Forget it. I'm just stressed."

"I know." He kept his voice soft. This wasn't Ellie he was talking to. Anything he said might send Gwyneth over the edge. "Honey, I'm coming to help you, but I need for you to do something before I get there."

"What?" Her voice went flat.

"They won't give me any information unless my name is on the HEPA form. Would you add my name to the list? Please."

After a pause, Gwyneth agreed, apparently wanting help even if from him. Maybe a small step in the right direction.

"Thank you." He bit off calling her honey again. Reconciliation was a slow process. "I'm leaving for Washington today. I'll call again when I land, and I'll make plans to come to Texas tomorrow."

"Okay."

Her voice, at least, had lost some of its edge. Brock ended the call, grabbed the water bottle he kept beside the bed, and stared blankly into the dim space of his bedroom. Plans for the next month had just taken a sharp detour—to Texas, the place he'd left so many years before, hoping never to return.

Do the next thing. His failsafe plan whenever he didn't know what else to do. He rose and headed to the bathroom. Just enough time to dress and catch the sunrise one last time.

Brock made an appearance at breakfast, then stole away to the chapel and seated himself on the front bench. He had prayed for Rozalynde for years, a faithless prayer, at best. Roz had made it crystal clear; she wanted nothing to do with him or his God. But still, he prayed, for Roz as well as Gwyneth, because they needed the truth just as much as he had. And if God could change his life—

Brock's shoulders slumped as he looked up at the stained-glass image of the risen Christ. "God, I need guidance."

At the back, the chapel doors creaked open.

"May I join you?" Moses remained poised at the door.

"Of course." Brock patted the bench with his hand. "Come sit with me."

Moses moved down the aisle with characteristic grace and sat, folding his hands in his lap. "I welcome this time to bid you a private farewell."

"As do I, my friend."

"You ate nothing at breakfast. You are burdened?"

Brock smiled and gave Moses a sideways glance. In his quiet way, Moses was offering his ear and possibly his help. "Yes. I received some bad news last night. Ellie's mother has suffered a stroke."

"I see." Moses let out a heavy sigh. "This will change

many things."

"Yes. I'm praying for guidance."

"I will pray with you."

"Thank you." Brock leaned back and shot him a grateful look. "I can think of no one I'd rather have praying for me."

"It is my honor." Moses stared ahead with squinting eyes. "Ah, and do you remember that day?"

A rhetorical question. A reference to the day Moses had shown up at Brock's modest one-room house and used his bloody foot to push open the door. He'd stood there, wild-eyed and panting, looking as if he might pass out. In his arms, a woman, unconscious and barely breathing. Brock's first patient, and within days, his first two converts. It was a story Moses never tired of telling and one Brock usually never tired of hearing. Today, however, his mind was on more pressing things.

Moses continued, his deep, mellow voice reverting back to its strong Angolan accent. "You take her from my arms and lay her out on a table, praying to your God. He help you bring her back to me. You tell me true things about this God. Things that make my heart burn to know more." Moses turned to him, unshed tears reddening his eyes. "Do you remember what I called you in those early days?"

"*Pula Kamba.*" Brock mouthed the words.

"*Ya, Ya.* My white-skinned friend who cared enough to speak hard things. You say to me, 'Our God is a jealous

God. You must decide who is the one true God and let all other gods go.' I listen, and my heart tell me these things are true."

"It was a great day when you both came to Christ."

"I ask you to give us new names to go with our new hearts. You call me Moses and my woman Miriam."

Brock nodded. "I found them much easier to pronounce than your given names. And then, you left your village for good and became my trusted dark-skinned friend."

"Ya. Ya. I found it wise to leave my village. You say to me, 'God has one woman, *bumbo Kamba*, one woman.'" Moses repeated, holding up a slightly crooked index finger, "'not many wives, for us to join our lives and our bodies to.'"

Moses scratched the side of his head. "I think long on this, and I ask you how one woman be enough for one man. You say, 'God is enough.' You tell me to pray to God to give wisdom to make the right choice. So I pray, and I choose Miriam as my one true *Damo*." Moses's smile deepened the creases of his cheeks as he leaned in and nudged Brock. "Other wives not pleased."

Brock chuckled then quickly sobered as the realization of what Moses was really getting at hit him with the force of a monsoon gale.

One woman, not two. Brock tried to swallow, even though his mouth had suddenly gone dry. Somehow, he managed to choke out, "Your eyes see what most others

187

don't, my friend."

Those brown eyes, now full of compassion, gave Brock a penetrating gaze. "It is because I see with my heart. It is now you who must make that choice. I will pray for God to give you wisdom."

Brock wondered, not for the first time, if Moses might actually be an angel sent by God to help him in this lonely land. "Thank you. I very much need your prayers."

Moses rose. Brock started to stand as well, but Moses extended his hand out flat. "No need. I leave you now."

Brock managed a weak smile as Moses gave him a deferential bow and backed into the aisle.

Brock shifted and focused again on the stained glass, this time not asking for guidance but for grace to do what he knew God was asking him to do.

CHAPTER 24

Give Joy up?

The thought sent a crushing weight to Brock's chest. He needed time to hash it out with God. A luxury he didn't have at the moment. He left the chapel and waved to Toby who was already doing a pre-flight check on the helicopter.

Brock forced a smile. "I'll grab my bags and be right out."

"I got ya, Dr. Brock." Mac jogged from the side of the clinic and fell into step beside him. "I'll load while you say your goodbyes."

It was pointless to refuse the offer. Mac rushed ahead to open the dormitory door. Brock gave Mac's shoulder a friendly pat as he entered. "Thank you."

"Whew. A bit cooler in here." Mac took out a hanky and swabbed his forehead and the back of his neck.

"Yes. I think it'll be a hot one today." Brock's bags stood ready beside the bedroom door. "These two, if you don't mind."

"Yes, sir." Mac stuffed the hanky in his back pocket and scooped up the bags.

Brock placed his Bible in a carryon bag and scanned the room one last time. With a heavy sigh, he clicked off the light and pulled the door closed, no longer looking forward to the trip.

The crowd beside the helicopter cheered as he rounded the corner of the building. Such dear people, all happy for him to get away and spend some time with his grandchildren.

Heaviness in the heart of a man maketh it stoop, but a good word maketh it glad.

The verse popped into his mind from out of nowhere and got him through the next few minutes. Brock smiled and made a point to hug each person.

Someone tapped him from behind. Brock turned, then gripped Neal's extended hand.

"Just wanted to wish you a safe trip."

"Thank you. Don't hesitate to call if you run into problems."

Neal's face broke into a wide grin. "Do you have phone service in the plane?"

Brock laughed. "No, but this guy right here will be good help."

Iyegha moved closer. "Yes, I will certainly try, and I also will pray God to bless your travels, Dr. Brock."

"Thank you. I'm leaving the clinic in good hands."

Brock pivoted to Moses and nudged him toward the helicopter. "Walk with me, friend." He leaned in and spoke low for only Moses to hear. "I wanted to thank you for talking to me this morning. You said things I needed to hear."

"May God be praised." Moses brushed past and propped open the door.

Brock paused and placed his hand on Moses's spindly arm. "Keep me in your prayers." His knees creaked and popped as he grabbed the handle above the seat and pulled himself up into the chopper.

Beside him, Toby positioned headphones and gave a thumbs up. Brock had barely buckled in when Toby revved the engine and took off, leaving behind a swirling trail of red dust and debris.

Brock leaned forward to catch a quick glimpse of the compound. The oblong clinic, inpatient hospital, and staff dormitories intersected at the dining hall to form a cross visible only from the air. Brock's tribute to the One who had led him to come to Africa. How different it all looked from the little shack Moses had stumbled into over twenty-five years ago.

Toby began talking as soon as the chopper leveled. "Looks like you'll have good weather."

Brock dragged his gaze away. "Yes."

"We'll sure miss you around here, especially Nicci. Myself, I'm kinda glad you're getting away, tell ya the truth. 'Bout time you took some R and R, you know what I mean? Spend some time with them grandbabies." Toby gave him a toothy grin and nudged with his elbow. "Maybe spend a little time with Miss Joy?"

Brock chuckled and played along, not ready to delve into the sudden change with all its ramifications, especially not with Toby.

Toby rattled on, hardly pausing to take a breath. Brock half-listened, giving well-placed nods whenever Toby glanced his way. Brock didn't mind. In fact, he found the mindless chatter entertaining, even oddly relaxing. At any rate, it certainly kept his mind off more troubling thoughts.

"We're getting close. I'm gonna contact air traffic control and ask for permission to land close to your plane."

"That would be nice. I have to confess, flying to the Luanda airport is much nicer than driving ten miles of bad roads to the grass airstrip like we used to. It's a great blessing having you around full-time, Toby."

"Works both ways, Dr. Brock. Yes, sir. Should've made the move a long time ago. God had to get me kidnapped to give me the kick in the pants I needed. Like Eric says, I always have to learn the hard way. 'Bout got me killed."

Toby radioed the tower, then went silent until he landed, as promised, close to the Gulfstream. "Okay. Let's get you on your way."

A strong breeze whipped his door back as soon as Brock cracked it open. Toby came around carrying Brock's two bags and shook his head when Brock attempted to take them. "I got 'em, Doc."

Brock followed Toby up the steps of the Gulfstream and shook hands with both pilots who stood ready to welcome. Toby returned from the luggage hold and gave Brock a crushing hug. "Have a good time with that family of yours."

"I will. Thank you, Toby."

With a nod and a wave to the pilots, Toby bounded down the steps. The co-pilot turned to Brock. "Can I get you anything, Dr. Whitfield?"

"Some water would be great."

"Sure thing. Here you go." He handed Brock a water bottle from the galley drawer. "How about a snack?"

"No, thank you. This is fine."

"Very good. We'll stop for lunch in Paris when we refuel."

Brock smiled and thanked him again even though he had every intention of fasting for the duration of the trip. Brock settled by his usual window seat and waited until the cockpit door clicked shut to blow out his breath in a grateful sigh.

Finally. The passenger cabin became as much a sanctuary as his beloved terrace where he usually talked things over with God.

As the plane climbed to its cruising altitude of 37,000 feet, the scene outside his little window became a canvas of brilliant blue above patches of puffy white clouds. A great backdrop for prayer, and right now, he had a lot to pray about.

It had been a long time since he'd been so troubled he'd felt the need to fast. A bittersweet reminder of how far God had brought him.

"You've always come through, no matter how bad

things seemed." Brock spoke the words, but in a soft voice, the conversation between him and God a very personal one about quite possibly the greatest challenge he'd ever faced.

He began the way he always did for his most serious prayers. "Father, I come into your holy presence asking for an audience." He envisioned approaching God's holy throne *to obtain mercy and find grace to help in time of need.* "Lord, my heart is heavy. You know how much I've come to care for Joy."

Thoughts of Joy warred with his prayer. In the span of one brief year, Joy Stockman had changed the paradigm of his life, much as Ellie had when she came to Africa. Only Joy was a peer and not a daughter.

He'd grown accustomed to Joy's kindness, to her encouragement, and most of all, her companionship. Something he hadn't known he craved until Joy came into his life.

"I was perfectly content before. Why, Father? Why did You let her come into my life in the first place?"

Brock paused, his heart too heavy to mouth the words. Joy, by far, was the most beautiful and inspiring person he'd ever known. Her very presence added life to a part of him long dead and shined light into the dark lonely places in his heart.

Was God turning off the light and closing the door to any future he might have had with her?

Brock's mind drifted to their last moments on the terrace before Joy left. "Was that it, Father? Was that the last time we'll have together?"

Brock sighed, then opened his Bible to Genesis 22 where God asked Abraham to do the unthinkable, to take his only son Isaac and sacrifice him back to God.

The same chapter he'd once shown Eric. Brock looked up and stared hypnotically out the window. Was it as hard for Eric to give up his leg as it was for Brock to let go of Joy?

Was this only a test? Maybe God would step in at the last minute like he had for Abraham? Roz might die and—

Brock's stomach twisted. Had he really sunk so low?

"God, forgive me." Brock leaned forward, his head in his hands. "If this is a test, I have failed miserably. Forgive me."

He read the passage again, his tears dripping onto the page. He kept reading until he came to the place where Jacob wrestled with the angel.

He read and prayed for hours, stopping only to stretch his legs in Paris. For most of the trip, the conversation between God and him remained one-sided as Brock poured out his heart. He tried bargaining. "I'll give Joy up for now. I'll devote my life to helping Roz, but please, I'm begging you, God, give Joy back. Please."

By the time the plane began its final descent into Washington, Brock's heart felt bruised as if he really had been wrestling with God Almighty.

God had already spoken, very clearly, back in the chapel before Brock ever left the mission compound.

Brock stared at his hands folded on top of his closed Bible. The answer was very simple.

But not easy.

Easy or not, Brock knew he could not leave this plane until things were made right. He did not have to understand it, or even like it. Disobedience was not an option.

"I give up." Brock raised his hands, palms up. "Joy was never mine to keep. I give her up. No strings. My heart is fixed, O God. Whatever You ask of me, give me the grace to do."

The peace that had eluded him since Ellie's early morning phone call now cushioned his heavy heart. Peace tinged with sadness, but still peace—that could not be explained or understood, a gift from his heavenly Father in response to obedient surrender.

The plane slowed, then glided smoothly onto the runway, braking sharply as it taxied to its designated spot. Brock's high metabolism reminded him the minute he stood that he'd gone a whole day without food.

At least, now he could eat again.

God had won, as He must.

Brock left the plane resolute, ready to face the one woman he had never truly loved and to end a relationship that never had the chance to get started.

CHAPTER 25

In the span of twenty minutes, the phone rang twice, turning Joy's world upside down.

David's call came first with the bombshell that he had put in for a transfer to D.C.

With barely enough time for Joy to catch her breath, a noticeably shaken Ellie called with news of her mother's stroke.

"Oh, Ellie." Joy grabbed a chair and sat. "How terrible. What can I do?"

"I don't even know what to do myself."

"Does your dad know?"

"Yes. I called him as soon as I heard. He said we'd figure out what to do when he got here."

"Listen, why don't I drop off the salad and bow out for tonight? This is a family crisis."

"No. You're family, too. You have to come. In fact, I was hoping you'd come early."

Joy ended the call and moved fast, energized into action. A crisis seemed to bring out her best, but two at the same time?

Joy grabbed a bowl and calmly went about the process of making the salad she'd offered to bring, tearing prewashed romaine and leaf lettuce into bite-sized chunks. A task to keep her fingers occupied while her mind sorted and categorized the startling information she'd received.

My life's a mess, David had said. He'd asked if he could stay with her until he could scout out an apartment.

Finally, the chance to reconnect with her son. Something she'd hoped and prayed would happen, but under happier circumstances.

Of course, she'd said yes. Her boy needed her. To deny him would be to cut her heart out of her body.

But it meant postponing her return to Africa. Something she hated to do, for entirely selfish reasons.

Joy opened a jar of Kalamata olives, and let them tumble into a strainer, then spread Roma tomatoes on the cutting board, slicing through each one with firm, deliberate strokes.

She'd have to let Brock know, the sooner the better. He'd be supportive and gracious, as always more concerned for her than how he'd manage short-handed.

Poor Brock. He had his own family problem to deal with, and he would do everything in his power to help, of that she was sure.

She stood at the sink and stared out the kitchen window. The trajectory of their lives seemed to be leading them in opposite directions.

What if she never returned? What if she could never again sit on the terrace with Brock, watching the sunrise? A sick thud landed in the pit of her stomach.

Joy stretched plastic wrap over the salad bowl, pulling it taut, then set it in the fridge. Time to stop these dead-end thoughts and go to the One who could give her peace. With a new purpose to her step, she grabbed her Bible and entered her bedroom. She got on knees and spread the Bible on the bed before her.

"Show me something, Father. I need to hear from You."

Her Bible fell open naturally to the book of Psalms. Without flipping the page, her eyes were drawn to Psalm 61. *Hear my cry, O God. Attend unto my prayer. From the ends of the earth, will I cry unto thee, when my heart is overwhelmed. Lead me to the rock that is higher than I ...*

Joy buried her face on the open Bible. "Father, my heart is too overwhelmed to pray. Give me wisdom. And peace."

It took three trips to load the car. Cherry cobbler, still warm from the oven on the back floorboard sat wedged between sandals and makeup bag. Greek salad on the other side and her nice clothes to change into hanging on a hook above the back-passenger door.

Joy slid into the hot leather seat and started the car. Bright green numbers appeared above the car radio. Not even noon yet?

Her stomach rumbled, not just from hunger. In less than seven hours, she'd see Brock again.

Her hair fell forward as she rifled through her bag for sunglasses. Joy adjusted the rear-view mirror and stole a peek. At least her hair looked good. The stylist had taken off a little more than requested, creating a bouncy, chin-length bob that swished as she moved. Even made her look younger, a vain thought she knew, but still a comfort given all the unsettling news from the morning.

Ellie met her at the door, a crying baby in each arm. "Thank God, you're here."

"Oh, my goodness." Joy puckered out her lower lip as she eased passed Ellie. "What's the matter with my babies?"

"They're hungry and cranky." Ellie followed Joy into the kitchen. "And so is their mother. Do I have to wait until tonight to dig into that cobbler?"

Joy set the cobbler on the counter and went back for another load, speaking over her shoulder. "Of course not. You can let me know if it's good."

"I'm joking," Ellie called after her. "If it tastes as good as it smells, it'll be amazing."

Joy hugged the salad bowl to her chest and grabbed her makeup bag and hanging clothes, determined to get the rest in one trip. She set the salad in the fridge, then washed her hands. "Okay, hand me one."

Joy took Nicky from Ellie's left arm and followed her up the stairs to the nursery, settling in one of the rocking chairs. Nicky clutched the bottle and stared up at Joy, occasionally breaking into a grin. She slid her finger down his cute, button nose. "You're a charmer, just like your daddy."

"You've got that right. He knows just when to throw a smile to disarm me."

Joy smiled and nodded, not really sure if Ellie meant Eric or Nicky.

Both babies made satisfied hums interspersed with slurping sounds. Nicky finished first. Joy raised him to her shoulder, loving how he snuggled close in the crook of her neck. His baby fine hair tickled her chin.

"I wish I could stay like this the rest of the afternoon," Ellie whispered, her eyes never leaving Bek's cherub face. "But duty calls." Ellie rose and placed Bek on her side in the crib.

Joy reluctantly did the same with Nicky, holding the pacifier in place until he drifted back to sleep.

Together they tiptoed from the room and down the stairs. Back in the kitchen, Ellie leaned closer to the baby monitor, then straightened, crossing her fingers. "With luck, they should be down for a couple of hours."

Joy rummaged in the meat bin in the fridge and pulled out turkey and Swiss cheese. "Want the usual?"

"Yes, please."

Joy went to work while Ellie sat at the table.

"My sandwiches never taste as good as yours."

Joy smiled and made a diagonal cut across each sandwich. "Everything always tastes better when someone else makes it." She placed a pickle wedge on each plate.

Ellie scraped back her chair. "I guess I should make myself useful." She took two water bottles from the fridge, then returned to her seat.

"Would you like for me to pray?"

Ellie nodded and slid icy fingers into Joy's hand. Joy prayed for the food, and also for wisdom for the decisions that had to be made. "Any updates?"

"Just spoke to Gwyneth before you came. It's bad, mainly because Mom lay on the bathroom floor for hours before Consuela found her."

Joy listened, at a loss for words, envisioning the carefully groomed woman she'd met the year before, lying for hours on the cold tile helplessly waiting for someone to find her. It would be a hard blow to someone so obsessed with her appearance.

"Gwyneth's freaking out. She doesn't handle stress well, and she's definitely not the nurturing type. Wants me to come, but I don't see how I could."

"I'll be glad to stay here and take care of the babies if you think you could trust me."

"Trust you?" Ellie reached across the table for Joy's hand. "I've seen you in action. But I'd hate to ask you. Taking care of twins can be exhausting."

"Please. I want to help."

The garage doors creaked open. Seconds later, Eric came through the side door lugging two bags of groceries.

"Yay!" Ellie clapped her hands. "You're home early."

Eric set the groceries on the counter. "Pit stop." He turned and hugged Ellie, smiling over her shoulder. "Hello, Joy. Looks like you showed up early, too."

"I'm ready to help."

"Just having you here helps." Eric moved quickly and with purpose, unwrapping four thick steaks. "Look at these beauties." He spread them on a foil-lined baking sheet and rubbed a mixture of seasonings on each side. Every so often, he would glance up and smile at Ellie who stood next to him, watching him work.

No wonder they had such cute babies.

Joy shook herself, remembering she had come to help. "Have you had lunch, Eric?"

He washed his hands and dried them with a paper towel. "No. I'm starving."

"Turkey and Swiss?"

"Oh, yeah. Heavy on the turkey." Eric dumped four potatoes into the sink.

"I can handle this part." Ellie nudged him aside with her hip. "I'll wash, you wrap."

"Deal."

Joy built Eric's sandwich, stealing peeks at the couple. A homey scene she loved being part of.

Eric set the foil-wrapped, boat-sized potatoes on the top rack of the oven.

Joy stood to the side holding his plate. "Ready for this?"

"Yes, ma'am. Thank you." Eric took the sandwich and leaned back against the counter. "Catch me up."

"Nothing new except Joy has offered to stay with the twins if I decide to go."

"Really?" Eric used his finger to wipe mustard from the side of his mouth and cut his gaze over to Joy. "You are one brave woman."

"I'm game, as long as you leave detailed instructions."

Ellie handed him a napkin. "So, do you think I should go?"

"Do you want to go?"

"That's a loaded question. Yeah, I guess I do, so I can live with myself."

Eric stared at the floor and ate his sandwich. After a couple of minutes, he spoke again. "Wait until your dad gets here. See what he thinks."

"Good plan."

Eric put the last bite into his mouth and crumpled the napkin on the plate. "I'm about to head out."

"Already?"

"I'd rather wait at the airport than get stuck in traffic. Need me to pick up anything while I'm out?"

"No, but I'll need to stock up if I leave for Texas tomorrow."

Eric grabbed his phone from the kitchen counter and paused to read his last text before looking up. "Make a list. Maybe we can make a run to the store after the kids are down for the night."

He turned to Joy and gave her a sideways hug. "That sandwich was delicious. Think we can talk you and Brock into babysitting after dinner?"

"I think you can probably twist our arms."

"Great. Okay, Babe, I'm outta here." Eric gave Ellie a kiss on the forehead, then left through the side door.

Ellie rubbed the back of her neck. "I've got so much to do, I don't even know where to start."

Joy smiled. "I find at such times, it's best to take a nap."

Ellie laughed. "You and I are kindred souls." Ellie bit her lower lip, making her dimple more pronounced. "Trust me, I wish I could."

"I'm serious." Joy took Ellie by the shoulders and moved her like a robot toward the stairs. "Go, while the twins are down. Then after your power nap, you can brief me and walk me through a typical day."

"Okay. You talked me into it."

"Good." Joy grabbed her makeup and clothes bag and followed Ellie up the stairs. "I'll freshen up a bit."

Joy tiptoed past the nursery to the bathroom at the end of the hall. Its ceramic-tiled floor was dated, but pristine, as was everything else in the Templeton household.

She left the door ajar and spread the contents of her makeup bag on the ledge above the sink. Her compact teetered off the edge and clattered onto the floor. Joy froze, listening for movement from the nursery.

She'd have to be more careful. Two babies at one time? Her stomach went queasy just thinking about it.

Twenty minutes later, she finished changing and eased out of the bathroom, just as Ellie opened her bedroom door. "I feel like a new woman."

"Were you able to sleep?"

"As soon as my head hit the pillow." They started down the stairs, but the sound of a baby cooing made Ellie do an about-face. "So much for a couple of hours."

Joy held down one of Bek's flailing legs and secured the diaper. "There, little miss. You smell much better." She held Bek up and kissed the dimple on her cheek, then straightened as Ellie returned with two warm bottles. "Do they usually wake up in such good moods?"

"Most of the time. I hope they stay this happy when Dad gets here."

"Oh, I don't think he'll mind if they don't."

"You're probably right. He hasn't held them yet. Only caught glimpses through the NICU window."

"He's in for a treat." Joy settled in the rocker and laughed at Bek, whose open mouth strained toward the bottle. "Has your mom been to visit?" Joy asked, then wished she hadn't.

"Twice, believe it or not." Ellie took Nicky to the changing table. "Although I must confess, she was more work than help. It's a good thing Gwyneth and I had nannies. I seriously doubt my mother has ever changed a diaper."

Ellie finished dressing Nicky and tried to smooth down his fine hair that stood up like an overgrown wheat field. "I think the babies melted her cold heart a little. She seemed happier—" Ellie broke off, her mouth drawn in a tight line. "Sorry."

Joy stopped rocking and tilted her head to one side. "This is a hard time for all of you."

"I can't imagine how scared Mom must be. Without her perfect image, I'm afraid she'll shrivel up and die." Ellie wiped her face and sat in the other rocker, with Nicky in the crook of her arm. "The woman's had more cosmetic procedures than Cher." She stared past Joy, an amused look on her face. "I remember one time, I couldn't have been more than seven, I think. Anyway, I went into Mom's bedroom. She was asleep, and her whole face was wrapped up like a mummy. Scared me so bad, I backed out and ran for my nanny. She told me that's what my momma had to do to look beautiful."

Joy listened without comment, sensing Ellie needed to talk.

"I wished she cared more about us than looking beautiful. By the time I was nine, I quit caring." Ellie shrugged and looked down at Nicky. "I just pray I won't be that kind of mother."

"I don't think there's any danger of that." Joy said quietly.

The familiar creaking of the garage door made them both jump and stare wide-eyed at each other. Ellie grabbed her phone and checked the time. "They're back already?"

With no time to think, Joy followed Ellie downstairs, trying not to jostle Bek too much and make her spit up on her shoulder.

They made it to the kitchen. Joy smoothed down her

top as Eric pushed open the door. "Guess who was already at the airport when I got there?"

Joy's breath caught as Brock entered and with him the aura of love that seemed to emanate from him.

Brock wore khaki pants and a mint green polo and with his full silver hair and close-cropped beard, he could easily pass for a male model on the cover of *Mature Living.* Her stomach fluttered, and she prayed her face didn't reveal too much of the giddiness she couldn't help feeling.

Joy hung back as he made a beeline for Ellie, taking the baby from her arms. "Hello, sweetheart." He leaned in and kissed Ellie's cheek. "I've been waiting a long time to hold this little guy." Brock rubbed his hand over Nicky's head and turned to Ellie, a twinkle in his eye. "This hair."

Ellie chuckled and moved closer, placing her hand on Nicky's back. "I know, right? Absolutely untamable."

"Brings back memories of you."

"Me? My hair stood straight up?"

"I'm afraid so. But look at you now. There's hope."

Eric stood back, grinning like a proud papa. Then he started toward the living room, carrying Brock's bag. "I'll take this upstairs to your room."

Brock thanked him, then turned to Joy. "Hello." His warm smile made her knees go weak. "I see you have my other little beauty." He brushed the side of Bek's cheek with the back of his fingers.

She held Bek out to him. "Think you can handle two at one time?"

"I'll certainly try. Come here, sweetheart." He cradled Nicky in one arm and extended the other.

Joy leaned in and situated Bek in Brock's free arm. "Got her?"

"Yes." He wrapped his fingers securely around their bellies and gave her an uncertain look. "I think so."

Bek stared up at him, her eyes wide, totally mesmerized by his short, white beard. She stretched her dainty fingers to touch it. Brock lowered his chin and captured her fingers in his mouth which made her cackle. "You and I are going to be great friends, little angel."

Nicky squirmed, kicking out his feet. Brock laughed. "Yes, you, too, little man."

Brock glanced up at Ellie, unshed tears brightening his eyes. "I feel like Simeon. 'Lord, let now thy servant depart in peace.'"

Ellie snapped a picture with her phone. "Don't you dare leave this earth now. I'm not ready to lose you ... or Mom."

Eric returned to the kitchen and grabbed the steaks from the fridge. "Taking orders. Rare, medium or well-done?"

"Medium." All three answered in unison.

Joy tore herself away to take the potatoes out of the oven, then set the table.

Ellie took the twins from Brock to strap them into their chairs.

"Honey, I'm going to step outside and keep Eric

company." Brock rubbed the top of Nick's fuzzy head and walked toward the patio door.

Joy caught herself staring after him. She turned and opened one of the cabinets. "What shall it be tonight? Veal with spring vegetables or chicken with mac and cheese?"

"Either one. They aren't finicky eaters, thank the Lord."

"Oh, wait. Here's a couple of jars that have beef and potatoes. Perfect. That way the twins can eat what we're eating." Joy emptied the contents of the jars into microwavable bowls. "How long?"

"Forty seconds." Ellie finished snapping on bibs.

Laughter filtered into the kitchen. Joy punched in the time on the microwave, then glanced out the back door. Brock stood next to the grill, a swath of smoke curling toward him. His eyes were crinkled in amusement at something Eric was saying. "Sounds like they're having a good time." Joy stirred the pureed baby food and tested it with her pinky. "Brock seems very happy to be here."

"I'm happy, too. I've missed him so much." Ellie took one of the bowls from Joy. "Maybe when we get Mom settled someplace, Dad'll return to Washington for a longer visit."

After a few minutes, the men came in, surrounded by the delicious smell of smoke and charcoal-grilled meat. Eric placed the steaks, still sizzling on the platter, in the center of the table. "Hope you're hungry."

"Starved." Brock rubbed his stomach and nodded to

Joy as he took the seat next to hers. "I see you killed the fatted calf. Do you know how long it's been since I had a good steak?"

"Us, too. We took advantage of the occasion." Eric sat next to Ellie and looked across the table to Brock. "Would you pray?"

By some miracle, the twins kept still while everyone joined hands. Brock prayed a short prayer of blessing for the food and for the ones gathered around the table.

For a man who claimed to be starving, he ate little. Instead, he pulled Nicky's chair closer to himself. "Mind if I feed him?"

Ellie pushed Nicky's bowl over to Brock. "I think I'm going to keep you two around. Taking care of twins is so much easier with help."

Watching Brock feed his grandbaby was just about the sweetest thing Joy had ever seen. Nicky opened his mouth like a little bird greedy for his next bite.

Joy fed Bek between her own bites, listening but remaining as quiet and invisible as possible, a habit acquired from her hospice days.

"Joy offered to watch the twins so I could go with you to Texas."

Joy felt Brock looking at her, so she became very focused on scraping the last bite onto the baby spoon.

"That's wonderful. I have to confess, I didn't want to make that trip alone."

Ellie wiped Nicky's face. "What time do you want to

leave?"

"I'd like to give the pilots time to recoup. Maybe after lunch?"

Ellie turned to Joy with a raised eyebrow. "Would that work for you?"

"Of course. I'll get here by eleven and take over from there."

After dinner, Joy went with Ellie to give the twins their bath and put them to bed. "I hope I remember everything. Do they always go down this easily?"

"Yes, thank God. He knew if He gave me two, they needed to be low maintenance. They love their beds. Good sleepers. Good eaters. I'm very blessed. And don't worry. Eric will be a lot of help. I couldn't do this without him."

She spoke the truth. By the time they made it back downstairs, the kitchen was spotless. Eric stood as they entered. As soon as Ellie cleared the doorway, she asked Brock. "Do you two mind babysitting while Eric and I do some shopping?"

Brock looked at Joy. "I think I'm up for the challenge. How about you?"

She nodded.

"Great. The baby monitors are on, but I don't think they'll wake. We shouldn't be gone too long."

Eric grabbed Ellie's hand and tugged her toward the side door. "You've got my number in your phone, don't you?"

Joy smiled and followed them to the door. "They'll be

fine. Don't worry."

"It's you I'm worried about, not the twins."

"Between the two of us, we'll figure it out."

Joy eased the door closed and turned back to Brock. Left alone, they eyed each other, an awkward transition made seamless by the warmth and amusement in his expression.

"It's good to see you again. How are you, Joy?"

The genuine connection she'd been hoping for, not just a superficial greeting. She relaxed and returned his smile. "I'm doing very well, Brock. It's good to see you, too."

She moved past him into the living room, speaking over her shoulder. "You must be tired." She chose the upholstered chair, and not the sofa, having enough sense to take the guesswork out of where they would sit. "I hope you were able to rest on the plane."

Brock took the other chair. "Not much." His shoulders slumped as if by some invisible weight. "I had some things to work through." He stopped talking and leaned forward, his hands clasped in front of him. Then he looked up and smiled, even though the spark had left his eyes. "It's kind of you to take care of the twins so Ellie can go with me to Texas. It means a lot. To both of us."

"I'm happy to help. I wish I could do more."

"I'd appreciate your prayers." He dropped his gaze to his folded hands and continued, his voice almost a whisper. "I hope to have an opportunity to make amends. Heal old wounds."

A silence, heavy with things left unsaid, settled between them. She found herself in the delicate position of lady friend discussing ex-wife and somehow knew deep in her soul what God had been trying to tell her for a long time.

She could, at least, make it easy. For his sake. She cleared her throat. "A lot has changed for both of us in the last twenty-four hours."

He looked at her, and her words spilled out before she lost her courage, answering the question in his eyes.

"Brock, I won't be able to return to Africa."

CHAPTER 26

The aftershock of Joy's words hit Brock full force. He swiveled his chair to face hers and tried to hide his disappointment, even while realizing how much easier she'd just made his earlier resolve to give her up. "What do you mean?"

"My son called this morning. Abby is going through with the divorce."

Compassion took over, at least for the moment. "I'm so sorry, Joy. I hoped and prayed they would work through things."

"So did I." Her pitiful attempt at a smile further threatened his resolve.

He balled his fist to keep from reaching for her hand. His chair creaked as he leaned forward. "How's he taking it?"

"Not very well." Her pitch rose as she blurted out, "I can't leave him right now, Brock."

"No." He said quietly. "Of course not."

"But I'm heartsick. About David. About leaving you shorthanded."

He raised his hand and interjected. "Don't let that trouble you. God always sends exactly what we need." A statement he'd made many times before and one he believed, but at the moment, didn't quite feel. Brock gave what he hoped was a reassuring smile. "It seems God is moving us in different directions."

Joy looked him square in the face, her eyes narrowed as if she were thinking. After a few seconds, she leaned closer and reached for his hand. "You're absolutely right."

Her hand trembled slightly in his, the only indication this might be hard for her, too. He closed his fingers around hers, grateful she had initiated the contact but incapable of ending it.

"I'm thankful for the time I had with you, Brock." Her face softened and her voice became more tremulous. "To work with you and get to know you."

For a long moment, neither said anything.

Then she smiled even though her eyes had filled with tears. "I can't deny that I—" She sat straighter as if bolstering her courage. "Rozalynde needs you, Brock. Your daughters need you, and my son needs me. I just wanted you to know I have no regrets. Only gratitude."

No regrets, only gratitude.

Her words killed any lingering doubt about the course God would have him take. His fingers tightened around hers, and he stared at their clasped hands.

God, please.

Every fiber of his being pressed against the God-given restraint, wanting to cross the boundary into more intimate territory with a lingering look, or a touch. Anything to somehow let Joy know how deeply he cared and how hard it was to walk away. That he wanted to spend the rest of his days with her—and not with Roz.

He glanced up and somehow found strength, not inside but from Joy, whose kind eyes held no hint of hurt or longing. Only a sense of peace and acceptance.

She seemed to be all right. He would have to find a way to be all right, too.

Brock smiled, with a cheerfulness he didn't feel and probably would never feel again. "I'm grateful, too."

She returned his smile, then gently pulled her hand from his. "Now, how about some cherry cobbler?"

By God's grace, Joy held it together the rest of the evening. Eric and Ellie returned while she and Brock sat around the table finishing off their dessert and drinking decaf coffee.

Brock helped Eric and Ellie carry in the rest of the groceries and supplies. She dished out cobbler for them and assured Ellie the twins hadn't stirred.

If either noticed their strained expressions, they said nothing, and thankfully, no one questioned when she announced that she needed to get home.

She retrieved the salad bowl from the dishwasher and said her goodbyes. Brock took the bowl from her. "I'll help you to the car."

She thanked him, secretly relieved to have another

moment alone with him. After grabbing her clothes and makeup bag, she left through the same door she'd entered what seemed a lifetime ago.

Brock placed the salad bowl on the back seat and turned to her, extending his hand. She took it, then he placed his other hand on top, holding hands for a moment longer.

Brock's hair gleamed even more silver in the moonlight. A faint breeze blew her hair across her face. Brock reached up and smoothed it back, giving her a tender smile. It was their last goodbye. She knew it, and from the look on his face, so did he.

He stepped around her and opened the car door. "Get some good rest." His voice was soft and held the huskiness of restrained tears.

Joy slid into the seat, and Brock closed the door. He stepped back and watched as she backed out of the driveway. The tears she had successfully held in check, now had free reign to fall. They tickled her chin, but she wouldn't let herself wipe them away. Not until she was sure he couldn't see and guess that she was on the verge of falling apart.

At the end of the block, she adjusted the rearview mirror to see if he was still there. He was, and she thought she saw him bring his hand to his mouth before giving one last wave.

With one hand on the wheel and the other clutching her chest, she drove a few blocks away, then pulled over and gave vent to the sadness and loss. It'd been a long time since she'd had such a gut-wrenching cry. It felt good.

By the time she made it home, she was physically and emotionally spent. She unloaded the car and like a mindless robot went through her nightly routine of cleaning her face and brushing her teeth. She took her blue satin nightgown from the hook on the bathroom door and slipped it on. It was old and had seen some wear, but settled around her body like a comforting friend.

Her mind and body felt numb which was actually a blessing. She curled up on her side of the king-sized bed and blew out her breath in a long grateful sigh.

There had been some hard goodbyes in her lifetime, but saying goodbye to Brock hurt more than she ever thought it would. It was worth it, though, and she meant what she'd said. No regrets, only gratitude.

"God, I don't know why you allowed our lives to intersect for such a brief time, but I thank you."

She stretched out on her back and prayed out loud, a comfort she'd discovered when Frank no longer shared her bed. "The future seems bleak now without Brock or the ministry in Africa. Father, I'm asking again for Your help. For Brock, for David and for me. Fill our lives again with joy and purpose ... And Roz. Do a work in her life, too."

Brock's favorite verse came to mind. God is able to do exceedingly, abundantly, above all that we ask or think.

"O precious Father, how could I help but fall in love with him? He's so much like You."

CHAPTER 27

It seemed nothing about this trip would be easy.

An afternoon rain shower only intensified the August mugginess. Steam rose from slick pavement making the loading area feel like a sauna.

Brock hugged Eric, then climbed the steps leading up into the Gulf Stream. Ellie followed, her eyes red-rimmed. She kept her head low as she slid into the window seat he'd left vacant for her.

"We make a pathetic pair, you and I." He held out his handkerchief.

"Thanks." She folded it and held it tight against both eyes like a bandage on an open wound.

"Eric and Joy will take good care of the twins," he ventured, hoping to cheer her.

"Oh, they'll be fine." She raised the corner of the handkerchief and sent him a sideways glance. "It's me I'm not so sure about. I've never left them for more than a two-hour stretch."

Brock nodded apologetically but could find no encouragement for her. He was fighting his own inner battle.

He helped her free a stubborn seatbelt, then buckled

his own into place. Neither talked as the plane taxied into position for take-off. Ellie leaned forward, apparently hoping for one last glimpse of Eric before the plane revved and sped down the runway.

Brock watched the buildings and trees whiz by through the window across the aisle, until the plane lifted, making his stomach plummet. Within seconds, the Gulf Stream sliced through cloud cover, immersing them in thick darkness.

His immediate future seemed as dark and menacing as the angry clouds surrounding the plane. He grabbed his Bible from his leather carry-on satchel. It fell open naturally to Romans 8. He scanned the chapter, stopping at verse 18.

For I reckon that the sufferings of this present time are not worthy to be compared with the glory which shall be revealed in me.

He looked up, staring straight ahead. He'd known some suffering in his life, mostly from his own doing.

The ache he had now in his chest wasn't actually suffering. The loss was somehow tempered with peace that came from knowing he was in God's perfect will.

Still, the pain was real.

Ellie leaned her head on his shoulder. "That's why you are a spiritual giant, and I'm not."

He shot her a puzzled look.

"When I'm sad, I cry. A lot, as you might have noticed. You, on the other hand, take out your Bible."

Apparently, he was doing a sorry job of hiding his sadness. "I cry, too, honey."

She slid her hand through his arm. "I noticed both you and Joy looked a little sad last night. Eric told me I shouldn't ask, but I've got to know. Is everything all right?"

He gave her a reassuring nod and patted the hand curled around his arm, buying time to figure out what to say and what to leave unsaid. "Joy won't be able to return to Africa as she had planned."

She turned to him, her eyes wide. "What?"

"Her son David is going through a divorce. She wants to be around to help him get settled."

"I guess that makes sense." She paused, then added. "So, the original plan has just been postponed, right?"

"We'll have to see."

Ellie blew out her breath in a huff. "I've always hated that phrase. When Nannie Jo used to say 'We'll see,' it always meant No."

He smiled but inwardly winced. It should've been him and not Nanny Jo helping raise her.

The plane broke through cloud cover. "Ah! There's the sun." He pointed, staring past her to the tiny window. "The clouds hid the sunrise this morning."

Ellie followed his gaze with an unenthusiastic nod, then returned to the topic at hand. "I can't believe Joy isn't returning. That messes up everything, especially since Eric and I won't be returning anytime soon."

Brock's eyes widened. "Is he going to take the Chaplain's job?"

"You know about that?"

"Eric mentioned it when he was in Africa."

"Hmm. We're praying about it. It would mean he'd have to go to seminary. But back to Joy. You need help. I was counting on her to be there for you, and well, it's just— I thought you and Joy were developing feelings for each other." She withdrew her hand from his arm and picked at a cuticle.

He smiled at the dejected droop of her cute little mouth. Granted, he wasn't there when she was growing up, but at least he was here now, with something far greater than anything a nanny could ever provide.

He reached back into his bag and pulled out a leather-bound book almost as worn as his Bible. He turned to the page dedicated to Ellie and tilted it to her. "Remember this?"

Her expression brightened. "Your prayer book." She took it from him and placed it open on her lap.

"Five years ago." He leaned closer and pointed to one of the top entries. "You and I were in this very plane flying over the ocean to Africa. As I recall, you slept most of the way."

"Five years." She traced her finger across the words. "It seems longer." Her lips thinned to a tight line. "That was a really dark time. I never dreamed I could be so happy now."

He weighed his next words. Was she spiritually mature enough to handle what he wanted to say? He reached across her lap, flipping back a couple of pages. "This is your mother's page. The next one is Gwyneth's. You see they remain almost blank." He shifted and took her hand. "Honey, listen to me."

Ellie turned to him, her eyes wide and trusting.

"I've prayed for my family for years, sometimes with little or no faith, but deep inside, I've always known God would answer. Just like he did for you. And Eric."

She dropped her gaze but nodded.

"Your mother is a broken shell of a person, much like I was when I was married to her. I owe it to her to try to offer the only real help available to her."

Ellie shook her head and fumbled for the wadded up handkerchief. "Mom will tell you to go to hell. You know she will."

He chuckled in spite of himself. "She's free to respond any way she chooses. But I'm thankful, not even she has the power to send me to hell, no matter how much she wishes it on me."

Ellie's dimple appeared for a brief moment. "You're amazing, to put your relationship on hold with Joy so you can help Mom."

Brock didn't respond.

"Dad?"

"Honey, there is no relationship with Joy."

Ellie shook her head in disbelief. "Why not? I know

you both care for each other."

He sighed, not bothering to deny it. "Because I'm committed to helping your mother. I don't know what that will entail or how long it will take. I won't keep Joy on the sidelines waiting for my return."

"I love Mom and want to help her all I can. But I love you, too. Why do you have to sacrifice your happiness, and Joy's, for a woman who—" she paused, then blurted out the rest, "who probably won't appreciate anything you do."

"I realize that. But God made it very clear He wants me to give Joy up."

Ellie stared at him several seconds, then gripped her head with both hands, pulling on her hair. "Ugh! I thought I'd worked through all of this when my babies were in NICU. I don't understand why God would bring the perfect woman into your life and then ask you to give her up. It doesn't seem fair."

Brock waited until he was sure the rant was over, then spoke in a soothing tone. "It wasn't fair for Jesus to give up His position in heaven to suffer and die for my sins, but He did it because of His great love for me."

Ellie gave him a troubled look. "Can you honestly say you love Mom more than you love Joy?"

"No." He stared down at his Bible, still open on his lap. "But I do love God more than either of them."

Ellie remained quiet, her warring emotions transparent on her face. Finally, with a resolute sigh, she turned to him. "I've said this before: I want your faith."

Brock slid his arm across her shoulders and pulled her close. "By the time you're my age, I think your faith will far surpass mine."

Ellie rested her head in the crook of his arm and splayed her hand across his chest. "Thanks, Dad. I feel better now."

He felt better, too. The heaviness he'd been carrying since that early morning phone call had somehow dissipated like the clouds outside the plane's window.

No. The clouds were still there. He just had to go high enough to see over them.

CHAPTER 28

The smell of antiseptically purified air hit Brock the moment he stepped through the automatic doors of Baylor University Hospital. A weird feeling of déjà vu swept over him as if the last thirty years of his life had been edited out. Strange, since he'd never actually practiced at this particular hospital. Still, his mind drifted back to a darker time when he was a cocky plastic surgeon, with patrons as self-consumed as they were wealthy.

His last visit to Dallas five years earlier had not produced any such feelings of nostalgia. His only agenda then had been to rescue his suicidal daughter and take her with him to Africa.

He placed his hand on the small of Ellie's back and guided her into a crowded elevator. The sixth-floor button was already illuminated. Even though the outside temperature was pushing one hundred, Ellie's fingers felt like ice as she gripped his arm for support. He suspected she was experiencing her own inner demons as she revisited the hospital where they had pumped her stomach and snatched her from the jaws of death. He leaned in and whispered, "Are you doing okay, honey?"

She lost the faraway look in her eyes and smiled up at

him. "Yes. I'm okay."

The elevator jolted into place, and the doors yawned open. He gestured for two elderly women to go first before following them out. Gwyneth sat in a secluded corner in the waiting area. She didn't look up as they approached, but remained focused on her phone, scrolling with her index finger.

Ellie shot him a *here goes* look and said with a cheery voice. "We're here."

Gwyneth finished typing a text before huffing, "Finally. You said you'd be here by four. I canceled an appointment to meet you."

"Sorry, honey. The rental car place took longer than we anticipated."

She looked at him with contempt, her green eyes narrowed into angry slits. "You could've taken a taxi."

Brock was struck by how much she resembled Rozalynde—in beauty and in personality. He changed the subject. "How's your mother?"

"Sleeps a lot. When she's awake, she's difficult, as always. Oh, and she talks slower. Drives me nuts."

From the corner of his eye, Brock felt Ellie staring at him with a silent plea to put Gwyneth in her place. Maybe he should, but right now he had more pressing matters to attend to. "Were you able to get my name on the HEPA form?"

"Your name was already there. I assumed you'd bribed them into adding it yourself."

Brock gritted his teeth but held his tongue. Maybe if he'd been around more, his eldest daughter would've become a better human being.

"Who knows?" Gwyneth shrugged. "I told Mom you were coming with Ellie. Maybe she added your name."

"Your mom knows I'm coming? What'd she say?"

"Nothing. In fact, she almost seemed relieved. Probably so doped up, she would've agreed to anything."

Brock placed a restraining hand on Ellie's arm. "Why don't you girls visit your mom? I'd like to speak to the attending physician."

Each looked at the other as if waiting for the other sister to make the first move.

He turned. "I'll walk with you as far as the nurses' station."

They trailed after him through double doors to the acute care unit. He paused at a horseshoe-shaped counter and waved them on. One nurse stood with her back to him, her laptop positioned on a portable cart. Another remained seated, studying her own computer screen. Her glasses sat low on her nose, and her face was pinched in a frown making her look more like a stern schoolteacher than a nurse.

No doubt she was aware he was standing there. He resisted the urge to clear his throat.

Finally, she glanced his way, peering over her glasses. "May I help you?" Her voice was brisk but not unkind.

"Yes. I'm Brock Whitfield. I'd like to speak with

someone about my—about Rozalynde Whitfield."

"Just a moment." She took a phone from her pocket and sent a text. Then she returned her focus to the screen.

Brock glanced around. The nurse with the portable cart had moved to the adjacent hallway. He spoke again to the tight-lipped nurse. "Shall I wait here?"

"Yes." She responded, her eyes never leaving the screen. "The doctor's on the way."

Brock's thank you remained unacknowledged. This woman could take lessons from Joy who went out of her way to show courtesy and respect, no matter the interruption. For possibly the hundredth time, he forced his mind away from Joy and back to the present.

A short, dark-complexioned man approached wearing a white coat with a Baylor name badge over the left pocket.

"Hello." He extended his hand and spoke with a thick accent, possibly Pakistani or Hindi. "I'm Dr. Seirafi."

Brock gripped the man's hand. "Brock Whitfield."

"Please. Come with me."

The doctor gestured for Brock to follow. He took him back through the double doors and past the waiting area to a small room containing an oval table and four swivel chairs.

"Please. Sit."

Brock braced himself. A visit to a conference room usually meant something bad. He sat and placed his folded hands on top of the table.

Dr. Seirafi sat across. He had a kind smile, brown

soulful eyes, and bushy eyebrows that made Brock second-guess the man's Indian heritage.

"I understand you also are a doctor." He spoke each word with precise deliberation.

Brock nodded.

"Your former wife has suffered an ischemic stroke. As you may be aware, early treatment can minimize the damage created by the loss of blood flow to the brain. Upon arrival, we were able to perform surgery to alleviate pressure and swelling of the brain. There is some weakness and possible paralysis to her right side that we hope will improve over time."

A daunting diagnosis to a relatively strong person. To Rozalynde, it might as well be a death sentence. "Is she conscious and aware of what has happened?"

"We have consulted with the patient. She became quite agitated and required sedation. Perhaps you will be able to offer support and encouragement."

Brock nodded even though he was probably the last man on the planet Rozalynde would listen to. "You have her on blood thinners?"

"Yes, the tissue plasminogen activator we are using is very effective in dissolving blood clots that hinder circulation. The case manager will discuss rehabilitation options."

"Sounds good. May I see her now?"

"Yes. Of course."

Brock rose and shook the doctor's hand, struck by how

different it felt to be on the receiving end of a diagnosis. He retraced his steps back to the nurses' station, his mind too numb to process the information. His love for Roz— if he could call it that— had died long before their marriage ended. Still, his compassion was stirred. He'd seen her fall apart over a broken fingernail. How would she ever handle something as serious as a stroke?

He passed a dimly lit room, no larger than a walk-in closet. Inside were two recliners, a small table with a lamp and Bible on top, and a framed painting of Jesus carrying a lamb.

He pulled up short. Not once had he prayed since entering the hospital. He ducked into the prayer room and sank onto the nearest chair, the gray vinyl, cold and unyielding to the weight of his body. He leaned over and rested his head in his hands, his heart heavy. "Father, I'm asking for Your wisdom and help. Tell me what You want me to do, then give me the grace to do it. Thy will be done."

The nurse behind the counter gave him Roz's room number. His soft-soled shoes made no noise as he eased down the hall. He gave a soft knock, then entered not waiting for a reply.

Ellie stood beside the bed, wiping drool from Roz's chin. Roz lay as if unconscious, in a hospital bed that dwarfed her fragile form. She'd lost weight, giving the line of her jaw a sharp angular look. Her hair had not been washed or combed and lay plastered to her head. The entire right side of her face drooped like she'd been given a massive dose of Novocain.

He gave a cursory glance around the room, scanning for mirrors to remove. "Where's Gwyneth?"

"She left." Ellie stood and leaned closer, whispering in his ear. "To tell you the truth, I'm glad. Gwyneth's even worse than I remember."

"I know, honey. Let's focus on getting your mother through this first."

"What'd the doctor say?"

"Ischemic stroke. They performed surgery to relieve the pressure, probably at the base of her skull. He has her on a tissue plasminogen activator. He also has her sedated. Apparently, she didn't take the news well."

Ellie reached for Roz's hand lying limp on the stark white sheet. "I can't imagine how hard this must be for her. How scared she must be. What will she do now? What will you do?"

Questions he'd asked himself with no real answers. "I don't know, honey. Right now, I'm going to get you settled in a hotel. Then we'll get some dinner and maybe discuss a plan of action. It looks like she's out for the night. That'll buy us some time."

"I like that plan. I'm exhausted. You must be, too."

She was right. The emotional roller coaster of the last two days, as well as jet lag, had taken their toll.

"I am a bit. Remind me to request a suite of rooms with a balcony facing east."

CHAPTER 29

Brock pulled into the parking deck and drove through three levels before Ellie pointed to an empty space. "There's one."

He eased the Chevy Impala into the spot and loosened his death grip on the steering wheel. "Whew." He shifted to unbuckle. "I hate to admit it, but Gwyneth was right."

Ellie paused, her legs poised to swing out the door. "About what?"

"I should've called a taxi. As soon as we leave the hospital, I plan to return the rental car. I'll take a washed-out road in a Land Rover any day over this Dallas rush-hour traffic."

"No arguments there, although you dodged those early morning commuters like a pro."

"Thank you. I think I gave our guardian angels a run for their money."

Neither spoke as they entered the building. One elevator closed, but the one beside it opened, this one empty. Ellie pressed six, then stepped back and stared at the numbers above the door, her fingers fidgeting.

Peace bolstered him as the elevator doors slid open. He walked past the prayer room with only a cursory glance.

He'd already started praying long before his feet hit the floor this morning.

Ellie slowed as they approached Roz's room. The door opened before he could open it, and a large woman dressed in neon pink scrubs greeted them. "Good timing. I'm Lindsay, the day nurse." She pushed a portable cart out of the room and let the door close behind her. "We just got Miss Roz cleaned up. You must be Gwyneth. She's been asking for you."

"No, I'm Ellie, her other daughter. This is my father."

Lindsay looked at him and nodded, her expression pleasant. Nothing like the nurse from the night before.

"How is she?"

"She's holding her own. More alert today." She pushed the cart away from the door. "Go right in. Company will do her good."

He highly doubted that but thanked her anyway and followed Ellie into the room.

Roz lay at a forty-five-degree angle. Her hair had been brushed and every vestige of makeup scrubbed from her face which somehow made her seem more vulnerable than she had the night before.

She turned as they entered the room and focused her left eye on him. Her right eye remained partially closed. She opened her mouth and pursed her lips with studied deliberation. "You … came. Didn't … think … would."

Her words were slow but at least intelligible. Definitely some weakness on the right side of her face that might improve with time.

"Hello, Mom." Ellie's shaky voice held a forced cheerfulness. "We were here last night, but you were pretty out of it."

Roz slapped her left hand on the bed like a frustrated teacher rapping her desk. "Don't … t-tell."

Ellie glanced at him then back to Roz. "I don't understand."

Roz beat the bed more violently. "N-no … one … know." Roz flailed her arm and gripped Ellie's sleeve pulling her closer. "Guwinf … not … t-tell."

It didn't surprise him the one thought on Roz's mind was to preserve her image at any cost. "Honey, why don't you step into the hallway and give Gwyneth a call? Tell her to keep your mom's condition on the down-low."

Ellie gave a reluctant nod and turned to go. Roz started beating the side of her bed again. Ellie paused and pivoted back, but Roz dismissed her with a wave and trained her left eye once again on him.

He filled in the spot Ellie had left. "I'm so sorry, Roz. I'm here to offer any help I can."

She stared at him a long time, then moved her left hand to the right side of her face pushing the sagging skin upward. She curled up her lip and blew through her teeth until she got out the word "fix" along with a spray of saliva.

The word came out slowly but plain enough for him to read her loud and clear. How could he even respond to such an outrageous request? Did she think he could fix this with plastic surgery?

She slapped her hand on the bed again, more demanding this time, like a child throwing a tantrum. "Fix." Her voice screeched. "F-face." The part of her face that could move crumbled, and she balled her hand into a tight fist. She whimpered and started rocking back and forth.

The frightened woman, scrunched in a heap on the bed, bore no resemblance to the scathing Roz he once knew. She looked up at him with a face so bleak it reminded him of some of his patients at the clinic who'd lost all hope. He choked back his tears and spoke soothingly to her. "All right, Roz."

She stilled and faced him, her left eye widening.

He continued before she could start slapping the bed again. "I'm going to talk things over with the doctor and see what we can do."

"Fix ... face?"

"I'll discuss possibilities with your doctor." He hedged. "It's important that you rest and not worry." He smoothed back a strand of hair that had fallen across her face. "Try to relax, Roz. You're going to get better."

She nodded with child-like frailty, and her mouth quivered as she spoke. "F-fraid."

"I know." He whispered and brushed away a tear trailing down her cheek. "But you're not going to go through this alone."

Brock waited until the furrow on her brow smoothed,

and her breathing became heavy and regular, then eased out of the room. He paused outside her door and drew a long, measured breath, collecting his thoughts and composure.

In the thirty years since they had gone separate ways, Roz had reached out to him only a handful of times, usually when some crisis arose.

Roz now faced perhaps the greatest crisis of her life. Instead of the sarcasm and contempt she usually displayed, she'd welcomed his help, probably because she had no choice.

Seeing Roz so broken assured him more than ever he was where he was supposed to be. His next step wasn't so clear.

Ellie paced beside the large window at the end of the hall. He came closer, the frustration in her tone coming through louder than her words.

"I'm not asking you to cancel, Gwyneth. Just postpone for a couple of months."

Brock eased beside her. Ellie glanced up at the ceiling, frowning. "Okay, okay … We'll figure something out."

Ellie dropped the phone into her bag and fell into step beside him. "Apparently, Gwyneth leaves for Sweden tomorrow morning."

He pulled up short. "Sweden?"

"I know, right? Some high-end cleansing spa. According to her, if she postpones, she'll be at the bottom of the waiting list, and it'll take up to two years to get another opening."

He admired her restraint in not pointing out how selfish her sister was and was grateful Ellie seemed to be made of different cloth. "Has she told anyone about your mother?"

"She swears no." Ellie's fingers pumped air to indicate double quotation marks, then flipped her hair back and gave a surprisingly accurate impersonation of Gwyneth. "I'd be mortified for anyone to know my mother's an invalid."

"Your mother's secret is safe, at least for now. We'll spare her the reason why."

Ellie paused at Roz's room and peeked in. "Looks like she's out."

"Let her sleep. It's one of the ways the brain heals itself. Right now, I have a couple of errands I could use your help with, if you're up for it."

"Sure. What's first?"

They joined a group already waiting for the next elevator. "I'll tell you in a bit."

Neither spoke until they made it to the car. Ellie buckled in before turning to him. "Are you going to return the rental car first?"

"Not just yet. First stop is your mother's house." The ancestral home he'd given up. Had he been in his right mind during the divorce, he would've fought harder to keep it. "I don't think there's any staff there now that knew me, but I'm pretty sure they will know you and be glad to see you."

Her phone pinged. She pulled it out of her bag and read the text. "Eric says they just got the twins down for their morning nap, and he's going for a run. Mind if I call him?"

"Of course not."

She punched the speed dial. "Will it distract your driving if it's on speaker?"

"No. Go ahead."

Ellie held the phone on the console between them. After a couple rings, Eric's voice came through loud and clear. "Hey, babe. How's it going?"

"I'm with Dad, and I've got you on speaker."

After Brock and Eric exchanged greetings, Ellie updated Eric on Roz. "It breaks my heart to see her like this."

"I bet. It's got to be tough on Roz, too. Honey, I'm putting you on speaker so Joy can talk, too."

"Okay. Hi, Joy. How are you holding up?"

"Hello. I'm doing great. Eric's so organized. He has everything running like clockwork."

Brock passed the car in front of him and tried to ignore the flutter Joy's voice sent to his stomach.

Ellie chuckled. "Yeah, he's pretty amazing."

Eric spoke again. "Joy's the amazing one. Bek's been bombing her diapers. Joy had to bathe her and change her outfits three times yesterday."

"Oh dear. Sorry, Joy."

Joy's laughter filled the car. "No worries. I'm loving every minute of it. I'm no substitute for their Momma, though. We're just trying to hold it together 'til you come back home."

Eric piped in. "Speaking of coming home … got an estimated time of arrival yet?"

Brock spoke for the first time. "Possibly tomorrow morning. I've got some things to run by Ellie. We'll let you know for sure later today."

"Good to hear from the man with the plan," Eric replied.

"That's definitely not me, then." Brock chuckled. "I'm trying to follow through on God's plan, but He hasn't quite revealed it to me yet. Would appreciate your prayers."

"Yes, sir. You've got'em. Joy and I pray whenever we can snatch quiet moments, which are few and far between around here."

Ellie chimed in again. "Dad and I will take what we can get. We're pulling into Mom's driveway now. I'll call again when we know more."

"Sounds good. Love you both."

"Love you, too. Kiss my babies for me." Ellie's voice choked on goodbye. She grew quiet and stared out the window.

Brock reached over and patted her hand. "Missing your babies?"

Ellie nodded, her mouth drooping. "Gwyneth's leaving, and we can't stay indefinitely. Mom'll be all alone. Who's going to take care of her?"

Brock answered without hesitation. "Me." He ignored

Ellie's wide-eyed stare and pulled up close to the security keypad. "I don't suppose you remember the password that opens this gate?"

She held up her hand. "Seriously? You plan to stay here and take care of Mom?"

"I haven't quite worked out all the logistics, but yes."

"What does Mom say about this?"

"I hinted, but I don't think she fully comprehended what I was saying. Do you remember the password?"

Ellie shook her head as if coming out of a trance. "I think so, but it's been over five years. She might've changed it."

"Let's give it a try." Brock lowered his window, his fingers poised over the keypad. "I'm ready."

"One zero-one, one, one-nine eight zero."

Brock paused, then punched the last four digits with deliberate jabs.

The gate lifted, and Ellie cheered. "Yay! It worked. You know, for the life of me, I still can't figure out why Mom picked that random combination of numbers. I thought it might be a date, but as far as I know, nothing spectacular happened on that day in 1980."

Nothing spectacular, all right, just the date their divorce became final. Apparently, a day Roz had no intention of forgetting. Brock gave Ellie a sideways glance. "Have you ever asked your mother?"

"I did once. She waved her hand in that way she does and said she picked eight random numbers."

"Hmm. Sounds like your mother's logic."

Brock eased the Impala forward, surprised that the long driveway, though now paved and not a dirt road, still looked the same after all these years. The oaks that lined both sides of the road had grown, their massive limbs now meeting in the middle, forming a magnificent canopy. "North Texas must've had good rainfall this summer. Look how green everything is."

"I've always loved this place."

"Me, too. My grandfather spared no expense when he had this house built. I think he wanted the world to know he was now a very rich man."

"Wait a minute. This is your house?"

The paved road changed to decoratively tiled pavers. Brock pulled around the circular driveway, placed the car in park, and shifted to look at her. "Not anymore. It belongs to your mother."

Ellie stared at him, shaking her head in disbelief. "There are still so many things about you I don't know. This was your family home. Why did Mom get it?"

Brock sighed, kicking himself for bringing it up. "I didn't have it in me to fight for it." He stared straight ahead remembering that dark time. "And I didn't want to uproot you girls from the only home you'd ever known."

He opened the door and started to get out.

"Wait a minute." Ellie grabbed his arm and pulled him back. "Tell me this before we go in. Is it hard for you to be here, you know, after all this time?"

"Yes." He saw no reason to deny it.

She held his gaze, her eyes filling with tears. "I'm sorry, Dad. I wish I could make it better for you."

His face softened. "You, my sweet child, are the sunshine of my life. You make every day better for me."

He took her hand and squeezed it. "Now, help me get my foot in that door."

CHAPTER 30

Brock had the sensation he was stepping back in time as he approached the mansion. The portico, supported by four stately columns, filled a good three-fourths of the width of the front and was as impressive and imposing as ever.

He pretended not to notice Ellie's frequent glances his way. The poor girl had enough on her plate without worrying about him, too. He looked past her shoulder and pointed. "See that weeping willow?"

Ellie turned and nodded.

"My mother planted that tree the day after I married your mother."

Ellie grinned. "Was she making a statement?"

"Probably, now that I think about it." He pressed the doorbell, and they both stood facing the door like a couple of traveling salesmen.

The woman who opened the door had black wiry hair interspersed with gray. If he had to guess, he'd say she didn't quite reach five feet but stood like a fierce terrier ready to guard her territory. She cocked her head to one side and pressed her lips into a tight line.

He inhaled and started to introduce himself but

stopped when the woman gasped and placed her fingers over her gaping mouth.

"Oh, my." She flung her arms wide. "Come here, chica. Ellie, is it really you?"

"Yes, it's really me." Ellie laughed and embraced the woman, then stepped back placing both hands on the woman's plump cheeks. "It's so good to see you again."

The woman took Ellie's hands in her own and brought them to her lips. "I did not think to ever see you again."

The sweetness of the gesture warmed Brock's heart and brought tears to his eyes.

Still smiling, Ellie pivoted and placed her hand on his arm to draw him closer. "Consuela, this is my father, Brock Whitfield."

All fierceness gone, Consuela gave him a deferential nod. "Pleased to meet you, señor."

"Thank you. Nice to meet you." He would have shaken her hand had she offered it. At least, she greeted him with politeness, most likely for Ellie's sake.

"Please." Consuela opened the door wider. "Come in, and tell us, how is your poor momma?"

Ellie paired off with Consuela, while he lagged behind, like a tourist trying to ditch his tour guide. Their voices trailed off as they entered what used to be the formal dining room, leaving him free to scan everything from the polished marble floors to the grand staircase. Apparently, Roz had seen no need to change anything, including her last name, most likely because the Whitfield name would open more doors to society than her Scandinavian maiden name of Holmstrom.

He wandered into the room to the right of the foyer. Still a sitting room, now with two floral Queen Anne chairs facing an oversized sofa, upholstered in a heavy burgundy, befitting old Texas money. Brocade panels, held back with tasseled sashes, draped the floor-to-ceiling windows. The room held few memories except the pungent smell of old furniture and polish, a smell that, as a child, made him feel more like he was in a museum than a home.

"Señor Whitfield?"

Brock whipped around like a guilty thief caught casing the joint. He raised his eyebrows and tried to look dignified. "Yes?"

"Would you like something to drink? Some coffee, perhaps?"

"Yes. That would be wonderful. Oh, uh Consuela, I have something I need to discuss with the staff. Would it be possible to have all of them meet with me before I leave?"

She hesitated, no doubt weighing whether to risk Ms. Roz's disapproval. "Si, señor. I will let them know."

"Thank you." He sat in one of the chairs and pulled reading glasses and a notepad from his shirt pocket. The list of things he had to take care of was growing. *Call accountant. Meet with case manager.*

A girl, possibly early twenties, brought a tray and set it on the coffee table. He thanked her. She nodded, without making eye contact, then left as quickly as she had come.

He welcomed the coffee. It was hot, tasted good, and sent an unexpected wave of homesickness. He checked his watch. It would be four in the afternoon in Africa. Crunch time with Neal and the rest of the clinic staff working in as many patients as possible before calling it a day.

The distinct clip-clop of Ellie's sandals brought him back to Texas and his present situation. "Dad?"

"In here, honey."

More clip-clops, then Ellie appeared in the doorway, the strap of an overnight bag slung over her shoulder. "I prowled through Mom's things. Grabbed everything I thought she might need."

She sat and plopped the bag on the floor beside the chair.

"Good thinking."

"Wanna bet she'll complain about the one thing I didn't bring?"

Brock merely chuckled and sipped his coffee.

Consuela returned with five others in tow, walking single file, heads lowered as if going to a police line-up.

He stood, folding his hands in front of him. "Thank you, Consuela. Would you introduce everyone?"

"Si." She turned to the girl on her left, the one who'd brought the coffee. "This is my granddaughter Mia."

"Mia." He repeated and smiled.

Mia's wide mouth drooped at the corners. That, and the silver pierced ring on the edge of her lower lip, gave her the appearance of a hooked fish. She looked up long enough for him to catch a glimpse of sadness in her eyes. He made a mental note to add her to his prayer list.

Next, Consuela gestured to two middle-aged women, possibly Filipino. "Marina and Teresa work in the kitchen." Brock made eye contact with each and smiled.

"And this is Davis, the groundskeeper. He sometimes has his grandson to help him, but today it is only him."

He dipped his head to the tall, long-armed black man that reminded him a great deal of Moses.

Davis returned Brock's nod and said, "My daddy worked for the late Mr. Whitfield."

"You don't say. What's his name?"

"His name Leroy."

Brock jerked his head up. Leroy. The wiry gardener, who'd always had a kind word for him. "I remember him. He took me fishing a time or two."

"Yessir. My daddy, he love to fish. He getting on up in years."

Brock nodded and did the math. Had to be in his upper nineties by now. Maybe even one hundred. "I'd love to stop in and see him. Do you think he'd remember me?"

"I reckon he would. He don't hear too good no more, but his mind sharper'n mine."

Brock turned to the rest of the group, who had remained respectfully quiet during their little interchange. "Please. Have a seat. I won't keep you long."

No one moved. Consuela, who seemed to be the one

in charge, gave a brief nod and led the way. The four women wedged themselves on the sofa, sitting close to the edge.

Davis slid his hands down the sides of his sweat-stained shirt and shuffled his feet. "I'll jes stand, if that's alright."

"Of course." Brock felt all eyes trained on him as he returned to his chair. "I wanted to meet you and thank you in person."

The group stared at him, apparently unaccustomed to receiving praise of any kind. Consuela placed her palm against her heart and blew out her breath.

"Which one of you found Ms. Roz?"

Consuela halfway raised her hand and blurted out, "I felt so terrible, señor. Ms. Roz, she never like for me to interrupt her, but she no come down for dinner, so I go to her room and knock." She leaned forward cupping a hand to her ear. "No answer, so I open the door and peek in. There she was, on the floor, and I think to myself, she dead." She made the sign of the cross against her chest. "I call the paramedics. They say she alive, but they take her away." Consuela fidgeted with the handkerchief she had taken from her pocket. "Perhaps, if I had found her sooner."

He waited until he was sure she was finished, then said softly, "You did exactly what you were expected to do. You couldn't have known."

She raised clasped hands to her lips as if in prayer. "Ellie say Ms. Roz have a stroke?"

"Yes." He spoke in a matter-of-fact way, like a physician consulting with family. "There's some weakness on the right side of her body. She'll need physical therapy." He paused, then added, even though he had no way of knowing for sure. "With time, she might make a full recovery which brings me to another reason I wanted to meet with all of you."

An invisible force field of tension emanated from the group on the sofa. They frowned and looked at each other. He glanced at Ellie, who continued to study her hands, folded tightly on her lap. No help there.

He licked his lips, determined to muddle through. "Ms. Roz is ... um, sensitive to ... she's concerned that no one know about her ... health issues until she recovers a little more." He cleared his throat and continued. "I have confidence in you as her staff that you will honor her request to keep all of this confidential."

"Si, señor." Consuela stiffened and sat erect. "We never discuss Ms. Roz's personal matters with anyone, do we?" She cocked her head to the ones seated beside her. They looked first to her, then back to him, their heads bobbing in a circular motion as if uncertain whether to shake or nod.

Good enough. His chest started to feel lighter. "Thank you. I know she will appreciate that very much." He leaned forward in his chair, tapping the tips of his fingers together. "One more thing. I want you all to know that your jobs are secure. In fact, I'd like to ask you to keep working your regular schedule even though Ms. Roz may not return for several weeks."

The force field lowered considerably.

Once again, Consuela raised her hand. "What if someone calls and wishes to speak with her?"

Brock paused, rubbing the stubble of his beard. "Say she is away on personal business. Then let me know if I need to relay a message to her."

"Si. You will be in the area?"

"Yes. I plan to stay until she's well enough to go home." He pulled out his phone and reading glasses. "In fact, let's exchange numbers in case I think of anything else."

Consuela took her phone from her pocket and nodded as he called out numbers.

Then Brock stood as did Consuela and the rest of the women. He reached across the coffee table and systematically shook each hand. "It was very nice meeting you. God bless you."

Last, he came to Davis, who wiped his hand down his shirt again before gripping Brock's hand. "I'm going that way. I'll walk out with you."

Consuela hugged Ellie, then led the women from the room.

Davis rushed ahead to open the front door. A blast of hot, humid air fogged Brock's reading glasses. He pocketed them and gave Davis a friendly pat on the back, then joined Ellie in the car. Still smiling, he eased the car around the circular driveway. "That went well, don't you think?"

Ellie waved to Davis. "Better than I thought it would." She turned the air up full blast, then adjusted the vents. "Now what?"

"I thought we'd grab some lunch, then I'll drop you off at the hospital."

"Drop me off— as in you're leaving me alone with Mom?"

"Only for a little while." He glanced over and found Ellie staring at him. He added, "I need to run some things by the accountant, then talk with your mom's case manager."

Still no response.

"Or would you rather stay with me?" He ventured.

After a few seconds, she responded with an airy lilt to her voice. "Actually, just drop me off at the airport. I think I'll join Gwyneth at that Swedish spa."

He laughed, more than a little relieved she was able to joke about it. "Actually," he said, mimicking her, "I do plan to take you to the airport first thing in the morning, but to send you home, not to Sweden."

"Even better." She sighed, then added with a hint of resignation. "But I can't leave you, Dad. I'm not a lot of help, but I'm all you've got right now."

"That's sweet of you, honey, but Eric and Joy need you more than I do." He reached over and patted her hand. "And you're more help than you know. You're the one who thought to get some of your mom's things."

She opened the bag she held in her lap and peeked inside. "I guess I should take this stuff to Mom. Maybe help her fix up."

He paused at the end of the long driveway waiting for a break in the traffic. "I think she'd like that."

Ellie dropped her chin and shot him a disbelieving look. "I'm pretty sure she won't like anything I do."

He grinned and eased onto the highway. "I'll hurry. I promise."

CHAPTER 31

Brock left the case manager's office on the first floor and bypassed the elevator. Maybe by the time he climbed six flights of stairs, he'd have a plan of action. He paused on the sixth-floor landing to catch his breath, now sporting a stiff knee but still no plan. The door, which apparently got little use, creaked loudly as he pushed it open and entered the hallway. The thin nurse from the night before looked up, then returned to the screen without moving one muscle in her face. He smiled at her anyway and said, "Hello."

He tapped the door to Roz's room with his knuckles and eased it open. Ellie stood beside the bed holding a spoon close to Roz's mouth. "Come on, Mom. One more bite."

Roz jerked her head away, her mouth clenched shut.

Ellie set the spoon back on the tray with a deliberate clank.

Brock eased beside her and tweaked her elbow.

She turned to him and rubbed her forehead. "I hope you had better luck than I did."

"Rough afternoon?"

Her look told him all he needed to know. Roz

remained turned away with her eyes shut.

"Did you tell your mother the good news?"

Ellie shook her head. "What good news?"

He walked to the other side of the bed and reached over the safety rail to touch Roz's arm. "Ellie and I went to your house today and had a little talk with your staff."

Roz's good eye flew open.

"Consuela seemed very concerned about you."

Roz shifted to lie on her back and started slapping the bed with her left hand. "R-r-raise."

He pushed a random button, sending her head even lower.

She made a deep guttural growl.

"Sorry. Wrong button." He pushed another. This time the bed creaked, propelling her head forward. "Is that enough?"

He took her grunt to mean yes. "The staff promised not to talk about your condition to anyone. In fact—" He broke off as Roz raised her left hand, and with an amazing show of force, shoved the supper tray. It happened fast, but Ellie's reflexes were faster, blocking it before it went flying across the room.

Ellie shot him a *see-what-I-mean* look and turned toward the door, grabbing her purse as she went. "Time for me to get some air and check on the twins."

Roz remained with her eyes closed. As soon as the door clicked closed, Brock nudged the tray table well out of reach and tried again. "I arranged for the staff to continue working indefinitely. I figured keeping business as usual would rouse less curiosity among your friends."

The news he thought would ease her mind, seemed to agitate her more. She gripped his hand, pinching the soft skin above his knuckles. "T-take ... out."

He looked at her, his forehead wrinkled, and repeated what he thought she said. "Take out?"

She nodded.

"You want take-out?"

She nodded again.

"You want Chinese take-out?"

She gave another guttural growl and started beating the bed. "Ahway."

His first thought was that she wanted him to go away. But she was staring up at him, not with anger but with desperation.

The no-nonsense nurse entered the room, pushing a portable medical station. She didn't speak or make eye contact, but went about her business with single-minded efficiency. His respect for her grew a notch. She could still take lessons on bedside manner, but it was clear this woman's one agenda was to take care of the patients on her watch. She checked and recorded Roz's vitals and gave the nighttime meds. A blood thinner and what looked like a tranquilizer, possibly Xanax.

She pushed the button to lower Roz to a prone position and looked at him for the first time since coming into the room. "Visiting hours end in fifteen minutes."

His eyes automatically went to the clock above Roz's bed. "Thank you." He said to the retreating figure.

Roz was already drifting off and would probably remember none of their little interchange in the morning. Her head drooped to one side. He rearranged the pillow and positioned her head more in the middle.

Roz opened her eye and searched for him, curling the left side of her mouth in a lopsided smile when she saw him.

It was the drugs, he knew. But still, it warmed him. Maybe there was hope, after all.

He left the room and shot Ellie a text. *Ready to leave?*

Phone in hand, he started walking down the hall toward the elevators and glanced in the prayer room. "There you are."

Ellie's head jerked up. "That was fast. I just responded to your text."

She slung the strap of her handbag over her shoulder and started to rise, but he held up his hand and stepped into the room. "Let's talk a minute."

She eased back down. He took the other chair and angled his bent knees toward her. "My meetings took longer than I expected. Sorry you had a rough afternoon."

"That's okay, especially since it was partially my fault."

"Let me guess. You forgot the one thing she really wanted."

Ellie grinned and rolled her eyes. "I forgot the all-important jar of anti-sag nighttime moisturizer. But that wasn't the worst thing."

"Worse than forgetting the all-important moisturizer?"

Ellie closed her eyes and scrunched up her face. "I gave her a mirror."

Brock inwardly winced. "Oh."

"You should've seen us, Dad. I sat on the edge of her bed and emptied the makeup onto the covers. I experimented with different colors. She seemed to be enjoying it and looked pretty good when I got finished. Looking at her from the side, you couldn't even tell anything was different." Ellie slowed her animated tirade and slapped her palm to her forehead. "Then she asked for the compact, and without thinking it through, I gave it to her."

"What happened?"

"You can imagine. She let out a screech that sounded a lot like those crazy night owls in Africa. I tried to take it from her, but she snatched it back and flung it across the room. It shattered into a million pieces, and I cleaned up every sliver. Cut my finger in the process." Ellie held up her forefinger as proof. "My penance for being stupid enough to hand her a mirror."

Brock smiled. "Don't beat yourself up, honey. She asked me to fix her face, so she already knew it was drooping."

"That makes me feel a little better." She leaned forward with her forearms propped on her thighs. "But

259

seeing herself for the first time must have been a big shock. I wish it had been someone else that handed her that mirror and not me."

"I know, honey, but it was probably good it *was* you. The hospital staff might not have handled her tantrum so calmly."

"Good point. Did you learn anything from the case manager?"

"Technically, your mom could be released as early as tomorrow. After that, she'll be moved to one of the local rehab facilities. I won't leave until I know she's all right and on the mend."

"What can I do to help?"

"You have your hands full right now. I was planning to send you back home tomorrow morning."

She shook her head. "I can't leave you or Mom right now."

"Your mom has a long recovery ahead. Down the road, you can come back. Maybe even bring the twins."

Ellie leaned back in the chair with her hand at her throat. "Can you imagine toddler twins running amok in the Rehab place?"

"Hmm. Maybe by that time, she'll be back home. I have a feeling Consuela would love running after the twins."

Ellie laughed, then sobered. "You *are* going back to Africa, aren't you?"

"I want to. I promised Nicci I'd be there when the baby

comes." Brock studied the pattern on the tiled floor and shrugged. "At some point, I'll have to go back. Right now, I'm taking one day at a time."

A voice over the intercom announced visiting hours were now ended.

Brock pushed up from his chair with a grunt, vowing to take the elevator and not the stairs. "Let's go."

The heavy night air felt like a sauna as they exited the automatic double doors of the hospital. Brock nudged her toward a well-lit parking deck. "This way."

"You still have the rental car?"

He nodded. "I'm getting the hang of driving in the city again. I figured if I haven't killed us yet—" He pushed a button, and the car winked back at them. "I'm a little hungry. Have you had dinner yet?"

"No. What sounds good to you?"

"I don't know. How about Chinese take-out?"

CHAPTER 32

Roz roused and knew before she opened her eyes she was still in the living nightmare that was now her life. She'd lost track of the days since it happened. Her brain felt like a couple of dice that had been shaken and thrown hard against the side of a table.

The room was dark. She shivered and yanked the covers, trying to free them from the deadweight of her right hand.

The effort left her drained. Where was the nurse call button? She pushed random buttons on the bed rail. The top of the bed jolted up, then back down again.

With gritted teeth, she balled her fist and hit the panel as hard as she could with what was left of her wimpy strength.

She lay there helpless to do anything as if somebody had unplugged the right side of her body. She raised her left hand to her face, tracing both sides with her fingers. The right side still drooped. She slapped and shoved it up, hoping this time it would stay when she let go.

But it never did.

She'd rather die than let any of her busybody friends see her like this. The gossip would never stop, even after her face was back to normal. They'd stare at her the rest of her life, trying to see if they could detect even a hint of sag.

Her breaths came in shallow gasps, as she dug her nails deep into her right cheek, clawing the hateful ugliness.

Brock had to fix her face. Soon. Before anyone found out. They'd have to go someplace private. Far away from snooping gossips.

She'd have to find a way to make him understand. He wasn't getting it last night.

Brock, take me out of here. Far away and fix my face.

She squeezed her lips together and puckered. "B-bu-ruh."

Maybe skip Brock. *B*'s and *R*'s were too hard, especially together.

Take me out of here and fix my face.

Out won't work. Can't be anyplace local.

Take far away and fix face.

Too many f's.

Take away fix.

Brock was many things, but he wasn't an idiot. He'd figure it out, especially if she pointed to her face.

Take away, fix. Take away, fix. Take away, fix.

The words were so clear in her mind. Why couldn't she make them come out of her mouth right?

She placed her tongue on the inside of her front teeth and blew out like she was trying to spit. "Ttuh." She wiped her chin and started over, this time trying to control the amount of spit that actually left her mouth.

"T-tayk. T-take. Take."

She wiped sweat from her forehead. At least, she wasn't freezing anymore.

"Take ... ah.way ... f-feesk."

She tried it again. And again. Each time a little smoother and louder until she was certain Brock would understand.

"Take ... away ... fix."

But what if he lied? What if he didn't come back?

She gripped the sheet, rocking back and forth as much as her half-numb body let her and humming with a sort of high-pitched whimpering sound.

What she wouldn't give for a cigarette. She brought her thumb and forefinger to her mouth and pretended to take a drag, then closed her eyes and blew out a long slow breath from the side of her mouth.

Brock couldn't let her down. He'd take her away and fix her face. And if she had to, she'd move to Washington when it was all over.

A nurse jolted Roz out of a good dream and back to reality. That was her first mistake.

"Good morning. Time to take your blood pressure." Her sugary tone grated on Roz's last nerve.

Too young and cute to be a nurse. All the things Roz would never be again. She fastened the cuff, then stepped back to her computer. The blasted thing kept inflating, squeezing the life out of her one good arm. Roz grunted and slapped the bed with the hand that was turning blue.

The nurse grabbed Roz's arm and pinned it down. "Hold still." Prissy Pants lost the sugar in her tone.

From then on, it was war.

The nurse stuck a thermometer in Roz's mouth, which she promptly spit out.

The nurse huffed and stuck it in again with a firm grip on Roz's chin. Roz was about to jerk free when the meter clicked, and the nurse removed it.

"Okay. I need you to take your medicine."

The head of her bed started to rise. Movement at the foot of her bed caught her eye. Brock stood at her tray, pouring water into a cup.

When had he gotten here?

"Want some help?"

He spoke to the nurse and not to her, which, if possible, made her even angrier.

Prissy Pants smiled and handed the pills over to him.

Brock came close with one of the pills between his thumb and forefinger. "Open up, Roz."

She tried to shove his hand away, but he moved it out of her reach.

Brock handed the water to the nurse and held Roz's left arm down. "These pills will make you better. Why are you fighting this?"

She didn't know. She just knew she couldn't let them win, not without a fight.

Brock managed to wedge the pill into her mouth. The nurse was ready, sticking the tip of the straw in next.

"Okay, Roz. Take a sip and get it down."

She sucked in, then spewed out both pill and water, soaking the front of her hospital gown.

There. That's what she thought of Brock, Prissy Pants, *and* their stinking medicine.

Brock stepped away and returned with a hand towel. He methodically dabbed Roz's chin and neck, then turned to the nurse, "Looks like you'll have to bring them in suppository form."

Her heart raced. She fished for the pill in the folds of the sheet and put it in her mouth.

Brock guided the straw back to her lips. "Good girl. Was that so hard? Now, two more, and you'll be done."

She took them without a fight.

The nurse left the room. Brock stayed by her bed and reached through the bed rail to take her hand. Normally, she would've snatched it away, but the battle over the pills had left her sapped.

"Would you like your head lowered again?"

She nodded and braced for the lecture about cooperating with the staff.

Brock released her hand, pushed the button on the panel, and her head started going back down. He adjusted her pillow and smiled. "Better?"

She stared up at him. Why was he being so nice?

She must be dying. Of course. And he was sticking around to make sure he reclaimed her part of the fortune.

Brock rested his forearms on the bedrail. "Ellie's on

her way back to Washington. She said she'd try to come back when you get settled in a rehab."

"Guywinff?"

"Gwyneth's in Sweden. Something about a—uh—prior commitment."

Roz nodded and closed her eyes, feeling more alone than ever.

She felt Brock's hand on her arm.

"I know this is hard, Roz. But you're going to get better."

The unexpected kindness in his tone made her crumble. She sobbed, a gross unnatural groan from somewhere deep inside. The tears flooded her cheeks, and she pulled her arm loose to cover her face. She cried a long time, snuffling and hiccupping with loud heaving breaths.

Brock didn't stop her or comfort her. Not that it would've helped, but he could've at least tried.

She peeked through wet fingers. Brock had left. Was gone, just like everyone else. She curled her hand into a fist and brought it to her mouth, biting down hard on the edge of her forefinger.

Now what would she do?

She felt a warm, wet cloth on her face. She stilled, knowing it was Brock who had put it there and was wiping away the slimy mixture of tears and saliva from her swollen face.

He didn't say a word. Just bathed her face. She kept her eyes closed, acutely aware of how ugly she looked when she cried, especially now with a deformed face.

She felt him pull the sheet up to her chin, then his hand lingered at the base of her throat, slightly above her heart. It warmed her. Made her feel safe.

Until he took his hand away.

With effort, she forced her left eye open. Brock was still there, unsmiling and staring at his folded hands propped on the bedrail.

He turned to her, and his expression softened. "You don't have to get to shore, Roz. Just drift for a while. I'll be here when you wake."

His words soothed her even though they made no sense. She nodded and let herself drift.

If there was anybody in this world who needed a miracle, it was Rozalynde. His heart ached for her, knowing what a fragile person she had always been. It was why he'd made sure she had plenty of money. The woman was incapable of taking care of herself.

Brock stayed by her bed, taking the opportunity to study her unobserved. She had been blessed with good genes and natural blonde hair, a gift from her Scandinavian heritage. That, together with her classic heart-shaped face, had caught his eye in the first place.

Even with the right side of her face drooping, Roz still looked far younger than her sixty-eight years.

He grinned and made a mental note to tell Consuela to

find the miraculous anti-sag cream. And the loose-fitting clothes Roz would need in Rehab.

He stepped over to the window and peeked through closed blinds. It would be another hot, humid day. His one ally had left early, shortly after sunrise. Right now, he'd give all he owned to be on that plane with Ellie. She'd be landing soon, welcomed by four who would be very glad to see her.

He glanced at the clock that had barely moved since the last time he'd checked. Reminded him of the long and tedious days in prison before he'd earned the privilege of work detail.

Now it was Roz who was imprisoned in her own disabled body, no doubt hating it as much as he had hated his jail cell.

He moved back to stand beside her bed. Roz lay on her back breathing heavily with occasional sniffs from her meltdown. He couldn't leave no matter how much a part of him wanted to. Even if God allowed him to leave, his own code of honor wouldn't. Roz had no one else who really cared about what happened to her.

He moved back to the recliner in the corner and sat, placing his bowed head in his hands.

"Father, it looks like I'm back in Wilderness 101, and my stubborn heart is still longing for the leeks and garlic of my life back in Africa … and Joy." He whispered, ashamed to admit he still struggled to get thoughts of her out of his mind.

"Only You can take this longing from me. Fill my heart with Your own sweet presence. And help Rozalynde. She needs a miracle.

So do I, Father." He clenched his hands and glanced at Roz. "So do I."

CHAPTER 33

If nothing else, he would return to Africa with a new appreciation for the long hours his patients and their families had to wait to be seen.

Brock shifted position in the recliner. Roz slept most of the time. A mixed blessing. Certainly gave him some peace. He scooted closer to the window and scrolled through every article he could find about Ischemic stroke recovery.

The door opened and a man wearing a white physician's coat entered. Asian and younger than Dr. Seirafi.

Brock bounded from his chair and extended his hand. "I'm Brock Whitfield."

"Hello. I'm Dr. Hoy." He shook Brock's hand. "You are the husband?"

"Ex-husband."

Dr. Hoy nodded and flipped through a couple of pages, no doubt verifying Brock's access to information.

He went to the bed and spoke loudly. "Ms. Whitfield?"

Roz's eye fluttered open. She turned her head and stared blankly.

"Hello, ma'am. I'm Dr. Hoy." He lowered the bed rail.

"Would you sit up for me, ma'am?"

Roz shook her head and did not move. Brock tensed, praying she wouldn't pull another stunt like the one this morning.

The doctor seemed undeterred. He pushed a button, raising the head of the bed to a near ninety-degree angle, then took Roz's arm, propelling her forward.

Brock stepped in and swung her right leg around, then stayed close to steady her.

Dr. Hoy positioned his stethoscope and listened to several areas of Roz's chest, and seemed to make a point to end every request with *ma'am.*

"Deep breath, ma'am. And again. One more time, ma'am."

Each time Roz complied with whatever he asked. A small miracle in itself.

"Thank you, ma'am." He folded the stethoscope and put it in his pocket. Next, he lifted the back of her hair to the shaved area and pulled up the square piece of gauze. "Yes. A small incision where they relieved the pressure from your brain. Looks good," he said and reattached the gauze.

Brock remained quiet, appreciating a fellow doctor's skill.

"You are doing well, ma'am. Dr. Seirafi would like to keep you here through the weekend. Then you will be able to return home. Many of the rehabilitation facilities in the area have a waiting list. The case manager will arrange for some in-home assistance until something becomes available."

Dr. Hoy gave a deferential nod and left the room.

Brock turned to Roz with feigned cheerfulness. "Three more days, then you'll get to go home."

Roz formed a fist and beat the bed beside her, knocking herself off balance.

Brock lunged and caught her before she tumbled off the bed. He gripped her waist and set her further back. "Would you like to sit in the recliner a little while?"

Roz shook her head and grabbed his face, tugging him closer.

He gently pried her fingers loose from his beard but remained close. "I'm listening, Roz." With effort, he kept his voice soft. "What do you want?"

"Take … ahway … fix." She touched the right side of her face and repeated. "Take … away … fix."

Brock nodded and took her hand. "I'll do what I can, but first you have to go to Rehab. They'll help you talk again. And walk again."

Roz jerked her hand from his and tapped her face. "Fix!"

Brock took her hand again. "Listen to me, Roz. I can't fix anything yet. You've got to give nature time to repair things on its own." He touched the right side of her face. "It's already better. In one month, you'll be amazed at how much you'll improve. I'll get you good help, I promise. They'll come to your house, and then when a place opens up, you'll—"

She shook her head again and slapped his arm, shoving him away.

Brock's jaw tightened. He took a step back to humor her. Attitude was everything, and right now, hers was definitely not good.

"Roz."

She looked up, so small and frail in her oversized hospital gown.

He took a deep breath and softened his tone. "Help me. Tell me what you want."

She pursed her lips, and he waited for her to get it out.

"Take ... away."

"Where, Roz? This is where you'll get the best help. This is where Gwyneth is. And your friends."

Roz grunted and grabbed his arm, poking his chest with her forefinger. "F-far ... wif you."

Take with you? The light started to click on. "To Africa?"

She nodded.

"You want me to take you to Africa?"

She nodded, more forcefully.

He raked his hand through his hair and looked at her dumbfounded. "Why?"

"Ahway." She made a sweeping motion with her left hand. "No ... one ... see."

"Roz, I'm not equipped to give you the best help." Even as he said it, he knew it wasn't quite true. He had the means to equip that clinic with anything she needed, just like he'd done for Eric.

She poked his chest again and puckered her lips. "You … hep."

He stared at her. She was sitting on the side of her hospital bed, pleading with him to devote every waking minute of the foreseeable future to her recovery, so she could save face.

He'd laugh at his own pun if he wasn't feeling so sick inside. "I'll talk it over with the doctor. See what he says."

She leaned against the bed, clearly spent.

He lowered the head of the bed and helped swing her legs back under the covers. "Get some rest. I have some things to take care of, but I'll be back to help you with lunch."

He returned her lopsided smile and left the room.

Roz in Africa? What doctor in his right mind would agree to let her travel halfway around the world to a little clinic ill-equipped to give her the help she needed?

Was this the miracle God was sending?

If so, why wasn't he happier about it?

CHAPTER 34

Brock rolled up his socks, underwear, and T-shirts and laid them systematically across the bottom of his luggage with the same precision he often used to lay out surgical instruments. Each item positioned at exactly the same angle with the exact same distance between, an effort to try to bring order out of chaos, perhaps?

The night before leaving Africa, he'd packed for what he thought would be a month. Hearing of Roz's stroke the night before his departure was the first of many detours taking him down roads he'd rather not travel. Now, he painstakingly refolded and packed the shorts and shirts he'd brought, not letting himself dwell on the weeks he wouldn't get to spend with Ellie and the twins.

At least, he hadn't left anything behind at Ellie's house. It was as if he'd known then he wouldn't be back.

He zipped up the luggage, then set it beside the door. It had been a tough two weeks, with him walking the floor more than one night trying to work out the details in his head. Which room to put her? Did she have a passport? What about vaccines? Could he find a physical therapist willing to come to Africa for an extended time?

The case manager had been a godsend, arranging for

Roz to be transferred to another floor and given speech and motor skills therapy.

Just one example of how God met and answered every question almost before he asked.

Except the one he struggled with the most. Why didn't he want her in Africa?

Brock went to the window and pulled back the vertical blinds, staring out at the Dallas skyline from his fourth-floor, hotel window. The humidity settled a haze over the horizon like a coming cloud bank even though the sun was shining.

His rotten attitude was like that haze, putting a damper on everything God was trying to do. He placed his palm on the window sill ashamed to admit he was acting no better than Roz. Not outwardly, like Roz slapping the bed, but inside, the balled-up fist of his heart was beating against the air in a full-blown tantrum.

He looked at the sky. "Roz isn't the problem, Father. I am. Show me what I'm missing."

Brock sighed, then went to the bathroom, laying out his toiletries around the sink. He leaned closer to the mirror to trim his beard.

Forgive.

Brock stilled, as he always did whenever God spoke to his heart. He set the scissors down and stared at his reflection.

It all came rushing back as if it were yesterday. Another hotel room, much nicer than the one he now occupied. The honeymoon suite, with Roz in a white negligee emerging from the bathroom like a Scandinavian goddess.

For one brief moment, he'd felt like the luckiest man alive.

"Congratulations." She'd said, then raised her champagne glass to him in a toast. "You get your trophy wife, and I get your millions."

His fingers curled around the smooth porcelain edge of the countertop.

He could still hear her laughing at his shocked face, scoffing at his pain. From then on, he'd closed his shattered heart, and did everything in his power to hurt her, treating her more like a high-end hooker than the woman he'd once adored.

The pain eventually subsided, replaced by disgust, and ultimately indifference.

The puzzle piece that had been missing started to fall into place.

He had never truly forgiven her, and a root of bitterness he didn't even know existed had been poisoning every facet of his relationship with her even now.

"God—" Brock dropped to the floor and lay prostrate on the cold tile of the bathroom, resting his forehead on his clenched fists. "God, I'm done. I can't fight this anymore." His shoulders convulsed with his broken sobs. "Take it— my selfish pride. My rebellion. God, You've forgiven me for the worst of sins. Help me forgive Rozalynde. Shine your light into the closed part of my heart. Help me love her, Father, with Your love."

Brock unclenched his hands and held them up.

Then, the real miracle happened. It felt as if tight cords around his heart were being cut, leaving him free to breathe deeply. The struggle was gone, and his spirit was light.

Brock finished trimming his beard, showered, and dressed in the khaki pants, white shirt, and sports jacket he had brought for special occasions.

In less than four hours, he would carry Roz up the steps of the Gulfstream, like a groom carrying his bride. He would vow to himself and to God, once and for all, to lay aside his own rights and desires and with God's help, do all he could to show Roz what the redeemed side of broken looked like.

CHAPTER 35

Roz settled herself in the seat where Brock had placed her. It took having a stroke, but here she was, at last getting to ride in style in the Whitfield personal plane, a privilege denied her since the divorce. Brock had driven the rental car past the gate and parked next to the steps of the plane. No security red-tape. No lines of screaming children.

The cabin was quiet and spacious. She slid her hand down the tan leather seat next to her. She could get used to traveling like this. What a fool she'd been not to fight harder for her fair share of the flying privileges.

Heat emanated from the tiny window beside her. She started to pull down the screen but caught a glimpse of Brock. He had removed his jacket and rolled up his sleeves and was helping the pilots load the rest of the luggage. A handsome man. One of the few men who actually got even better looking with age. She leaned back in her seat and lowered the screen. They would've made a stunning couple had they stayed together.

She didn't hate him anymore. Maybe it was the stroke. Or maybe it was the fact that he was the only one helping her.

She needed him. So what was his angle? Why was he

going out of his way to be so nice to her? It had to be for the money. Did he seriously think she'd ever marry him again and give him total control of her half of the money?

Even so, she was going to have to try harder to stay on his good side, at least until he fixed her face.

Brock bounded into the plane again with his jacket slung over his shoulder. "All set?"

She nodded even though her speech had improved markedly in the last two weeks. Brock said it was because the swelling in her brain had gone down. It still took a long time to get the words out. Brock said that would get better, too.

He lay his jacket over the armrest of an empty seat, then reached for her shoulder strap, leaning in close to fasten the buckle. She closed her eyes and breathed in the warm scent of clean sweat mingled with a faint hint of his cologne. A masculine scent she found attractive, though she'd never tell him so.

He took the seat to her left and strapped his seatbelt into place. The plane revved and taxied to the runway for takeoff.

"Are you comfortable? Would you like a blanket or a pillow?"

She shook her head.

He smiled and placed his hand on top of hers and gave it a squeeze. Something he'd done more than a few times over the past two weeks. It was strange at first, but she'd gotten used to it and even secretly enjoyed it. But today, it made her more than a little nervous.

"Brock?"

"Hmm?"

She hesitated. Her words came out slow, especially when she wasn't sure what to say next.

He looked up from his iPad and waited, his eyebrows raised.

"I ... can't ... be ... wife."

His head jerked back and he stared at her with wide eyes. "Roz, what are you talking about?"

"Why ... did ... you ... agree ... to ... help?"

Brock's expression softened. "Because I wanted to."

"Why?

"Because you needed somebody to take care of you."

"Won't ... sleep ... with ... you."

He lifted his hand from hers. "Roz, I—that's not why I—"

She heard his sharp intake of breath as he turned his face away. After a long pause, he turned back and reached for her hand again, this time lacing his fingers through hers. When he spoke, his voice was surprisingly tender. "Roz, I don't blame you for being concerned. I did you wrong when I was married to you, but I promise you, I have no intention to ... uh ... you don't need to worry."

She dropped her gaze unable to look him in the face.

"I wish I could go back and right some of those wrongs. I know I can't. But listen to me. I'm not the same man you married. I've changed, and I know you don't want to hear this, but it was God who changed me. He took the mess that I was and forgave me. His love changed my life."

He leaned forward to make eye contact. "He loves you, too. You just don't realize it yet. God is the one who sent me to get you. He's the one who worked out all the details for you to come to Africa."

She snatched her hand away. "He ... did ... this." She pointed to her face.

Brock's nod was almost imperceptible. "He allowed it. Sometimes the only way we'll ever turn to God is when we don't have any other place to go."

She wanted nothing to do with that kind of God. "Don't ... push ... me."

"I won't. But I give you fair warning. All the people at the mission compound are followers of Christ, and they love to talk about God."

She rubbed her sweaty palm down the side of her pants, then twisted the loose fabric in her balled-up fists. Maybe she should tell him to turn the plane around before it was too late.

"Roz, right now I don't want you to worry about anything. My goal is to help you get better. Period. No strings attached. You can trust me, and if I do anything that makes you uncomfortable, tell me."

Her racing heart slowed, and her breathing returned to normal. She was so tired. All she wanted to do was sleep the rest of her life away.

"I brought your prescription of Xanax. Do you need

one?"

She nodded and took the pill like a junkie craving her next fix. Within minutes, the tenseness left her chest. Before she drifted off, she raised her head and looked at Brock.

He glanced up from his iPad. "Need something?"

She shook her head. "Won't … mind … if … you … hold … hand … sometime."

The side of his mouth quirked up. "Do you want me to now?"

She nodded, and out of nowhere, her eyes filled with tears.

He slid his hand under her arm and curled his fingers around hers. "Better?"

She did feel better, but she couldn't explain why. She really didn't care. She just wanted to sleep.

Brock stared at the article he'd downloaded, *Stroke Victims and Air Travel,* mentally checking off every item except the recommended foot and leg massages to prevent blood clots.

Roz had been asleep for the past three hours. He hated to wake her, especially to tell her it was time for a foot massage. In her present state of mind, she might think he had ulterior motives.

Maybe the compression hose he'd insisted she wear, no matter how ugly, would be enough to keep her from getting a clot. He, on the other hand, wasn't wearing them. He unbuckled and got up to stretch his legs a little, pacing from the cockpit to the bathroom in the back. Each time he passed Roz's seat, he glanced at her. Even the left side of her mouth drooped in a little frown, and her brow remained furrowed.

What a troubled, twisted little mind she had. If there was anybody who needed peace, it was Roz, who wanted nothing to do with the only One who could give it to her. Brock had a new appreciation for what Eric had gone through when he spent three months with his atheist father. If God could break the stubborn will of someone like Bob Templeton, surely there was hope for Roz.

Thankfully, his meltdown back in the hotel had caused a dramatic shift in his own attitude. Miraculously, he no longer considered time spent with Roz as wasted.

The plane hit a pocket of turbulence. Brock lurched forward, grabbing hold of an overhead compartment to keep from crashing into the galley at the front.

Roz jerked upright. "What's … wrong?"

"Nothing. Just a little turbulence." Brock made it back to his seat and buckled.

Roz reached over with her left hand and raised the shade over the window. "How … long?"

He had become somewhat of an expert at reading between the lines of her stilted language. Thankfully, she no longer pounded with her left hand. "About ten hours."

She gasped and visibly slumped in her seat. "Can't—

do—this."

Brock showed her his iPad and told her about the article, leaving out the part about being a stroke victim. "If you'll prop your left leg over the seat, I'll give your foot a massage."

He helped move things along by reaching for her leg and propelling it across the armrest. "There. Comfortable?"

She nodded even though her body looked contorted.

He removed her shoe and began to knead with both hands, working his way from the sole of her foot to her calf.

Her appreciative moans told him he must be doing it right.

"Would you like for me to tell you a little bit about the mission compound?" He shot her a sideways glance.

She kept her eyes closed but nodded.

"I guess I should warn you, the buildings are nothing like you're used to."

Her eyes flew open.

"They're plain and functional. Most have concrete floors. Some have tile, but the hospital rooms and staff living quarters are air-conditioned, which is quite a luxury in Africa."

He tucked her foot back into its shoe. "This one's done." He moved to the seat facing hers. "Can you inch your right leg toward me?"

She looked at him just like some of the clinic patients who understood nothing of what he said. He tried again, this time pointing. "Your leg. Ease it toward me." He could've easily done the work for her but wanted her to try.

She bent and used her left hand to push her leg toward him.

"Good." He praised her effort and met her more than halfway, lifting her leg to his lap. "The staff live on a long hall like a dormitory. The rooms are small, but each one has its own bathroom."

Her eyes had closed again.

"Your room has French doors that open to a terrace." He'd already notified Miriam to get his room ready for her and move his things across the hall to Eric's old room. "Beyond the terrace, there's a field with wild grasses and shrubs and wildflowers. It's so beautiful. And peaceful. One of my favorite things to do is sit on the terrace and watch the sun come up just above the hill at the far side of the field." One day, when the time is right, he would tell her why sunrises mean so much to him.

"There's a physical therapist coming in about two weeks. She'll stay for a whole month, working with you and helping retrain your weak muscles. The brain is an amazing vessel, Roz. It can rebuild pathways and repair itself."

She opened her eyes and looked at him. "Fix ... face?"

Apparently, talking and walking were low on her list of priorities. "It will take at least six months before we'll know how much your face will recover on its own. After that, we'll see."

"Six?" Her lips tightened, making the drooping part of

her face more pronounced.

"It'll go by fast, you'll see," he said, for his sake as well as for hers. The last three weeks had seemed like a lifetime.

CHAPTER 36

The sun was already low on the horizon by the time their plane arrived at the Luanda airport. The return trip was always brutal with the six-hour time difference tacked on to the already grueling sixteen-hour flight time. By the time Brock and Toby transferred luggage from the Gulfstream to the helicopter, Brock was just about done in and Roz, even more so.

Toby remained uncharacteristically quiet, even though Brock had already briefed him about the abrupt change of plans.

Roz, never one to be overly friendly with strangers, barely acknowledged Toby when Brock introduced him.

"One more hour, then you can finally get settled in your new home." Brock second-guessed his choice of words the moment he spoke. The closer they got to the compound, the more Roz fidgeted.

Toby swooped over familiar hills and angled the helicopter's nose down causing Brock's pulse to race. He strained against his shoulder strap to watch the stream of staff flooding the compound, much as they had done just three weeks ago.

Roz gripped his arm, digging in with her nails. "No …

one … see."

He nodded, not really sure if she meant she didn't want to see or didn't want to be seen. Not that it made any difference. Either way, he faced the dilemma of how to keep the enthusiastic crowd from overpowering them as soon as the blades stopped twirling.

"When we land, you stay put, and I'll deal with the people."

Roz didn't respond but kept her head lowered with her left hand acting as a shield, shutting even him out.

The moment the wheels touched the red gravel, Brock leaped out and moved fast, steering the crowd as far as possible from the helicopter.

Moses lingered near the back of the group, but Brock motioned him closer. "Rozalynde is exhausted and isn't up to meeting anyone just yet. Let everyone know there'll be a short staff meeting immediately after dinner."

Brock continued to work the crowd, all the while stealing glances back to see if Rozalynde was all right.

Moses announced the meeting, then herded everyone back to their jobs with his long arms.

With a final wave, Brock turned back to the helicopter that appeared now to be empty. Toby stood beside the open cockpit door, systematically cracking his knuckles.

"Where is she?"

Toby shrugged but gestured with a quick jerk of his head toward the back seat. Brock looked at the still empty seat and gave Toby's arm a squeeze. "Leave us alone for now. We'll get the luggage later."

Toby nodded and followed the rest of the group going toward the dining hall.

Brock opened the back door, then froze. Roz lay in a heap, taking up most of the floor space in front of their seats.

Was she dead? He pulled himself up and stepped gingerly around her body. She lay facing him, curled in a fetal position. "Roz?" He touched her thigh.

She was staring straight ahead. Possibly having a seizure.

She spoke, barely moving her lips. "Can't ... do ... this."

"Roz, sit up so we can talk about this."

She made no response.

He placed his hand on her shoulder. "Let's get you inside. It will all seem better after you're settled."

"Mis ... take."

"Give it a chance. Give it one week. If you still want to go back, I'll take you back."

She shook her head.

"Roz, the pilots can't take you back tonight, and you can't sleep out here." He slid his hand under her waist and shifted to get leverage. "Let me help you, okay?"

"No!" She became a she-devil, twisting out of his grasp and pounding on his face and chest with her fist. "Go ... away ... leave ... alone."

Brock tried to protect his face by grabbing her flailing

hand and holding it close to his body.

Roz shrieked like a trapped animal and leaned in, latching onto his index finger with her teeth.

"Let go, Roz." He winced and tried to snatch his finger free.

She clamped down harder, almost biting through to the knuckle, drawing blood.

"Roz, please let go!" He cried out and brought his other hand up to break the hold she had without hurting her in the process.

Only by God's grace was he able to speak once more. He lowered his tone and spoke slowly, keeping his voice soft and gentle. "Rozalynde, let it go."

The winning combination that made her mouth go slack. He immediately pulled his finger free and loosened his hold on her. Blood spurted from the puncture wound. He grabbed a shop rag that didn't look soiled from the back of Toby's seat and wrapped it around his finger.

Roz went limp with her face flat against the filthy floorboard of the helicopter. Her whimpers grew louder becoming heaving sobs. "Can't … live … like … this."

The door of the helicopter opened, sending a welcomed breeze to Brock's sweat-covered face. Moses stood with his hand on the top rim of the door. "May I help?"

"Yes. Get Iyegha to draw up 10mg diazepam and bring it to me as quickly as possible."

Moses disappeared before Brock finished speaking.

Brock used the back of his hand to wipe the tears mingled with sweat running down her cheeks. "You're hot. Let me get you inside where it's cooler."

"Can't."

"I know. But just for one night." Brock shifted to give his knee some relief and rolled her up against his chest, stroking her hair back from her face. He spoke as if she were a frightened child, his one goal to keep from setting her off again. "It's not safe for you to stay out here. And we'll take these ugly hose off your legs and get you comfortable. Okay?"

Her eyes remained closed. Brock let his back recline against the edge of the seat. Moses reappeared, his chest heaving with shallow breaths, and handed the hypodermic to Brock.

"Thank you." He lifted Roz, and removing the cap from the needle with his teeth, he slid the needle into the muscle of her arm. She barely flinched, clearly too exhausted to put up any more fight. Maybe she didn't need the sedative after all, but he couldn't take the chance.

The dead weight of her body presented another challenge. He gritted his teeth and hoisted her up like a very heavy rag doll. Moses guided Brock's foot to the step as he backed out.

"Let me take her." Moses didn't wait for an answer but lifted Roz from Brock's already cramped muscles.

"Thank you." Brock grabbed Roz's luggage and rushed ahead to open the terrace doors.

Miriam stood at the doorway of his bedroom. She stepped aside then followed them into the room.

Moses set Roz on the side of the bed. Brock gripped her shoulders and leaned closer, looking into her glazed eyes. "Roz, we're going to help you use the bathroom and get ready for bed." Brock carried her to the bathroom, then steadied her in front of the toilet while Miriam pulled down her slacks.

Miriam nodded. "All right. I've got her now."

Brock returned to the bedroom and rummaged through her bag for a nightgown.

Miriam called out. "She is finished."

Brock returned and held Roz steady while Miriam removed her top and slipped the gown over her head. He gripped her under each arm and straightened his back, using his legs to bear the brunt of her weight, then pulled her up to a standing position. "I'll leave the compression hose on her for tonight. She might be out for a long time."

Brock swooped her up in his arms and carried her to the bed. Miriam squeezed through the door with them, supporting Roz's head, then she eased ahead to pull down the covers.

He felt the strain on his lower back as he set her on the bed and covered her with the sheet and blanket.

Miriam adjusted Roz's head on the pillow, then gestured to his hand. "You should see to your finger."

Brock glanced down. Blood had seeped through the rag. He unwrapped the makeshift bandage and checked the damage. His finger was stiff and swollen. The gash made by her teeth was deep and still oozed blood.

She nudged him toward the door. "I will stay until she is fully asleep."

"Thank you."

Moses remained outside the door like a sentry on red alert. He fell into step and reached for Brock's hand, taking a closer look at the swollen finger. He shook his head, clucking with his tongue. "Brother, this is the woman you chose?"

Blood slid down his finger to his wrist. Brock dabbed it and gave Moses a crooked smile. "God chose this woman for me."

Moses slapped his hand to his forehead. "I will pray harder."

Brock chuckled for the first time since their trip across the ocean began. "Yes. Pray harder. We both need it."

He paused at the outside door, a shortcut to the clinic. "Please tell the rest of the team to eat dinner without me, but stay for the meeting." He held up his finger. "I'm going to clean and dress this, then I'll meet you there."

Moses pressed his long fingers into Brock's shoulder. "I will let them know."

The clinic staff had transitioned to the night crew. Brock waved with his left hand, keeping the wounded one tucked out of view, and eased into one of the cubicles used for outpatients. He sucked in as he poured peroxide and watched it fizz and bubble into a pink froth. Then he dabbed and examined more closely. Jagged and deep, almost to his knuckle. Already sore as the devil. He wiggled it up and down. Blood spurted again, filling the lines and creases in his palm. It would leave a scar. He almost hoped it would.

"Jesus, if you could endure a spike through your hand, I will endure an eyetooth to my finger."

He applied triple antibiotic salve, then wrapped gauze around the wound. A slow and awkward process, especially using the less dominant left hand. By the time he finished, his index finger was securely bandaged and twice the size of the others.

He returned to the dining hall and waved everyone back down. "Please, keep your seats and continue your dinner."

Everyone complied except Nicci, who pushed back from her seat and waddled to the kitchen.

Brock singled out Al, before taking his seat. "Before I forget, would you bring a cot to my bedroom after the meeting?"

"Sure thing, Doc."

Brock took his usual place at the head of the table with Moses and Miriam to his left and Neal and Dottie to his right. Nicci returned and placed a steaming bowl of black beans and rice in front of him.

Brock stood and pulled her into a sideways embrace. "Thank you. I smelled them the moment I stepped into the building. You take good care of me."

Nicci predictably covered her cheeks. "Toby told me he was going to get you and bring you back. I say to baby, 'You can come now.'"

She laughed, and Brock laughed with her, patting her firm round stomach. "Not just yet, little one. Stay in there a few more weeks."

He sat and knew he'd have to make a dent in the food. Maybe Nicci would understand if he took what he couldn't finish as a midnight snack. He took a couple of bites and hummed appreciatively. "Mmm. Nobody makes beans and rice like you."

The fat gauze around his finger made eating awkward. It seemed the joint on that one finger was essential to everything else he did. With reluctance, he covered his bowl with his napkin and pushed back from the table.

"I'll get started if I may." He decided to stay seated to draw less attention to his finger. "In hindsight, I apologize for not telling you about Ellie's mother before I left. Ellie called just hours before my departure with the news her mother had suffered a stroke. I informed Moses but no one else because I really had no details."

He reached for his glass of water and took a sip. "Her name is Rozalynde, but she prefers to be called Roz. She suffered an Ischemic stroke three weeks ago. It affected her motor skills, speech, and balance, all of which are improving. I've contacted a physical therapist who will be coming in a couple of weeks to work exclusively with her.

"There is some weakness on the right side, and that's

why I needed to speak with you. Ellie's mother is—" he paused, thinking through the best way to handle the whole Roz situation. He decided to be honest.

"Roz is sensitive about how her face looks. That's why she came to Africa, so none of her friends would see her. She is extremely fragile and broken right now, and that brings me to the real reason I wanted to meet with you.

"Roz is not a follower of Christ, nor does she want to be. But I feel that God has her here for us to show her Christ's love. Just like some of you did for Ellie when she first came and later for Eric as well.

"Every day, we need to add her to the staff prayer list and ask God to soften her heart and draw her to Christ."

Everyone remained quiet and thoughtful. After a few moments, Neal spoke up. "What happened to your finger?"

Brock held it up as if on display. "It got caught in between something when I was getting out of the helicopter." He shot Moses an innocent look. Technically not a lie and much easier to explain. "But I'm afraid I won't be much help to you for a while."

Neal gave a dismissive wave of his hand. "Dottie and I have already discussed it. We're here for as long as you need us."

"I really appreciate that." Brock dropped his gaze and traced an imaginary pattern on the table, his jaw working as he fought to regain composure. He continued, his voice husky. "I would also covet your prayers. My relationship with Roz has been strained for quite some time. God is giving me an opportunity to right some past wrongs and maybe cause her to come to Christ. If you don't mind, I'd like a couple of you to pray out loud as we commit the next few weeks into God's all-powerful hands."

Everyone, as if by some unspoken consent, joined hands. Al, the handyman who talked the least of anybody on the team, prayed first. He often went about his duties so quietly and efficiently he was almost invisible. His soft-spoken voice filled the room with his heartfelt requests.

Toby prayed next, his voice loud like he was bursting into the throne room of grace, storming it on Brock's behalf.

Mac was next, followed by Neal and the two men who'd accompanied him on this trip.

Moses ended the prayer, his mellow African accent making his prayer sound more like an African song.

At the final "Amen," Brock wiped wet cheeks and placed his hand over a full heart. "Thank you. I'm so blessed to work with you, my friends."

Chairs scraped on the concrete floor as everyone left the table. Brock caught up to Miriam and tugged her aside. "Walk with me, please. I need to discuss some things with you."

She nodded and waved Moses away. Brock grabbed his bowl of beans and rice and joined her at the doorway. "I'll need your help with Roz for the duration of her stay."

"Yes, of course. How is it that I can help you?"

"Roz can be a difficult person, and right now, she is

especially fragile. I will do all I can, but I think she would be more comfortable if you helped her get cleaned up and dressed. Maybe brush her hair. And I don't have to tell you because this is one of your strengths, but if you could praise her as often as possible. Tell her she is pretty. Something like that. Roz seems to thrive when she is praised. I would be very grateful."

Miriam stopped walking and turned to him, her long fingers splayed across her chest. "It is my honor to serve you in this way. I will do my best."

Once again, Brock's eyes filled with tears. "You must promise to let me know if she is ever unkind to you in any way."

Miriam merely smiled, her countenance radiating with an inner glow. "Would you allow me, Dr. Brock, to sleep on the cot beside her so that you can rest?"

"That's very kind of you, but no. Maybe when she's had time to meet you and feel comfortable around you. I don't think she'll remember much of what happened tonight."

"It is well."

Brock agreed and touched Miriam's arm. "Yes. It is well. Come to this room perhaps by nine in the morning. Bring her a tray. Oh, and let Nicci know that Roz will need a low-sodium diet. Then we'll go from there."

Miriam left, and Brock stood in his former bedroom, feeling more than a little displaced. He set the bowl of beans and rice on the bedside table and wondered if he could get away with feeding them to Lady, who never turned down a scrap. They were very good, but his stomach was all twisted in knots and had been ever since Roz's meltdown.

Brock retraced his steps down the hall, not allowing himself even a glance at the room Joy once occupied. He did, however, steal a quick look into the now darkened dining hall. A thin line of light shone from the kitchen's double doors. He heard a loud clattering sound like a stainless-steel pot or platter bouncing off the floor followed by Toby's "Oops, My bad."

Brock grinned and continued to where three other hallways intersected, the very hub of the cross-shaped buildings. He took a right turn down another dark hallway. The knot in his stomach loosened as he entered his office. It seemed to welcome him, with the comfortable smell of his leather chair, his books, and the musky scent of potpourri that Nicci kept on the edge of his desk.

It would be close to four in the afternoon in Washington, and Ellie would be watching the clock, waiting for his call. He sat in his swivel chair and grabbed one of the extra pairs of reading glasses he kept in his top right drawer. He pulled Ellie's name up for a Skype session, and within seconds her smiling face filled the screen.

"You made it!" Ellie held Bek in her lap and raised her little arm up. "Wave to Poppy." Bek started beating the top of the desk with the teething ring in her other hand.

"Poppy?" He chuckled. "Is that what they'll call me?"

"Nothing's set in stone. We're open to suggestions."

"I like that one."

"We do, too. So how are you, Dad? How'd it go?"

"Good. Your mom slept for most of the trip. We stopped in Paris to let her stir around a bit."

"That's good. So she's behaving?"

"Yes. She panicked a little when we landed at the compound."

Ellie turned, and for one brief second, he caught a glimpse of Joy taking Bek from Ellie's lap. Ellie tugged Joy back. "Wait a minute. Say *Hi* to Dad."

Joy leaned in and smiled. "Hello, Brock. I'm glad you made it. We're praying for you."

"Hello, Joy." The longing he'd kept at bay for days, now reared up so strongly, he clenched his fist to keep from touching her smiling face on the screen. "Thank you. We need those prayers."

He didn't ask her any questions, even though he very much wanted to know how she'd been and what the status of her son was. He couldn't even tell her he'd been praying for her, too, because he'd given the care of her over to God and stopped praying. For his own sanity's sake.

With a wave, Joy left the screen, and Ellie swiveled back. "You had to sedate Mom, didn't you?"

Brock pushed away thoughts of Joy being in the same room, listening to him talk and made a conscious effort to keep his bandaged finger out of the camera's view. "Yes.

Understandable. It was a long trip."

"Uh-huh. If I'd been on that plane, I'd have needed some sedation, too."

Brock chuckled. "I understand. Thankfully, I won't need any help tonight. I'll be out the minute my head hits the pillow."

"Where is she? My old room?"

"No. I put her in my room."

"Really?"

He answered the next question before Ellie asked. "I moved across the hall to Eric's old room."

Ellie paused, then asked, "Have you been able to speak to Gwyneth yet?"

"No. I've left some messages, but she hasn't answered my calls. Maybe she's on telephone silence at the Swedish spa." Or maybe she didn't want to speak to him.

"Would you like for me to try?"

"Yes, if you don't mind. So how are things there?"

"Twins are doing great. A little cranky. From the amount of drool, I'd say more teeth are coming in. And Joy's son, David, arrived two days ago. Eric's going to play racquetball with him when he gets settled." She turned her head and smiled, no doubt at Joy. "We're supposed to go over there for dinner tomorrow night. Joy's making her famous lasagna."

"I haven't had lasagna in years. Not one of Nicci's specialties."

"Let me guess. She served beans and rice for your

welcome home dinner."

He grinned. "Yes. Do you know, I don't think she's served beef tips and rice since you left Africa."

"How sad. It's so good."

"I know. I think that means you'll need to visit soon."

"We're actually talking about coming soon after Nicci's baby is born. Maybe around the first of November."

"That would be wonderful." Three months. Gave him something to look forward to. "Okay, honey. I'm going to call it a night. Kiss those babies. Give my love to Eric, and keep us in your prayers. Oh, and check your email. I'll try to send you daily updates."

"I will. I love you, Dad." She blew him a kiss, and the computer screen went dark.

He swiveled his chair toward his window and let his head rest against the back of his chair, forcing his thoughts away from Joy and back to Roz.

He'd dealt with a handful of violent patients since coming to Africa. Hurting people who were also frightened often lashed out at the people around them. Usually, he had no trouble calming the situation down to keep both staff and patient safe.

His own ex-wife had been the only patient who'd managed to almost bite through his index finger. At least, he was the only one who'd been injured. He replayed the scene in his mind, wondering what he could've done differently. Nothing came to mind.

Ironically, he felt no anger toward her. Roz was a broken person who needed Christ. It was crazy, but he was almost excited to see how God was going to pull that miracle off.

CHAPTER 37

Roz felt someone shaking her arm, then heard Brock calling her name. She tried to shrug him away. "Let … sleep."

"You can sleep again soon. Right now, you need to wake up and eat."

"Uh-uh."

He shook her arm again. "Sit up and try to eat something."

"What … time?"

"Almost eleven."

She blinked a couple of times. Her eyes felt dry and gritty like there was sand in them. She raised her hand to rub them. Brock sat in a straight-backed chair next to her bed. Had he been there staring at her all night?

"I have a surprise for you." His cheerful tone grated on her nerves.

"What?"

"I'll tell you after you eat." He reached for her arm to help pull her into a sitting position.

"Not … hungry. Want … cigarette." She added, just for spite and to get a rise out of him. From the tight line of his lips, it was working.

"You don't need a cigarette, but you do need food. You need to take your meds."

He stood and stuffed another pillow under her head, then moved the tray from the bedside table to her lap. "Then I'll tell you about the surprise. You'll like it, I promise."

"Stop ... it!" She swore and shoved the tray, slinging hot coffee and scrambled eggs across the bed and onto him. The rage inside her reared up with all the force of a fire-breathing dragon. "Stop ... pachontiz ... patriontiz." Her voice became louder and shriller. "Stop ... talking ... down. Not ... a ... child."

She glared at him, ready to take him on.

He brushed eggs from his lap, then looked up at her, his eyes full of kindness and not the anger she expected. "You're right. I probably did sound like I was patronizing you. I apologize, Roz. That wasn't my intention."

He rose without waiting for her reply. The eggs he'd missed earlier dropped to the floor as he left the room. He returned with a damp hand towel and methodically scraped the rest of the food from the bed back to the tray. "I ordered some botox injections from a friend of mine who practices in the U.K. The shipment will arrive early next week. It'll help pull up those muscles, especially here." He touched the right side of her face under her eye. "Studies indicate botox is also helpful with muscle spasticity. Sorry, with the stiffness in your weak muscles. So, I thought we could try injecting some botox into your arm and wrist and also in your thigh. It can't hurt to try it. Well, it might hurt when I inject it, but it won't be harmful to you, and may actually help."

She nodded without making eye contact. It was crazy, but his kindness just made her madder, making her lash out again. "Don't … pity."

He moved the tray out of her reach and returned to his seat. "Roz," he said with no hint of impatience. "You barely ate anything yesterday. Tell me what you feel like you could eat."

"Coffee."

"Okay." He grinned. "That's a start. Anything else?"

She shrugged, then turned her face away. The bed shifted as he sat beside her on the soiled part of the cover.

"Tell me what you want, Roz."

"Make … this … go … away. That's … what … I want." She clamped her lips tight, gritting her teeth. When he didn't respond, she looked up. He was staring at the floor.

Finally, he spoke, his voice almost a whisper. "I wish I could."

She raised her chin as if to challenge. "So … you … could be … rid of me?"

He reached over with his hand and cupped her face. "So you could be happy again."

She grabbed his hand and flung it away. "I'll never … be happy … again."

He didn't comment or try to argue. Instead, he stood.

"I'm going to get you some coffee. Miriam, one of our staff, is going to help you get cleaned up and dressed."

She curled her hand into a fist and brought it to her mouth. What was wrong with her? She didn't want him to leave but lashed out at him when he was there. It was like her evil twin was pushing her down a dark tunnel with her incapable of stopping.

He had already taken far more than she ever thought Brock Whitfield capable of taking. What would she do if he flew her back to Dallas and dumped her?

She bit down on the knuckle of her hand. A faint memory of her biting something flickered in her mind but disappeared every time she tried to remember what. Or when.

A tall black woman appeared in the doorway. "Hello. My name is Miriam. Welcome to our home." Her dark eyes seemed to sparkle. "And you are Rozalynde, my sweet Ellie's mother."

Roz stared, too mesmerized to speak, as the woman moved to the foot of the bed.

She was very black and very beautiful with a smile that seemed to light up her entire face. "And look at you. So beautiful, with your hair the color of sunshine and your eyes the color of the sky. You have passed your beauty to your daughter but lost none for yourself."

Roz liked everything about this woman. The way she talked, with an accent that made ordinary words come out sounding like poetry. And the way she moved, with more poise than anyone Roz had ever met like she was somebody special. But most of all, Roz liked the way Miriam made her feel, like she was somebody special, too.

"You and I will be great friends, *linda mama*."

Linda mama? Was she calling her Linda or calling Ellie Linda? Either way, she had to set her straight. "My name ... is Roz."

Miriam laughed and moved around the bed, taking Roz's hand. "Ya. Ya. Linda in our language means beautiful. I called you beautiful mama. And now, I will help make you a clean mama." She disappeared into the bathroom.

Roz heard water splatter on the floor of the shower. Miriam returned and flipped back the sheet and blanket without commenting on how wet and soiled they were.

Miriam took Roz's left hand with fingers that were rough and calloused, yet gentle. "Let me help you sit on the side of the bed." She pulled and supported Roz's back, then swung her legs over the side. "Very good. Now, place your arm around my waist." With a low grunt, Miriam lifted Roz to her feet. "We will walk like we are one person."

Miriam propelled her forward, with Roz dragging her right foot along, and not stopping until they reached the toilet. "Now, mama, I will put you on this pot while I ready the water."

Roz complied without hesitation, her earlier temper now soothed.

Miriam squatted and removed the ugly opaque hose

from Roz's legs. Then she slipped the nightgown off, leaving Roz completely exposed.

"Two steps."

With Miriam doing most of the work, Roz made it into the shower where there was a white plastic shower chair for her to sit on. "You will get ... wet."

"Don't worry about me. I'm here to take care of you."

Miriam detached the water nozzle. "Is the water too hot?"

Roz shook her head, keeping her eyes closed. She felt glorious and pampered and pretended she was back in Dallas at her favorite day spa. Miriam scrubbed Roz's hair, massaging her scalp with her strong fingers. "Smells ... good."

"Ya. Ya. A special soap our Nicci makes for us. She also makes our food. We are blessed to have such a gifted woman."

The shower left Roz's skin soft and tingling. Miriam plopped her back on the toilet, this time with the seat down. She took a towel and wrapped it around Roz's hair. Next, she put some pink cream on her hands and rubbed them together, then slathered it on Roz's moist skin.

"Stay still while I get your clothes." Miriam returned with clothes Roz didn't recognize. Loose fitting slacks with an elastic waist, made of some kind of lightweight material that was the color of sand. The tunic top was the same color and made the outfit look like lounging pajamas. Very soft and comfortable.

"You like?"

Roz nodded.

"I will make more for you." Miriam removed the towel from Roz's hair and brushed through the tangles without hurting. Her stylist back home never bothered to be gentle with Roz's sensitive scalp. "Shall I braid it as I used to do for Ellie?"

"Yes … would like that."

Miriam used her long fingers to separate Roz's hair into strands. It felt so good to have someone fix her hair. Roz closed her eyes and let herself relax and enjoy the moment, something she never did at the high-end salons in Dallas.

Miriam finished, long before Roz was ready for her to, and placed both hands on Roz's cheeks. "*Mwatu wawa Kwuiba.*"

"What did … you say?"

"I say, 'You are very beautiful'."

Roz hadn't looked in a mirror lately. She frowned and raised her hand to the right side of her face, hoping it would feel less droopy, but of course, it didn't.

Miriam stooped until she was at eye level with Roz. "What's the matter, mama?"

"I'm not … beautiful."

"You sound like our Nicci." Miriam smiled and helped Roz stand. "She came from a tribe that cuts deep ridges in the cheeks of all girl babies born in their village. She, too, does not understand her true beauty."

Miriam gripped Roz around the waist, and together

they walked back, this time to the recliner.

Roz sat, while Miriam stripped the bed and wadded the sheets along with her clothes from the night before stained with dried blood.

"Why ... blood?"

Miriam picked up the blouse and examined it. "That came from Dr. Brock's finger. I will leave you in this chair while I go for clean sheets. You will not try to walk?"

Roz shook her head, still processing the blood from Brock's finger.

Miriam left the room. Within minutes, Brock came and stood in the doorway. Her ill mood was gone now, and she was actually glad to see him. He must have showered, too. His hair was still damp, and he wore a brightly colored shirt untucked over Khaki shorts.

He smiled at her. "Feel better?"

She nodded.

"Good. Would you like some coffee?" He held two cups in his hands.

"Yes." She hesitated, then added "Please." Because she was feeling especially gracious at the moment.

Brock's eyes widened a little, but he seemed pleased. "Here you go."

She held it with her left hand while supporting it as well as she could with her right.

Brock sat across from her on the edge of the stripped bed.

"What happened to ... your finger?"

313

Brock shrugged. "I hurt it trying to get you out of the helicopter last night."

Roz stared at the finger, then looked up at him. "Did I ... bite you?"

He hesitated, then said, "You were a little out of your head and very frightened."

Tears filled her eyes. She remembered nothing about the ride in the helicopter or what happened when they arrived. It must have been bad. She sipped her coffee, trying hard not to let any dribble down her chin and onto her tunic.

"I will ... try ... better."

"Thank you." Brock's eyes crinkled with warmth. "I will try better, too. You look very pretty with your hair like that."

She liked hearing it, even if it wasn't true. Her hair maybe, but nothing about her face was pretty, no matter what Brock or Miriam said. "I like ... Miriam."

"She likes you, too. When you finish your coffee, I can show you around if you feel up to it. Or you can sleep some more after Miriam makes up your bed."

"Will ... eat ... now and ... take meds." She offered as a goodwill gesture to make up for the bite.

"Really? All right. What would you like?"

She stared, trying to remember the right word. "Warm ... bread."

Brock's gaze narrowed. "You mean toast?"

Toast! Of course. She nodded, repeating it in her mind.

"Good choice. The toast is made from homemade bread. Anything else?"

"More coffee."

"It's good, isn't it? Our cook's special blend. Her name is Nicci."

The woman Miriam told her about. "Niecey?"

"That's right. She's married to Toby, the guy who flew the helicopter here. They're expecting their first baby in a couple of months."

"Miriam talked ... about her."

Brock stood and took her half-empty cup. "When you feel up to it, you can eat in the dining hall and meet some of the other people who work here. All nice people, just like Miriam." He walked to the door, then turned. "Don't try to get up. I'll be back soon."

Left alone, she got her first good look at the room that wasn't much larger than her walk-in closet back in Texas. French doors with a cot pressing against closed vertical blinds. A smooth concrete floor that felt cool under her bare feet. A three-drawer dresser and half-sized bed. Between her recliner and the bed, a small table with a lamp, a Bible, and a 5-by-7 framed picture of Brock. A good picture of him, but then Brock always had been photogenic. She reached for the picture and studied it up close. A profile shot with the sun shining full on his uplifted smiling face. He looked happy, a lot happier than he seemed now. She placed it back on the table, but it fell flat, revealing a note taped to the back. She glanced at the door and listened for footsteps, then read the note, her hands shaking from the adrenaline rush.

Forgive me for leaving the party before you made it back, and forgive me for my intrusion into your bedroom. I wanted to give you this small token of appreciation. This year has been life-changing for me, and I've loved every minute, especially those shared sunrises.

Thank you, Brock. The love of Christ shines through all that you do.

God bless,

Joy.

So, Brock had a lady friend.

Roz read through the note again, looking for juicy details. Intrusion into your bedroom? Shared sunrises? Seemed like Brock had a few secrets. He probably left this picture in here, knowing she'd find it and read the note.

She flipped it over and looked at the picture, this time with new eyes. A woman named Joy took it. That's why he looked happy. She wanted to throw the picture at him the minute he walked through the door, but she wouldn't give him the satisfaction of thinking she was jealous.

Because she wasn't.

Livid, yes. But not jealous. She certainly didn't want Brock back, but she didn't want him to be happy either. He didn't deserve it.

She placed the frame back, positioning it as close as possible to the original place on the table. Within minutes, Miriam returned carrying a set of folded sheets.

"You are alone. I thought Dr. Brock would be here."

"Getting ... toast," she said, proud of herself for getting the word right.

Miriam flapped the fitted sheet in the air, then let it float down to the mattress. "Ya. Ya." She spoke, tucking in corners. "You will enjoy."

Roz licked her dry lips and decided to snoop some more. "Who is ... Joy?"

Miriam tucked in the top sheet at the foot of the bed, then straightened, her hands supporting the small of her back.

"Our Joy? Did Dr. Brock tell you of her?"

Roz shook her head. "Her name ... is on ... picture."

Miriam cut her gaze to the bedside table. "Ah, *sim.* Yes. Joy take that and give to Dr. Brock for his birthday." Miriam placed the bedspread over the sheet, then folded the sheet and bedspread back. "It is ready to welcome you back."

Roz shamelessly pumped for more information. "Is she ... here?"

"No. No. Joy worked here long time but left before you came to this place. Maybe one day you will meet and be great friends."

The corner of Roz's mouth curved in a sneer. One thing was certain. She and this Joy woman would never be friends.

CHAPTER 38

Brock walked down the hall to Roz's room with a tray of warm bread and coffee, this time in a Styrofoam cup that could not be broken if thrown.

Strokes could cause mood swings and depression, no doubt about it, but he suspected something even worse. Roz might actually have a much deeper problem like bipolar disorder. That would certainly explain not only her impulsive decision to come to Africa but also her meltdown once she actually got here.

He returned to find her surly mood had returned again.

"I'm back. I see Miriam has been here to make the bed." He stated the obvious for lack of anything better to say.

Roz made no attempt to make eye contact but sat staring at the floor, an ugly twist to her mouth.

"Sorry it took me so long to get back. Nicci had a fresh loaf of bread baking in the oven. I thought you might like this instead of toast." He eased around the bed with the tray in hand, second-guessing the decision to place it on her lap.

He sat directly across on the freshly made bed. This time if she shoved the tray, he'd be ready.

An awkward silence ensued as Roz picked up her

coffee and sipped, staring at him like an angry cat.

He swallowed hard and tried to think of something to say to break the tension that had filled the room.

Roz set her cup back on the tray and looked at him, pursing her mouth.

He could tell by the set of her jaw that whatever she was about to say was not going to be good. Every muscle in his neck tensed.

"Who is Joy?"

Where had that come from? Brock raised his eyebrows but kept his expression neutral, fighting guilt he didn't have to feel. "She's one of the volunteers who helped at the clinic."

Roz's lips curled in a lopsided sneer. "Same ... old Brock." She took the frame from the table, flipped it over, and read with mock sweetness. "Loved every minute ... shared sunrises." She gave him a smug look. "You ... almost had ... me fooled."

"Roz, what are you talking about?"

"You're sleeping with this Joy person, aren't you?"

Brock's mouth dropped, and it felt as if every bit of blood had drained from his face. "What?" He blurted out when he could talk. "Why would you ask such a ridiculous question?"

Her eyes narrowed without blinking. "I know you ... better than you ... think. Don't bother to ... deny it."

He stared at her and muttered under his breath.

"What?" Roz shifted, and Brock lunged to steady the

tray that almost toppled to the floor.

"I said unbelievable." He raked a hand through his hair, well aware anything he said, could and would be used against him. He leveled his gaze at her. "No, Roz. Joy was a volunteer here and a friend, just like all the other volunteers who come and go at this mission."

"Do others watch … sunrise?"

"Sometimes. Ellie rarely missed one. It's like a tradition." He decided to go on the offensive. "Roz, what is this about? You don't love me. I don't think you ever did. Why are you of all people acting like a jealous ex-wife?"

"Jealous? Ha! But now I know … what a hypocrite … you are." She waved her left hand in dismissal. "No matter … I'm done talking."

"No," he said with more force than he meant to. "You opened this door, and I'm not going to close it until we get some things hashed out."

Brock took a moment to take the tray from her lap and set it far from her reach. It gave him enough of a pause to tamp down his own anger. He had learned a long time ago *the wrath of man worketh not the righteousness of God.* His silent prayer was answered, and the things he had been about to say took a drastic one-eighty shift.

He sat on the bed again and spoke, keeping his tone soft. "Look at me, Roz."

She turned her head away, her mouth clamped.

"The day we were married, it devastated me when you

said you'd married me for the money." He dropped his gaze to his folded hands. "But I realized something the other day. You were right."

She raised her chin and looked at him, her expression defiant.

"I think that's why it hurt so much. I didn't want to admit it, but I did marry you because of your beauty. Like you said, I wanted a trophy wife, and you called me on it. I hated you for saying what you did, and I wanted to hurt you back and make you pay. And sad to say, I did a pretty good job of it. But I'm not the same man I was back then. When I think about how I treated you and how many women I paraded in front of you and everyone else, I can hardly look at myself in the mirror. I wish I could go back and undo so many things."

He slipped off the bed and knelt beside her chair. "I wronged you, Roz. I know you may need some time, but it would mean so much if you would forgive me." He reached for her hand, willing to take the risk that she might snatch it away and possibly even slap him. Or maybe bite him again. "Listen to me. I care about you, and I need you to quit fighting against me and start fighting with me to get you better."

She looked at him, tears welling up in her eyes.

"Do you think you can find it in your heart to forgive me?"

She dropped her gaze. "I don't know."

He nodded. "I understand. So, while you're thinking

about it, can we call a truce? Can we be friends?"

The tear that rolled down her cheek was answer enough.

His stiff knee balked as he stood. "Ready for a nap?" Totally on impulse, he leaned in and kissed the side of her face above her temple. "I'll get Miriam to help you use the bathroom and get you back in bed."

He started to grab the tray but stopped. "Would you like the rest of your bread?"

She nodded and managed a lopsided smile that sent a little catch to his heart. "And … meds."

He slapped his palm to his forehead. "Thank you. I totally forgot about that." He placed the tray back on her lap. "I'll be back with Miriam and your medicine."

He left the room, his heart a little battered but at peace. At least he'd been able to answer Roz with complete honesty. Had she asked him if he was in love with Joy, the conversation might have gone a whole different way.

Praise be to God! Satan had lost some ground today.

What just happened?

Roz ate the rest of the buttered bread, staring at the empty doorway. She had never seen Brock this way, so humble and transparent. Nothing like the man she had been married to. She raised her hand and touched the place he'd kissed.

What had happened to bring about such a drastic

change? He said it was God. Was that even possible?

Roz inched forward in her chair and hoisted the tray up with her left hand, being very careful not to let it tip to one side. She placed the tray on the bed and reached past the picture of Brock to pick up the Bible beside it.

She had seen Bibles but had never owned one. Certainly, had never held one in her hands. She flipped through the pages, stopping at random parts. *The spoilers came out of the camp of the Philistines.* She turned more pages. *But the Lord sent a great tempest in the sea, and there was a mighty tempest in the sea, so that the ship was like to be broken.* She sighed and flipped pages all the way to the back. *And whosoever was not found written in the book of life was cast into the lake of fire.*

Strange words that didn't make sense. She started to put the Bible back but opened the front flap. Brock's unmistakable signature was written at the top of the first blank page. Underneath was something that looked like a short paragraph. With a quick glance at the door again, she read what she hoped would be another private note. The words were printed and more legible than his signature.

God is able to do exceedingly, abundantly above all that we ask or think according to the power that worketh in us. Ephesians 3:20

Her heart thumped against her chest, but she didn't know why. She read it again. God could do more than we could ask or even think?

If this were true, God could make her face go back to

normal.

A crazy thought popped into her head, but she'd have to act fast. If Miriam or Brock caught her praying, she'd never hear the end of it.

She closed her eyes and slid her left hand over to her right, palm to palm, in what she assumed was the proper position for prayer. She couldn't actually raise her folded hands to her chest, but maybe God would make allowance for that. Her heart raced again like she had rubbed the magic lamp, and the Genie had appeared asking what she wished him to do.

She prayed, but not out loud, much better at thinking the words than saying them.

God, if You really are real, would You let me get back to normal? Especially my face. If You will do that for me, I'll believe.

She ended her prayer and tried to raise her arm. Still as weak as ever. She slid the fingers of her left hand across her face. Still numb and drooping.

Roz closed the Bible and placed it back on the table, disappointed but not really surprised that her prayer had not worked.

Maybe there was a God. But apparently, he had his favorites, and she wasn't one of them.

CHAPTER 39

Brock welcomed the rains that came in September, washing away the months of accumulated dust from the dry season and giving everything a cleaner feel. The heaviest rains would not come for another seven or eight months. Roz wouldn't handle that well. Dark, rainy days seemed to worsen her depression, but he'd cross that bridge when the time came.

The memory of crossing the bridge with Joy last spring popped up and made him smile. Thoughts of her still invaded his mind throughout the day but no longer made him sad. Mostly, he was grateful for the memories and tucked them away to be savored when Roz was not his main priority.

But today was not that day.

He had to admit life with Roz had gotten better. Her recovery had been almost miraculous. The arrival of Meredith Langley was one big reason. One of the most gifted and efficient physical therapists he'd ever seen. Just a scrap of a girl, but she had what it took to handle difficult patients. Within the first week of her arrival, she had Roz doing things he didn't think she'd ever do again.

The Botox injections played a huge part in her rapid

improvement, too. Well worth the thousands he had to pay to get them. The injections did wonders, not just with her facial muscles. With just a tiny injection to strategic areas on her right arm and leg, the weakened muscles gained strength and flexibility much faster than they would have on their own.

With this rate of improvement, Roz might be completely back to normal within weeks and not months. No doubt, God was graciously honoring all the prayers that had been lifted up on her behalf.

Brock checked his phone for the time and picked up his pace, unloading the last box of supplies. He was cutting it close, but he managed to skid into the physical therapy room with one minute to spare. "All done?"

Meredith stood with her back to the door. She glanced at him over her shoulder, then back to Roz. "Want to show him what you can do?"

Roz's mouth tightened as she pushed up from her chair without help and walked to the door, no longer sliding her right foot but actually picking it up.

Brock whistled. "Look at you!"

"Watch this." Meredith pulled a set of keys from her pocket and tossed them to Roz. "Look quick."

Roz caught them with her right hand but couldn't hold on to them.

Meredith swooped and snatched them from the floor. "Let's try that again. Remember. Close your fingers as soon as they connect." Meredith demonstrated with Roz nodding. On the second toss, Roz caught and held the keys. Brock clapped his hands. "Very good!"

"Her hand strength and coordination get better every day. I think it's all those video games you play with her." Meredith took the keys from Roz and gave her a hug. "I want to see you eat with your right hand tonight at dinner."

"I will try."

Brock smiled, more than a little proud of how well she was talking. Six weeks of intensive work sounding out consonant and vowel combinations had finally paid off.

Maybe the biggest change of all was the way their relationship with each other had evolved into a companionable friendship. Something he hadn't thought would ever happen. They still had very little in common, but at least they were able to treat one another with respect.

"Two hours until dinner. Do you need a nap?" Brock angled his arm toward Roz, and she slid her hand through the crook at his elbow.

"No. I feel pretty good."

"Okay. How about sitting outside? The sun is making one of its rare appearances."

"I would like that."

They walked slowly down the hall and turned at the intersection, going by the dining hall. Already the rich aroma of meat and vegetables spilled out into the hallway. Brock breathed in. "I can't make out what she's cooking, but it smells good whatever it is."

"I'm tirst—t. Can't say that word."

"Want a bottle of water?"

"Yes."

Brock ducked into the dining hall and grabbed two waters from the cooler. He twisted the cap off and handed one to her. "Here you go."

"Thank you."

"You're welcome. The mail came while you were with Meredith. Ellie sent you some more yoga pants."

Roz perked up. "Good. Anything else?"

"Uh-huh. Some pictures of the twins."

Roz slowed her steps to take another drink of water. It took a while, but thankfully, the sun was still shining when they made it to the double doors leading out to the terrace.

"Wait here. I'll grab a towel from my room to dry off the chairs." Brock returned and pushed open the door. Humidity was high with steam rising from the puddles on the concrete, but the rare sight of a rainbow arching over the hills to the east made it worth their while to bear the stickiness. The field next to the terrace held dappled blotches of afternoon sun mingled with shade. Brock could hardly tear his gaze away from the beauty of it all as he dried off Roz's chair, then his own.

Roz plopped into her chair blowing out a breath. "This feels good. Worked hard today."

"I know you did. I'm proud of you."

Lady came running as she always did whenever they were on the terrace and as usual, rushed first to the one who had no love for dogs, nudging her arm for attention.

"Go away! You stink." Roz shoved, but Lady didn't take the hint. "Brock, call this stupid dog."

Brock chuckled and leaned forward. "Come here, girl."

Lady bounded over to him, licking his arm as he scratched the fur on her neck. "Okay. That's enough. Go lie down." To his surprise, Lady actually obeyed.

Roz rested her head against the back of her chair and closed her eyes. He was used to her silence and even welcomed it if the truth were known.

He still hadn't found a way to approach the subject that weighed heaviest on his heart. What good would it do her to recover physically if her soul remained in the dark about God? Maybe it was time to take the direct approach.

"Roz, can I ask you a question?"

She lifted her head and squinted, opening one eye to look over at him. "What?"

"Do you believe there's a God?"

"Oh, please." She closed her eyes, effectively shutting him out. Or trying to.

"I'm just curious. I really don't know what you believe about God. I'd like to know, but we can always talk about it later."

She remained quiet for about a minute, then breathed out with a huff and sat up. "No. Let's get it over with. I do believe there's some kind of force in the universe. There. Happy?"

He ignored her sarcasm. "Do you believe there's life

after death?"

"Are you asking me if I believe there's a heaven?"

"No. I'm asking if you think there is something after this life ends. You know, you could've died when you had that stroke. What do you think would've happened to you?"

"I really don't know, Brock," she said, her tone laced with exasperation. "It scares me to think about it." She leaned back against the chair, closing her eyes again. "I don't like talking about it, either."

"I know. But you are going to die one day, Roz. Wouldn't you like to be prepared to face death?"

She shot back up. "Brock, why do you have to bring this up? You promised not to push your religion on me."

"Roz, I push lots of things on you that you don't like. Your medicine. Your exercises."

She looked away, rubbing the back of her neck.

He shifted toward her. "I'll make you a deal."

She turned to face him, her eyebrows arched in a challenging scowl.

"Give me one chance." Brock felt like a traveling salesman trying to get his foot in the door knowing once he did, the product would sell itself. "Roz, haven't you ever wondered why Jesus died? I mean, think about it. I know you've heard about Jesus dying on the cross. Why would he do that?"

Roz looked at him and shrugged. "I've never thought about it."

"I'm asking you to think about it now. Let me tell you

the story of why Jesus came to this earth and died on the cross."

She let out a heavy sigh. "Would you leave me alone if I do?"

Brock hesitated, not willing to make a promise he probably couldn't keep.

She spoke, her voice resigned. "I guess I owe it to you to hear you out. Just this once."

A door opened that had been closed, locked, and bolted for years. Brock's heart leaped inside him as he sent up a silent plea for help.

He began at the very beginning, as he did with the patients who came his way, knowing nothing about God. He covered everything: God, the creator. Satan, the deceiver. God's great love for mankind and His gift of free will. How sin came about and the subsequent fall of man. Most importantly, how God was not willing that mankind would perish but was willing to redeem them with the sinless sacrifice of His only Son, Jesus.

Brock felt God's anointing the moment he opened his mouth. Roz listened, without interruption as Brock poured out the wonderful story of God's redemption. It was a story he never tired of telling, and a couple of times, he had to stop, overcome by his own emotion.

He talked for over an hour with Roz hanging on his words and looking at him with a raw vulnerability he'd never seen in her before.

"And the best part is that God offers eternal life in

heaven as a free gift. Something that can't be earned or bought, but simply received. I received that gift when I was still in prison, and it changed my life. Nobody deserved to have his sins forgiven less than I did, but nobody could possibly appreciate it more."

He paused, feeling in his heart the time was right. "That's what I want for you, Roz. You can receive that gift right now simply by admitting to God that you need His forgiveness and asking Him to come into your heart and make you a new person. He can restore your broken soul, just like your broken body is being restored. Wouldn't you like to do that now?"

Roz stared at him, her eyes floating in unshed tears. She spoke in a quiet voice, "I'm not ready."

Her words jolted him. To him, he'd never seen anybody more ready. He had to respect her decision to wait, even though every fiber of his being wanted her to make that leap of faith today before she could talk herself out of it.

"Thank you, Roz. It meant so much to be able to share my faith with you." He smiled, hoping the disappointment didn't show on his face. Then he added, not really knowing why. "But you don't have to have anyone with you. You can pray to Jesus anytime and any place. He loves you and wants more than anything for you to accept His free gift."

The wall of her resistance seemed to go back up as she turned her gaze back to the field.

He did the same. Early evening fog so typical of the

rainy season had started to hover over the lowest spots of the field. He sent up another prayer, this time thanking God for the opportunity to share the wonderful story of redemption with Roz.

Roz went through the nightly routine of cleaning her face and brushing her teeth, unable to get Brock's words out of her mind.

God can restore your broken soul just like He's restoring your broken body.

She leaned closer to the mirror, sliding her fingers across her right cheek. It was almost completely back to normal and even looked tighter and more sculpted in some places. Brock said it must be the Botox.

But deep in her heart, she knew it was God who'd answered her prayer to fix her face, even better than she'd hoped.

Her soul was broken, too. Brock had been right about that. She stared at her reflection with troubled eyes. A perfect facade that masked the shallow person she really was, full of emptiness, anxiety, and even loneliness. Was it possible God could fix that, too?

Roz clicked off the bathroom light and went to the bedroom door and locked it. She settled in the recliner by the bed and reached for the Bible, not knowing what to do next. Why was it so hard to understand? And how did Brock of all people become such an expert about God?

Something that can't be earned or bought.

Roz opened the Bible to the front and read again what Brock had scrawled on the first blank page. The same words that inspired her to pray for God to fix her face. She touched her right cheek, no longer misshapen and drooping.

A tear rolled down her right cheek, then another. She slipped from the chair and got on her knees beside the bed, ready to do serious business with God. But how? Maybe she should've done it when Brock gave her the chance.

"God, I believe You fixed my face. Thank You for that. And Brock said You could fix my broken soul, too."

She was broken. So broken, maybe even God couldn't fix her. She started crying so hard, her shoulders shook and her breaths came out like heaving sobs, but she had no idea why. Finally, the tears quit flowing, even though they left a damp circle on the bedspread where her head rested.

Taking a shaky breath, she continued, repeating as best she could the words Brock had told her to say. "I would like for You to come into my heart and make me a new person on the inside." She paused, then added something on her own. "Like You did for my face and arm and leg."

She remained still a moment longer, not really sure what had just happened, but a good feeling that had never been there before bubbled up inside of her.

She rose and started to click off the lamp when the photo of Brock caught her eye. She picked it up and studied him. Warmth and joy were all over his face. Who was this man? Certainly not the person she used to know.

An unexpected tenderness came over her. She put the photo back on the table, clicked off the lamp, and crawled into bed.

Maybe it was time for her to go back to Texas.

CHAPTER 40

Clouds stretched across the eastern horizon like pink ribbons and would soon change to gray, dropping a good two inches of rain on the compound. No breeze stirred the heavy air that smelled of moist leaves and red dirt. No birds sang their morning chorus. Even the two cats remained hunkered down in the shed. The quiet before the storm, and yet Brock sat in his usual place on the terrace hoping for a glimpse of sun, no matter how brief, to help start his day.

If only he could determine the next step with Roz as easily as he could predict the changes in the weather.

To his left, the blinds and draperies from Roz's bedroom brightened. He pulled out his phone and checked the time. What was she doing up before five?

Curiosity won out over restraint. He entered the dorm hallway and knocked on the door. "Roz?" No answer. He twisted the knob with his heart pounding. Didn't she know not to lock her door? He leaned in, speaking louder, "Roz? Are you all right?"

The door flew opened, and he had to grab the doorjamb to keep from falling into the room. Roz stood there, her hand splayed across her chest. "For heaven sake, Brock, you scared me to death. Why are you banging on my door this early in the morning?"

He straightened and took a step back, releasing his pent-up breath. "I saw your light and ... Is everything all right?"

She sighed heavily and spoke with an edge to her voice. "I was in the bathroom, if you must know. I answered you, but the banging was so loud, I guess you didn't hear me."

"Sorry. I didn't expect you to be up so early." Especially fully dressed and not in clothes she'd worn the night before.

"Well, I was going to surprise you and join you on the terrace. I peeked through the blinds and saw you sitting out there."

He stared dumbly at her.

"I thought you wanted me to watch the sunrise sometime. You said you did." She backed up and started to close the door. "But if you don't want me to, fine. I'll go back to bed."

"Roz, wait." He shot his hand out and caught the door before it closed. "I'd love for you to join me."

She gave him a skeptical look. "Of course, you'd say that now."

"Please." His expression softened as he stepped to the side and gave a sweeping wave with his arm. "I want you to."

Without meeting his eyes, she walked past him into the hall. He eased around her and pushed open the terrace door.

He gestured toward a chair, then waited for her to sit, before taking his usual place. "Looks like we're just in time."

Roz nodded and looked at the sky.

The pink clouds were now a fiery red with orange and yellow shafts of light shooting out between the hills. God was outdoing Himself this morning. Brock relaxed against the back of his chair but cast occasional glances Roz's way, bracing for the inevitable complaints. *You've got to be kidding me.* She would say with disgust. *I got up at the crack of dawn for this?*

The sun was fully up before he chanced another look. He expected to see disappointment or even disgust, but not tears streaming down her cheeks. Brock shifted in his seat and studied her, weighing whether to press or let her alone. He decided to ask, keeping his voice gentle. "Why are you crying, Roz?"

She slid her hands across her cheeks and said without looking at him, "That was beautiful, Brock."

He smiled, more than a little touched by the sincerity of her tone. "I'm glad you liked it."

The shed door creaked open. Lucy ambled over to where they were sitting. Not long after, Bitsy came, too.

"Go." Roz arched her foot and tried to nudge Lucy from her leg. "You're rubbing cat hair all over my pants."

"Sorry." Brock reached over and scooped up both cats. "They make a point to pester people who don't like them."

The show was over. He thought Roz would get up and

leave the terrace, but she remained where she was. An awkward silence followed with him petting both cats to keep them from jumping from his lap to Roz's.

Roz gripped the armrest of her seat and turned to him. "I thought I should tell you I did it."

At the sound of Roz's voice, both cats poised to make the leap to her lap. He tightened his grip on the back of their necks and cocked his head to her. "Did what?"

"You know." Roz met his gaze with the same vulnerable look he'd seen the night before. "I—um—prayed last night."

He stared at her, too stunned to reply. The cats wiggled from his grasp and ran toward the field. Then adrenaline surged for the second time that morning, and he found his voice. "Roz, that's …" He faltered, unable to find a word that could possibly describe how he felt. "That's so wonderful." He'd been granted a rare glimpse of the real woman he suspected had been there all along. Just to be clear, he couldn't resist asking, "What did you pray?"

"You know." She shrugged and looked away as if embarrassed. "I asked Jesus to come into my heart and fix me on the inside like He did on the outside."

He slid his chair closer to hers and reached for her hand, stroking the inside of her wrist. "You don't know how happy that makes me. Thank you for telling me."

The self-assured, prickly mask went back up as quickly as the sun had disappeared. She straightened and tugged her hand from his.

The sky darkened as his weather app had predicted, and fat drops of water started to splatter the concrete around their feet. "I guess we'd better go in before—"

The bottom seemed to drop out. Roz squealed and moved toward the building, her right leg dragging a little. Brock ducked his head and gripped her elbow to steady her, propelling them along a little faster.

"Whew." She paused at her bedroom door, catching her breath. "Do you think I might catch another sunrise before I return to Texas?"

He smiled. "Most likely. The monsoons won't hit until after Christmas."

"Good. I'll be long gone before then."

She turned and went into the room, closing the door behind her. He crossed the hall to his room, went to the window, and raised the blinds. Rain was falling now at a fairly good clip already dotting the red gravel road with puddles.

Still one hour before breakfast, he pulled his journal from a stack of books on his bedside table. He sat in the recliner and flipped to Roz's page. Today, he could check off one of two faded requests he'd scrawled on the blank page so many years ago. *For Roz to come to Christ.* He placed a check beside her name and dated it. For years, he'd prayed for her to come to Christ, yet he'd been shocked to hear she had. Was he still so shallow in faith?

Make amends for all the ways I wronged Roz.

The second request stared up at him. Could he finally

check that one off, too? Part of him said yes, especially after all he'd done in the last two months.

Still, he couldn't bring himself to place a checkmark and call it done. It seemed God had more for him to do in Roz's life, and he was almost afraid to discover what that might be.

CHAPTER 41

Brock jolted awake from a dead sleep and reached for his phone on the table beside his bed. He pulled back his covers and clicked on the light, rubbing his hand through his hair.

Two fifteen. Way too early to think about getting up. He went to the bathroom, then quickly washed his hands, hoping he'd be able to go back to sleep.

He had just returned to bed when he heard the familiar creak of the double doors leading to the terrace, followed by the sound of bare feet slapping against concrete.

"Doc?" Toby called out in a failed attempt to whisper. "Nicci's water broke. You gotta come quick."

Brock smiled and started to rise. "Looks like your baby's birthday will be September 26."

"Ain't that too early?" Toby cracked his knuckles and remained at the door in his boxers and T-shirt.

Early or not, this baby was coming. "Ten days. It's within a good range." Brock dressed quickly even though with the first baby it could be a long wait.

He slipped on his shoes and followed Toby out the door. "Don't worry. Everything will be fine."

Brock considered himself to be a fast walker, but

tonight he was no match for the guy who was already halfway across the field. Brock caught up as they both bounded onto the front porch. "Hold up a minute." He paused, catching his breath. "Here's what I want you to do."

Toby leaned in, his feet shuffling like a quarterback, waiting for instructions for the game-winning play.

"I'll check on Nicci while you get dressed. Then I want you to go to the clinic and round up a wheelchair. Meet us at the terrace doors."

Toby shot ahead and opened the door. "I'll hurry."

Brock trailed behind Toby to their bedroom, then knocked on the bathroom door. "Nicci? It's Dr. Brock."

The door whipped open. Nicci stood on a pile of towels with a hand splayed across her large round stomach. "I'm so sorry to have to wake you."

Brock gave her a reassuring smile. "I was already awake. Are you ready to have this baby?"

She nodded, then doubled over, gripping his hand.

"Let yourself relax. Breathe in through your nose and out through your mouth." He checked his watch, then demonstrated, breathing with her. "Good. Just like that, each time a contraction hits."

Toby stuck his head around the bathroom door. He was now wearing athletic shorts and white Nikes but the same T-shirt. "Everything okay?"

"Everything is good. Find Sonja and let her know we're on our way."

Toby nodded and took off, plowing into Miriam. "Oops. My bad." He gripped her shoulders to steady her, then took off again.

She placed her hand over her chest and laughed, catching Brock's eye. "Even on the ground, he is flying. How is our little mama?"

"I'm glad you're here." Brock stepped aside so Miriam could crowd in. "Nicci's doing great. Toby's the one I might have to sedate."

Nicci doubled over again, unable to talk.

Brock checked his watch again, and as soon as Nicci straightened, he nudged her to the door. "Toby's getting a wheelchair. Let's start walking that way and meet him on the terrace."

The number of babies he'd delivered since arriving in Angola was relatively few. Angolese women were stout and hardy and had been known to deliver in the afternoon and help cook the evening meal on the same day. Something Ellie referred to as "hardcore."

Nicci was no different, although Brock definitely would put his foot down if she tried to help with their evening meal.

Three hours later, Elzira Pearl Williams made her appearance, apparently getting her size from her mother and her lung capacity from her father.

Miriam cleaned, measured, and weighed her with quiet efficiency, then handed the little bundle back to Nicci.

She held her baby close and slid her finger across the

tiny cheek. "So smooth and beautiful."

Toby stood beside the bed and brushed Nicci's ridged cheek with the back of his fingers. "Just like her momma."

A sacred and tender moment that sent a hush through the room and an unexpected longing through Brock's chest. He glanced up and smiled at Miriam. *The only thing that could make this day more perfect would be to have Joy standing here, too.* He eased closer and slung his arm around Toby's shoulder. "I'll leave you now."

Toby turned, his eyes bloodshot and full of tears. "Thanks for everything, Doc."

"It was my joy and privilege." He leaned over and covered Nicci's hand with his own. "Get some rest. I'll check back a little later."

Nicci tore her eyes away from Elzira and gave him a grateful look.

He wadded up his scrubs and tossed them into the basket, then left the clinic through the side doors. The clouds hung low in the sky making the possibility of a sunrise almost next to nothing. But he headed to the terrace anyway, if only to spend some time alone with God.

It would be a little past midnight in Washington. He sent Ellie a text, hoping it wouldn't wake her. *It's a girl!*

Within two minutes, he grinned and swiped the screen to answer. "You're up?"

"Yes. Twins are restless tonight. Okay. Give me details."

He laughed. "Elzira Pearl Williams ..."

Ellie interrupted before he could continue. "Elvira?"

"Elzira with a *z*. It means consecrated to God. Pearl came from Toby's grandmother."

"I love it!"

"She measured forty-three centimeters. Uh ... that would be seventeen inches, and she weighed a little over two kilograms."

"Six pounds. I remember when the twins finally reached six pounds. They looked huge."

"Elzira doesn't look huge. Such an adorable baby. I wish you could've seen Nicci when she stroked the baby's smooth cheek."

"Aww. How sweet. I can't wait to see everybody. I'll let you know when we nail down a date."

"Perfect. By the way, if you're not too sleepy, I have more good news."

"I'm always up for some good news."

"You'll really like this. Are you sitting down?"

"Yes! Tell me!"

"Your mom has become a Christian."

A brief pause followed by the sound of a door closing, then an ear-piercing squeal. "Oh. My. Goodness. Are you serious?"

He laughed. "Yes."

"I have no words. How did it happen? Tell me everything."

"Two nights ago, I told your mom the whole story of Jesus. Honey, it was amazing. She listened without interrupting and seemed to be taking it all in. But when I asked her if she wanted to pray and make that commitment, she balked. So, you can imagine my surprise the next morning when she joined me to watch the sunrise. That's when she told me she'd prayed."

"Unbelievable." There was another brief pause, then Ellie continued, her voice back to normal, "Do you think I should call her or wait until she tells me herself?"

Brock leaned forward, watching two ants struggle to drag a dead beetle across the concrete. "It's hard to say. Hold off and let me think about it. She seemed hesitant to talk about it. I'll keep you posted."

He heard Ellie release a long sigh. "I still can't believe it. I've prayed for her, but I really didn't think she'd ever come to Christ. God is so good, in spite of my weak faith."

"My sentiments exactly, sweetheart."

"When do you think she'll return to Texas?"

Brock hesitated before replying. Now was probably not the best time to tell her about his latest crazy idea. "I don't know. She mentioned leaving before the real monsoons hit."

"Hmm. I hope she plans to stay at least until after our visit."

"As far as I know, she does. By then, she'll almost be completely back to normal." He moved the subject to safer territory. "Now. Your turn. How are things with you?"

"Twins are doing great. Nick got his first big boy haircut."

"You took him to a barber? Did he cry?"

"No, on both counts. Eric cut his hair, and I'm the one who cried."

Brock chuckled. "How's Eric's job situation?"

"He's decided to keep training recruits for now, but he's doing something on the side. I'll let him tell you about it when he comes. Eric's a lot like you, Dad. He's always looking for ways to help people. He's spent a lot of time with Joy's son."

"Really?" He tried to sound nonchalant. "How is David?"

"Better than when he first moved here. Eric plays racquetball with him three days a week. David's started going to our church, and we usually eat Sunday dinner over at Joy's house."

"I'm glad to hear it. Does he still live with his mom?"

"No. He actually lives in an apartment not too far from us. He's a nice guy. You'd like him, Dad."

"Yes, I'm sure I would." If he ever got the chance to see Joy again and meet her son. "Well, I'll let you go. When you and Eric get here, I have something to run by you."

"Tell me now. I'm too wired to go back to sleep."

Brock chuckled, happy to keep the conversation going. "I've been thinking of building some more houses in the field behind your house."

"That's a great idea! Who gets to live there?"

"I'm still working on that."

"Okay. We'll talk about it when we come. I have a

feeling our two weeks in Africa won't be long enough."

"I know, honey. But we'll certainly make the most of it."

"Yes, we will. Give my love to Toby and Nicci and … oh, dear. What was her name?"

"Elzira."

"I'll say it ten times a day and maybe by November, I won't forget."

"Just ask Eric. He never forgets anything."

"True. Hey, if you get time, send some photos of Elzira." Ellie said the name with emphasis. "I'll show them to Joy. She's always hungry for news from the compound."

His heart went to his throat, and on impulse he asked, "How is she?"

"Joy's fine, Dad. She comes over almost every day to help out. I don't know how I'd manage without her."

He smiled but didn't respond.

"Why don't you call and talk to her yourself. You could tell her all about the baby. She'd love that."

He'd love it, too. That was the problem. It would stir up longings he'd fought so hard to keep at bay. "Maybe it'd be better for you to tell her. But I'll send some pictures."

He heard Ellie expel a long sigh. "I still don't quite understand, but I respect your decision. Can I at least tell her you said hello?"

"Yes." He hesitated, then added. "And that I'm happy to hear David's doing better."

"Deal." Ellie sounded appeased. "I'm going to check

on the twins and try to get a little sleep before they wake again."

"Sounds good, honey. Kiss the babies and give my love to Eric."

"I will! Love you, Dad."

The screen went dark. Brock stood and stretched his tight back muscles, then ventured off the terrace to the field. The rain-soaked grass darkened his soft-soled loafers as he walked behind Toby and Nicci's house. He scanned the vacant field, picturing a line of small one-bedroom houses, much like bungalows. A massive building project that would take quite a bit of planning. He'd have to run the idea by Neal and Dottie first since they had agreed to move here permanently and take over the mission. He had planned to work another physician in at some point considering he was now sixty-seven, but the episode with Rozalynde sped up the process.

No official announcement had been made, and other than Moses and Neal, and their wives, no one else knew. Ellie would take the news hard until she realized the change would make it possible for him to visit Washington more often.

Nicci would struggle with it, too, but she had bonded with Dottie and Kasemba even more than he'd hoped. And now, with a daughter to care for and love, Nicci would be all right.

He hadn't quite worked out the other problem in his life. Somehow, he'd envisioned helping Roz recuperate from her stroke, then sending her back to Dallas to resume her life. But God had a way of taking his plans and turning them upside down and inside out until the final outcome was nothing like he imagined it to be.

What God seemed to be asking him to do now was almost unthinkable.

But it would take two miracles to pull off: The first, for him to ask Roz to marry him again ... and the second, for Roz to actually say *yes.*

CHAPTER 42

Joy grabbed Ellie's phone and was halfway up the stairs before she realized it was Brock calling. She barreled into Ellie's bedroom and called through the bathroom door. "Your dad's on the phone."

"Great." Ellie hollered back. "Talk to him while I finish up."

"Hello, Brock?" She placed her hand over her chest and tried not to sound so breathless. "Ellie's in the shower. She said for me to talk to you until she gets out … but I can give her a message if …"

"No hurry. How have you been, Joy?"

"I'm doing very well." She backed up to the bed and sat, keeping an eye on the bathroom door. "David moved into an apartment. I guess Ellie told you when you talked a couple days ago."

"She did. She also said Eric and he play racquetball."

"Eric's been wonderful." Early afternoon sunlight streamed through open blinds and made horizontal bars on the carpet. Joy flexed and pointed her foot, tracing the shadows with her toe. "David still has some low moments, but on the whole, I think he's going to get through this." If she were completely honest, she would have to say the same about herself. "And how are you doing?" Before he could answer, she added, "How are Nicci and Elzira?"

"They're doing great. I wish you could—"

He paused leaving her to fill in the rest. *Be here? See the baby?* The mellow sound of his voice pierced her heart and made her want to respond with the same longing in her tone. Joy folded in her lips and tightened her grip on the phone, pressing it hard against her ear.

Finally, Brock inhaled and continued, his tone now back to normal. "I think they're planning to visit Toby's mother at Christmas. I'm sure they'll spend some time with Eric and Ellie, too. They'd love to see you again. Oh, and here's something you might be interested in hearing. We're expanding our ministry."

"Really?" She crossed her legs and shifted away from the bathroom door. Ellie could take as long as she wanted. "Going to more outlying villages?"

Brock gave a low chuckle. "Even better. We're praying about starting an orphanage. In fact, we're drawing up plans to build some bungalows in the field behind Toby's house."

Joy closed her eyes and imagined them nestled against the tree line at the edge of the field. "I love it. Kasemba is somehow involved, isn't she?"

"How'd you guess?"

Joy smiled to herself. "I've seen her in action. Kasemba's like a child magnet." The bathroom door clicked opened, and Ellie emerged fully clothed.

353

"Here's Ellie. Good talking to you, Brock. Please give my love to everyone." Without waiting for a reply, she handed the phone to Ellie.

"Hey, Dad. Thanks for returning my call." Ellie tugged Joy's sleeve and mouthed *don't go.* "We'll be flying in on November fifth ... That's right. We both wanted to celebrate our anniversary in Africa."

Joy smiled and with a polite wave, left the room, closing the door behind her. She paused in the hallway and took a deep breath, her heart thumping hard in her chest. One brief conversation with Brock had knocked her back to square one. But it was worth it, and the memory still warmed her heart as she crossed the hall and eased the nursery door open. Nicky stuck his head up like a turtle and saw her before she could dart out of view.

She tried but failed to reach him before his wails woke his sister. Bek gripped the bars of her crib and pulled herself up. Her tousled brown curls looked like a bird nest in a windstorm. She raised her arms and started to cry.

A wet brown stain on Nicky's leg gave him priority status. Joy swooped him out of the crib and held him away from her body as she transferred him to the changing table. Bek's cries amped up, and Joy worked faster, talking over her shoulder. "I'm coming, princess."

Ellie swept into the room. "Me, too, Dad. Take care."

Joy managed a quick glance, then focused again on Nicky who seemed to be all legs and arms in an attempt to flip over onto his stomach. "Maybe I should give him a quick bath."

"Good idea. Bek's a mess, too." Ellie plopped Bek next to Nicky. "If you'll start the bath, I'll get them ready."

"Deal." Raising children was definitely for the young. Joy zipped into the bathroom and bent over the tub, letting the water stream through her fingers until the temperature was right. "Ready," she called over her shoulder.

Ellie came with a naked baby in each arm. Joy took Nicky and set him in the water next to Bek. "Good thing they love their baths."

Ellie knelt on the floor, propping her forearms on the side of the tub. "I know. This summer when they were teething, I must've bathed them six times a day."

Joy grabbed the low stool they kept in the bathroom just to spare her knees. "Teething diarrhea is the worst."

"It wasn't so much the loose bowels, it was the loud crying. Baths were the only way I could get any peace." She grinned and held up her thumb and forefinger. "I came this close to asking Dad to put you on the next plane back to Washington."

Nicky slapped the water with both hands, sending a spray over the side that made wet splotches on Joy's navy slacks. She grabbed a towel and placed it on her lap. How different her life would've been had she stayed here instead of going to Africa for a year. She would never have gotten dengue. Or fallen in love with Brock Whitfield. Two things that seemed to require a long recovery.

"It's crazy and a little sad." Ellie scooped water in her

355

palm and poured it over Bek's back. "But I feel much closer to you than to my own mother."

Joy's expression softened. "That's sweet of you to say." Thoughts of her own daughter pierced her soul. Had she lived, Vannah would've been thirty-eight, only one year older than Ellie. Comparisons were inevitable. Vannah would've made a wonderful mother, too, but died long before she got the chance. Unbidden tears pricked her eyes as she reached for Ellie's wet hand. "Now that your mom has Jesus, I have a feeling she'll realize how blessed her life really is. Who knows? You may grow much closer to your mom than you ever thought possible."

Ellie nodded, though from the droop of her mouth, she didn't believe it. "That's certainly what happened with my dad. It took me over thirty years to find out what an amazing man my father is."

"Yes." Joy held out her finger for Nicky to grab. "Your dad is one of those rare men who is fully surrendered to the will of God." She switched gears before she choked up. "I guess we'd better bathe these babies before they wrinkle up like little prunes." She tugged the washcloth from Nicky's other hand and poured body wash on the center, then handed the bottle to Ellie.

"Thanks." Ellie took the bottle and set it in the corner, apparently in no hurry to bathe Bek. "I'm going to say this only once, then I'll never bring it up again." Ellie gave her a sideways glance. "Unless you want me to."

Joy raised her eyebrows and waited, knowing in the pit

of her stomach what Ellie was about to say.

"I know how much you and Dad care for each other. I'm really sorry things didn't work out."

Joy stopped washing Nicky and looked up at Ellie. "Thank you. I'm sorry, too, but I'm very thankful I had the opportunity to work with him and get to know him." She returned her focus to Nicky and scrubbed his already clean back. "Like you said, he's an amazing man. Okay, this one's squeaky clean." She shifted and started to bathe Bek.

"You're amazing, too."

Joy gave a self-deprecating chuckle and shook her head. "If you only knew how fragile I am most of the time."

"You never show it." Ellie took the washcloth from Joy and finished washing Bek. "I think I owe you an apology. I might have taken longer than necessary to give you and Dad a chance to talk."

Joy laughed outright. "I did notice, but don't apologize. I enjoyed our chat." She sat on the side of the tub with a towel spread across her knees.

Ellie lifted Nicky out of the water and placed him on Joy's lap. "Will you ever go back?"

"I doubt it. At least, not in the foreseeable future."

Ellie picked up Bek and swaddled her in a pink towel, pulling the cuffed corner over her damp head. "I guess that means you won't consider going with us when we visit next month."

Joy smiled and shook her head, even though she'd considered the possibility at least a hundred times since she'd found out about their visit. Definitely not something that would be good for her. Or for Brock. She cuddled Nicky close to her chest, breathing in his sweet, clean smell. "But would you do something while you're there?"

Ellie's expression sobered, and she kissed the top of Bek's head. "Of course."

"Give your mom a chance. I'd give anything to be able to spend an afternoon with my daughter, the way you and I do almost every day. Now that your mom's a Christian, spend time with her. Get to know her like you've never been able to before. Maybe even tell her about how you came to faith. But don't expect her to have it all down pat yet. This is all new to her, and she'll need time to grow just like we did. But I'm praying for God to do something really spectacular in all of your lives."

Deep in her heart where it really mattered, Joy knew she spoke the truth, even if it meant losing Brock forever.

CHAPTER 43

Roz sat still while Miriam worked magic on her hair, pulling it up in a French braid. It was her favorite way to wear her hair. Made her face look thin and sculpted and gave her an overall younger look.

"Today, you must look very pretty for your family who is coming to see you."

"Yes," Roz answered without moving her head.

"I will braid ribbons into your hair and make you look colorful like a white-skinned African princess."

"*Ya. Ya.* I would like that."

Miriam leaned in and tilted her head. "Listen to you talk my talk."

Roz smiled and sat a little straighter in the chair. "Teach me more."

"*Sim.*" Miriam pushed Roz's head forward. "Hold your head like this. *Kuyava.* Good. Now tell me something you wish to know."

"Hmm. How would you say money?"

"*Kumbu.*"

"Kumbu." Roz repeated. "And how would you say somebody with money."

"*Mandrov.*"

"Mandrov. And how about someone who gossips."

"*Curibota*. No. That is not the word. It is *Zongola*."

"Zongola." Her lips thinned in a smug smile. A word to keep handy when she returned to Texas. Her neck started to ache. "Are you almost finished?"

"*Sim.*"

"Why do you sometimes say *Sim* and sometimes say *Ya Ya?* Don't they both mean yes?"

Miriam laughed. "You are a smart one. *Sim* is the Portuguese way to say yes. *Ya Ya* is Angolan slang for yes, yes."

"We have slang words where I'm from."

Miriam's hands stilled. "Is it so? Teach me your English slang."

Roz raised her head, thankful for the break. "It's called Southern slang."

"Would Dr. Brock know this Southern slang if I talk it to him?"

"*Ya. Ya.* Most definitely. The next time you see him, instead of saying 'How are you?' say 'How y'all doing?'"

"How yaw'll doing."

Roz clapped her hands. "Perfect. I hope I'm there when you say it."

"How yaw'll doing."

"Say it a little faster. 'How y'all doing?'"

"How y'all doing?"

"*Ya. Ya. Kuyava!*" Roz had that feeling inside again. That good feeling that bubbled up like fizz in champagne.

She'd first noticed it after she'd prayed to Jesus to come into her life. Sometimes it was stronger, like now. Other times, it felt like it was there, just lying dormant.

Miriam finished braiding Roz's hair. "Come see how beautiful you look."

Roz followed her into the bathroom and stared at her reflection with tears filling her eyes.

"Why is it that you cry? Do you not like the ribbons?"

Roz turned and grabbed Miriam's rough, leathery hand. "I am crying because I didn't think I'd ever like the way I look. I feel like God has given me my face back."

"Yes. Yes. It is God who has done this. Do you know this to be true, my linda Kamba, my beautiful friend?"

"I know." Roz dabbed her tears without smearing her mascara. "I prayed for a miracle, and God gave it to me."

Miriam grabbed Roz, smashing her against her chest. "*Louvado seja Jesus.*"

Roz stiffened, mostly worried about her hair. "What did you say? Something about Jesus?"

"I say, Praise be to Jesus! It is wonderful to see that you are growing in your faith."

"Maybe a little." Roz turned back to the mirror and surveyed the damage. At least the ribbons were still intact. She patted some stray hairs back into place. "It still feels as unfamiliar as the dialect you've been teaching me."

"You are a baby Christian, a little over a month old, like our sweet Elzira. But look how you both have grown. Already, you give praise to God for the miracle of His healing." Miriam smiled and placed her hand over Roz's heart. "Jesus now lives here. He will help you with His truth, just like I help you with my language."

"That's what Brock said."

"What did I say?"

Roz whirled. Brock stood in her bedroom, still dressed in scrubs with a surgical mask hanging loosely around his neck. "Brock Whitfield! How long have you been standing there eavesdropping on us?"

He threw both hands up in surrender. "I just walked in. I promise."

"Dr. Brock." Miriam gave Roz a knowing smirk. "How y'all doing?"

Brock's face crumbled in laughter as he cut his glance over to Roz. "What have you been teaching her?"

Roz returned his smile and shrugged. Sharing a joke with Brock was new territory, for both of them.

Miriam answered, sounding very pleased with herself. "It is an English dialect called Southern slang. Have you heard of this before?"

Brock's eyes were still crinkled with amusement. "Oh, yes. Many times. You'll have to try it out again when Ellie comes. She'll love it." Brock touched Roz's arm. "I'm going to take a quick shower, then I'd like to talk something over with you before the kids get here."

The bubbly feeling in her chest went away. "It's not something bad, is it?"

A strange look came over Brock's face. "I hope you

won't think it's bad. We'll see."

Brock was going to ask Roz to marry him. Today. Before Ellie arrived. Ellie, who, with all the best intentions, might try to talk him out of it.

His stomach felt queasy even though he was now certain this was what God wanted him to do. This was his final and complete surrender to the will of God.

It had taken him a while to get there. In the first few weeks with Roz, he'd still struggled, and underneath, he'd harbored the secret hope that one day God would let him go back to Joy.

Today, he would lay aside that dream forever.

No angel was going to stay his hand. Today, he would unconditionally commit to Rozalynde, but it was going to be all right. He could be content to live out the rest of his days with Roz because God, not any person, was the one who filled the longings of his heart.

He didn't exactly love Roz, but he had grown fond of her. Her mood swings were far less frequent and severe, and her tendency to be vain and self-absorbed didn't bother him anymore. Maybe because she seemed to be trying to do better.

Roz didn't love him either. He had no illusions about that. But in a crazy way, he knew she was fond of him, too. She no longer seemed to stiffen when he entered her room. In fact, she seemed glad to see him.

Whether she was fond enough to give their marriage another shot remained to be seen.

Brock finished his shower and dressed in the clothes Ellie had sent via Eric for his birthday. White long-sleeved shirt, khaki slacks, and burgundy and tan checked sports coat. He even dabbed on his favorite cologne. It was a special day for more reasons than one. He slipped on his lightweight brown loafers and checked himself out in the mirror. Their daughter had good taste.

He crossed the hall to her room and found Roz in the bathroom studying herself in the mirror. Her recovery from the stroke had been nothing less than a miracle. One would have to look very closely to detect any lingering weakness on the right side of her face. Something Roz apparently was doing now as she leaned in, scrutinizing every inch. She gave a little jump and straightened as he eased behind and smiled at her reflection. "You look lovely, Roz."

"Brock!" She pressed her hand against her chest and met his gaze without turning around. "That's the second time today you've sneaked up on me."

"Sorry. That really wasn't my intention."

"Well, don't do it again." Her smile took some of the sting out of her words.

He took his phone from his pocket and aimed it her way. "Stay just like that, looking at your reflection."

As soon as he snapped the picture, she turned and grabbed the phone. "Let me see."

Their heads almost collided as they both leaned in to

view the shot.

"Do you know what I love about this shot?" Brock said, angling the phone for her to see. "It captures you twice. Your right profile here and your full face in the reflection."

What he said must have pleased her. The corners of her mouth curved into a slight smile as she stared at the picture.

"We should've gotten some before shots of your face when it was drooping."

"Are you crazy?" She shoved the phone back toward him. "I looked hideous. Why would we ever want to take a picture of that?"

"So everyone would know how far you'd come."

She gave him a scathing look and spoke to his reflection in the mirror. "I don't want everyone to know. That was the whole point in my coming here, if you recall."

Brock smiled and reached for her hand. "Let's get out of this bathroom. There's something I want to show you."

"What?"

"You'll see."

"Brock, I hate it when you deliberately leave me hanging."

He tugged her through the bedroom and out through the French doors. "This way."

"Across the field? You know I don't like walking out there."

"Humor me."

"Fine." She hitched up the sarong she was wearing. "But I'm not going where it's all muddy."

"Fair enough." He slowed his pace to hers and sneaked a sideways glance, not sure if she really was annoyed or just pretending to be. "By the way, that color looks really nice on you."

"I thought so, too. Kind of a melon-salmon color. Miriam wove some matching ribbons into my braid." She touched the side of her hair. "What do you think?"

"I think you look very pretty, Roz. That's why I took your picture."

"Then I should take your picture. You look very dashing in your sport coat." Roz stepped around a clump of tall weeds. "How much farther do we have to go?"

"This is far enough."

They were standing in the middle of the field behind Toby and Nicci's house. The midday sun was beating down through a haze of humidity, but the temperature remained moderately pleasant. "I thought you'd like to see where we plan to build some staff bungalows."

She lowered her chin. "Why?"

Roz was clearly in one of her negative moods. It'd been a mistake to bring her out here, he could see that now. Maybe he should shelve his plan to propose until another day. "Let's go sit on that bench."

"Who's the idiot that put a bench so far from the buildings?"

He felt his jaw tighten. "Mac was the one who brought

it, and I was the idiot who asked him to."

"Oh." She stared at him, then resumed walking. "Well, I'm sure you must have had a reason."

He fell into step beside her, already regretting his terse response. He gripped her elbow and maneuvered her around a clump of weeds. "Next month, we'll break ground to build five bungalow-type cottages, and I wanted to test out how the sunrise would look from this vantage point."

She pointed to the left of Toby's house. "Is that east?"

He nodded. "The sun rises between those two hills beyond that far line of trees."

Her expression softened. "Looks like this would be the perfect spot."

"I thought so, too."

He led her to the wooden bench that until last week had been beside the back steps of the clinic. He wiped the seat with his handkerchief, then gestured for her to sit. Brock sat next to her and closed his eyes, inhaling deeply. The air smelled different during the rainy season. The dense humidity and abundance of rain brought out the rich, pungent scents of decaying leaves, red dirt, mosses, and wild grasses the same way Nicci's herbs brought out flavors in the food she prepared. The result was an earthy, musky scent he loved.

Roz spoke, her voice tinged with her typical sarcasm. "When did you get all crazy about a sunrise?"

He opened his eyes and looked at her. "In prison." He could leave it there but decided to explain. "It was a very dark time in my life. One morning, just as the sun was coming up, I prayed and turned my life over to Jesus. Light flooded into my cell and into my heart." He shifted toward her and took her hand. "The sunrise took on a whole new meaning for me after that. It was like God was saying it was a new day for me."

Roz looked away but didn't pull her hand from his.

"What are you thinking, Roz?"

A tear inched down her cheek. She used her other hand to wipe it away.

"Please … I'd like to know."

She shrugged. "Until this moment, I'd never given one thought to how you felt in prison. It must've been terrible."

"It was." He admitted, touched more than he could say by the unexpected sympathy in her tone. "But I deserved it. That and so much more."

Not too long ago, Roz would've agreed.

"Roz, I want to tell you again how sorry I am for being such a terrible husband. I wish I could undo so many things I've done in my life."

She gave a heavy sigh and looked away. "We both made mistakes, Brock. Let's just call it even."

"I'd like that very much, but I'd like to take it one step further."

She eyed him suspiciously. "What are you saying?"

"I'm asking you to marry me again."

"What?" She jerked her hand out of his grasp. "Are you crazy?"

"No. I'm actually saner than when you married me the first time."

She glared at him, her lips pinched in a tight line. "Just like that? You expect me to pick up where we left off and be your wife again ... and all that might entail? Have you lost your mind?" She looked up at the sky, her expression as dark as the clouds hovering over them, then whirled back with fire in her eyes. "I don't need or want your pity."

"I know you don't." He'd forgotten how easily she could get him sidetracked. He took a deep breath and tried again. "Listen. I made a mess of it the first time. I'd like a chance to make things right and be a better husband. No strings. No expectations."

Roz picked a piece of fuzz from the folds of her sarong and flicked it into the air, an angry scowl on her face.

In the distance, he heard the mating call of the black swallow, a hauntingly beautiful sound, heard only during the rainy season. Brock shifted and scanned the woods. What were the odds of hearing this particular bird at this moment? God indeed had a sense of humor.

Finally, she turned to him, her expression bleak. "Face it, Brock. I'd never make it here, and you'd never make it in Texas. We'd end up hating each other, just like last time."

"You're wrong, Roz. We both have God in our lives. It won't be like last time." She opened her mouth, but he held up his hand to stop her. "Don't answer today. It's a lot to think about. Give yourself some time to sort things out."

His phone pinged. He slipped it from his pocket and read the text. "Toby says Eric and Ellie and the kids are loaded into the helicopter and should be here in about an hour."

He tightened his grip on the edge of the bench and started to rise, but Roz tugged him back. "Brock, wait."

He stilled and looked at her.

"Just because I ..." She closed her eyes and pressed her fingers against her forehead, then tipped her head back to him. "I am grateful for all you've done."

His expression softened. "I know." He smiled and reached for her hand that now lay limp on her lap. "Let's grab some lunch before the kids get here."

CHAPTER 44

After dinner, Brock and Roz finally got Eric and Ellie and the twins all to themselves. The rain held off, so the group went out on the terrace. Brock held a chair for Roz, then settled in his usual chair and held up his hands. "Okay, I'm ready. Hand me one."

Ellie and Eric exchanged looks, and by some telepathic agreement, Ellie handed Bek over to Brock. "Here you go."

Roz spoke up. "I guess I'll take the other one."

Eric swooped Nicky up high in the air before stepping over Brock and handing him to Roz.

Ellie let out a gasp which made everyone else jump. "Look! A shooting star!"

Brock glanced up in time to see the tail as it fizzled and disappeared. "I think that was yours, honey. Make a wish."

"All my wishes have already come true." Ellie relaxed against the back of the seat with a contented sigh. "You don't know how I've missed this place. I feel like I'm home."

Bek twisted in Brock's lap, and tapped his face, grabbing a handful of his beard. He gently pried open her fingers and kissed them. "Have the twins learned any words yet?"

"They jabber to each other all the time. It's like they have their own language." Ellie smirked at Eric. "We had this running bet whether they'd say Ma-Ma or Da-Da first. Guess who won." She crooked her thumb and pointed to Eric. "But I think he cheated."

"Me? How did I cheat?"

"Oh, don't give me that innocent look, mister. I heard you coaxing Bek when you thought I wasn't listening. I wouldn't be surprised if you had some kind of speaker hidden under their cribs playing 'Da Da' over and over while they sleep."

Eric raised his eyebrows and shot Brock an amused look. "See what I put up with?"

Brock chuckled, and Bek craned her head around to stare up at him, her big blue eyes making her look like a little bird. He folded in his lips and said with exaggerated emphasis, "Pop … py. Pop … py."

"What do you want them to call you, Mom?"

"Oh, I don't know. As long as it isn't one of those old grandmother names like Maw-Maw."

"How about GiGi?" Eric ventured. "We could tell everyone it stands for Glamorous Grandma."

"Ooh, we like that one, don't we, Nicky?" Roz took Nicky's hands and clapped them together. "Yes, we do. Yes, we do."

It was a surreal moment, with him sitting on the terrace

next to Roz, each holding a grandchild. A moment as rare and fleeting as the shooting star Ellie had seen. Brock smiled his thanks to God, then turned to Eric. "Ellie said you're doing something on the side. Catch us up on all your news."

Eric leaned forward, tapping his fingers in front of him. "I decided not to train for the Chaplain's position. I weighed the pros and cons and did a lot of praying. Bottom line: Training recruits is my passion. I love it—"

Ellie placed her hand on Eric's shoulder. "And, he's good at it."

"So, I found a way to be involved with a ministry-type project without giving up my job."

"That's even better," Brock said while bouncing Bek on his good knee. "Best of both worlds, so to speak."

Eric reached for Ellie's hand. "We thought so, too. It's called Third Option. It's specifically geared for families of fallen CIA agents and offers critical support to families that lose loved ones in the line of duty. We offer resiliency programs and provide counseling and financial support, basically anything they need."

"When Eric found out about this organization, he signed up and tracked down the family of one of his mentors. A guy named Stuart Harris."

Brock remembered the name. "Was he the one who was killed in Honduras?"

"That's right. And because of the nature of their service, often their deaths get swept under the carpet. This organization is changing all that. Stu's dad was so thankful I was able to reach out to him and bring him some closure."

Nicky started fidgeting, and Brock whispered to Roz. "Want to switch?"

For reply, Roz handed Nicky over, plopping him next to Bek.

"Here, I'll take him." Eric reached across Brock's lap and hoisted Nicky up. "Come here, buddy."

"Well, Eric, that sounds wonderful. I'm so proud of you. To think, not that long ago you were in Central America, closing in on the leak responsible for Stu's death."

Eric smiled and nodded. "Look at me now. I'm married to the most amazing woman on the planet and the proud father of twins. Only God could've done something like that. And speaking of amazing, Ellie now has a part-time job."

Ellie chimed in. "I was volunteering at the Crisis Pregnancy Center. When they found out I'm a licensed nurse practitioner, they hired me on the spot. I told them I could only work three afternoons a week. They were so desperate, they were willing to be flexible. I absolutely love it, and Joy graciously comes over and watches the twins so I don't have to worry about leaving them."

Brock ignored Roz's sharp intake of breath at the mention of Joy's name and kept the smile he had plastered on his face.

"Your daughter probably won't tell you, so I will. She

funnels most of her paycheck back into buying supplies for the Center."

Brock grinned at Ellie. "I'm not surprised."

"I learned from the best." Ellie waved her hand in dismissal. "That's our big news. Now, it's your turn."

Brock hesitated and cut his gaze over to Roz. Even though he'd already told Ellie himself, this would be the perfect opportunity for Roz to make a public declaration of her newfound faith in Christ. But she didn't speak or even look up from her folded hands.

Ellie filled in the awkward silence. "Joy mentioned you were going to start an orphanage. I can't wait to hear details."

Brock felt Roz's laser-like stare bore a hole into the side of his face. "Yes, we're very excited about that. In fact, tomorrow I'll show you where we plan to build the bungalows I told you about. Kasemba is going to be the one running it."

Ellie laughed. "I met her this afternoon. Joy told me Kasemba would fall in love with the twins. Boy, was she right. I think I'll have a lot of help while I'm here."

Brock inwardly cringed and reminded himself he had nothing to feel guilty about. He chanced a look at Roz. Her lips were clamped in a tight ugly twist as she studied one of her fingernails. Definitely not be the time to announce he'd asked Roz to marry him again.

He straightened and took a fortifying breath. His other news might hit Ellie equally as hard. "I decided to ask Neal and Dottie to stay here on a permanent basis."

"That's great, Dad. I was a little worried about who was going to help you now."

Brock nodded, relieved Ellie didn't mention Joy's name again. "Honey, he won't just be helping. I've asked Neal to take over the ministry."

"What?" Ellie shrieked, making Nicky start to wail. "Sorry, buddy." She took him from Eric and stood, bouncing him on her hip. "Does that mean you'll be leaving Africa? Dad, you can't. This is your passion. Wait a minute." She stilled, her eyes huge. "Are you all right? Is there something wrong I don't know about?"

Brock shot up his hand and shook his head. "No, honey. I'm fine. I'm just looking down the road. Now that I have grandchildren, I wanted to spend more time in Washington."

She pressed her palm to her chest and smiled. "That part I like, as long as you don't leave the ministry altogether."

"No. I'll still be very much involved."

"That's a relief, but it'll take me a while to get used to the idea." Ellie turned to Eric and blew out her breath. "We need to get the twins in bed."

Brock kissed the top of Bek's head and handed her off to Eric. "Sleep as late as you want to in the morning. We have two weeks to catch up."

"I wish, but the twins take after you. Up before dawn." Ellie eased around the patio table to give Roz a hug. "I'd like to spend some time with you tomorrow."

Roz nodded. "Just don't make it too early."

"I won't. Kasemba is coming around eleven to play with the twins. How about then? We have some catching up to do."

Brock stood and gave them all a hug. "Eric, tomorrow Mac said he'd take you hunting if it isn't too wet."

"It's never too wet to go hunting."

"Next time, we're coming in June when it doesn't rain a drop." Ellie stifled a yawn. "Okay, we're going to bed now. Good night."

The terrace became very quiet after the Templeton family left. Brock turned to Roz. "Ready for bed?"

"I need a pill, Brock."

Brock nodded. "You can take a melatonin."

"I need an Ambien." She said flatly, then stood and walked toward the building.

Brock rushed ahead and opened the door. His big mistake had been to mention the studies that showed Ambien effective in stroke recovery. He preferred not to give it to her, but she wouldn't sleep without it. Maybe the Ambien could help reset her sleep cycle, then he could wean her off it. He walked her to her bedroom door. "Get ready for bed. I'll bring your medicine."

At midnight, Brock was still up, reading and praying.

The familiar knock at the door was Ellie. He knew it

before she tentatively stuck her head in and asked, "Are you awake? I saw the light under your door and took a chance you would be."

He rose and gestured to the recliner while he took the straight-backed chair.

"No, Dad. I can't take your chair. I'll sit here."

He took her by the shoulders and nudged her to the recliner. "Please. I would rather have this chair."

"Every time I enter this room, I have a flashback."

He nodded and gazed around the room. "I remember that day like it was yesterday. It was just after sunrise. Remember? You and I were on the terrace when Toby flew Eric into the compound. Only God could've orchestrated events so perfectly to change so many lives."

"Especially Eric's." Ellie pulled her legs up to sit Indian style. "It's like God literally dropped my Prince Charming out of the sky."

Brock chuckled, then grabbed a couple of peppermints from the bedside table drawer and tossed one to Ellie. "You're up late, honey."

"The plight of motherhood, I'm afraid." She popped the mint into her mouth. "They usually sleep through the night, but they're not used to the travel bed we brought."

"I'm glad you're here. I wanted to give you more details about why I decided to hand the ministry over to Neal and Dottie."

"You don't have to. As long as I know it's not about your health, I'm totally for it."

He smiled and relaxed against the back of his chair. "That's good to know. Your approval means a lot to me ... which is why I think I need to talk to you about your mother and me."

Ellie leaned forward. "This sounds like something I won't like."

"Hear me out, then decide. I've asked your mom to marry me."

"What?" She stared at him, her eyes wide. "Why?"

The feeling of love for this child of his was so overwhelming it almost took his breath away. He prayed, pleading with God to help him make her understand. "Honey—"

She shook her head. "Don't try to tell me you've both fallen madly in love with each other." She swiped at the tear that ran down her cheek. "And Mom said, 'Yes'?"

"Not exactly." He rose and got some tissues from the bathroom and handed her the entire box. "She's thinking about it."

"I don't get it. Why do you have to sacrifice the rest of your life to marry her? From what you've told me, Mom doesn't like it here. You just wait, she'll draw you away from everything you love and suck the life out of you." She straightened, squaring her shoulders. "Wait a minute. Is this why you decided to hand everything over to Neal?"

Brock shook his head, but couldn't keep from smiling at the adorable picture she made even with her red nose and tear-streaked cheeks. She was barefooted and wore a T-shirt and pajama pants. Her hair hung in loose waves framing her face which had been scrubbed clean. She looked like a younger version of Roz but had a sweetness about her that Roz would never have.

He waited to see if there was more. There was.

"And I know you don't want me to bring this up, but what about Joy? I know she loves you more than Mom ever has or ever could."

"Has she told you so?" He asked, then immediately wished he hadn't.

"No. She's too much like you to bring up anything about her own feelings, but she can't hide the sadness even though she tries to. She misses you, Dad. She misses everything about this place. How can you walk away from a woman like that?"

"I told you once before, honey. Because God asked me to."

"Yes, I remember. But Mom's doing so much better. She's even a Christian now. You achieved everything you set out to accomplish. Isn't that enough?"

"I thought it would be." He answered honestly. "But after your mother arrived, God began to work on my heart. Ellie, I know you don't understand, but one day, you will. It's like God has given me a chance to become the husband I should've been the first time."

He could almost see the wheels turning inside her head.

"Are you sure it's God asking this of you and not an

attempt to make up for past sins?" She clamped her hand over her mouth. "I'm so sorry, Dad. I had no right to say that."

"Don't apologize, honey. Believe me, I've asked myself the same question. But I could never make up for my past sins. Only Jesus could've done that. And I feel like the woman who anointed Jesus' feet with costly ointment. I love Him so much because He forgave me so much."

Her mouth curved into a slight smile. "No one who knows you could ever doubt that you love Jesus." She gave him a direct look and asked point-blank, "But are you happy?"

He met her gaze without flinching and answered truthfully. "Not exactly."

She opened her mouth, but he raised his hand to stop her. "Let me explain. I may not feel especially happy, but I do feel joy. That's so much better than something as unpredictable as happiness. Happiness is like a firecracker. Or like that shooting star you saw earlier this evening. Exciting and beautiful but only for a moment, then it fizzles. I want something that will last and sustain me through life's dark moments. Honey, when I take my last breath on earth and go to meet God, I don't want to leave one thing undone that He's asked me to do. I want to finish well, with no regrets."

He slid his chair closer to hers and reached for her hand. "If she is willing, I'm going to marry your mother, but I don't want you to spend one second worrying about me. Who knows? It may not be as bad as you think it will be. Your mother's changing. Getting better. God's already done so much, and I'm excited to see what He's going to do next. I can promise you this. Whatever it is, it will be good."

He stood and extended his hand. "Now, come here and give your dad a hug."

She uncurled the pretzel shape of her legs and walked into his outstretched arms, sliding her hands around his waist. "I love you so much, Dad." She burrowed her face against his chest.

He placed his hand on the side of her head and pressed her close. "Feel better?"

She nodded. "I always feel better after talking with you. Thank you for letting me vent and talk it out. I hope you know I really do love Mom. It's just that I love you so much, too."

"I know, honey."

"Is there anything I can do to help you?"

"You could help me the most by spending time with your mother while you're here. I know she can be prickly on the outside, but she's actually more fragile than she appears."

Ellie nodded. "I had already planned to. Joy basically said the same thing before we left Washington." She raised her head and looked up at him. "It almost sounded like she was praying for you and Mom to get back together. Did you mention to Joy you were going to propose?"

"No." Brock swallowed hard. "I didn't discuss anything about your mom and me. But while we're on the subject, maybe it would be a good idea for you not to bring up Joy when you're with your mom."

"You told her about Joy?"

"I ... No. Joy wrote a note to me before she left. Your mom read it and had some ... questions."

Ellie's eyes grew huge. "I mentioned Joy tonight, didn't I? Was that why Mom was so quiet?"

"Your mom was tired." He gave her a reassuring smile, then walked with her to the door. "I just wanted you to know in case the subject came up."

"Good to know." She kissed his cheek and turned to go.

"Wait a minute, honey." He stepped over to the bedside table and grabbed a flashlight, then hurried back to the door. "Here you go."

"Thanks, Dad." She pressed the button on the end, flooding the darkened hallway with bright LED light. "You know me well."

He watched her pad noiselessly back to her room, then glanced across the hall. The course of the rest of his life lay behind that closed door.

After tonight, he had a pretty good idea what Roz's answer would be.

CHAPTER 45

Roz brushed aside the vertical blinds and stared listlessly at the rain-soaked terrace. Why did Brock have to spoil everything and ask her to marry him again?

She rubbed her throbbing temples, then slid her fingers down the smooth curve of her cheek. If only her decision-making skills had returned to normal as fast as her drooping face had.

She stepped away from the French doors and studied the tiny bedroom. The half bed, with the orange and red flowered bedspread Miriam had made. The leather recliner with signs of wear on the armrest. The braided rug on the concrete floor. In many ways, more home to her now than the palatial mansion she'd left behind in Texas.

At least, here she didn't have anything to prove. Maybe she should accept his proposal after all. She laughed to herself. Wouldn't that give the biddies back home something to gossip about.

There was a soft knock on the door. "Mom?" Ellie stepped in, her hair damp and loose around her shoulders.

Roz glanced at the clock on the bedside table. "Is it eleven already?"

"Not quite. Kasemba showed up as I was getting out

of the shower." Ellie hovered at the door. "Would you rather I come back later?"

Roz waved her hand in dismissal. "No, that's all right. I just have a little headache."

"So do I. How about walking down to the dining hall for some coffee?"

"Sounds good."

Ellie followed her into the hall. "I love your outfit. Miriam made a similar one for me."

Roz glanced down, smoothing the sides of her tunic with her hands. "They're like lounging pajamas. Very comfortable. Sometimes I wear the tunic with the yoga pants you sent me."

Ellie slowed her steps. "Hold up, Mom. I'm going to duck into my room and grab some ibuprofen."

"Get me some, too."

Ellie sat on the bed, rummaging through her purse. "I always get a headache when I sleep later than usual."

Roz stayed at the door. The tiny room was cluttered with luggage. Clothes and baby blankets were strewn over the recliner, and two travel-sized baby beds were shoved against the wall next to the bathroom.

"Sorry about the mess. I'm going to tidy up before Eric returns from his hunting trip. Clutter like this drives him crazy."

"So, why doesn't he clean it up himself?"

"He usually does." Ellie stood, bottle in hand. "He's so much help at home."

"I should hope so. And why didn't Toby and Nicci make room for you at their house instead of expecting you to crowd into this little room?"

"Mom." Ellie turned to her, a scowl on her face.

Roz raised her hands, palms out. "What? Your dad said the house was originally meant for you."

Ellie opened her mouth, then closed it and resumed walking. "I need coffee. And for the record, they begged us to stay with them, but we both agreed we'd rather stay closer to you and Dad."

Gracious. When did Ellie get so testy?

Neither spoke again until they entered the dining hall. Ellie placed the bottle of pills on the table and went to the sidebar. "Cream and sugar?"

Roz nodded and sat. "Eric went hunting in all this rain?"

"Nothing stops that man." Ellie returned with two Styrofoam cups. At least, the edge had left her voice, and she was smiling again. She sat and shook four pills into her hand, then shoved two across the table. "Here you go."

"Thanks." Roz took a tentative sip and scrunched up her face. "Too hot."

Ellie scraped back her chair. "I'll grab some water from the cooler."

"For heaven's sake, Ellie, quit flitting around. You're making me nervous."

Ellie paused midway to the cooler and pivoted back.

"Well, you're halfway there now. You might as well

get it."

Ellie nodded and headed back to the cooler. She returned, plopped two water bottles on the table, and sat.

"Thank you, but I could've gotten it myself."

Ellie downed two pills, then closed her eyes and blew out her breath.

Roz tried twice to twist the cap from her bottle. With gritted teeth, she tried again, twisting harder.

Ellie reached across the table. "Hand it to me."

Roz shook her head. "I can do it."

By now, the inside of her palm was raw. Her pulse revved, and the pounding behind her eyes intensified.

"Mom, let's swap. This one's already opened."

Roz jerked the bottle from Ellie's grasp, and before she knew what she was doing, she belted out a string of expletives and flung the bottle across the room, barely missing Ellie's head. "I'm not an invalid."

Ellie gave her a stricken look and scraped back her chair again, no doubt to get as far as possible from her mother.

Roz propped her elbows on the table and covered her face with her hands, feeling like the miserable wretch she was. What was wrong with her? She hadn't pitched a fit in weeks.

Seconds later, she felt a soft touch on her shoulder. "Mom?"

Roz dragged her hands from her face.

"I'm sorry." Ellie knelt beside her. "The last thing in

the world I wanted to do was make you feel like an invalid."

The kindness in her voice made Roz crumble even more, and she could no longer hold back the tears that had been welling up. "You know, you sound just like your father."

Ellie smiled and handed her a napkin. "Is that a good thing or a bad thing?"

Roz dabbed her wet cheeks. "A good thing. Since I've been here, he's had to put up with a few of my tantrums, too. It's hard to believe he's the same man I used to be married to." She tilted her head to Ellie. "He actually asked me to marry him again. Can you believe that?"

Ellie rose and slid into the chair next to her. "What was your answer?"

"I said no." Roz picked up her cup and took a sip. The coffee had cooled to the perfect temperature. She took the two pills and washed them down. "At first."

"So, you're considering it?"

"Your father can be pretty persuasive. He told me it would be different this time since we both have God in our lives."

Ellie smiled. "Dad mentioned you're a believer now. I've been dying for you to tell me all about it yourself."

Roz stared into her half-empty cup. She could hold her own in any crowd of superficial socialites. Why was it so hard to open up about God? "I prayed one night, not really knowing what I was doing. I just knew I wanted what your father had. And Miriam. She and I have had some good talks." She lifted her chin and turned to Ellie. "I said a lot of things to you when you chose to stay in Africa. I was convinced your father had brainwashed you. I know you and I have never been especially close, but it didn't seem fair that after all these years he could waltz back into your life and steal you away."

"Oh, Mom, it wasn't like that."

"I know that now. I don't hate him anymore."

Ellie reached for Roz's hand and held it close to her chest. "I love you both. And Dad's right. It *would* be different this time. Why don't you take a chance and say yes?"

"Because I'm not like your father." Roz jerked her hand from Ellie's grasp. "Just look what happened a few minutes ago. I can't be nice all the time."

"Dad knows what you're like. He wouldn't expect you to be anything other than yourself." Ellie scooted closer. "Tell me this. Would you like to be married to Dad again?"

If she knew the answer to that, she wouldn't be all tied up in knots. "I honestly can't say. Marriage is so … threatening. I swore I'd never marry again …"

"Do I detect a "but" in there?"

"But …" Roz drew the word out and placed her fingers on her lips to hide her silly grin. "Your father's winning me over. He can be quite charming sometimes."

"Yes." Ellie smiled. "Yes, he can. Listen, Mom, I can't tell you what to do, but since God has already done some incredible miracles in your life, maybe this is your chance for a fresh start."

That good feeling started to bubble up inside her again. Maybe Ellie was right. But before she made any life-altering decisions, there was one thing she had to know. Roz shifted in her seat. "Ellie, last night you mentioned someone …"

Ellie's phone dinged. "Excuse me, Mom." She slipped it from her pocket and scanned the text. "Eric says he'll be back in about an hour." She tapped out a reply to the text. "Which means I've got to get busy."

Roz pushed back from the table and walked across the room. The water bottle she'd thrown had rolled under the sidebar. The old Roz would've left it there, but the new Roz felt the need to atone for her earlier tantrum. She contorted her body to reach it but only succeeded in pushing it further from her grasp.

"Want help?" Ellie slipped her phone back into her pocket.

"No." She said through gritted teeth and went down on her all fours, grunting with the effort.

"Sure?"

"The blasted thing is just out of my reach."

Ellie handed her a plastic spoon. "See if you can knock it closer with this."

She whacked the bottle hard enough to send it skidding across the floor, then gripped the edge of the sidebar counter. She caught a glimpse of Ellie's face as she pulled herself up. "What are you smirking about, young lady?"

"Nothing." Ellie covered her mouth but couldn't hide the amused sparkle in her eyes. "It's just, I'm seeing a side of you I've never seen before."

"You mean seeing me on my hands and knees with my backside in the air?"

Ellie laughed out loud. "Exactly. Now that I've seen what you can do, follow me to my room. It's a disaster."

Roz rolled her eyes and played along, secretly loving the banter. "I can promise you this: I'll think twice before throwing another water bottle."

"Then it was definitely worth it." Ellie slid her hand through the crook of Roz's arm and they walked, arms linked together down the hall to Ellie's room.

Roz's chest swelled with pride as if she'd just been accepted into the very exclusive Brock and Ellie club. Suddenly, it didn't matter who this Joy person was. Brock was right. Things could be different this time.

"So, what were you going to ask me?"

"Hmm?"

"You were about to ask me something when Eric sent a text."

"Never mind." Roz smiled and patted Ellie's hand. "It wasn't important."

CHAPTER 46

The next morning, Brock tried again to convince Neal to take the head of the breakfast table but to no avail. Instead, Neal and Dottie moved to the far end to make room for Ellie and Eric. The twins had already taken a morning bottle and were still fast asleep in their travel bed.

The table was full, as was Brock's heart, as he led the group in prayer to bless the food and their day.

Roz sat next to him, looking especially pretty in the sarong she'd worn on the day he'd asked her to marry him. She smiled at him and even gave his hand an extra squeeze when he ended the prayer. It was going to be one of her good days.

The women had plans to spend the day together. He sat back and listened to the chatter filling the air with happy sounds of people who love each other and share the common bond of being brothers and sisters in Christ. At that moment, he could honestly say he was the most blessed man on earth.

He caught Ellie's eye and winked at her as he sipped his coffee. Today, he would help in the clinic, then work in his office, catching up on some paperwork. Later, this afternoon, he hoped for some one-on-one time with Eric to chat more about the Third Option Organization and maybe even about David Stockman.

All in all, it was shaping up to be a great day.

"Ellie, did your mom tell you what she taught Miriam?"

Ellie smiled at her mother. "Tell me."

"It'd be better if Miriam showed you herself." Roz looked across to Miriam and gave her an encouraging nod.

Miriam finished chewing her last bite of eggs and wiped her mouth with her napkin. "Ellie, how y'all doing?"

"Priceless!" Ellie grabbed Roz's hand and laughed out loud. On impulse, Brock slipped out his phone and snapped a picture of them laughing together. Then he asked them to pose. "Look this way, girls."

They both looked, but Roz balked as soon as she saw his phone. "Oh, Brock, not now. Just look at me. I'm a mess."

"I am looking at you." He held the phone up, getting them in focus. "You look beautiful."

The compliment made her smile, and he snapped the picture, which turned out better than he could've hoped with Roz smiling at him and Ellie smiling at her mother.

He touched Roz's hand. "I'm getting myself more coffee. Would you like more, too?"

She checked her cup. "No. I think I'm good."

Brock scraped back his chair and went to the sidebar where Eric was stirring creamer in his personal stainless steel travel mug. "Mac and I are about to head out."

"Sounds good, son. Try to stay dry."

Eric grinned while securing the lid on his coffee. "Not likely."

"Hey," he said with a touch to Eric's arm. "Look me up when you get back.'

"Will do." Eric gripped Brock's shoulder with a hearty squeeze.

Having Eric and Ellie back at the compound seemed to make everyone a little happier. Brock leaned back against the sidebar and watched with fondness Eric's progression around the table. He and Toby exchanged fist bumps, then Eric placed his hand on Elzira's head, caressing her thick curls. "Your momma's gonna spoil this little angel."

"Don't I know it." Toby shooed him away. "Go on and get out of here and don't you be messing with her, waking her up'n all. She may not look it, but this little girl's got one powerful set of lungs."

"Now, I wonder who she gets that from." Eric grinned and eased around the table, stopping between Roz and Ellie. With one hand on Roz's shoulder, he leaned in to kiss Ellie's cheek. "You ladies have fun today." Then he nodded to Mac at the end of the table. "Ready, man?"

Mac pushed up and nodded to everyone, then headed out the door with Eric. Brock seized the opportunity to slide into Mac's vacant chair next to Toby. "Mind if I hold her?"

Toby handed the tiny bundle over to him. Brock cradled her close to his chest, rubbing her head, much as

Eric had just done. "Such a little beauty." Brock craned his head around Toby to speak to Nicci. "Does she keep you up much at night?"

"Only when the moon is full. On those nights, we walk the floor …"

The rest of what Nicci said was lost as his ears picked up Ellie's panic-stricken cry. "Mom?"

Chaos erupted with chairs flying back.

"Mom!"

Brock didn't remember handing the baby over to anyone. He flew around the table penetrating through Miriam and Ellie to find Roz slumped over, her arm hanging slack beside her.

"Moses, Defibulator!"

Stroke or heart attack?

The professional in him took over as he slid Roz's unconscious body from her chair, cradling her head as she collapsed on the floor.

God, help! He probed for a pulse with one hand while lifting one of her eyelids with the other, then immediately straightened her body lying crooked by the table. Determining the airways unobstructed, he began CPR.

Come back, Roz.

He was mindless of the crowd of people hovering around and was only slightly aware of a baby's screaming that soon faded away as he concentrated on counting thrusts, interspersed with two quick breaths given in measured intervals.

God, bring her back.

Moses skidded into the room, already opening the AED case.

Brock checked again for a nonexistent pulse, then hit the button on the machine while preparing the electrodes to attach to her chest. Ellie knelt beside him, ripping away the material of Roz's sarong and grabbing one of the electrode pads to place slightly under the right collarbone.

He did the same, moving with fast, deliberate skill, placing the adhesive pad slightly under and to the left of Roz's heart. The analysis registered she needed a shock.

"Clear," he called and pressed the button, sending a jolt that raised Roz off the concrete floor.

Still no pulse, he immediately resumed the manual thrusts to Roz while the AED charged. Experience and his own gut instinct told him she was gone, but he wasn't ready to give up. Not yet.

Two minutes later, he went through the process again. "Clear." Roz jerked again, collapsing back with her mouth slack.

His fingers probed the side of Roz's neck while Ellie probed the inside of the wrist. His eyes met hers and saw the same resigned desperation she no doubt saw in his.

"Let's give it one more try." He continued manual thrusts, then gripped her nose and chin and blew his breath into her inert body.

God, please bring her back!

The machine beeped. Brock leaned back. "Clear."

Once again, Roz's torso went airborne, then fell back, her mouth gaping.

Brock searched for a pulse he knew would not be there.

A hush fell over the room as he, with his tight jaw working, removed the adhesive pads and eased the torn material of her sarong back into place.

He glanced up, searching for Moses, whose reddened eyes met his with compassion. "Eight thirty-two," Moses said quietly.

Still on the floor beside her, he opened his arm to Ellie, who fell into his embrace. They clung to each other, their shoulders convulsing and their broken sobs the only sound in the room. Brock felt a soft touch on his shoulder, strengthening and warming him with its comfort.

His tears overflowed from a heart too full to contain the shock, grief, and sadness of losing Roz so quickly and being powerless to stop it.

Their torrent of emotion eased after a couple of minutes. Brock drew in a shaky breath and kissed the side of Ellie's face, his own wet cheeks brushing against hers. Only then did he open his eyes and find that he and Ellie were alone in the room with Roz, the rest of the group respectfully letting them say goodbye in private.

Death was certainly no stranger to Brock, and through the years, he'd learned to detach, for his own sanity's sake.

Somewhere over the past twenty plus years, he'd made peace with the fact that God alone was sovereign over life and death.

But Roz's death blindsided him. He swiveled his desk chair to face the window. The mopane's rain-soaked leaves drooped as if in sympathy.

He tapped his lips with steepled fingers. What happened? She'd been doing so well. One minute she was smiling at him, and the next, she was dead. Just like that. And she'd never actually responded to his proposal. Now, he'd never know what her answer might have been.

Maybe it was better this way.

He was sad and still in shock, with the reminder she was actually dead hitting him repeatedly at random moments. But there were no more tears after that first meltdown. Gratitude for all God had done far outweighed any sadness he felt. In the span of a little over three months, God had brought Roz from the lowest low only to lift her up to the splendor of heaven. His full heart held no regrets. A deep sense of peace seemed to be carrying him along, and in his heart, he knew he'd done all he could. *Jehovah-Shalom.*

Before he dealt with the international logistics, there was a very personal matter he had to attend to. He retrieved his phone from his pocket and swiveled back to face his desk. On impulse, he pulled up his last photo, the one with Roz smiling at him, looking happier than he'd ever seen her.

His smile faded as he pulled up Gwyneth's number. *God, I need Your help. Pour Your grace all over this conversation.*

He rubbed his eyes as he counted rings, silently praying it wouldn't go to voicemail. But, of course, it did. His jaw clenched, and he cut off the recorded message, refusing to leave a message that would probably not be opened. He shot her a quick text instead. *Please call me. 911.*

By some miracle, his phone rang in less than a minute.

"Hello, Gwyneth." Relief replaced his earlier frustration. "Thank you for calling me."

"What's wrong?" The edge to her voice reminded him so much of Roz.

"Honey, I have some bad news."

He paused to give her some time to brace, then continued. "Your mom passed away this morning."

He heard her quick intake of breath, proving the call had not dropped. Then silence. He waited a few seconds, then continued, assuming she would want to know details. "We had just finished breakfast and were about to leave the table. She slumped over and never regained consciousness."

He paused again, hoping she would ask questions.

"I'm so sorry, honey. I know this is a big shock. It was to all of us, too. Your mother had almost fully recovered and had talked about returning to Texas by Christmas. I'm sorry you didn't get the chance to say good-bye."

"Yeah. Me, too." Another long pause, then she finally spoke, her voice low and subdued. "Does Ellie know?"

"Yes." He didn't think it wise to expound. At least, not now. "We've talked about laying her to rest here in Africa. How would you feel about that?"

"That's fine." She sighed. "It doesn't really matter where you spread her ashes."

"We're not having her cremated, honey."

"Oh. I just assumed …"

"No. We'll be making plans today or tomorrow. I'll let you know as soon as I know the details. I'd like for you to be here, if possible."

"Uh … I don't think so."

"We'll delay the funeral until you can fly in. Say the word, and I'll make sure the company jet—"

"Listen, Dad, I appreciate the offer. I really do. But I can't deal with it right now. I'm really sorry to hear about it, but Mom's gone. What's the point of my coming?"

Brock let it go, relieved at least that her expression of sorrow seemed genuine. He could bide his time. Gwyneth didn't stand a chance against the mighty God he served who had just shown the limits He would go to save a broken soul.

"I understand, honey. I have some pictures and even a little video from one of her physical therapy sessions, if you're interested."

"Okay."

"Great. I'll be coming to Texas soon to handle some

of the legal matters. Maybe I could see you then."

Another long pause. He waited, resisting the urge to give her an out.

Finally, she spoke, her tone resigned. "Sure. Give me a call when you get back in town."

A call that would probably go to voicemail. "I will. Take care, honey. I love you."

She didn't respond, and his screen went dark. No matter. He was a patient man, and God was on the move.

Brock knew the procedure in case an American died in Angola. The next day and a half went by in a haze with his contacting the American Embassy and providing the necessary documentation required by both governments. Arranging for the burial of an American citizen was a technical nightmare full of bureaucratic red tape that Eric offered to handle for him. Brock thanked him, but declined, needing to take care of this final thing for Roz on his own.

He wanted Roz to be buried in Angola in the small burial plot behind the chapel. It was where he hoped one day to be laid to rest, as well as Moses and Miriam when their time came. It surprised him to realize how very much he wanted Roz there, too, close to the only real friends she'd ever known.

Everyone connected to the mission attended the graveside service. He almost choked up when a group of nationals in traditional dress belted out in perfect harmony "We'll Understand it Better By and By" in their native dialect. Roz, who'd taken delight in learning bits of

Angolan slang, would've loved it.

Eric and Ellie and the twins were such a comfort to him during the entire week, and it took very little persuading on their part for him to go back to Washington with them. Though he suspected Ellie thought otherwise, his decision had nothing to do with Joy, but rather a deep need to be close to family. His heart was still reeling with the suddenness of it all, and he needed time to sort things out. How long that would take, he had no idea.

Brock still slept in Eric's old room, not ready to move back to the room Roz had occupied since she'd arrived. The night before they were scheduled to leave, he awoke in the middle of the night unable to go back to sleep. He stuck his feet into his slippers, feeling a pull to go outside.

He eased open the door leading to the terrace, scrunching his face at the inevitable creak, then grimacing when he remembered she was no longer there to be disturbed by it. The November air was predictably cool and moist on his face. He stood on the wet concrete breathing in the musky scent of damp earth from the late evening rain.

As kind and wonderful as everyone had been, it felt good to be alone. He wandered around the building not caring his soft-soled slippers were getting caked with red mud.

It was dark, but he needed no light.

He felt his way around the chapel, then fell to his knees beside Roz's grave, again not at all concerned he was now soiling his pajama pants. One thing drove him: To be alone at Roz's grave. Just him and God.

He bent, with his forehead resting on his folded hands on her grave. He remained quiet for a long time, letting his full heart communicate with *groanings that could not be uttered.*

Then he spoke aloud but with a hushed tone. "Gracious Father, my heart is so full of love for You and all You've done. I can never thank You enough. Your way is perfect. Forgive me for doubting You and resisting You. And thank You so much for never giving up on me. Rozalynde is now with you, Father. Thank you, O God, thank You. Help me to finish well, Father. Lead me and guide me, and help me to finish well."

He stilled, and once again the still, small voice of the One his heart loved the most spoke to him and said the words he'd been waiting, longing to hear.

Go get Joy.

CHAPTER 47

I found him whom my soul loveth.

Joy spent most of the day in the kitchen, hoping it would calm her nerves. Cooking usually did. In less than two hours, the Templeton family would return to Washington. And Brock Whitfield would be with them.

Every part of her wanted to be there when the plane landed, waving her arms like a banner. *Welcome home. Welcome back into my life.*

But was God really bringing Brock back into her life? She had no way of knowing for sure. Three months was a long time. Maybe he'd changed.

She certainly hadn't. If anything, her feelings for Brock had gotten stronger, which is why she graciously refused joining them for dinner their first night back. She was far too transparent, and Brock far too perceptive.

No. If Brock wanted to see her, he'd have to make the first move.

The timer beeped, and she pulled two steaming pans of lasagna from the oven. If she wouldn't be there to welcome them, she could at least give the weary travelers some food.

But not before she tasted it first herself. No matter how

many times she'd made it, her lasagna varied from batch to batch. Her stomach rumbled as she spooned out some from the smaller pan she'd made for David, then covered both with aluminum foil. She brought the spoon close to her mouth and blew, testing it with the tip of her tongue.

A good batch. She took another bite, closing her eyes in appreciation. Maybe even her best yet. Her stomach clamored for more, but her fear of running into Brock far outweighed her hunger.

She placed the homemade bread she'd made earlier and both pans on the backseat floorboard. Templeton house first, then she'd swing by David's.

In forty-five minutes, she was back home, with the warm aroma of garlic, herbs, and marinara still lingering in the air. The dishwasher clicked to the drying cycle as she grabbed a bottle of water from the fridge and the plate she'd left cooling on the counter. She took them to the smaller table beside the bay window, ready to sit and let herself uncurl from the frenzied activity of the afternoon.

David called not long after she finished eating. He thanked her for the food and raved about how good it was.

Then the clock seemed to stand still. As the evening wore on, she checked her phone twice to make sure she hadn't accidentally switched it to silent mode. Each time, she turned up the volume a notch, just to make sure she wouldn't miss a call. By the time she pulled back the cover on her bed, her imagination had gotten the best of her. She slid into bed and lay on her back, wide awake and staring into the blackness. The plane could've crashed. They'd be stranded in the middle of the ocean, clinging to their flotation devices. Or they'd all be killed on impact, and nobody would know to call her. It might take days for—

A bright green light filled her darkened room, followed by the shrill ring of her phone. Adrenaline surged as she threw back the covers and snatched her phone from the bedside table. Brock's name and not Ellie's popped up on caller ID. She answered on the first ring. "Hello, Brock? I'm so glad you called. I was getting worried." Her words tumbled out in a rush.

She heard a soft chuckle, then the voice she'd been longing to hear, sounding warm and mellow and a little tired. "Hello, Joy. Air-traffic control put us in a holding pattern. The twins let everyone know they weren't very happy."

"I bet." She smiled and untangled her legs from the covers, then swung them over the side of the bed. "Are you at the house now?"

"No. We're still in the terminal. I'm standing outside the family bathroom. Eric and Ellie are changing the twins, then we'll load up and head home. I wanted to call and let you know we were back."

"I'm so glad you did. I left some food at the house for you, but it's probably too late to eat. Ellie can stick it in the fridge and heat it up tomorrow."

"Thank you. I don't think any of us will want to wait." He paused, then added, "Actually, I was hoping to catch you before you went to bed. I'd like to see you tomorrow, if you're available. Maybe take you to lunch ... that is, if you'd like to."

"I'd like that very much, Brock," she blurted, sounding more eager than she'd intended.

"Great. Noon, okay?"

She nodded as if he could see her, then answered, "Noon is great."

"Good. Well, they're coming out of the bathroom now. I'll see you tomorrow, Joy."

"Yes. I'm looking forward to it. Give my love to everyone." She ended the call, then fell back on the bed, grinning up at the ceiling. They hadn't crashed into the ocean. And Brock had been the first to call.

All was right again in her world.

The last time Brock took her to lunch, she had the same dilemma. Joy stared into her closet, wanting something special, but not too dressy. Not too casual either.

She went with a mid-length skirt, black and flowing, paired with a white cashmere sweater and a colorful scarf draped around her neck.

One more bathroom check. Hair and makeup still good. She added a little more lipstick and folded in her lips, then checked to make sure none was on her teeth.

What was she getting all worked up about? This was just a lunch date between two friends who hadn't seen each other in a while. Perfectly normal.

Who was she kidding? This wasn't like any of her usual lunch dates. This was Brock Whitfield, and in five minutes, he'd be at her door. She was going to cry, she knew it already. Tears of joy at finally reconnecting with a good friend. Tears of sadness if he chose to tell her anything about Rozalynde, which she hoped he felt comfortable enough to do.

Maybe she would have the grace to hold it together for a while, but there would be tears. Of that, she was sure, which is why she'd used waterproof mascara and tucked a travel-sized tissue pack in her clutch purse.

The doorbell rang sending a jolt to her pulse. She paused at the door, took in a deep breath and slowly blew it out. She opened the door, and Brock stood there, the warmth in his smile telling her more than with words that he was happy to see her again.

All the things she thought she might say at this moment, left her, along with every other conscious thought in her body.

He reached for her hand and enveloped it in both of his. "Hello, Joy."

She shook herself from her stupor and returned his smile. "Hello, Brock."

"Shall we go?" He continued to hold her hand as he escorted her around the black Mercedes in the driveway and opened her door. She slid into place, breathing in the hint of his cologne.

He walked around the front, giving her a chance to observe him without making it too obvious. He'd never looked more handsome with black slacks, white button up shirt with the first two buttons left undone. Charcoal gray sports jacket. He looked and moved like a man who had money and taste, which of course he did. His silver hair was full and styled without looking styled, and it was clear he'd put as much thought into his appearance as she had.

He eased into his seat and smiled at her again. "All set?"

"All set." Just like he used to ask when they were on their two-week trek into the outlying villages. "Nice car, by the way." Living with a man who sold cars for a living had taught her a thing or two about quality cars.

"Thank you. I thought I'd rent a car while I'm here. Makes it easier on everyone."

"How long do you plan to be here?"

"I'm not sure."

That's all he said, and she didn't press for more details. For now, just being with him was enough. She stared out the window. "Beautiful day," she mentioned casually.

"Gorgeous. I don't know if you remember, but last year the monsoons came early. November was one of our wettest months."

"I do remember. Except for the occasional Nor'easter, November's one of our driest. It's actually my favorite month."

"Really?" He cocked his head and smiled. "And why

is that?"

Joy thought for a moment. "I guess, for one thing, I love the way it smells. You know, that first whiff of winter that's in the air. The days are usually pleasant, and the nights are chilly enough for a fire. I love a good fire, especially a real one, with wood and not a gas log. This is crazy, but I love to smell smoke of any kind. Leaves. Logs. And I'm embarrassed to admit it but even the smell of a good cigar or pipe. I've never smoked one myself, of course, but I've been known to sidle up to someone who did and take a whiff or two."

Brock looked amused. "Good to know. If I see you inching toward some stranger on a park bench, I'll know what you're doing."

She laughed. "I'll try to warn you first. And I just realized I've been babbling again. I do that when I'm nervous. So, I'm going to be quiet now and let you have a chance to talk."

"I'd be happy to listen to you babble all day." He braked for a red light and turned to her. "And why are you nervous?"

She shrugged and spoke to her window. "I don't know. It's been a long time since we've seen each other. I guess I'm still breaking the ice." She turned back to him when the light changed. "Do you have a favorite month?"

"Hmm." His eyes narrowed as if he were thinking. "It's hard to narrow it down. Every month that rolls around is like an old friend who shows up for a good visit." He paused, then added, "I love the rainy season for the same reason you love November. Affects the way everything smells. Makes it smell earthy." He caught another red light and slowed to a stop.

An old friend who shows up for a good visit. What a lovely thing to say. On impulse, she told him so. "That was beautiful, Brock. I forgot there's a bit of the poet in you." The truth was, she hadn't forgotten anything about this man. She changed the subject to keep it from becoming awkward. "Where are we going for lunch?"

"I have to confess. I did some snooping. Ellie mentioned you love pizza, so I asked Eric if he had any suggestions. He said we have to go to a place called "We, the Pizza." Ever heard of it?"

"No, but I love the name! And she's right. I love pizza."

"I do, too, and I rarely get it. Eric is all about details. He told me where to park and some places we could go after we eat."

"Sounds great!"

"Except there's a good walk from the parking deck to the restaurant."

"I'm game. It's a lovely day." Her low-heeled boots might not be ideal for walking, but she'd never tell him that.

The walk to the restaurant was pleasant. Brock offered his arm, and she gratefully accepted, sliding her hand into the inside crook of his elbow. She breathed in the pungent smell of moist earth and dead leaves with new appreciation as they walked along the cragged sidewalk.

The place was a small, but quaint hole-in-the-wall storefront with tables and red umbrellas on the street. They went inside and stood before a counter with scores of slices labeled for selection.

She stared at the choices, tapping her lip. "Everything looks so good, I can't make up my mind. I usually get a pizza with everything, but that spinach and artichoke pizza is calling my name."

"Tell you what, I'll order the one with everything if you'll let me taste the one with spinach."

She grinned at him. "Deal."

They carried their food to a set of stairs next to an entire wall decorated with round aluminum pizza platters.

"Sorry to make you climb. Eric said we should eat on the second floor."

"Lead the way. I have total trust in Eric's advice."

She followed him up the stairs to a table somewhat isolated from the rest. Their chairs were red and cushioned. Brock pulled out her chair, then sat across from her. The memory of the last time they were at a restaurant together flashed through her mind. At least, here Brock wouldn't be speaking Portuguese and a server wouldn't be hovering between ficus trees spying on them.

Once they were settled, Joy broached the subject they both seemed to be avoiding. She took the initiative and reached across the table, placing her hand on his. "I wanted to tell you I'm so sorry about Rozalynde."

"Thank you." A glimmer of sadness appeared on Brock's face. "It was definitely unexpected. I don't know how much Ellie told you, but Roz had a miraculous recovery. Someday, I'd like to tell you more about the wonderful things God did before she died. I guess Ellie might have mentioned Roz became a Christian while she was there."

"She did. That must be a great comfort to you now." As it was to her when Frank died.

"Yes." He nodded and finished chewing the last bite he'd taken, then wiped his mouth with his napkin. "Very much so."

She said no more about Roz, and neither did Brock.

Other than commenting on how good the pizza was, they ate in silence.

Then the somber mood lifted, as quickly as it had come. Brock took a sip of water and smiled over the rim of his glass. "Still nervous?"

She shook her head. "I'm settling down now."

He grinned and gave her a tender look. "I've missed you, Joy."

The pricking at the back of her throat reminded her there would be tears today. She swallowed hard and was about to tell him she'd missed him, too, but before she could reply, he asked about her son. A subject that thankfully no longer made her cry.

"David lives in an apartment about four blocks from

my house. He's doing great, thanks to Eric and a lot of prayer. Eric and David have a lot in common. I guess that was one reason I was so drawn to Eric in the first place. David has started going to our church and attending the men's prayer breakfast on Fridays. I think he's going to be all right."

"I'm glad to hear it. I'd like to meet him while I'm here."

"Yes, he wants to meet you, too. I'll have to cook Sunday dinner and have everybody over."

His eyebrows shot up. "I almost forgot. Joy, your lasagna was outstanding. No wonder it's David's favorite."

"Thank you. I'm glad you liked it."

"I loved it. In fact, I ate some for breakfast. Didn't even bother to heat it up."

"Are you serious?" She asked, more pleased than she let on. "Right now, I don't think I'll ever want to eat again. Will you excuse me while I visit the ladies' room?"

"Of course." He stood as she pushed her chair back and placed her wadded up napkin on the remnants of crust on her plate.

She left, mostly to freshen up and reapply lipstick and gloss. After she washed her hands, she took a moment to collect her thoughts. She placed a hand over her heart and stared at her reflection. It seemed that Brock was now back in her life, and it was as if the last three months, as long and hard as they had been, had never happened. He said he'd missed her. She needed to hear that most of all because she, too, had missed him so much and hadn't been able to shake it no matter how she'd tried.

Now he was back, and she didn't know what exactly that meant or where it would lead. She just knew, now more than ever, that she loved this man, and she didn't know how much longer she could keep from showing it.

Brock threw away their trash, then returned to his seat, propping his elbows on the table with folded hands tapping his lips. He was the nervous one now even though he'd practiced what he wanted to say many times in his mind.

Maybe he should scrap it for now. Just enjoy being with her. Get to know David. He had almost convinced himself that was the thing to do when she came out of the restroom, and he experienced the same rush of butterflies he'd felt when she opened her door and said "Hello." She was so beautiful he could hardly tear his eyes from her. He loved that her beauty was natural and unpretentious and radiated from within. There was character in her face, in the lines that crinkled around her expressive eyes. There was kindness in her face as well. She smiled easily and often, with a genuineness that warmed him. Quite frankly, he adored everything about her, especially the way she made him feel when he was with her.

She met his gaze as she approached. He stood and rushed to pull out her chair.

"Why thank you," she said and gave him that smile

that always seemed to make his mouth go dry.

He returned to his seat and reached for his water, but accidentally bumped it instead, almost tipping it over. His surgeon's dexterity saved the day and her clothes from an ice water shower.

"Good save." She grinned and picked up her glass tilting it toward him like a toast.

"Thank God. I think my guardian angel was on his toes." He took a quick sip and decided to quit stalling. "I still laugh about the time we were crossing that bridge."

She nodded and covered her sheepish grin with her hand. "I think both our guardian angels were on the ball on that trip."

He would have to agree.

"I have such fond memories of those two weeks." A faraway look came to her eyes. "Do you remember that one village where they had a big feast in our honor? We all gathered under this huge tree, I think it was in the chief's courtyard, and we squatted in the dirt eating rolled up sticky rice and dipping it in a community bowl of hot peanut oil. That was one of my favorite memories of the whole trip."

Brock smiled, mesmerized by her animated features. "There was something that happened in that village I never told you about."

"Really? What was that?"

"It was a village we had never visited before," he began.

"They certainly seemed glad we were there. They were so friendly, especially the chieftain."

"Exactly. That was the problem."

She tilted her head. "I don't understand."

"Whenever we arrive at a new village, especially one we've never been to, Moses is the mediator and interpreter. He knows many dialects and can figure out words in the dialects he doesn't know. So, it's his job to talk first to the chieftain, the *soba,* and get his permission for us to stay in the village."

She nodded. "I remember the chief had quite a few tribal markings on his bared chest. He seemed quite proud of them the way he was strutting about. So, what happened that I didn't know about?"

"When we first arrived, he took a liking to the silver-headed *pula nboa.* "

"White-skinned woman." Her eyes widened. "Oh. You mean me?"

Brock nodded. "And he asked Moses if you were my *damo.* "

"He thought I was your wife?"

"It gets worse."

"I'm not sure I want to hear."

"Moses told him 'No,' but that you were a *kamba.* "

"A friend."

"The chieftain then said we were welcome to stay if you would share his tent for the night. I could tell you more things he said, but I'm sure you get the picture."

Joy slid her hand up to her throat and shuddered.

"When Moses told me, I was ready to pack up and leave but only after I took care of a little business to set him straight."

"As I recall, we stayed that night."

"Yes. Moses let the chieftain know that you were a princess and were under the protection of a very powerful king, and it would be unwise for him to violate you or show you any disrespect."

She nodded. "That was brilliant. It must have worked."

Brock took another sip of water. "That night, after we went to our tents, I couldn't sleep. I didn't trust that chieftain to honor a king he didn't know, so I decided to take matters into my own hands."

She leaned forward, licking her lips. "Brock, what did you do?"

He laughed. "Not what you think. Moses and I took down our tent and moved it directly in front of yours. I decided if he was going to make any moves on you, he'd have to go through me to do it."

"Oh, Brock." Joy's eyes filled with tears. "That's just about the sweetest thing I've ever heard."

Her praise made him sit a little taller. "I don't think I closed my eyes at all that night. We got up early, before anyone else stirred, and took down our tent so you wouldn't know." He reached across the table and took her hand. "There's something else you should know."

"Oh dear." She stared, her eyes wide. "There's more?"

He gave her a reassuring smile. "Actually, you might already know because we talked a little about it when we went to the coast. I'm in love with you, Joy. I have been for quite some time."

She looked at him, her eyes soft, radiating with an inner glow. "And I've wanted to hear that for quite some time."

"The day I was scheduled to leave for Washington, Ellie called about her mother's stroke. I knew things would change, but I had no idea how much until I went into the chapel. Moses, in his subtle and wise way, had a little talk with me and basically let me know I was going to have to choose between you and Roz."

He paused, finding it hard to talk about even now.

"I knew he was right. Every fiber of my being wanted to choose you, but I knew in my soul, God wanted me to choose Roz. So I did, or at least I tried to before I got off the plane. Then I saw you, and it tore me up inside to think I'd have to walk away from the greatest happiness I'd ever known."

Joy's expression softened. "I knew you were struggling. That's why I decided not to return to Africa."

Brock continued to hold Joy's hand, stroking it with the edge of his thumb. "That night when I watched you drive away from Ellie's house, I knew that ... I might never get the chance—" He broke off and swallowed hard. "Anyway, when Roz and I arrived back in Africa, I couldn't go anywhere without thoughts of you invading my mind and heart. It was a battle I fought constantly and often lost. But God is so gracious. He helped me, and I somehow knew He was helping you. I had to believe that, or I would've gone crazy."

"God did help me. I can't deny I had some hard moments, especially when I was at Ellie's, and you would call." Joy smiled and squeezed his hand. "But deep in my soul, I knew that God was doing something great. Something far more important than my feelings for you."

The respect he'd always felt for Joy grew even stronger. If there was going to be any kind of future with her, he owed it to her to tell her everything, as much as he hated to. "Joy, I asked Roz to marry me."

Her expression was a mixture of pain and acceptance. "I know."

"Did Ellie tell you?"

She shook her head. "She didn't have to. I know what kind of man you are, Brock. Once you commit, you're all in. I think I knew ever since the night you arrived in Washington. You asked me to pray. And my heart broke for you because you looked so sad. You said you were hoping for a way to make up for past wrongs. I knew right then, I needed to step aside."

"You're an amazing woman."

She smiled and shook her head. "God knows, I'm a fragile lump of clay."

He leaned forward and brought her hand to his lips. "An amazing and beautiful lump of clay."

She fanned herself with her other hand. "You're making me blush."

They had been at the table so long, the lunch crowd had long since left, leaving the entire upstairs vacant except for them. Brock released Joy's hand, rose from his chair, and eased around the table.

She gave a little gasp as he dropped to his knee beside her. He reached for her hand again and held it close to his heart. "Joy, I moved my tent closer to yours because I wanted to protect you, but that's not enough for me. I don't just want my tent close to yours ... I want you in my tent."

Joy dropped her gaze, and he wasn't sure if she was laughing or crying. Or both.

Brock smiled at her sweetness and with the back of his fingers, brushed away the tear that trailed down her cheek. "I love you, Joy. I know this is sudden, and if you want to wait and get to know each other better—"

She fell against him, wrapping her arms around his neck. "Oh, Brock," she said, her voice choked with tears. "You dear, dear man. I already know everything I need to know about you. Pitch that tent. I'll gladly be your *damo* and follow you anywhere."

His breath caught. He closed his eyes and held her close, breathing in the warm sweetness of her perfume.

Powerful, all-consuming love, much like he'd felt so many years ago in that prison cell, swept over his heart, carrying away all the tension and sadness from the past few weeks.

"My sweet Joy." He leaned back and caressed her cheek. "I don't know how much time God will give us."

She smiled, with her very heart in her eyes, and covered the hand on her cheek with her own. "This one day has been more than I dared hope for."

"I'd have to agree." He grinned and brought her hand to his lips. "Best day ever!"

"Yes!" She laughed and leaned closer, her eyes sparkling. "And I'll be so grateful for every other day that God gives us."

"So will I." He smiled, his full heart praising his great God who never failed to do exceedingly, abundantly, above all that he could ask or think.

FROM THE AUTHOR

The Bible is the ultimate love story that reveals the very essence of God.

Sometimes, God asks the unthinkable, like when He asked Abraham, to take his son, his only son Isaac, whom he loved, and sacrifice him back to God.

It was a test that had far-reaching ramifications about which Abraham had no knowledge. He only knew, as unthinkable as it was, he must obey. There was no other option.

LOVING BROCK

In *Loving Brock*, Brock Whitfield was put to the ultimate test because God wanted to do something far greater than bring two people together. God was once again doing exceedingly, abundantly, above, and He wanted to use Brock to do it.

Often, when a person becomes a Christian and decides to go "all in" for Christ, God will ask something similar. I think we all have our "Isaac"—that one thing we hope God won't ask of us.

But the truth is that God wants all of us, holding nothing back, because He wants us to fully experience the truth in verse 19 before we witness the power of verse 20.

"To know the love of Christ which passeth knowledge, that ye might be filled with all the fullness of God." Ephesians 3:19

Only then can we understand that God is "able to do exceedingly, abundantly, above all that we ask or think." Ephesians 3:20

God's love can transform a broken person. I know this because He transformed me.

I'd love to hear your story. Contact me at www.joandeneve.com

God bless.

Joan Deneve

ABOUT JOAN

Joan Deneve enjoys being a wife, mother, grandmother, teacher, and author, but her favorite role and defining title is that of Christian. Joan teaches English in a Christian school and has a passion to help young people fall in love with Christ and equip them to become all God wants them to be.

Joan shares her life with Rene', her husband of forty years. Together they reside in Prattville, Alabama, a quaint city with southern charm and hospitality.

Joan loves to laugh and spend quality time with family and friends. Learn more about her at her website: JoanDeneve.com

ACKNOWLEDGMENTS

I very much appreciate Marji Laine Clubine and Write Integrity Press. I'm honored to be a part of this great company.

I owe much gratitude to my editor Deborah Raney. I'm been so blessed by her expertise and guidance, and I could not have finished or polished this manuscript without her help.

I used these books to research life on the mission field in Africa. *Hand on my Scalpel,* by David Thompson, M.D., and *Mine Eyes Have Seen the Glory,* by Lowell A. Gess, M.D., provided valuable stories about medical missions in Africa. Many of the cases at Brock's clinic were based on real-life episodes found in these books.

I consulted Dr. Wes Stafford's excellent book *Too Small to Ignore* for insight into tribal life in Africa.

Hope Heals by Katherine and Jay Wolf and *My Stroke of Insight* by Jill Boyte Taylor were especially good resources for information about stroke recovery.

SPECIAL THANKS

Please bear with me as I attempt once more to thank everyone who played a part in this glorious process.

My wild and wonderful writing journey began when an imaginary door opened on my back porch, and I walked through it to see where it would lead. I rummaged for that "great idea for a book" I'd placed in a drawer some twenty years before and then played around with it, thinking no one would ever see it but me.

Seven years later, I've completed the third and final book in the Redeemed Side of Broken Series, and it is with bittersweet fondness that I say an emotional farewell.

First, I must thank God. I feel like a three-year-old kid who absolutely loves to play with LEGOs but is given a gigantic LEGO kit that is clearly beyond his skill set. So his dad, who definitely has the necessary skills, sits down at the table, pours out the LEGOs, and says with loving patience, "Here, buddy, let's build this together. I'll hand you the pieces, and you can connect them."

You get the picture? I love to write, but I often felt it way beyond my skill set to accomplish. God sat at the computer with me and helped me with every word, phrase, sentence, scene, and chapter until the massive project was done.

He did that for me because He loves me so much. So, thank You, God, for giving me the gift of writing and then actually doing the lion share of it Yourself.

Writing a book opened up a whole new world of experiences and friends that I never knew existed. We writers feel a kinship with each other that "normal" people wouldn't understand. I fell in love with this world and the people in it and have made lifelong friends. These dear people love God and love the craft. They have shared their knowledge and their heart with me. I could not have taken this journey without these dear friends, and I know it was God who caused our paths to cross.

Carolyn Hill was the first writer to take me under her wing and has been a part of my journey almost from day one. She is a skilled writer who is the absolute queen of imagery and characterization. As a critique partner, she has a great eye and knows how to take a phrase and make it better. She also knows when to encourage and when to instruct. I am so blessed to be your friend, Carolyn.

Through Carolyn, I met Nancy Kimball. With phenomenal patience, Nancy taught me the rudiments of writing, and I owe ALL of what I know about deep point of view and other writing skills to Nancy. Nancy has been my faithful critique partner for all of my books and helped turn my "ugly" drafts into something beautiful. She is an amazing author and an amazing friend. Nancy, your "Atta, girls" gave me wings! Thank you, Phoenix. Your friendship changed my life.

Jessie Bush is another name in my writers' hall of fame. Jessie is also my daughter and far surpasses me in natural talent and creativity. She is a selfless and fierce supporter and encourager who knows my characters almost better than I do and is the one who often pointed me in the right direction when I'd be stuck in plot purgatory. Thank you, Jessie. I am in awe of your talent, and I love driving the angels crazy with our "craft talk."

Tracy Ruckman and Fay Lamb, thank you for helping to make this fledgling writer's dream come true. I will always love you and thank God for you.

Thanks to all of my writer friends whom I've met along the way: Marji, Jebraun, Jack, Tim, Joy, Gretchen, Diane, Nikki, Linden, Jackie, Kathleen, Betty, Elizabeth, Harriet, Cynthia, Deborah, Ann, Peggy, Marie and all my other dear writer friends at Write Integrity Press. Thank you for your help, encouragement, and prayers. I wish you all great success in your ventures!

I'm also blessed to have a host of "normal" friends who love me and encourage me.

Michele Bradley is the angel God sent to bless me with love, encouragement, prayer, and "fun" entertainment. She is quite possibly the most Christ-like person I know and has been the "best" of friends to me.

Beth Wasson, your friendship has been a constant in my life. Thank you, Beth, for your generous heart and unconditional love.

Carol Parks is one of my beta readers who helped point me in the right direction. Thank you for your time and encouragement!

Big thanks to all my church friends and teacher friends

who loved me and prayed for me: My book was finished because of you. THANK YOU!!

My students (past and present) occupy a huge chunk of my heart. Thank you for your love, respect, and delightful personalities: You make my day job a joy!

I would not be the person I am today without the support and love of my dear family.

My mother is my friend, my prayer warrior, and my biggest cheerleader.

My husband, Rene, is my rock and the soft place where I fall.

My son, Jeremiah, is a constant joy and an encouragement to me. He also is my "go to" guy for medical research and advice.

My daughter, Jessie, is my heart and my "real-life" Ellie.

I'm blessed to be mother-in-law to Sarah and Michael. They show unfailing love and respect and mean the world to me.

My grandchildren own prime real estate in my heart and are the joy of my life. Auston, Ethan, (and, of course, their girlfriends) Lacey Jane, Cloe, Hannah, Haley, and Christian are unique, talented, and fun. They're all really cute, too.

My nieces and nephews (especially Shane, Steve, and Shonna) are quick to run to my rescue, and I thank God for you.

Finally, Phalia Smith and Sheila Parrish, my sweet

sisters who both lost their husbands within a three-month span. Nobody knows me, understands me, or loves me like you do. And nobody on earth illustrates better what the "redeemed side of broken" looks like. I love you.

OTHER BOOKS BY JOAN

Templetons don't break down. Even when their world is falling apart. Eric Templeton's well-ordered life as a top CIA agent is shattered when a traitor within the agency plots to have him eliminated. Sent on a bogus mission to Africa, Eric is ambushed and critically wounded. A helicopter pilot flies him to a remote mission hospital where Dr. Brock Whitfield and his daughter, Ellie, work to save his life. If Eric survives, his life may never be the same, and he still has to deal with the traitor who wants him dead. Eric wants justice, but Brock and Ellie know that Eric's survival is the least of his worries. What he needs most are mercy and truth.

Life couldn't be better or sweeter for Eric and Ellie Templeton as they begin their life together as new Christians and a newly married couple. But Ellie enters her marriage with some baggage of her own. What if Eric goes back on another mission? What if she loses this man who has become her life? Even worse, what if God never lets them have a child of their own?

God has some spiritual surgery He must perform on Ellie to free her from the deep-seated feelings of guilt and doubt that have bound her soul for years.

God painstakingly and lovingly creates the perfect storm of events designed specifically to bring Ellie to the place where she can "let go" and fully trust God.

No. Matter. What.

RECENT RELEASES FROM WRITE INTEGRITY

Young Adult Action/Adventure

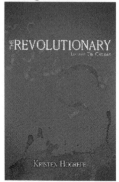

Book 2 of The Rogues dystopian series by Kristen Hogrefe is enthusiastically received!

Liberate the Captives!

Revolutions run on sacrifice ... and blood.

Three months a satellite prisoner, Portia wonders if the Brotherhood has left her to die—until she plunges into the domain of a smuggler contacted by her brother. But her rescue comes with a price tag, and now, she must forfeit her identity to act as a spy. She learns that her enemies want the Dome to approve mass satellite executions, though no one knows why. Worse, they're using her friend Luther, now a Court Citizen intern, to sign the short-term orders. She wants to confide in Luther, but can she still trust him with the company he keeps?

Women's Fiction

How can one man save the town he loves when he's the reason for the destruction?

David New has guarded his secrets for years, but when two brothers arrive in town, he gets news that the daughter he's never told anyone about has disappeared, possibly the victim of a heinous crime. The lives of many of the town residents begin to unravel in the gale force consequences of David's past, he has nowhere else to turn. God is the only one Who can calm the storms, but can David and the good folks of Serenity Key survive until He does?

A tempest has been brewing for thirty years, with only one island town in its path.

Thank you
for reading our books!

Please consider returning to the Amazon page
and leaving a review for the author!

Look for other books
published by

Write Integrity Press
www.WriteIntegrity.com

Made in the USA
Columbia, SC
27 December 2021

52845949R00239